TRICKS FOR FREE

An *InCryptid* Novels

SEANAN McGUIRE

DAW BOOKS, INC.

DONALD A. WOLLHEIM, FOUNDER

375 Hudson Street, New York, NY 10014

ELIZABETH R. WOLLHEIM
SHEILA E. GILBERT
PUBLISHERS

www.dawbooks.com

First Printing, March 2018

1   2   3   4   5   6   7   8   9

For Michael and Deborah.

Rock and roll.

Price Family Tree

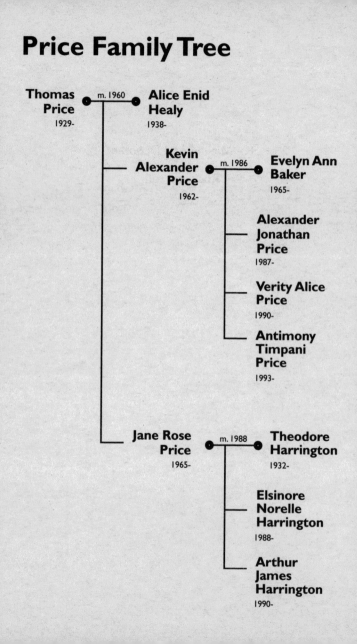

Baker Family Tree

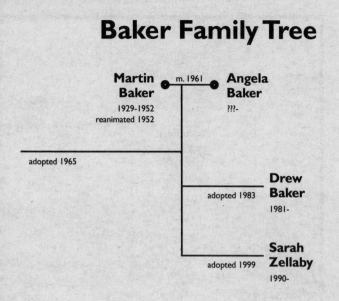

Martin Baker
1929-1952
reanimated 1952

m. 1961

Angela Baker
???-

adopted 1965

adopted 1983

Drew Baker
1981-

adopted 1999

Sarah Zellaby
1990-

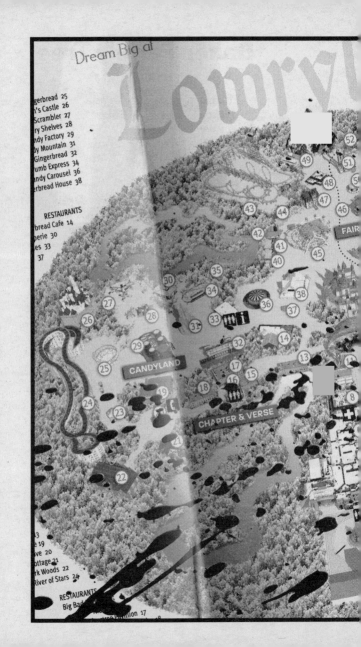

DEEP DOWN

57

59

58

60

66

65

64

ATLANTIS

67

79

69

70

76

71

77

METROPOLIS

75

73

72

74

LOWRY'S
WELCOMING WORLD

Priscilla Spencer

Payment, noun:

1. The act of paying for something; reward or punishment.

Penance, noun:

1. Punishment for past actions.

2. An attempt to pay for what can't be bought.

3. See also "exile."

Prologue

"Woe betide the damned soul who tries to get between me and my children. I'm only the nice one in this family because I don't care enough to hurt you."

–Evelyn Baker

The locker room of Lewis and Clark High School, Portland, Oregon

Six years ago

CHEERLEADERS FILLED THE ROOM. Most were half-clad; all were getting dressed with the ruthless speed and lack of artifice universal to teenage girls with no one they needed to put on a show for. The show would come later, when the Trailblazers football team took the field with their loyal spirit squad behind them, waving their pom-poms and cheering for victory.

A new girl rushed into the room, forcing the others to make room or get knocked over. Her game bag was slung over her shoulder and her auburn hair was pulled into a sloppy ponytail, tied off with a wilted spirit ribbon in Trailblazers blue and gold. A freshman girl straightened from her crouch too slowly; the newcomer placed a hand between her shoulders and used her as an impromptu vault, landing on the other side of her without breaking stride.

A diminutive peroxide blonde with the figure of a Tolkien elf and the presence of a pop star dropped her mascara wand and turned away from the mirror, planting her hands on her hips in a classic superhero pose. "Melody West!" she snapped, voice a whip cracking through the room. "You are *late*!"

The new arrival stumbled to a halt, momentum lost in the face of her captain's disapproval. She turned, spirit bow somehow looking even more wilted. "I'm sorry, Sophie," she said. "My family—"

"Sorry doesn't stack our pyramid when you don't show up, Mel," said Sophie. Then she stopped, eyes going wide. "Wait, are you—are you bleeding?"

Melody West, better known in some circles as Antimony Price, youngest daughter of the Price family and cryptozoologist in training, barely managed to conceal her wince. She'd been hoping to get to her locker and her emergency first aid kit before anyone noticed that her lip was split and her knees were skinned severely enough to impress a six-year-old.

"You should see the other guy?" she said weakly.

Sophie lowered her arms and moved toward her teammate, irritation forgotten. The other cheerleaders clustered around them as Sophie seized Antimony's hands. Antimony swallowed another wince. Sophie clearly hadn't noticed that her palms were almost as raw as her knees.

"Who did this to you?" Sophie asked, voice low. A murmur of angry curiosity rose from the rest of the squad, formless and violent. Melody was one of their own. Melody was part of the team. If they needed to no-show on the game to kick somebody's ass on her behalf, well, that was a price they were willing to pay to protect a fellow Trailblazer.

Antimony dropped her eyes, looking to the side and away. It was a practiced motion, and one she'd been using when people asked about her frequent injuries since the start of high school. It wasn't *fair*. Her older sister, Verity, got the skill with makeup to conceal her bruises and scrapes without looking like she was enrolling in clown school. And Alex, her older brother, was a boy:

people generally shrugged off anything less severe than a broken bone as long as he looked stoic about it.

(She was pretty sure that wasn't fair either: Alex had as much right to concern and compassion as she did, and being a boy didn't mean his injuries hurt any less. But he didn't complain because a bruise ignored was a bruise not reported to Social Services. Under the circumstances, she would have swapped with him in a hot second.)

"Mel, you've got to talk to someone. If this is your loser boyfriend ..."

There was no loser boyfriend. There had never been a loser boyfriend. Antimony had fabricated him from whole cloth, a rough, slightly disreputable character who went to a different high school and had been portrayed — on the few occasions when he needed to be seen by her classmates, from a safe distance — by her nerdy cousin Artie in what he insisted on calling "jock cosplay," driving her Uncle Ted's 1969 Camaro and sneering. Thus far, she'd managed to keep any member of the squad from meeting him face-to-face, which was for the best, since Artie's pheromones tended to scramble the hormones of girls he wasn't actually related to.

"I'm fine," she said, and that was the truth, at least; all her wounds were the kind that could be handled with Band-Aids and antiseptic and extra foundation. The changeling-infested bear she'd helped her family kill couldn't say the same. It was dead and downed and probably on fire by now, since her mother had very firm ideas about disposing of hazardous material.

If she was being *really* honest, she was feeling a little smug. How many people could fight a murderous, technically undead bear and make it to campus in time for the big game? Not many, that was how many. She was crushing it.

Sophie sighed. "Okay, we don't have time to argue about this right now, but will you promise me you'll at least think about talking to someone? I'm scared for you."

"I promise," lied Antimony, without a twinge of guilt.

She'd been lying to her friends and teammates since kindergarten. What was one more?

"Thank you," said Sophie, and pulled her into a quick hug before turning to the rest of the squad and barking, "Anyone who's ready to hit the field, get your butt over here and get Mel presentable! What looks bad on one of us looks bad on all of us!"

Like a glittering cloud, the cheerleaders descended.

If there had ever been a triage team as efficient as cheerleaders helping one of their own get ready, Antimony couldn't think of it. In a matter of seconds, she was sitting on a bench, stripped from the waist down. One cheerleader bandaged her knees; another covered the gauze in Trailblazer blue athletic tape, making it look more "aesthetic" than "accident." Two more cheerleaders dealt with the damage on her face, expertly layering paint and powder.

"Arms *up*," commanded Sophie. Antimony put her arms up. The makeup team paused long enough for Antimony's sweater and bra to be removed. Antimony spared a momentary thanks for the fact that she'd been through this process before, and had no difficult-to-explain weapons concealed on her person.

"Arms *out*."

Antimony stuck her arms out. Sophie produced Antimony's sports bra and uniform top from the gym bag, pulling them onto the larger cheerleader's body.

Someone hit Antimony in the face with a fistful of glitter. She struggled not to cough. It might have thrown off the person who was brushing her hair. Then someone else was taping her hands, and her skirt was being fastened around her waist, and she was done: she was dressed.

"Good work!" shouted Sophie, clapping her hands and glancing at the clock above the door. "With two minutes to spare! Go Trailblazers!"

"*Go Trailblazers*!" shouted the rest of them, even Antimony, who wasn't really Antimony anymore: she was Melody West, high school cheerleader, without a care more complex than finally landing that perfect tumbling pass and seeing the world spread out before her in perfect, crystalline simplicity.

They moved as one, out of the locker room and across the grass to the glowing rectangle of the football field. The sun was long down, and floodlights lit the bleachers and the green, making it look like a slice of paradise, like something too perfect to be real. There was a cut between the sections of the stands, and the squad ran through it just as the announcer boomed, "Your Trailblazer cheer squad!"

Everyone in the bleachers cheered and shouted and waved their pennants and foam fingers in the air. It wasn't because they loved cheerleaders so much, Antimony knew. It was because the football teams would be out next, and then the game could finally start. That didn't slow any of them down. The squad broke into a new formation, the fliers going into an elaborate tumbling pass, the bases hitting their poses and waving their pom-poms high. Antimony hit her mark and froze.

It wasn't safe for any of them to go to the same school. She and her siblings had all been educated separately, using their education as an opportunity to test out their false identities and learn to blend. She'd never set foot on any of Verity's high school campuses—she'd had three, overachiever that she was—and had only seen Alex's school once, after he'd graduated, when an away game had taken her to their football field. Family didn't come to school. That was the rule. That was how they kept things distinct, and prevented future disaster.

And there, sitting in the front row, dressed in school colors and clutching school pennants and looking for all the world like students who'd decided to come and see what all the fuss was about, were her dead aunts, Mary and Rose. Rose was wearing a letter jacket, which explained the hot dog in her free hand. As a hitchhiking ghost, she could become temporarily alive again if she borrowed someone else's clothes, and she was always, always hungry. Mary just looked like, well, Mary, white hair blowing in the breeze, one fist thrust into the air.

Finally, her family had come to see her cheer.

Grinning ear to ear, Antimony shook her pom-poms,

and chanted, "Do your best to blaze that trail! You know our team never fails!"

The other team's cheerleaders answered, and the crowds roared, and the football players took the field, and everything was perfect. Everything was finally, absolutely, *perfect*. Antimony never wanted the night to end.

But of course, it did.

One

"Change is good. Change keeps us growing, and growing keeps us living. But don't ever change so much that you forget who you used to be."

–Frances Brown

The Cast Member Recruitment Office of Lowry Entertainment, Inc., Lakeland, Florida

Eight months ago

I SAT VERY STRAIGHT IN my uncomfortable plastic chair, trying to look like I wasn't freaking out. Judging by the way the other applicants kept glancing at me, I wasn't doing a very good job.

Let's see any of *them* stay this calm after spending four nights sleeping in the snake-filled bushes next to the Florida highway, waiting to be eaten by the next available alligator, wondering if that might be an improvement over waking up in the morning and resuming their walk. I hadn't eaten in two days. The only reason I didn't smell like a dumpster fire was the truck stop half a mile outside of town, which had attached showers available for rent. My last five bucks had gone for hot water and industrial soap, and the prayer of getting this job.

There were other jobs. Some of them might be easier to get, especially given my current circumstances, and if I had to resort to them, I would. There's no shame in flipping burgers or cutting lawns. But I wanted the anonymity of the crowd, the knowledge that my itchy polyester uniform made me part of a faceless mob. If the Covenant was looking for me, they'd be checking the greasy spoons and car washes. Those are the places people on the run are supposed to go to make a quick buck. This was a whole different league, and I was counting on that to protect me. If I could get through the door.

I'd burned most of my fake IDs when I ran away from the carnival. My cousin Artie tracks them for us, making sure the associated credit cards and address information will always ping as valid on government systems. The trouble there was that my cousin Artie *tracks* them for us. If I used any of those identities, he'd be able to find me, and that would completely undercut the point of running away.

But I still had one to fall back on.

Artie didn't create "Melody West," because he'd been too young when I first needed her. She'd been a gift to my parents from Uncle Al, a jink living in Las Vegas who got adopted into the family through the usual complex series of unreasonable events. We don't have much blood family left in the world, but we make up for it by acquiring honorary family everywhere we go.

As far as most people are concerned, "Melody West" disappeared after she graduated from high school, one more boring mystery for a world that's always been absolutely full of them. I've never liked to let anything useful go to waste. I'd been expanding upon and tinkering with her identity ever since, keeping her on the grid just enough to qualify as a real person. She'd never held a steady job, never anything lucrative enough to attract the attention of the IRS, but she'd never applied for benefits either. She moved around a lot. She was unremarkable, unnoticeable, and she was *mine*. No one else knew her ID was still active.

Antimony Price couldn't get a job at Lowryland, because Antimony Price wasn't here. Melody West, though, just might stand a chance.

"Melody?" The woman who called my name didn't look up from her clipboard.

I rose. "Here."

She finally glanced up. Her nostrils flared in barely-smothered dismay at the sight of me. There's only so much a truck stop bathroom can do for a body.

I'll give her this much: she covered her reaction quickly. "This way," she said, stepping back into the hall. People had been vanishing through that door all morning long. None of them had come back. There was another door that led to the outside, to keep those of us still waiting from either getting dispirited when we saw happy applicants, or cocky when we saw disappointed ones. Psychologically speaking, it was probably a good design.

In practice, it made me feel like everyone who left was being fed into a giant meat grinder somewhere behind the scenes. And now it was my turn. I forced myself to keep smiling and followed the nameless woman out of the room, toward what I hoped would be my future.

Children and parents all over the world speak the name of Michael Lowry with only slightly less reverence than the name Walt Disney. They were rivals once, after all, and while Disney proved to have the edge when it came to modern family entertainment, Lowry held his market share with an iron hand, producing innovative pictures and inexpensive alternatives for the family that couldn't quite afford the golden spires of Disney's enchanted kingdoms. Not managing to match Disney's towering successes didn't take him out of the game.

Like Disney, Lowry dreamed of amusement parks, immersive environments for the whole family to enjoy. Like Disney, Lowry saw California and Florida as the best locations to realize his dreams, since they were the states with the mildest winters and hence the fewest annual closure dates. They weren't the only ones to flee to America's vacation destinations, but they were the first to break ground on their great entertainments, and Florida's Lowryland opened only two years after Disney World.

Not that anyone would have known Disney World

even existed from walking down the hall of the Lowry-land recruitment office. Framed black-and-white photos of Lowryland were placed every few feet, each tastefully accentuated with a plaque or framed award certificate or article extolling the superior virtues of Lowry Entertainment, Inc. over all other children's entertainment companies. I'd been expecting team spirit from the Lowry folks—no point in being on a team if you can't find something to cheer about—but this was approaching pep rally levels.

My escort led us to a cubicle maze, where she gestured for me to take a seat on the petitioner's side of an L-shaped desk. She wrinkled her nose, ever so slightly, when my butt hit the chair. I was clearly even dirtier looking than I'd thought. My heart sank.

I could try Lowry again, of course. The nice thing about having a fake ID is that you can always get another one. But fake IDs cost money, and without contacting my family, I'd have to find a way to get that money on my own. Robbing convenience stores might play a big part in my future if I wanted to be able to buy clean clothes, a clean name, and a second shot at all the jobs I was about to not get.

"All right, Miss . . . West, what brings you to the Lowry family? Why should we consider you for the position?"

"I'm a hard worker, I'm motivated to meet and exceed any employment requirements, and I have experience working with traveling carnivals, which means I've worked with crowds, children, people experiencing ride-related vertigo, and entertainers." All of that was true. That's the key to a good lie: build it on a foundation of as much truth as possible, because the truth will shore it up even when the falsehoods begin falling away.

I'm getting awfully tired of lying about who I am. There's always been a veil of pretense between me and the rest of the world, thanks to my family and what we do, but there's a big difference between basic subterfuge and this "Bruce Banner on the run from the government goons" bullshit that has consumed my life.

The woman flashed me a frozen smile. My heart sank.

That wasn't the sort of smile that came before "you got the job." It *might* be the kind of smile that came before "Security is going to escort you off the premises." All in all, not a good sign. My fingertips grew hot as my anxiety about failing to get the job translated into adrenaline and the adrenaline translated, as it so often does, into my body trying to involuntarily set things on fire.

Being an untrained magic-user in the process of manifesting her powers is fun, and by "fun" I mean "only slightly better than being covered in wasps, like, all the goddamn time." Better yet, there's no one around to train me. The last magic-user in our family was my grandfather, Thomas Price, and he's been missing since long before I was born. My Aunt Mary could get me the lessons I need, but she's a crossroads ghost, and well . . .

Some prices are still too steep for me to pay, even if it means occasionally charring my clothes.

I stuck my fingers under my knees, smothering them as best I could, and met the woman's frozen smile with a weak, wavering smile of my own. *Please don't say what you're about to say,* I thought. *Please don't.*

She did. "Lowryland is not a traveling carnival, Miss West, and while we appreciate your enthusiasm, your lack of either references or a fixed address makes you—"

"*Melody*?" Excitement tinged my assumed name, causing it to climb higher with every letter, until it peaked in something just shy of a squeak. "Melody *West*?"

The woman with the clipboard blanched. I turned.

There, standing in the mouth of the cubicle, was my high school cheer captain, Sophie Vargas. Oh, she was older now—who wasn't?—and had traded her cheerleading uniform for a smart pantsuit in a shade of cream that set off her naturally tan skin gorgeously. It looked like it cost about as much as my cousin Elsie's car, and that wasn't even going into the accessories, which were all opal, and obviously all real. Her makeup was tasteful, her heels were both leather and low, and I could easily have walked past her on the street without a second glance, if not for one little detail:

She had a spirit bow—in the Lowry Entertainment

logo colors, red and silver—clipped above her left ear. It was a playful, almost juvenile affectation, and it made the rest of her make sense. Sophie was always an over-achiever. Now she was just overachieving on a corporate level.

I didn't have to work to make my eyes widen or my jaw drop. The sight of her did that all on its own. "Sophie?"

"Oh, my *God*, I heard your voice down the hall, and I thought 'naw, that can't be Mels,' but here you are—" Sophie paused, frowning. "Here you are. Clarice, what are you doing here? If this is an intake interview, it should be happening in one of the conference rooms."

"Miss West's credentials are somewhat . . . lacking," said the clipboard woman. She was less frightening now that she had a name and was grimacing like she'd bitten into something sour. "She does not have a fixed address, and while she's listed several relevant skills, she has no verifiable past employment."

"I see," said Sophie. There was a sudden, venomous sweetness in her tone. I remembered that voice aimed at cheer newbies on the field behind our high school, usually right after they complained about something trivial. "Did you not receive this quarter's memo on giving back to the community by working with people who lack work history but possess applicable skills?"

"That was meant to help us hire more seasonal college workers, not homeless people," said Clarice.

Sophie's face froze. "I see. Thank you for your candor; I'll be speaking with your supervisor. Melody, with me, please."

It had never been a good idea to argue with Sophie when she used that tone. I couldn't imagine that had changed. I jumped to my feet, grabbing my backpack from where I'd stuffed it under the chair, and started toward the cubicle exit. At the last moment I paused, offered Clarice a wan smile, and said, "Thank you for meeting with me."

Sophie took my arm and whisked me down the hall before Clarice could reply. That might have been for the best. I couldn't imagine whatever Clarice might have to say would be terribly complimentary.

The cubicle maze extended to the far wall, where Sophie took a sharp left, pulling me into a narrow hallway with walls only a few shades darker than her suit. I made a sound of impressed amazement as I realized her outfit was not only designed to coordinate with her accessories and her coloration, but with the building itself. She was dressed to look like the whole place had been painted solely to flatter her. It was either genius or proof that she'd spent too much time as a cheerleader. Or possibly both. Both was always an option.

We reached an open door with her name on a brass nameplate next to it. SOPHIE VARGAS-JACKSON. I blinked.

"You got married?"

"I would have invited you, but no one knew where you were." Sophie gave me a measuring sidelong look. It was the first time she'd visibly assessed me since stepping into Clarice's cubicle. It definitely wasn't the first time she'd done it. Sophie was good like that. People never knew she was sizing them up until it was done. "You know, most of the old squad has stayed in touch. You're the only one who dropped off the face of the planet."

"Yeah, well." I looked away before she could see more than regret in my eyes. "Things got complicated."

"Things always do."

Sophie's office was sleek, sophisticated, with leather chairs and glass-topped furnishings, all accented with little pops of Lowry red. (Literally "Lowry red." That's the name of the color. Isn't trademark law fun?) She stepped around the desk and sat in her high-backed executive chair, gesturing for me to have a seat. I sat.

The visitor's chair here was sure a lot nicer than the one in Clarice's cubicle. It was probably going to need to be steam-cleaned after encountering me.

"Did you marry him?" asked Sophie, without preamble. I blinked at her. "Uh . . ."

"Because I've been the hiring manager here for two years—don't laugh, I'm young, but I went to business school, and the company knows potential when it comes along. I've seen a lot of people come through those doors and run into the gatekeepers like Clarice. She's supposed to screen out the ones who aren't safe to be around children, the ones who aren't competent. Clearly, it's time to send her back to sensitivity training." Sophie rolled her eyes. "Some people can't get it through their damned thick skulls that if you're willing to see the potential in everyone, you're in a position to benefit from everyone. You'll never find a harder, more dedicated, more loyal worker than someone who's already been passed over by somebody else."

"You're running a corporation like a cheer squad?" Sophie had become squad captain when we were sophomores in high school, winning by a clear majority vote on a platform of inclusiveness and not being a jerk without good reason. She didn't quite have an "everybody into the pool" policy, but under her guidance, our squad had become a lot more diverse and a lot more successful than it had been under the previous regime's "we like skinny blondes who don't make good bases but sure can shake their asses" guidelines.

Sophie smiled thinly. "I'm not running the corporation yet. Give me ten years, and maybe I will be. Did you marry him? Because I'll be honest. I assumed you'd said 'no' when he asked, and that he'd murdered you and stuffed your body into a drainage ditch somewhere. It's not like your absentee parents would ever have noticed."

Just like that, everything clicked.

Melody West did not come from a warm and loving home, because if she had, I wouldn't have spent all my time making excuses for the absence of her—of my—parents. My home was warm. My home was loving. It was just that my parents couldn't come to my school functions any more than they'd come to Verity's or Alex's. We were as close to on our own as the system allowed. But that meant people looked at my naturally somewhat dour demeanor and frequent bruises and assumed I was neglected at best, abused at worst. I didn't work very hard to convince them otherwise. If they thought they had all the answers, they didn't look any deeper.

Unfortunately, it also meant that when my squad decided I was dating a boy who beat me, they didn't trust my parents to step in and stop it before I got seriously hurt. My high school career had been peppered with well-meaning interventions aimed at ending a relationship that didn't exist. When Melody West vanished after graduation . . .

It was easy to understand why they'd drawn the conclusions they had, and I felt terrible for doing that to them.

Not so terrible that I wouldn't take advantage now that I needed it. I cast my eyes down at my hands, clasping them together in my lap, and mumbled, "I didn't get murdered."

"Where is he now?"

I shrugged.

Sophie sighed, relieved. "Mel, did you finally leave him?"

I glanced up, reading her expression quickly before I said, "I was in a bad spot. I couldn't stay. So I just . . . I ran with what I had on me. The money ran out a couple of days ago. I know I look like hell, but I can work, you know what kind of work ethic I have, and I thought . . . I thought I might feel better if I went to work someplace that's about making people happy. I thought it might make me happy, too."

All of it was true, except for the last part. Working at Lowryland wasn't going to make me happy. It was going to make me harder to find. It was going to buy me the time to figure out what to do next. I needed to disappear before the Covenant used me to find my family.

Sophie nodded. "I can't do you any special favors just because we have a history."

"I know. I didn't expect to find you here."

"But I can do you the favor Michael Lowry wanted us to do for the entire world: I can give you a chance." Sophie leaned across the desk. "Do you really want a job?"

"I do."

"Then welcome to Lowryland," she said, and held out her hand. "And welcome back to your life."

I took her hand, and shook it, and smiled. Things were finally going my way.

Two

"If you live a lie too long, it turns into the truth. Be careful which ones you decide deserve that kind of power."

–Enid Healy

A shitty company apartment five miles outside of Lakeland, Florida

Now

MY ALARM WENT OFF before sunrise, shrieking shrill and piercing in the gloom of my bedroom. Only gloom, not darkness: both my roommates were already up, and while they were generously keeping their voices down until I crawled out of bed, neither of them could see in the dark. The hallway light crept around the edges of my door, painting everything in shades of charcoal.

I rolled onto my side and hit the alarm clock with all the pent-up aggression I'd collected over the past few days. It stopped shrieking. It did not, alas, break. Like all Lowryland Cast Member Housing (capital letters mandatory, unless you wanted an Official Lowryland Branding Lecture), our apartment came equipped with ancient, industrial-strength alarm clocks designed to wake the dead, if necessary. If you could break one, you'd be fined twenty dollars and issued a replacement that had been made less than ten years ago, which meant it could take an iPod hookup and wake you with something less violent than the screeching of a nuclear air raid siren.

(As to why we didn't just replace them: spot

inspections were a thing that happened because, apparently, we couldn't be trusted not to destroy company property. If one of the managers swung by and found us with an unauthorized alarm clock, we could be fined a lot more than twenty dollars. We'd also get a black mark on our records—all three of our records, even if only one of us had gone to Target for modern technology. Much as we hated the alarms, we hated black marks on our record even more.)

My name is Antimony Price, even if no one calls me that anymore, and sometime in the last eight months, this became my life. I worry about alarm clocks now. I worry about black marks on my record.

I worry about getting out of bed on time.

Groaning, I sat up and rubbed my eyes with the heels of my hands, trying to make them want to open. They did not. Opening was, in fact, low on their list of things to do today, right above "staying open" and "looking at the world." I respected their right to protest, but had to declare a fiat, since they didn't really have a choice. I needed to work if I wanted to eat, and I needed to eat if I wanted to stay alive. For all that things had turned to shit since leaving the carnival, I wasn't ready to lay down and die. Not yet. Not until I knew whether I'd managed to save my family by running when I did.

Most people have seen the footage, either live or on YouTube: a blonde girl in high heels and a sequined dress fighting a giant monster snake on national television, right before declaring war on a shadow organization, shooting the camera, and disappearing. (Oh, heads almost certainly rolled over that. Someone should have killed the feed before it hit the air. The network *did* kill the feed for all time zones after the first one. But we live in the age of instant gratification, uploads and downloads and viral videos, and once the cat—once the giant dimension-hopping snake—was out of the bag, there was no putting it back. The world was watching.)

That wasn't me. That was my big sister, Verity, she of the awesome dance moves and totally absent common sense. "We're in hiding from a global organization of monster hunters who thinks we're public enemy number one," she thought. "I'll just go fight a snake cult on national television."

To be fair to her—not that I'm usually inclined to be fair to her—she probably didn't say it *exactly* like that. And she wasn't the one who *summoned* the giant dimension-hopping snake during a live broadcast. My family sometimes charges into danger without thinking about it, but we're pretty good about not endangering civilians, or blowing our cover. Given a choice between blowing her cover and letting a lot of civilians die, Verity had taken the only real option she had available. It was the one I would have taken, too, if I'd been in her place.

But once her face was broadcast around the world, people saw her. People *knew* her. The Covenant was suddenly aware that our family was still alive, kicking, and getting in the way of their undoubtedly nefarious plans for the world. That was a problem. The Covenant of St. George didn't become the biggest, baddest monster hunting organization the human race has ever known by standing back and letting their enemies do whatever they wanted to. They're killers. They were going to come for us.

We needed to know how much they knew. And that's where I briefly digress from my digression about the Covenant of St. George to talk about monster hunter breeding programs.

See, the Covenant has been a closed wall against the rest of the world for centuries. They take new recruits when they can get them, but the monster hunters of old did way too good a job: they wiped out most of the dragons and ogres and giants and other really big, obvious, impossible to explain away monsters that evolution had to offer. They also believed that a lot of those creatures drew their power from being believed in, so they spent centuries trying to convince everyone that sea serpents were logs and crossroads ghosts were just a trick of the light. The end result? A world where no one believes in monsters and so nobody is really panting to sign up with a paramilitary monster hunting organization.

But they still need members, and like all good para-military organizations, they've been recruiting from the easiest available population: their own children. This is where I'd say something nasty about their parenting skills, except for the part where my parents raised me the same way. I always knew I was going to go into the family business, because I always knew we lived in a danger-ous, complicated world—one that needed me. Maybe that's the Covenant in us coming to the surface.

Up until five generations ago, we were members in good standing, as bloodthirsty and obedient as the rest. We got better. The rest of the Covenant didn't.

In order to avoid inbreeding and bad things, the Cov-enant started a genealogical branch right around the time they started having recruitment issues. Arranged marriages and predictable family traits became the name of the game. My family, my modern, American, non-Covenant family, looks a lot like a Covenant family called the Carews: short and blond and spunky and dan-gerous. Apparently, Carew genes are dominant, although Alex looks more like a Healy, taller and browner-haired and with slightly worse eyesight.

Me, though? I actually look like a Price. And since my grandfather, Thomas Price, was the last Covenant mem-ber of his line, no one in the modern Covenant really knows what that means anymore. Out of all of us, I was the only one who could be sent to find out what the Cov-enant knew, and what they were planning to do with that knowledge. I barely had time to tell my roller derby league I was going on sabbatical before my family had me on a plane to London, where I'd hooked up with the local Covenant recruitment center and been whisked away to a big manor house in the middle of nowhere to be tested, evaluated, and eventually dropped into a shal-low grave if they decided I wasn't what they were look-ing for.

I have always done excellently on tests. I passed them all, despite the stress of pretending to be a zealot while concealing my honor guard of talking mice, and the Cov-enant decided I was a great recruit deserving of a field trial. Which is how I wound up with the Spenser and Smith Family Carnival, having been sent undercover by the people I'd been sent undercover to spy on, and if that sentence feels like a headache waiting to happen, just imagine how I felt when all this was actually going on.

The Covenant wanted me to assess the Spenser and Smith Family Carnival for a purge. There had been some disappearances; there had been some questions raised. If there was something killing people, the Covenant was ready to step in and make it stop ... and the fact that they'd be doing it on North American soil, in territory my family had been struggling to protect for decades, was almost icing on the cake. They were testing my loyalty. They were testing my skills.

They were backing the wrong horse. In a move that was predictable to anyone who'd ever met me without my masks on, I betrayed them, saved the people of the carnival if not the carnival itself—we sort of burned that down—and then I got my mice to safety and ran, because they knew me. They had my blood, sweat, and skin, and if they were willing to bring their magic-users to the party, they could track me down. I wasn't going to be the reason they found my family.

The crowds at Lowryland are big enough to confuse that sort of tracking spell. See, everyone in the world is technically related, if you go far enough back along the family tree, and when you put a few thousand distant cousins in one place, the false positives are enough to overwhelm even the most focused magic. As long as I stayed where the people were, I would be safe, and as long as I had no contact with my family, I would be drawing no lines for the Covenant to follow.

All it cost was my home, and my name, and everyone I cared about. No big deal, right?

Right.

Rubbing the back of my neck with one hand, like I could massage away all the aches and agonies of the day before they even happened, I left my room for the dubious comforts of the rest of my shared apartment. Lowryland promised affordable housing to all their thousands of employees, in part, I assumed, so they could figure out how much of our paychecks we were socking away in preparation for heading someplace better. They didn't promise particularly comfortable housing, or that we wouldn't have to share it.

Enter my roommates. Banes of my existence, the only reason I was still sane, and best of all, the reason the hall outside my room smelled strongly of bacon and coffee.

"Coffee," I moaned, shambling toward the kitchen. The door to the room shared by Megan and Fern was shut, which probably meant they had suffered another laundry tornado and didn't want to risk guests seeing inside. Not that we ever had any. Inviting guests over would have meant allowing other people to enter our home, and we had reasons to avoid that.

Fern looked up when I appeared in the doorway. She was already beaming. "Morning, Annie," she chirped. "I made you extra bacon because I know you've got an extra shift tonight."

"I love you, don't call me 'Annie,'" I said, and made a beeline for the coffee machine.

Reason number one, and the main source of any mental stability I currently have: Fern. AKA, "the only person at Lowryland who could blow my cover at any moment if she chose to, but who has blessedly chosen not to." AKA, "one of the girls I used to skate with on the Slasher Chicks roller derby team back in Portland." AKA, "one of the few close friends I've ever had who wasn't related to me, and thank God for that."

Fern is a sylph, a humanoid cryptid capable of controlling her personal density. She's always short, skinny, and colored like a porcelain Bo Peep figure, all milky skin, golden hair, and vast blue eyes. It's just that sometimes she's light enough for a stiff breeze to carry away— literally—and other times, she's denser than tungsten. Watching her deal with people trying to shove her out of the way on the train to work is one of my life's small joys. As to why she's in Florida instead of Portland, where I left her, I have yet to get a straight answer. And, honestly,

I don't much care. I know she's not reporting on me to the family. That's all I need to know.

(As for *how* I know . . . that's another story, and involves my dead Aunt Mary, who checks in on me weekly. I have a weird family.)

Without Fern, I wouldn't have survived my first week with the company. Without Fern, I *definitely* wouldn't be in one of the nicer apartments—and yes, our tiny, cabbage-scented place was considered one of the nicer options available. Fern had spotted me across the quad during housing registration for new hires, and had come bounding over to grab me by the elbow and announce me as her long-prophesized second roommate, awaited and adored. I'd been too surprised to fight, and she'd dragged me home with her, where I was given my own room and added to the lease.

As for why I got my own room when I was the third person to come into the apartment, enter exhibit B: Megan. Short for "Magaere," because that's a name that modern people give to their children. Not that Megan's parents are modern. Megan's parents are Pliny's gorgons, which makes Megan a Pliny's gorgon, which means I couldn't room with her unless I wanted to be in constant danger of being temporarily paralyzed. Not my idea of a party.

(Fern didn't have the same concerns. Something about the way sylph density works—or doesn't—protects them from the gaze of the gorgon. Just one more mystery of science that we may never have the opportunity or the equipment to solve.)

Currently, Megan was wigless, letting the snakes atop her head breathe freely. Their tongues constantly scented the air, assessing their environment. Like all gorgon "hair," they looked like perfectly ordinary serpents, if I ignored the fact that their bodies ended at a humanoid scalp instead of in a snaky tail. (Gorgon X-rays are *fascinating*.) They were colored like delicate rattlesnakes in shades of dark brown verging on black and the very palest of peach. They were beautiful, as was the woman they were attached to, who was sipping from a mug of coffee with her eyes half-lidded behind her smoked glasses.

One of the snakes yawned, showing its fangs. Beautiful and dangerous.

"How did you sleep?" asked Fern blithely. Of the three of us, she was the only morning person. Megan and I were united in our hatred of her before noon. We were united in loving her the rest of the time, so it worked out.

"Not long enough," I said, splashing coffee into my cup. It was thick and black, brewed triple-strength, just the way I liked it. Just the way all three of us liked it.

"Word," muttered Megan.

"What's your shift today?" I asked, dumping sugar into my coffee.

The snakes on her head coiled into a striking position, responding to the change in her mood. "Noon to midnight," she said glumly. "I'm going to be a corpse tomorrow."

"Sucks," I agreed sympathetically.

I was a general employee, going where I was told and filling whatever positions needed to be filled. I could work a register, monitor a gate, set up a parade route, or help guests get to where they were going. Fern, with her delicate build, perfect features, and already cartoon-worthy voice, was what we called a "face character," one of the people who got to put on a fancy costume and spend the day embodying one of Lowry's cartoon creations—in her case, Princess Aspen from *Goldtree and Silvertree*, that 1989 masterpiece of soft-focus pseudo-feminism in a fairy-tale coating.

(The girl who played Elm was human, and shared her apartment with two other face character performers, and thought Fern was out of her mind for continuing to associate with riffraff like me. It takes all kinds to make a properly annoying world.)

Megan, on the other hand, was something elevated and rare, and wouldn't have been in general housing at all if she hadn't requested to be placed with Fern. Megan was a medical graduate student doing her residency at the Lowryland Hospital—which was, yes, a fully accredited and functional facility, with the necessary equipment for everything from delivering a baby to performing organ transplants and other major surgical procedures. Getting a position there was supposed to be difficult bordering on impossible, and no one could figure out how Megan had been able to get in, since she didn't come from an affluent family with a history of training on Lowry property. No one in her family tree was a millionaire, or possessed of much political capital, or even human. I would have been willing to bet she was the first cryptid ever to be accepted into the program.

That was probably part of how she'd been able to get in. Gorgon communities like the one she comes from always need doctors, and so do the dragons, the wadjet, and the other cryptids who look like mammals but are really reptiles or therapsids. Once she'd qualified for Lowry, it would have been easy to hire someone like my Uncle Al to give her application the push it needed to rise to the top of the heap.

As the only nonhuman in the program, though, she couldn't stay with the other residents without running the risk of blowing her cover and winding up in a biology lab. Hence her staying in the sticks with us, and dealing with the chaos of three competing schedules in one house.

Three competing . . . wait. "Okay, why are we all up?" I asked, lowering my mug. "I'm supposed to be to work at eight. Did I oversleep again?" I didn't look at the clock. If I was late, I was late, and nothing was going to change that. I was going to finish my coffee before I went off to get disciplined.

"My mom called this morning," said Megan.

"Her mother called at four o'clock, is what she means to say," said Fern. "She doesn't understand that we can't be fully nocturnal here."

"That, or she's punishing me for being a fussy baby." Megan yawned, wider than a human would have been capable of yawning, until my own jaw ached in sympathy. "I love my family, but I would swallow my own feet for a nap."

"So take one," I said.

She shook her head. "Can't. If I sleep now, I'll sleep through the start of my shift. Besides, if I'm up, I can give the two of you a ride to work."

I perked up. "Have I mentioned recently that you're a brilliant, talented doctor who's going to revolutionize the field of medicine?"

Megan's hair hissed at me.

It's not that the train between employee housing and the park is unreliable. Like most things in Lowryland, it runs with a precision that would make a watchmaker weep. It's not that it's expensive. A monthly train pass is included with our employment, and can be used to get on either at the employee parking lot or at any of the six housing stops.

It's that the trains are always packed, and the air-conditioning is broken about two-thirds of the time, and the upholstery smells like canned meat and old sweat, and there's no possible way to avoid people touching you, whether they intend to or not. It's that there are cliques and social groups anyplace there are people, and being on the outside of the majority of them can make the ride pretty damned uncomfortable.

(To be fair to them, it's not like I've exactly gone out of my way to try making friends. To be *un*fair to them, it's not like they would have made it easy for me if I had. Most of them don't even like Fern, and she's the walking, talking incarnation of a happy meadow filled with butterflies and flowers. Amusement park politics are like academic politics, only more so. The infighting's so vicious because the stakes are so low.)

Ten minutes after Megan offered us a ride, Fern and I were dressed—within reason—and crammed into her battered Toyota Corolla. I had a purse full of bacon, makeup, and small personal items. Fern had an entire garment bag, which she used as a pillow as she stretched out across the backseat and closed her eyes. That was probably a large part of how she could survive being a morning person: the girl was capable of napping anywhere, even places where it should have been physically impossible to nap.

"Our rear end's dragging," muttered Megan, before twisting around and jabbing Fern in the leg. "Hey. You. Lighten up."

"Sorry, Megan," mumbled Fern sleepily. The car's rear end rose six inches as she turned her personal density down, becoming about as substantial as her garment bag.

Megan flashed me a wry sidelong smile, a moment of camaraderie between unlikely roommates. I smiled back, more strained. At least I was trying. That was more than most people would have guessed I'd do. I was trying.

I never wanted my life to be a wacky sitcom about a human girl and her inhuman roommates struggling to get by at what many people consider to be the second-happiest place in the world. I'm not actually sure *what* I wanted my life to be. Figuring it out never seemed quite as important as living it. I'd been a cheerleader in high school and a roller derby player afterward. I'd taken my share of online courses, but I'd never bothered going to a "real" college. What was the point? The best I could do was get a degree I'd never use, since it's not like the Evergreen College in Olympia, Washington, offers courses in how to be a better cryptozoologist.

(That may be unfair. Olympia is prime Bigfoot country, and if any school in the world is going to offer classes about them, it's going to be Evergreen. It's just that those classes would be vilely, violently wrong, and I'd probably have gotten myself expelled for punching a teacher.)

On the rare occasions when I'd tried to imagine where I saw myself in ten years, it had either been on the track with my teammates, scoring points and skinning knees, or traveling with the Campbell side of the extended family, spending my days repairing rides and my nights slinging knives for the amusement of the paying audience. In a way, I guess I wanted what Verity wanted: I wanted a stage. I just wanted one that was smaller than hers, in warehouses and big tents rather than ballrooms, where no one remembered the performers, only the performance.

But I'd never seen myself isolated from my family. I didn't even have any mice with me. Whatever happened to me here, no one was going to witness or remember it. I was the first member of our family to be without a piece of our institutional memory since Elizabeth Matheson had discovered a colony of Aeslin mice worshipping a chicken in her yard.

Aeslin mice: hyper-religious, hyper-loyal, and totally devoted to my family. Oh, and they talk. Standard protocol says that none of us go anywhere without a mouse, since that way, if anything happens, the mouse might be able to make it back and tell the story. I'd started my journey with a mouse. Mindy, a member of my personal priesthood, had accompanied me to England to make sure that if something happened to me, word would get back to my family. We'd picked up another mouse there, Mork, a member of the colony that stayed behind when my great-great-grandparents quit the Covenant. He was the only English Aeslin I'd met. The rest preferred to stay in hiding, at least until their representative was able to come back and prove that our colony wasn't a bunch of mouse-eating monsters. It was clever. It was the right way to do things.

The last time I'd seen either Mork or Mindy, I'd been in the process of leaving them with my maybe-boyfriend, Sam, who'd promised to get them to the airport so that they could get back to the rest of my family. According to my dead Aunt Mary, they'd made it. They were fine. That was probably the only reason my mother wasn't burning the world down to find me.

Being the youngest child in my family has sometimes meant feeling like an afterthought, the kid conceived to be a blood donor to the two that actually mattered. But even when I'd been feeling like that, I never questioned whether my parents loved me, or whether they would charge into the gates of hell to snatch me back if they thought they could get away with it. That was one more reason I needed to stay in hiding. If they knew where to find me, they *would* come to bring me home, and then . . .

Most tracking spells work better when there's no interference around the person who's being tracked. My family lives in a survivalist compound outside of Portland. We've always used isolation as one of our greatest strengths. Put me in the building, and it could become an even greater weakness.

Context is everything.

The traffic was heavy around us, cars packed with tourists heading for Lowryland mingling with cars packed with employees heading for Lowryland. Part of why Fern liked to stretch out in the backseat when we got a ride to work was the crowd. When we went bumper to bumper—not an everyday occurrence, but not as rare as I'd like either—people got bored and peered into the cars around them, looking for a karaoke show, or a nose-picker, or an interesting dog. Even out of costume, there was a chance Fern would be recognized. Annual Pass-holders were notorious for learning to identify individual performers, and they could cause problems when encountered "off the clock."

(The scariest incident we'd had so far had been at the Target, of all places. Fern and I had been looking at canned goods when a hand clamped down on her arm and someone started dragging her away, pulling her several feet before she'd managed to increase her density to the point where she couldn't be moved anymore. And then I'd punched the asshole in the gut. He'd fallen over, threatening to call store security and to notify Lowryland about a misbehaving princess. We'd run. When Fern made her security report, she had left me out, claiming that the puncher was a "helpful stranger," and since it hadn't happened on Park property, it hadn't been pursued. But we'd been a lot more careful since then, and we always went shopping in a group.)

The employee turnoff loomed up ahead. Megan tightened her hands on the wheel, an involuntary gesture that broadcast, loudly, how much she didn't want to take it.

"I could keep driving," she said, voice light and

sincere. "We could head for the coast. Just the three of us, surf, sand . . ."

"Unemployment," I said. "I need this job. You need your residency."

"I need a bathroom," said Fern.

"Fern needs a bathroom," I said. "Sad but true: we have to go to work."

"Spoilsport," said Megan, and made the turn.

The traffic was lighter here. Most Lowryland employees take the train, and the rest of us tend to carpool, since the parking lot is a nightmare wasteland where people have come to blows over the "good" spots. Megan wasn't parking. She pulled up to the employee drop-off point, where a line had already formed of cast members waiting for the bus that would take them to the backstage entrance to the Park.

"Let the magic begin," I muttered and opened the door. "See you tonight?"

"Sweet Medusa, I hope not," said Megan. "You need to sleep, or you're going to wind up stabbing somebody."

"Only if they deserve it," I said.

Megan was laughing as I closed the door. Fern and I turned to wave before joining the line. In the distance, the bright lights of Lowryland were warming up for another day, splitting the sky into candy-colored segments, like something out of someone else's dream. Not mine. Never mine.

Clutching the strap of my purse, I shoved my misery and loneliness down as far as it would go. Time to go to work.

Three

"We all have to do things we don't want to do in this life. For example, right now, I have to keep not shooting you."

–Jane Harrington-Price

Lowryland

WE SEPARATED AS SOON as we were on Park property, Fern heading for the dressing room to join the rest of the face characters in preening, primping, and getting ready to face their public. Not a job I envy, or one I would aspire to, even if I fit the requirements for any of the Park's many featured characters—I'm too broad-shouldered and chesty to be a princess, too bitter and sarcastic to be a Fairy, and too tall in general to be shoved into a complicated costume that looks like something out of a child's nightmare. My Price genes may have gotten me into this mess in the first place, but at least those same genes are keeping me from being crammed into a cloth-and-plastic Goblin suit. There are small mercies everywhere.

I took the underground route into the heart of Lowryland. Most guests never realize that everywhere they walk, they're walking over more Lowryland. A complicated maze of tunnels and corridors runs from a point fifty yards outside the visible Park boundary, all the way under the Park itself, sometimes stacked two and three deep, so that it's possible to just keep going down, into an endless warren of laundry rooms, storage, and intra-Park transit tunnels.

(Do I know for sure that there's a colony of hidebehinds living under Lowryland? No. I do not. Am I pretty damn convinced that it has to be down there somewhere? Yes. Yes, I am. Because hidebehinds are smart, and they like it when other people do their work for them.)

The sound of laughter, conversation, and the occasional groan drifted out to meet me as I approached my assigned dressing room. I stood up straighter, pulling the veil of Melody West, grateful ex-cheerleader fleeing from a dubious past, down over myself. Then I stepped inside.

There are people who say you never really escape from high school, you just keep finding it in different forms, over and over again, until it finally kills you. Those people are assholes, and should not be allowed in polite company. That doesn't mean they're wrong. Entering that locker room was like falling down a dark tunnel to the first time I'd been Melody, when she'd been a lie I told the world to keep them from figuring out that I was a lot more Wednesday Addams than Marilyn Munster—not that Marilyn was a good option either, since being Marilyn implied living in a world where monsters were real, and that wasn't something I was allowed to share with my classmates.

They got to be ignorant. They got to walk in the world thinking humanity was in charge of everything, the peak of the evolutionary ladder and rulers of all we surveyed. Turns out, ignorance often comes with an exciting, unexpected side effect: cruelty. To people who think they're the best the world has to offer, kindness is an afterthought and an unnecessary one at that.

The women already in the locker room were no better or worse than me. We were all junior employees, all moving around the Park daily as management decided what our priorities were for the week. We did everything but serve food and sweep streets—and when there was a janitorial emergency, there was always a chance one of us would find ourselves holding a broom. I didn't mind. At the carnival, anybody could be asked to do just about anything in a pinch. I'm not too much of a fainting flower to mop up outside the Scrambler.

Try telling them that. They had better haircuts, better shoes, more friends, and everything else from the mean girl starter kit. Three of them laughed behind their hands when I walked into the room. The others continued getting ready. That didn't mean I could shake the feeling that they were watching me, waiting for the moment when I'd try to strike up a conversation and I could be slapped down hard.

Humans are monkeys, and monkeys like to have a pecking order. I'd sealed my place in ours when, during training, I responded to someone asking "where did you move here from?" with "Route 4." That was all it took. I was formerly homeless, a pity hire, and there was no possible way I could ever be as deserving of comfort or compassion as they were, because poverty is always a personal failing, no matter how it came about.

There are days when I want to punch absolutely everyone around me, and keep punching until they're no longer capable of fighting back. I'm told those desires are antisocial. Sometimes, I really don't care.

I crossed to my locker, opened it, and began to strip. I was going to spend my day in the Fairyland section of the Park, where Princesses Lizzie and Laura would be greeting their adoring public in between rides on the Midsummer Night's Scream (a roller coaster that seemed to have been designed by someone who *really hated* the kind of people who like to ride roller coasters) and trips around the artificial river in Lizzie's Goblin Voyage. I'd be swiping credit cards and making change at the Fine and Fair Gift Shop. Pretty standard, pretty boring, and pretty much a job I could do in my sleep.

I caught a flicker of motion out of the corner of my eye as I yanked on my uniform top. My fingertips warmed in anticipation of the coming fight. I tried to will the heat away. It had been more than a week since I'd set fire to anything I'd need to pay for, and almost three months since the last time I'd started a fire in the Park, period. That was a good thing. If I lost my job because I'd been caught burning company property, I was going to have a hell of a time getting hired anywhere else.

(The traditional destination for Lowryland Cast Members who lose their jobs due to minor rules infractions is Disney World, and vice-versa. Half the ride jockeys in Florida get passed back and forth between theme parks like trading cards on a playground. But there are things that render a person unemployable, and destruction of corporate assets is on the list. Also on the list, bizarrely enough, is chewing tobacco. I guess everyone has standards.)

"Hey, Mel," said a sweet voice.

"Melody," I replied, and finished adjusting my top. Fairyland has six separate themes, depending on which part of it you're working. The Goblin Market area is styled in a vague parody of the pre-Raphaelite aesthetic, all deep jewel tones layered over pale pastels. It's one of my favorite parts of the Park to work in, mostly because the costumes don't show blood as well as, say, the ones in Candyland.

"Sorry, hon?"

I turned, pasting on an artificial smile. The woman next to me was dressed for a day in Metropolis, all shiny silver chrome and breathable purple mesh fabric. She looked like she was getting ready to skate backup in a production of *Starlight Express*, even down to the spray glitter in her hair.

"My name is Melody, not Mel," I said. "That's all I said."

She frowned, nose wrinkling. "That's not friendly of you."

"Really? Because I thought I'd said I didn't like being called 'Mel' every day for the last eight months." The heat in my fingertips died back to comfortable embers. The magic was willing. The magic was ready and eager to go. That was soothing, even if I had no intention of using it. "Hello, Robin. What can I do for you today?"

My tormenter straightened, back on comfortable ground. Her cronies giggled behind their hands. I wanted to tell them they were acting like children, but that would have been an insult to children everywhere. Bullying isn't tied to age. It's tied to who a person is, and sadly, these people were more interested in being ugly assholes than they were in being decent human beings.

"Did you hear that raccoons got into the dumpsters out back again?" she asked, all wide-eyed and innocent.

A place as big as Lowryland makes a lot of trash, and it can't all be burned on-property. There's recycling, and sorting, and disposal to be dealt with. When a guest throws something away, it's carted off by custodial and added to the mountain of debris we dispose of daily, bussing it—literally—to the dumpsters. They're concealed from all public view by a concrete corral nearly half a mile from even the employee parking, where the garbage trucks can come and go without being seen.

It was no surprise when raccoons got into the damn things. If anything, it was a surprise when the raccoons *didn't*. "No, I hadn't. Thanks for the update. Does custodial know?"

"Oh, yeah," she said, and thrust a brown paper bag at me. "Here."

I didn't take the bag. I'm not that stupid. "What's this?"

"We just thought that if you had someone to bring you a lunch, you wouldn't need to go diving in the garbage anymore," she said, eyes wide. She dropped the bag onto the bench. The rest of the girls burst into triumphant laughter as she turned and sashayed away.

I watched her go, clenching my hands to keep myself from burning the whole damn place down. It's not that I hate my job. It's that I hate the people I have to do it with.

Fortunately for my sanity, none of the mean girls were assigned to my part of the Goblin Market, at least not this morning, and it wasn't like they'd risk their usual shenanigans in front of the guests anyway. Fighting amongst ourselves is fine, as long as we do it where no one could see. Upsetting a paying customer, now, that's grounds for immediate termination, no take-backs, there's the door. So I stood in Fine and Fair, helping guests find genuine Lizzie and Laura dolls, assisting lost children, and generally doing whatever needed to be done at any given moment.

"Excuse me," said a familiar voice. "Do you have this in a medium?"

I turned, already smiling, to face my Aunt Mary. "I'll check the back," I said.

She returned my smile. As was usually the case when she appeared at my work, she was dressed to blend in: jeans, sneakers, and a dark purple shirt she'd probably copied from a Hot Topic store window, with an art nouveau Lizzie surrounded by a border of pomegranate flowers stenciled down the side. Her long white hair was pulled into a braid. There was nothing she could do about her eyes, which looked like a hundred miles of empty highway, exit markers marching off toward the horizon, but most people either wouldn't notice them or wouldn't allow themselves to think too hard about what they'd seen. The dead walk among us. Denial keeps that from becoming too big of a problem. Usually.

Mary Dunlavy isn't a blood relative, but she's absolutely a member of the family, because family is more than blood. My Uncle Ted isn't a blood relative—not of me—but he's married to my Aunt Jane, and he's the father of two of my cousins. Mary didn't live long enough to marry in. She just babysat for my grandmother and my father and my aunt and my siblings . . . and me. She only crossed the country, traveling miles from her own grave, to stay with us and make sure we were safe. She's always a crossroads and a call away, and while there are rules that govern what she can and can't do, being a ghost who chooses to exist primarily among the living, she does as much as those rules allow.

She was also the only member of my family who knew where I was hiding. Because she wasn't a blood relative when she was alive, her presence wouldn't tip the balance toward the Covenant being able to find me, and because ghosts go wherever the hell they want, her showing up wasn't going to trigger any alarms.

"Thank you," she said, and leaned closer. "How you doing, kiddo?"

Being called "kiddo" by someone who looked like she hadn't even finished high school—mostly because she hadn't; she'd been dead before graduation—would have been amusing, if it hadn't been Mary. As it was, being called anything else would have seemed strange. Normal is what you make it.

"Getting by." I started walking through the store. She trailed behind me, still projecting the overall impression of a girl who wanted to know whether we had her size. As long as I kept smiling and kept my voice low, no one would notice anything out of the ordinary. That's what I was aiming for. "How's everybody else?"

Mary frowned. She didn't like it when I refused to give her the details on my life, saying that as my only aunt with access, it was her duty to keep an eye on me. She wasn't wrong about that. If she hadn't been able to check in, I would probably have been even twitchier than I already was. Mary was my last connection to home. I was holding on with both hands.

"Worried about you," she said. "Your mother wants you to call."

"My mother always wants me to call."

"Yes, and she's got the right idea. There are ways—"

"We don't know what resources they have. I wasn't there long enough, and I was only in one facility. They could have a whole division of Arties all tapping away, looking for ways in."

Mary gave me a disapproving look. "You don't believe that."

"Does it really matter what I believe?" Being a Lowryland Cast Member had done a lot for my ability to keep smiling even as the life drained out of my voice, leaving me a pleasant, amenable robot designed to please the guests without letting on that I was miserable. "It's not safe. Mom knows that, or she would already have threatened you with an exorcism to get you to tell her where I am. She tells you she wants me to call because she knows that's what a good mother would do, not because she expects me to do it."

My mother *is* a good mother. She has three kids and two kids-in-law, and she loves us all with the fierce protectiveness of a mama bear trying to keep its cubs alive. She's also a pragmatist. She wasn't raised by humans—my maternal grandparents are a cuckoo and a Revenant, and try explaining that when it's time to draw the family tree—and they taught her early that sometimes, when the door closes, the people on the outside are on their own. The survival of the whole matters more than the survival of the individual pieces. If bringing me home meant endangering the rest of the family, she would let me stay away. She would trust me to take care of myself. But she would keep asking me to call because that's what a human mother would do.

Mary sighed. "I don't like this."

"I know. I don't expect you to." We had reached the short corridor between the store and the backroom, where additional stock would be found, if we had any. I stepped into it. Mary followed me, coming as far as a guest reasonably could, while I hovered at the edge, out of the view of any cameras. There were no listening devices—yet. Give corporate a few more years and they'll figure out a way to cram those into their surveillance system.

Hopefully, I'll be long gone by then, having figured out a way to safely thwart the Covenant and return home. That's the trouble with going into hiding to escape from a multinational organization with unknown resources and capabilities. I don't have an exit plan. What I knew to do began and ended with "run." I'd run. I'd found a place to hide. Now I got to live with it.

"My hands are heating up again," I told Mary, keeping my voice low. We could get away with maybe five minutes of unauthorized break, assuming none of my managers wandered by and decided to ask why I was spending so much time on one guest instead of keeping the whole floor happy. "I've managed not to set anything on fire, but it's getting harder."

"You should do a controlled burn," said Mary. "On your next day off, find a trash can and just let loose."

"Arson is not a good thing."

"No, but until we find someone who can train you, it's a little bit inevitable, so we may as well make the best of it." Mary shrugged. "I'd help more if I could. I've been looking for books. Turns out, most magic-users don't like to share."

"Tell me about it." I'd been working from my grandfather's books when I was still at home. Grandpa Thomas had been a magic-user *and* a member of the Covenant of St. George. Somehow, he'd managed to conceal the first from the second for long enough to get away alive, which was no small feat.

There were days when I wished, more than anything, that he'd been as good at avoiding crossroads bargains and being sucked into dimensional rifts as he'd been at escaping from the Covenant. Maybe then he would still have been around to train me, and I wouldn't be living in fear of the day I went all *Firestarter* on my friends. Having most of my potential futures come straight out of Stephen King books is not reassuring.

Mary looked at me with concern. "Don't," she said.

"I wasn't going to!"

"No, but you were starting to think about it, and every time you do that, I'm going to tell you not to."

I glared at her. "You're not the telepath in this family. You don't get to tell me what I'm thinking."

My cousin Sarah is the telepath in the family. Our reunions are a *lot* of fun.

"No, I'm not the telepath." She folded her arms. "I'm just the girl who's been serving the crossroads since before your parents were born, and I can tell when someone's starting to think that making a deal would be good for them. It wouldn't be good for you. It's not good for anyone. So I'm going to tell you no over and over again, until you learn to listen."

"Mary . . ." I paused, and sighed. "I wouldn't do that

to you. You know I wouldn't do that to you. And there's no way the crossroads would send anyone else to broker a family deal, which means that even if I'm tempted, I can't do it."

"Good," she said coldly. Then she thawed a little, and said, "I saw Sam."

"What?" My voice broke at the end of the word, hitting a note too loud and too shrill to be safe. I looked guiltily around before leaning toward her and asking, "How is he? *Where* is he? He's not looking for me, right? He's smart enough that he's not looking for me?"

"The show has settled at a rented training facility in Indiana while they wait for the insurance money; they should be able to replace everything they've lost and be back on the road by the beginning of next season," said Mary. She paused, looking at me carefully before she added, "The Campbell Family Carnival is there with them. They're helping to get the show back on their feet, and making sure no one loses their edge due to idleness."

"But the Campbells—"

"Are family, yes. Not blood family. No one's going to have a tracking charm that can link them to you, or use them to hurt your friends. Breathe. You're not the only person in this family with a brain in their head. You can trust us to not fuck up completely just because you can't make all the decisions."

"Intellectually, I know you're right. Emotionally . . ." I paused, unable to put what I was feeling into words. It was like the words didn't exist. Maybe they didn't. Maybe I'd finally discovered the unspeakable.

Sam Taylor wasn't the love of my life. He wasn't even my significant other, whatever that meant, or my boyfriend, although he'd kissed me like he was, against a burning carnival sky, when everything had been crashing to an end. And then I'd walked away from him, because it was the only way to keep him safe. I didn't love him—at least I didn't think I did—but I might have, if we'd been allowed to take the time to figure out who we were to one another. We'd both been lying from the start of our relationship, and that sort of thing can take some time to get past.

God, I wished we'd had the time.

Unfortunately, while Sam wasn't blood family—and hence wasn't a target for tracking charms, and should have been able to safely come find me—he was something the Covenant viewed as even worse: he was a cryptid. A fūri, to be specific, a kind of yōkai therianthrope originally from China. He was a virtuoso on the flying trapeze, because when he wasn't forcing himself to look human, he had a prehensile tail and feet that could do double duty as hands, and he was one of the most beautiful men I'd ever met. Maybe not when he was standing still, but in motion . . .

I've always been about the motion. Whether it's the cheering field or the derby track, motion is where beauty lives. When Sam moved, he was a poem, and I wanted to memorize the whole damn thing, and for his sake, I could never see him again, and that sucked harder than I could say.

Mary leaned over and touched my arm. "I'll tell your family you're okay, and that you still don't need them to come get you. But you say the word . . ."

"I know," I said. "Thank you, Aunt Mary."

"Any time, kiddo," she said, and she was gone.

I wiped the tears from my cheeks and stepped out of the alcove, pasting my Lowry-approved smile back into place. Time to get to work. After all, this was my life now.

Four

"Loving too much is just as bad as not loving at all. Maybe it's worse. People who don't have anything to lose never have to worry about the inevitable."

–Alice Healy

Lowryland, eight hours and about sixty thousand inane questions later

I SAT AT A TABLE outside the Midsummer Night's (Ice) Cream Shoppe, back in civilian clothes, my glittery eyeliner scrubbed away, and wondered whether I would ever feel like standing up again. My feet were one solid ache, one that I could feel pulsing in time to the beating of my heart. In a way, the pain was a good thing, since it was distracting enough that I wasn't worried about setting anything on fire. And if that isn't the definition of making lemonade out of life's lemons, I don't know what is.

The Park was winding down around me. Parents dragged exhausted, weeping children in mass-produced costumes toward the trails that would take them out of Fairyland and back to the central hub, which was themed after Lowry's idea of a perfectly bucolic American town, half Ray Bradbury and half Lake Wobegon (without actually coming close enough to owe copyright acknowledgment to either, naturally—the man was a genius at dancing the thin line of public domain). I silently toasted them with my milkshake, wishing them luck at getting past that dazzling arcade of shopping and concessions and final opportunities to spend all their money. Lowry's

Welcoming World was designed to be a flytrap for wallets, and it stayed open a full hour after the rest of the Park shut down, making sure it would have time to suck out every last dime.

(I hate working in Lowry's Welcoming World. I *hate* it. The shops are too diverse for the area to have a cohesive theme, and while that might seem like a good thing, in practice it means that anyone wearing a Welcoming World uniform can be grabbed by a guest at any time to help them find a pair of earrings or shorts in their size or whatever piece of useless crap they've decided they need to make their theme park-loving lives complete. Which, hey, fine. I am a nerd, I understand that sometimes life isn't worth living if you don't have the commemorative tchotchke of your dreams. It's just that people want to do their shopping after midnight, when they have poor impulse control and—frequently—worse manners, and their feet hurt, and they're exhausted, and they tend to take it all out on the poor cast members who have to explain that no, they don't control the prices, no, they can't give a discount because there was a long wait to see Lindy the Lion in Candyland, no, they don't know where their managers are. Give me the rest of the Park, with its safe, sane closing hours, and leave the retail to the masochists and the heroes.)

The lights went out in the ice cream stand as the final food service employee booked it for the safety of behind-the-scenes, where no guests would be able to grab them and request one last double-dip cone. The glittering white fairy lights twined through the oversized toadstools and climbing morning glory flowers continued to twinkle, creating the illusion that tiny fairies were everywhere, watching everything that happened in their slice of Lowryland. I sipped my milkshake and let myself sink deeper into my seat, enjoying the sound of the area atmospherics. Crickets, and droning cicadas, and the occasional distant chime of bells: all the sounds Lowry's engineers had decided would say "Fairyland" to their young guests.

I couldn't say it had been a bad day. Sure, there'd been

a few rude guests, including one asshole who decided that screaming at a clerk in a shop filled with children was a great idea, and sure, there'd been the usual assortment of incidents, ranging from shoplifting to overly excited toddlers peeing in the middle of the store when they saw Oberon and Titania walking by with their handlers, but that was all pretty standard for Lowryland. I couldn't say it had been a good day either. Good days . . .

Good days were rare. Good days were the ones where I somehow managed to convince myself that Melody West was a real person, and that I wouldn't be wearing her name tag and her uniform if she wasn't me. Melody West didn't have any dark secrets to run away from, and she wasn't hiding from people who wanted to hurt her; she was just a woman with a job that wasn't too hard and wasn't too easy and came with free admission every day to one of the most magical places in the world. Melody West didn't have to worry about setting things on fire if she lost her temper. She didn't cry herself to sleep at night wondering whether she'd ever see her family again, or whether she'd walked away from the best shot she'd ever have at a relationship with someone whose jagged edges matched her own. Melody could be *happy*.

When Mary came to visit, it got harder to hold onto Melody, because Melody wasn't the sort of person whose dead aunt would haunt her. So while I was always glad to see Mary and the connection she represented to home, I resented it at the same time. As long as I couldn't let myself go and melt into Melody, I'd keep remembering how much I hated it here.

"Freedom!" announced Fern, dropping into the chair across from me with more force than should have been possible for such a diminutive figure. Ah, the varying density of the sylph. She could mostly control how dense she was, but she tended to get lighter when stressed and heavier when tired. There's probably a metaphor in there somewhere.

"You still have glitter in your . . ." I paused to give her a quick once-over. She was back in street clothes, and her fine blonde hair hung limp around her shoulders, pressed flat and lifeless by a day crammed inside her Aspen wig. Most of her eyeshadow was gone, but the ghosts of it haunted the creases of her face, sparkling in the fairy light. "Okay, you have glitter in your everything. You are a testament to the power of glitter."

"I'm like a slug," said Fern blissfully. She was holding a milkshake cup of her own, and took a long, snorting slurp before leaning back into her own chair. "How was retail?"

"Soul-destroying. How was the life of a fairy-tale princess?"

"Eh." She made a seesaw motion with her hands. "Most of the kids were okay. Adults, too. There were a few creepers who tried to grab our butts and got escorted out by Security, but it was mostly just people who loved the movie when they were little and wanted to tell us how much. They were harmless and sweet." She paused.

I recognized that pause. It was the sound of a "but" on the horizon, coming closer all the time. I frowned. "What happened?"

"There was a family. Two women holding hands, and two little girls who looked so much like them that it was . . . you know." Fern looked down at her milkshake. "I don't think they were human people. I think they were maybe dragon people."

"Could be," I said carefully. Dragons are notoriously cheap. For them, all money is potentially gold, and they need gold for both their physical and mental well-being. Lowryland isn't cheap. For a pair of dragons to bring their daughters here, well . . . it seemed unlikely.

But kids are kids, regardless of species, and kids love glitter and spectacle and rides designed to fling them into the sky while keeping them safely confined by straps and harnesses. Dragon mothers love their daughters as much as human ones do. Why shouldn't a pair of dragons bring their little girls for a day in a world that didn't really exist? If one of them worked for the Park—and quite a few dragons work for the Park—they could get in for free. Between that and their employee discounts, the trip would be a lot more reasonable than it seemed on the face of things.

There's no bad blood that I'm aware of between the sylphs and the dragons. They fill different slots in the global ecosystem, and they don't compete for resources. There are always surprises, though, and so I was even more careful with my tone as I looked at Fern, sidelong, and asked, "Did they do something to make you uncomfortable?"

"I couldn't tell them," said Fern simply.

"Oh," I said, as understanding dawned.

The easiest assumption in today's world is that anything that can pass for a human *is* a human. For me, as a human, the numbers said I was probably in the right. Humans are very, very efficient predators when we want to be. Life evolved on this planet in hundreds of forms, a daunting number of them intelligent, and it only took us a few centuries to put ourselves firmly at the top of the food chain.

For Fern, as a nonhuman, rational threat assessment said it didn't matter whether she was in the right. She needed to see everyone as a human until she was told otherwise, because humans were dangerous, and letting her guard down around the wrong people could get her killed. Even other kinds of cryptids could be dangerous. Some of them we'd hunted because they were predators, not because they were competition for the top billing on the world's list of intelligent species. A ghoul would devour someone like Fern as quick as they'd devour someone like me, and with even less concern for getting caught. A lot of cryptids won't call the police when something bad happens to one of their own. Too many of the cops are human, and sometimes the risk of exposure isn't worth the hope of justice.

I went very still as it struck me that, right now, I was living like a cryptid. I was hiding from people who wanted to do me harm as much because of who I was as because of anything I'd done. That was normal—being a Price meant I'd had a bounty on my head from the day I was born—but the isolation that came with it was new. The need to view everyone around me as a potential danger, to *hide*, it was all new, and it burned. There were dragons working all over Lowryland, and while none of them were part of my personal clique of Mean Girls, none of them knew my name either. It wasn't safe. It might never be safe again, not until we'd found a way to end the danger posed by the Covenant—and that was something we'd been trying to accomplish for generations.

Fern nodded gravely. "You understand," she said, and took another sip of her milkshake.

Fern had never been safe, not really. Fern couldn't afford the risk of telling a little girl that magic was for everyone, even children whose mothers had borne them without fathers, children who could set themselves on fire without fear of the flames, because what if she was wrong? Wrong could be easy, saying something weird to a human child and getting written up for breaking character, but wrong could be very, very hard. Wrong could be a Covenant family scoping Lowryland for signs of cryptid infiltration. Wrong could trigger a purge. For Fern, breaking cover had always come with the risk of never being safe ever again.

The target of my musings looked at me over the rim of her cup. Her eyes narrowed. "You're dwelling again," she accused. "You can't *do* that."

"Can, will, do, watch me," I said, and sighed. "What flavor do you have tonight?"

"Boysenberry chocolate maple vanilla banana with cookie dough and sprinkles," she said. "I can tell when you're changing the subject, you know."

"Yes, but you go along with it anyway." I wrinkled my nose. "That is a *horrifying* concoction."

"I like it." Fern took another slurp. "They let me clean out the machines."

"Couldn't someone get fired for that?"

Fern shrugged. "If someone got fired for everything that someone could get fired for, there wouldn't be anyone to keep the Park running, and then the alligators would reclaim the land. Alligators everywhere. As far as the eye can see."

"Right. Somehow it always ends with alligators for you."

Fern's grin displayed remarkably purple teeth. "That's because alligators are awesome."

The sound of the Clock of Ages striking one tolled through the Park, low and somehow ominous, like it had never been intended to be heard at this hour. That part was intentional: the engineers who controlled every aspect of Lowryland wanted the Clock of Ages to sound foreboding when it signaled the closing of the gates. Not enough to discourage repeat guests—heavens, no—but enough to put a bit of extra sparkle in their steps as they rushed for the exit. A dismaying percentage of them would be back tomorrow, ready to do the whole thing over again.

A cheer followed the tolling of the clock, rising from benches and cul-de-sacs all around Fairyland. Cast members who'd been hiding until the coast was clear began appearing as if by magic, rushing down the walkways that had been filled with tourists only a little while before. The smell of sweat and sunscreen still hung in the air, only slightly leavened by the layer of cordite left behind by the evening's fireworks spectacular. Sometimes it amazes me that anyone can fly home after staying to watch the Lowryland fireworks. They should all set off the TSA chemical detectors as soon as they get within twenty yards.

Fern and I stayed where we were, watching the others stream by. She sipped her milkshake. I did the same.

"Have you heard from Megan?" I asked.

"She got here half an hour ago," said Fern. "She brought the stuff."

"Everything?"

"Everything." Fern grinned at me again. "Still feel wiped out?"

"I think I just got my second wind." I got to my feet, offering her my hand. She grabbed it, laughing, and bounced to her feet.

Together, hand in hand, we ran into the fairy-lit gloom of Lowryland. Like so many guests before us, we left our troubles behind. Unlike so many guests before us, we disposed of our trash in the appropriate receptacles, because we're not assholes. Fine as that distinction can sometimes be.

Here's a secret about Lowryland after dark: yeah, it shuts down hard at one AM, except on those rare and horrifying occasions when the place stays open for twenty-four hours to punish us all for believing in mercy, and no, it's not possible to slyly turn a roller coaster back on for your own private edification. (Although the engineering teams do most of their testing and repair between the hours of two and six, and they're *always* happy to have warm bodies to play sacrificial lamb when they're messing with the settings.) But—and there's always a "but" when you're talking about something like this—that doesn't mean the place is ever truly *empty*.

Maintenance happens after closing. Construction happens after closing. Sanitation happens after closing. And while cast members aren't encouraged to stick around, since there are liability issues to be considered, we're also not tossed out on our rears if we happen to linger for a while. If we're willing to deal with the fact that the last bus from cast parking leaves at two, and don't mind riding in an empty, reportedly haunted train back to housing, we're free to do whatever pleases us.

According to a few of the cast members who swam downstream after getting booted from Disney, the Great Mouse has stricter rules about what employees can and can't do after the lights go out. Lowry Entertainment, Inc., however, is aware that they're the second choice for much of their target market, which means they have to keep their ticket prices just a sliver lower, their rides just a trifle better, and their employees just a bit happier. If being allowed to treat the Park as our private playground once the guests are gone aids in retention and keeps us all from trying to unionize or anything else profit-impacting like that, well, they can turn a few blind eyes.

Megan was waiting outside Lizzie and Laura's meet-and-greet area, a long brown wig on her head and an athletic bag in her hand, which she held up enticingly while wiggling her hips like the world's least erotic go-go dancer. It was like being lured by a happy children's show host. Fern and I raced toward her regardless, Fern falling back at the last second to let me snatch the bag from Megan's grasp. It was a shallow victory, granted more than earned, and I didn't care, because the weight of what I held was so familiar that I could cry.

"Bad day?" asked Megan sympathetically.

"Not the worst, not the best," I said. There was a bench about six feet away. I didn't feel like going that far, and sat down where I stood, beginning to unlace my shoes. "You?"

"Lots of vomit and sunstroke. It was a vomit-and-sunstroke festival."

"That's a bad festival," said Fern gravely.

Megan just laughed.

It can be easy to forget that gorgons aren't mammals. The snakes on their heads are a solid clue that they're not *human*, but head snakes are so biologically improbable that they don't flip the "actually a pseudo-reptile wandering around in a vaguely human disguise" switch. Which is, to be fair, not a switch that most people use in their daily lives.

Gorgons are warm-blooded and control their own internal body temperature, but they're not as susceptible to sunstroke as humans are, and they don't burn. Even the palest gorgons can sit in the sun for hours without anything to show for it beyond happy snakes. I don't know where they stand on vomiting, having never hated myself enough to ask, but since Megan regularly fed mice to the snakes on her head, and anything that goes down can come up, I sort of assumed she was capable of vomiting from a dozen mouths at a time. The extrusions of human children probably seemed like amateur hour to her.

Fern and Megan were chatting now, reviewing the minutiae of their days, and while I knew I was being a bad friend by shutting them out, I couldn't help it. There was so little left in my life that felt like it was normal. This? This was normal.

When I ran from the Spenser and Smith Family Carnival, leaving dead bodies and wounded friends and fire in my wake—leaving my *life* behind me—I'd taken nothing but what was already in my backpack, which had transformed somewhere along the way into a "go bag," always ready for the next evacuation. That it had happened without my really noticing probably said something about me that I didn't want to hear. I'd walked away with a couple of changes of clothing, a bunch of knives, a first aid kit, and my skating gear.

Maybe running away from home with a pair of roller skates, kneepads, elbow guards, and a helmet isn't the sort of reasonable, rational decision that an adult is supposed to make, and if I'd been in a position to pick and choose what I was carrying, I might have taken a few things out. Like the little house Mork and Mindy had built for themselves from scavenged pieces of the carnival itself, Popsicle sticks and ticket stubs and dead weight that I couldn't find the strength to throw away.

Sometimes planning is a luxury you just don't get. I'd found myself in Florida with no clean bras and a pair of professional grade roller skates, and while I couldn't say it was the best tactical decision I'd ever made, it was definitely the choice that was going to save my sanity.

I slipped my skates over my feet and the ache vanished like magic, replaced by a sense of serenity that I was going to pay for in the morning. That was fine. I was assigned to attend the actresses portraying Lizzie and Laura for the rest of the week, which meant I'd be standing mostly still, not catering to endless guest requests or running back and forth between the stockroom and the floor. I could handle a few bruises for the sake of tonight.

It only took a few seconds to do up my laces, my fingers moving on a swift, practiced autopilot that continued as I strapped on my kneepads and elbow guards, protecting my most vulnerable joints from the inevitable impact with something solid, like the ground, or the side of Princess Laura's Library.

When I finally looked up, Fern was sitting on the bench, lacing her own skates, and Megan was looking at me sympathetically.

"You *did* have a bad day," she said.

"That obvious?" I asked, strapping on my helmet. If my joints are susceptible to impact damage, my skull is even more so. One big advantage of roller derby over cheerleading: we're allowed to wear safety gear.

(Seriously. Cheerleading is not technically considered a sport, even though a competitive cheerleader is definitely an athlete, and anyway, giving us protective gear so we don't break our necks after leaping from the top of a six-level pyramid would make us less sexy and all that other bullshit. Because nothing says "hot" like "head trauma.")

"Yeah," said Megan. "What would you have done if I hadn't shown up with the skates?"

"I don't know. Punched a few walls maybe." Or gone into the swampy, undeveloped fields behind our apartment complex and thrown rocks at alligators. It wasn't nice, but it was mutually frustrating for me and the gators, and sometimes misery loves company.

Megan shook her head. "I worry about you."

"I worry about me, too."

"No, I mean it. Humans aren't supposed to function in isolation. You're pack animals. You need the rest of your pack around you to be mentally healthy."

I paused to give her a narrow-eyed sidelong look. "I can't decide whether you're teasing me about some of the things I've said about gorgons or not."

"Naturalism runs both ways," she said. "If you can play Animal Planet about my species, I can do the same with yours. You have to admit, I've had a lot more opportunity to observe wild humans than you've had to observe wild gorgons. You're like beetles. Your god must love you, because he put you *everywhere*."

"Jerk," I said mildly.

"Monkey," she replied.

I tried not to let my smile falter. She was technically

correct—humans are apes, after all—but all the word made me think of was Sam, and how worried he had to be. Thanks to Mary keeping me connected to the situation, I couldn't even lie to myself and pretend he no longer cared what happened to me. He cared. He might always care. He just couldn't do a damn thing about it.

A hand tagged my shoulder. I turned to see Fern go darting down a narrow nearby pathway, waving behind herself as she zipped away. "Catch me if you can!" she yelled, voice trailing off as her speed caught up with the sound.

Shooting Megan an only semi-apologetic look, I took off after Fern, and everything else—my day, my situation, the people I missed and my concerns about the people who were missing me—fell away, replaced by the sheer joy of *moving*.

My sister, Verity, is only really happy when she's doing something. When we were kids, our parents used to reserve time-outs for the absolute gravest of crimes, because using them for the little things that all children get up to would have been absolute torture for her. So she wrote lines instead, or did math problems concocted by Grandma Angela (an accountant, and an absolute monster where math is concerned), or raked the yard. Making her hold still was never on the table. My brother, Alex, is almost the opposite. He's an academic, and the reptiles he studies respond best to patience and pretending to be a rock. Time-outs were almost a gift where he was concerned, which meant he didn't get them either. Instead, he did dishes and sharpened knives and wasn't allowed to go back to his room, no matter how much he apologized for whatever it was he'd done.

Me, I fell somewhere in the middle. I loved the feeling of motion, the knowledge that I could run as fast as I wanted, jump as high as my legs would carry me, and count on the strength of the body I had built, one training session at a time, to carry me safely to the finish line. I also loved sitting quietly, saving my strength for when I'd need it, reading comic books and watching movies and arguing with my cousin Artie about who'd be in the objectively perfect X-Men lineup. It was a good mix. I got time-outs. I always came out of them swinging.

Skating after spending the entire day at a walking pace was like coming out of a time-out. It was freedom, it was flying, and the only thing that could have made it better would have been a wooden track beneath my wheels and the sound of my teammates grunting as they struggled to keep the opposing team from getting in my way. Fern's hair was a bright banner against the dark. I skated after her as hard as I could, trusting physics to be on my side.

As a blocker, Fern is one of the best, because everyone looks at her lithe build and assumes that she's an easy target. They'll slam into her without slowing down, only to bounce off and eat track when she somehow fails to yield before them. As a jammer, Fern is unrealistically fast, using her lowered density to turn the slightest momentum into terrifying speed. But that's on the track. The smooth, friendly, predictable track, that she knows like the back of her own hand.

The paths and walkways of Lowryland are different. They're smooth, sure, because a smooth walkway means less wear and tear on the feet of our guests, which means they stay happy longer and spend more money, but they're also unpredictable. They bend and twist in strange ways, looping those same guests past stores and little hidden snack bars, encouraging them to buy, buy, buy until their wallets run dry. Fern couldn't go full tilt without risking running into something she didn't know was about to loom up in front of her—and, maybe more importantly, she couldn't lower her density all the way, or the slightest irregularity in the pavement would launch her into the air. The lighter she got, the more chance there was of her becoming airborne.

It is a sad truth of humanity's casual dominion over the planet that most humans wouldn't believe they shared the world with another intelligent species if you shoved it in their faces. (Something that has happened, more than once, since the Covenant brought the population of most sapient cryptid species to a point where they could be dismissed as fables. For every devout Bigfoot seeker who gets a show on the SyFy Channel, there are thirty who talk laughingly about that prank their buddy Chuck tried to pull, even though Chuck has sworn since it happened that he wasn't anywhere near the woods that day. Humans believe what humans want to believe, and mostly what humans want to believe is that their dominion over the Earth will never be challenged. Certainly not by people with snakes instead of hair who can paralyze with a glance, or people who can control their density the way humans control their breathing.) Fern flying into the air wouldn't necessarily alert the tabloids, but it would mean fishing her out of whatever tree, decorative banner, or ride façade she managed to get snagged on *this* time.

Better, for me, was Fern's relative ignorance of Fairyland. Elm and Aspen do their meet-and-greets in Chapter and Verse, on the other side of the Park. That's where Lowry's designers crammed the movies that didn't fit with the dark poeticism of Fairyland, the pastel brilliance of Candyland, the caverns of Deep-Down, or the towering spires of Metropolis. The theming of each area was precisely calibrated to create as immersive an environment as possible, which meant most people only ever managed to memorize the zones where they spent the most time.

I hit the next corner with all the speed I could muster, turning right and striking off down a twisting little path through a series of equally twisting little trees. During the day, this area was consistently full of children, chasing the "sprites" generated by lights hidden among the branches. It was like watching a supersized version of a bunch of kittens playing with laser pointers, and as long as a few cast members were on hand to keep them from climbing, it was a good, harmless way for the kids to burn off a certain amount of nervous energy. There was something like that in every zone, and I personally thought that Fairyland had the best one, if only because ours didn't involve water.

The bricks lit up under the pressure from my skates, leaving a sparkling trail behind me that winked out a few seconds later. If we'd been playing hide-and-seek, this would have been a disastrous choice. Since we were playing tag, and more, I knew Fern was cutting a straight line toward the Midsummer Night's Scream, I kept going, emerging from the twisty little lane right next to the coaster.

Fern, finding herself skating *toward* me, squeaked and threw her arms out in front of her to ward off a collision. She clearly increased her density at the same time, because she lost speed for no apparent reason. As sometimes happened, the sudden change in momentum took her balance with it, and she toppled over, landing in one of the flowerbeds with a second, somewhat more muffled squeak.

There was nothing muffled about the scream that followed. It was high and piercing, the sort of good, clean sound that cuts through eardrums like a scalpel.

"Fern!" I skated toward where she had fallen as fast as I could, images of injury dancing unbidden in my mind. What if she had broken her arm? What if she had landed on a sprinkler and somehow impaled herself? What if —

"*Run!*" She popped up, waving her arms in a semaphore of repulsion, like she thought she could physically ward me away. I slowed down, too puzzled to continue skating forward with the same force, but I didn't brake, allowing the momentum I'd already gathered to keep me moving closer.

Close enough that I could see the oddly shaped splotch on the right side of her shirt, just below her collarbone. Close enough to see that it was blood. I gasped, the sound going from horror to relief as I realized there was no corresponding hole: she'd fallen into something that was already there, she hadn't hurt herself. Cold terror followed on the heels of relief. If it wasn't *her* blood . . .

"Annie, please, you have to *go*," pleaded Fern.

I didn't listen. I started my legs moving again, skating closer until I saw the pallid curve of limbs behind Fern, the arc of a broken neck, and worst of all, the beaded drops of arterial spray painting the flowers. This time, when I stopped, I actually managed to brake, freezing myself in place. My eyes were so wide they hurt, and it felt like there was a rock in my throat, preventing me from either speaking or swallowing.

"He's dead," said Fern miserably. "I screamed. I'm sorry, I shouldn't have screamed, but you have to go, Annie, you have to *go*—"

The reality of what she was saying slammed into me with all the force of the ground closing in after a bad fall. Someone was dead, murdered on Lowry property, and the way the body had been discovered meant Security was on the way. And I was right next to the crime scene. Me, with my paper-thin alias that had never been intended to stand up to more than casual scrutiny, currently hiding from an organization with the power to reach across continents.

Lowryland was enough of a psychic bruise on the landscape to scramble any attempts to scry for me or track me down telepathically. My picture being taken in conjunction with a murder victim wouldn't have any such protections. It would go into a computer, and someone, somewhere, would find it and use it against me. The Covenant knew my face. They had my fingerprints, thanks to the amount of time I'd spent on their home ground, and they had samples of my blood. If I was spotted here, they *would* find me.

"I have to go," I said, through numb lips.

"Yeah," said Fern. "Get Megan to drive you home. *Go*."

I turned, feeling like a coward, and skated back for the twisting little path through the trees as fast as I could go, while behind me, my friend stood alone and covered in someone else's blood, waiting for Security to arrive.

Five

"People will tell you death is just the beginning. They're sort of right, but they're mostly wrong. Death is an ending. Whether a new start comes after, it doesn't change the fact that something had to stop."

–Mary Dunlavy

A shitty company apartment five miles outside of Lakeland, Florida, waiting for the sky to fall

MEGAN SAT ON THE threadbare couch, watching me pace through the smoked lenses of her glasses. She looked as worried and weary as I felt. So did her "hair." It writhed around her shoulders and snapped at the air, never keeping still.

"Are you going to do that all night?" she asked.

"If I have to," I replied, hit the wall, and turned to walk the other way across the room, which seemed too large and too small at the same time, like a coat that didn't fit properly.

Megan had still been outside the ice cream shop when I'd come racing back down the path. Her first clue that something was wrong had been Fern's scream, but her second clue had been my silence. When Fern and I skated through the Park, we were *never* silent. We laughed, we shrieked, we traded insults when we were close enough to do it without calling down the wrath of Security, but we never held our tongues. It was a safety precaution. By making noise, we made sure anyone else in the area knew where we were, and we avoided collisions. For me to come skating silently out of the dark was a bad sign. For me to grab her arm and whisper, "Run," was a disastrous one.

So she'd run, and I'd skated ahead of her, and together, we'd managed to make it out of the Park without anyone putting two and two together and wondering why one girl on skates had stumbled over a body while the other got away clean. From there, it had been a short hop back to the apartment, and the dubious comfort of worrying about Fern.

I glanced at my phone, plugged in and charging on the kitchen counter. There had been no incoming texts or calls since leaving the property. It had been hours.

"Seriously, you're making me anxious."

"Then we can both be anxious," I said, but I stopped walking and stood in the middle of the living room, back so straight my spine ached, vibrating slightly, like a taut bowstring. Megan's gaze turned wary. Humans and gorgons are both predators, but humans are hunters and gorgons are trappers. Even coming from such similar backgrounds, we were so different, and we were always going to be.

Silence spread between us, filling the air until it seemed to drip down the walls. I held my tongue as long as I could, and when I couldn't anymore, I blurted, "I should move out."

"What?" Megan frowned, one sketched-on eyebrow rising. "Why?"

"If the Covenant decides to come here—"

"Then they'll kill me and Fern just as dead for being cryptids as they would for being your friends. I don't want to go back into the roommate lottery, and I don't want to deal with Fern moping around the place for the next, oh, *forever*." Megan shook her head, snakes hissing. "Stop, okay? Just stop. Eat some ice cream, or read a book, or sharpen all the knives, but stop. You're not leaving. Fern would have my hide if I let you leave."

"Fern takes team spirit a little far sometimes."

Megan smiled wryly. "Says the former cheerleader who got her job through nepotism."

"We do what we have to." I glanced at the door. "She should be back by now."

"She wasn't ..." Megan paused before continuing, sounding suddenly nervous, "She wasn't arrested for doing it, was she?"

"What? No. Lowry Security wouldn't let that happen, even if they had a way to pin things on her. It doesn't work that way in the real world." Television procedurals have a lot to answer for. They make it look like being within fifteen feet of a dead body gets people arrested for murder—which, to be fair, it can, but there are hundreds of other factors to be considered. Fern was a Lowry employee, carrying no weapons or obvious means of harming a person, and when she wasn't tinkering with her own density, weighed ninety-five pounds soaking wet. She might be suspected if the man had been shot *and* there was gunpowder on her hands, but since he'd looked stabbed and her hands were clean, she was going to be fine.

She was going to be fine.

She had to be fine.

"So what's going on?"

"I don't know." I gave the door another look, willing it to open, willing Fern to appear.

Neither thing happened. Instead, my phone rang. I lunged for it with barely a glance at the clock—three AM, swell—and swiped my finger across the screen to answer. "Hello?"

"Um, hi? It's, um. It's Fern." Her voice was shaking, and she sounded like she was on the verge of tears. That didn't necessarily mean anything beyond "had a long day" and "landed on a corpse."

I hoped it didn't. "Hi, Fern," I said, glancing at Megan. She sat up straighter, snakes once again hissing wildly. "Where are you?"

"I'm at Security. The main office. They, um, already called my shift supervisor to say I was going to be off work tomorrow. I have to go over everything with them, and then I have to talk to some people who are in charge of public relations. They don't get here until eight, so I'll be home sometime after that." Her voice quavered even harder on that last word.

I closed my eyes. "You probably can't answer this with anything but a 'yes' or a 'no,' but have they let you change your clothes?"

"No."

Meaning she was still covered in a stranger's blood. That was dandy. "Find someone in charge. Someone who looks . . . who looks like they pay a lot of attention to their clothes." Someone like my mother, who would have clucked her tongue and given Fern a new shirt hours ago, recognizing that no one really enjoys the feeling of blood drying on their skin. Not even Grandma Alice is that far gone. "Ask them if they have something else you can wear. They should get you a new shirt, at the absolute least."

"Oh," said Fern, voice going small. "Can you ask Megan if she works tomorrow?"

Fern knew my work schedule, and knew I had to be on-shift. Megan's was less predictable, thanks to the hours the hospital kept. "One of us will call in sick."

"*Not you*," said Fern. The steel in the words was enough to take me aback. She continued: "You have too many absences this quarter. I don't want to see you getting docked a vacation day for absenteeism. How can we go to Key West this year if you don't have the vacation days?"

I had no hobbies. I had no local family. Apart from Megan and Fern—and Mary, when she popped in—I had no friends. Put all this together, and I was possibly the most reliable employee Lowry had. I'd been late for work several times, but never late enough to get written up for it; most of the time, my managers didn't even notice, since years of cheerleading and roller derby and carnival work have left me incredibly efficient when it comes to getting ready. As long as I was standing where the guests could see me when I was supposed to, they didn't *care*. Fern didn't want me there for another reason.

"Fern," I said carefully, "are the police still with you?"

"Yeah," she said. "I'll see you in the morning, okay?

Tell Megan I'm fine." Then she hung up, leaving me with only the sound of empty air.

I lowered the phone and turned to the agitated gorgon. "She says she's fine," I said. "I think she's lying, but not too much. She's freaked out, not panicking, and not under arrest. She wanted to know if you were working tomorrow."

"I seem to have come down with a cold," said Megan, and coughed weakly into her hand. "Oh, no. That sounds serious. Better stay in bed."

"Uh-huh." I gave her a dubious look. "Can gorgons *get* human colds?"

"Nope, which is why I'm one of the only residents not to have had at least one sick day this quarter. My supervisors will be annoyed but understanding. Maybe even relieved." Despite her weariness and worry, Megan managed to twinkle. "They were starting to suspect I wasn't human."

Somehow, I found it in me to laugh.

Megan's smile faded. "Now you, on the other hand, *are* human, and you have to work tomorrow. Go to bed, Antimony. I'll make sure our girl is okay when she gets home, and you'll go to work like nothing happened."

"Because nothing happened, because I wasn't there," I said, with a quick nod.

Megan tapped her nose. "Bingo. Now sleep."

I flashed her a relieved smile and walked back to my room, where I stripped, checked that the knives beneath my pillow were where I needed them to be, and sank onto the mattress. I'm not ashamed to say that I was asleep almost instantly. When your entire childhood is spent training for a war that may never come, losing sleep over a little blood is not in the cards.

I dreamed of the carnival, walking down the midway to the distant sound of calliope music, and I knew that everyone I loved was somewhere nearby, trapped in the Hall of Mirrors or drowning in the Tunnel of Love, and I knew I could never save them, and I knew it would kill me to try. I tried anyway.

When my alarm shouted me back into the waking

world, there were char marks on my sheets and tears on my pillow, and somehow, that was exactly what I'd been expecting.

With Megan staying home and Fern still waiting to talk to public relations, I had to take the train by myself. I compacted my body into the confines of one seat, trying to look like I was half-asleep as I hugged my bag. Feigning unconsciousness wasn't a difficult trick. Between our after-hours roller skating and the time I'd spent pacing and worrying about Fern, I'd managed to get slightly less than five hours of sleep. Not enough sleep deprivation to kill me, but my breaks today were going to be spent sucking down coffee and praying I could avoid a fatal caffeine overdose.

My apparent doze meant the people around me didn't feel any need to keep quiet in my presence. If anything, I was encouraging the conversation, since I was Fern's roommate, and hence a constant reminder of her absence. By keeping my eyes cracked just a hair, I could see how many of them were glancing in my direction before they continued gossiping.

"So I heard from Eddie in Security that the little blonde one got *arrested* last night."

A gasp. "What did she do?"

"Murdered a man. A *guest*."

It was difficult to understand why murdering a guest would be worse than killing a cast member, but it was written plainly in the speaker's tone: by supposedly killing a guest, Fern had committed a mortal sin in the eyes of not just the law, but the entire Lowry entertainment complex. I swallowed the urge to snort derisively. Right now, it was too important that I listen.

Gossip is toxic, especially because it's often so much more interesting than the truth. The truth is provable, and dull, and difficult to change. Gossip, though . . . by the time there was a statement about the body that cleared Fern of all wrongdoing, she would already have been convicted a hundred times over. The man would be her lover, her brother, her blackmailer, her illicit son. Speaking up would only make things worse. The slightest attempt to defend her would be read as proof of her guilt, since innocent people don't need to be defended.

Again, sometimes I want to take a walk through the writers' rooms of all those police procedurals, and see how well bullshit television tropes can burn.

There were three good things about the situation, if I could call them "good." First, Fern was genuinely innocent. Being convicted in the court of public opinion might annoy her, but it wouldn't impact her life in any meaningful way. None of these people were her friends. She had me, she had Megan, and she had her bowling league every other Wednesday night. That seemed to be enough. Humans are among the most social of the world's various intelligent species. What would have been unbearable for me—what *was* unbearable for me— was just fine for Fern.

(Humans aren't *the* most social. I'm not sure who gets that label, but I'm betting on the dragons. They live in Nests that can contain hundreds of individuals, all piled on top of each other like a garter snake mating ball, and they seem perfectly happy that way. Which is good for them, given the cost of real estate in some areas.)

Second, and more importantly where Fern's job prospects were concerned, cast members don't gossip with guests, no matter how hard some guests may try to make us. It's not snobbery, although it can seem that way. It's a matter of drawing a hard, firm line between work and play. The fact that Lowry sometimes sends "secret shopper" guests into the Park to see whether we'll rise to the bait and start talking trash doesn't help. Even if the rest of the cast thought Fern was a murderer, she'd never be outed to the guests, and her job wouldn't be in danger. Princess Aspen would continue untainted, as she always had.

Thirdly and *most* importantly, at least for me, none of the people on the train were saying my name. Fern's instinct to shoo me away had been exactly right, and I'd managed to get out of there fast enough that no one was connecting me to the scene of the crime. I'd be able to keep my head down and stay out of the spotlight, and honestly, that was exactly what I needed.

The train pulled into the stop for the employee parking lot. I "woke up" and followed the others onto the platform, not bothering to conceal my yawn. When playing a role, it's best to fully commit.

The platform fed into two stairways and one escalator, with an elevator at the far end. I yawned again and joined the crowd thronging at the escalator entrance. I always tried to leave the elevator for people who needed it—hard to fit a wheelchair on the escalator—but I didn't feel up to stairs. Not with the night I'd had, and my balance as shot as it was. I'd try to descend normally, trip, fall, and spend the day trying to come up with an explanation for my stitches that didn't make me sound like a total klutz.

Someone grasped my elbow as I stepped off the escalator. My hands balled into automatic fists, fingers instantly red-hot. I clenched them and forced a smile as I turned to see who was touching me. Punching is frowned upon at Lowryland, and we had technically been on company property since stepping onto the train.

Setting people on fire is also frowned upon at Lowryland, which was a problem, since my hands were only getting hotter. I was going to start leaving blisters on my own skin soon, and that was never easy to explain.

Sophie smiled at me, the expression not reaching her eyes, and let go. "Melody, so glad I ran into you," she said, in the exact tone she had once used to call freshmen girls to task when they showed signs of buying into the bitchy cheerleader stereotype. It wasn't a tone I'd heard directed at me in years, and it still made my skin crawl and my clothes suddenly feel three sizes too tight. "Can I give you a ride the rest of the way to work?"

Translation: she needed to talk to me, preferably in private, and her "offer" was really a command veiled in a thin veneer of free choice. Oh, sure. I could refuse, but then she'd have to press the issue, and we both knew who was going to win that one.

As always, Sophie made me feel like an absolute mess just by existing. Her hair was perfectly groomed, and today's pantsuit was a shade of burgundy that made her skin seem to glow from within, tan and healthy and filled with wholesome goodness. The contrast it made against her cream silk shell top was almost criminal. I, on the other hand, was wearing Lowryland sweatpants and a black tank top, and hadn't bothered brushing my hair before leaving the apartment, since I'd need to style it in the locker room anyway. Goblin Market meant sausage curls for the long-haired girls, hairsprayed to within an inch of their lives to make sure they would never be knocked out of place.

"Sure," I said, unclenching my hands and trying to flex away the heat in my fingers, letting it disperse into the morning air. At least we were in Florida. Even the mornings were so warm here that the increase in the ambient heat around me was unlikely to be noticed.

It's too bad I didn't get a tendency to freeze things, instead of burning them. I could have gone to work for Disney instead of Lowry, made the big bucks as the most accurate Elsa they would ever have.

(Except I couldn't have. Consistency is the keyword across face characters at all the Parks that use them, regardless of the parent company: what one Princess Laura does or says or knows must be echoed across all the other Princess Lauras, lest they damage the illusion that they've casually wandered out of a cartoon. Sadly, this is why Princess Thistle and her husband, the dashing Prince Corwin, are the only face characters who speak American Sign Language.)

Sophie nodded, clearly having anticipated this outcome when she made her request, and turned to stroll out of the station, trusting me to follow. My coworkers stared as I left in the company of a hiring manager, and the first mutters started before I was out of earshot. Swell. I'd managed to keep myself out of the rumor mill where Fern's corpse was concerned, but now I was going to get my turn for a completely different reason.

Three spaces outside every Lowryland employee

train station and bus stop were reserved for managerial use. This was the first time I'd seen one of them filled. Sophie strolled toward her silver Lexus, pausing at the last moment to beep the doors open, and slid inside.

The interior of the car smelled of leather and cleaning fluid and money. It was like inhaling the inside of a very expensive wallet, and I couldn't shake the feeling that I was going to be charged for it. Sophie didn't say anything, just slid her key into the ignition and started the engine. Eyes watched from all across the station entrance as we pulled away, some jealous that I was getting a ride, others taking in every detail of what they saw so they could repeat it later to anyone who would listen.

"So," I said finally, desperate to break the silence, "how're you?"

"They make these cars so they don't even need a key anymore," she said. "You use your thumbprint to unlock it. Guess I shouldn't be surprised. We started using guest thumbprints to key to their tickets three years ago. Did you know, we've been sued for our guest information by the federal government six times? They say we have the largest private fingerprint database in the country, and even wanted felons have children who want to ride a roller coaster. We could help them solve a bunch of unsolved crimes."

"But we haven't," I guessed.

"Oh, hell, no. Imagine the headlines. 'Lowryland destroys family vacation by summoning the FBI.' Disney would make hay while the sun shone on *that* one. No, we'll keep fighting their requests, we'll keep shoveling money toward the lawyers, and we'll keep banking on Disney being a bigger, sweeter target. If they're the ones who allow the government to start arresting guests, our stock will go through the roof overnight. Always stick with the people who seem to care about your privacy."

I snorted. I couldn't help myself. Lowryland only "cares" about the privacy of their guests as long as it impacts the bottom line. There are cameras in all the rides and public areas of the Park. There are even more cameras in the company resort hotels. Nothing happens on Lowry property that Lowry doesn't know about thirty seconds later.

Realization hit me hard on the heels of that thought. My eyes went wide and my spine went stiff, my fingers not even heating up in the face of my shock. Sophie glanced at me and nodded, looking satisfied.

"Good," she said. "We're on the same page now—and in case you were worried, there aren't any microphones in my car. The corporate overlords, long may they reign, will probably be bugging the rank and file long before they get around to bugging management."

As a member of the rank and file, that probably shouldn't have been reassuring. Somehow, it was, if only because her need to explain meant that they weren't doing it *yet*. "How much did you see?"

"Not nearly as much as I wish we had." Sophie pulled a sour face. "The cameras in front of the Midsummer Night's Scream have been down since yesterday morning. A damn squirrel chewed through a wire. One of the electricians found the little bastard hanging off the transformer box, stiff as a board. They were supposed to get the cameras back on last night, and obviously, that didn't happen."

"Then how—"

"Ice cream." Sophie shrugged, turning onto the freeway. "There's nothing wrong with the cameras *there*. We have footage of you skating after Miss Conway, and then skating back alone, grabbing Miss Rodriguez, and exiting the Park. So my question for you is this: were you with Miss Conway when she found the body?"

I liked that wording. Sophie wasn't accusing Fern of murder, just of covering up my part in the victim's discovery. "What happens if I say yes?"

"I ask how confident you are that Miss Conway is going to stick to her current story, which is that she was by herself when she tripped and fell into the flowerbed, having already told her roommates to return to the apartment. Under normal circumstances, she would have been liable for any damage to the landscaping. Given she found a body that Security somehow missed on their initial sweep, we're willing to let this one go."

"Uh, yeah." In that part of Fairyland, in that sort of flowerbed—surrounded by a low hedge which was often full of birds and the hands of curious children—the odds that our victim would have been discovered by someone under the age of twelve were extremely high. Talk about bad press. "So *if* I had been there, and *if* Fern were lying about that part, I would be very confident in her ability to stick to her story. I...I knew her before we came here. She and I were sort of in the same situation."

Sophie nodded thoughtfully. "I understand why you ran."

"You do?"

"Of course, I do. I wasn't born yesterday, Mel." Sophie sighed, shaking her head like this was the sort of burden she would rather push onto someone else's shoulders, but was nonetheless compelled to carry on her own. "You still won't tell me what that bastard finally did to make you leave, and that's fine, I'm not going to push; you have a right to your privacy. That's something I would never try to take away from you, especially not after what you've already been through. If you'd been with Miss Conway when she found that...unfortunate soul, the police would have questioned you. They might have taken your picture. I suppose the other thing I have to ask is whether there's anything out there for them to find that might embarrass the company. Because you're my friend, we did a shortcut on certain aspects of the hiring process and background check. Was that a mistake?"

"No, ma'am." If Sophie had set Lowry's lawyers to digging, the worst thing she could have discovered was that Melody West didn't technically exist. Since we'd gone to high school together, shared locker rooms and buses and late-night pizza parties, she *knew* Melody existed. She would have written all that off as nonsense, an artifact of my dropping off the grid for so long. My fingerprints weren't in any systems except for Lowry's.

And the Covenant's. That was what I needed to be worrying about. That, and Fern—and my job. I caught a glimpse of the dashboard clock and yelped.

"Sophie, I'm going to be late!"

"Don't worry. Your manager has been informed that you're needed in Public Relations, and your shift is being covered, with no black marks on your record."

The inside of the car suddenly felt very cold. "I told you, I wasn't there."

"I know you did. We're calling in everyone who closed in Fairyland last night, to make an announcement about what happened and hopefully squash wild speculation." Sophie's frown was fleeting. "Gossip is poison."

"No argument there."

Sophie sighed. "Do you ever miss high school? The squad? I cheered in college, but it wasn't the same, was it?"

"You're doing it again," I said.

"Doing what?"

"Fishing. You want me to say 'no, it wasn't,' and then you'll know that not only did I go to college, but I was on a cheer squad while I was there. Or 'I wouldn't know,' and then you know at least one of those things isn't true. I told you, I can't—"

"Talk about the past, yes, yes, I know, but you'll forgive me for being concerned?" Sophie frowned again, harder this time. "If that bastard shows up here, I want to know how hard I need to kick his ass."

The thought of Sophie kicking Artie's ass under the assumption that he'd kept me locked in a closet since college would have been funny, if I hadn't been so sure she'd do it, and equally sure that the stress would make him lose control of both his empathy and his weird incubus mojo. Being whammied into falling hopelessly in love with my cousin probably wouldn't do anything good for her as a person.

(Artie's father, my Uncle Ted, is an incubus, which makes Artie a half-incubus, which means he's been taking longer than normal to get the walking porn soundtrack that is his body chemistry under control. Since incubi are by and large *very* focused on consent and making sure no one is doing anything they don't want to do, Artie spends a lot of time locked in his basement, avoiding the sort of girls who might accidentally decide they want to marry him and have his quarter-incubus geek babies. Which is all of them, barring close relatives and people like our Cousin Sarah, whose body chemistry is too far from the mammalian norm for pheromones to work on her. She's in love with him because she loves him. Weirdo.)

"He's not going to show up here," I said.

"But if he does—"

"I will call you so you can come and help kick his ass." I took a deep breath. "So if I had been there last night, and I had seen the body, I guess I'd want to know what happened."

"Are you asking me to gossip?"

"No, I'm asking you to help me sleep better at night, and to equip me to help my roommate who is, if you remember, an avatar of fairy-tale goodness and purity for children the world over looking for a little magic in their lives. Unless you want Princess Aspen to start telling kids how to get blood out of velvet."

Fern probably didn't know how to get blood out of velvet. I did. I could lead a goddamn master course in getting blood out of any kind of fabric, with a bonus session on getting blood out of hair without washing away all the hairspray. Alas, there isn't much call for that sort of thing in my current occupation.

Sophie was quiet for a minute or so, thinking it over. Finally, she said, "It looks like there was some sort of altercation, probably toward the end of the evening, fortunately out of sight of any of our younger guests. The victim was a local man named David Wilson. It doesn't seem to have been an intentional murder; the officer I spoke to said it looked more like an accident that he had been hurt badly enough to bleed out. Just sheer dumb luck."

"Sheer dumb luck doesn't usually go around stabbing people."

"No, but angry kids sometimes do, and all the metal detectors and casual security in the world won't stop people from smuggling knives into the Park. We can't get too intrusive, or we'll lose business. We couldn't even justify metal detectors to our shareholders until Disney did it without collapsing under the weight of the resulting outrage. Pat-downs and full-body screening are never going to happen, and if you ever tried to quote me on this, I would call you a liar and have you fired on the spot, but I'm glad that they won't."

I blinked. "Even with the folks in PR spinning full-time to keep this out of the papers?"

"Even with ten bodies, I'd be saying this," said Sophie firmly. "I don't know if you've looked at me recently, but you may have noticed that I am not, in fact, a white person. I am, rather, quite brown."

"I did notice that," I said carefully.

"One of my great joys here at Lowryland is walking through the Park and knowing that people from all over the world, from all walks of life, are able to come and enjoy what we've created without fear of racial profiling from the cast. We can't control what the other guests do, and yes, we've had a few incidents over the years, but every cast member treats every guest with equal courtesy, at least to their faces." Sophie's expression turned hard. "Bring in guards and thorough searches, and that changes. Suddenly it's the guest with the unfamiliar accent who gets 'randomly' selected for further screening. Suddenly it's the man with the faded gang tattoos who has to walk through the metal detector three times. David Wilson died because someone snuck a knife into the Park. That's tragic. All my sympathy goes to his family. I will lose a hundred Davids before I let children who look like me—children who look like anyone—start feeling like their skin color means they aren't allowed to have access to the magic we give to children who look like you."

I didn't say anything. Sophie glanced at me and grimaced apologetically.

"Sorry," she said. "I guess that was sort of heavy."

"No, I'm glad you said something," I said. "I hadn't really thought about it."

"You never had to." We had reached the gates to the

back lot. Sophie pulled up to the guard booth and smiled, flashing her ID badge. The man on the other side of the barricade nodded, giving me only a cursory glance before he raised the barricade.

We drove down the winding driveway that connected the gate to the parking lot in silence. Lowryland was designed to look like an entirely different world once guests were inside its borders. What most of them never realized was how much work went into creating—and maintaining—that all-important illusion.

The walls surrounding the Park were higher than anyone realized at a casual glance, built into the environments around rides, concealed behind shop facades and cunningly designed greenery. All told, the lowest point in the Lowryland wall was twelve feet high, and the Park designers were hard at work coming up with ways to bring it up to the otherwise standard fifteen. Only the wrought iron front gates were lower than that, affording a tantalizing view of the entry plaza to the people standing in line every morning or looking over their shoulders every night. Once inside the Park, the rest of the world might as well have been a story told to frighten children.

That included the administrative offices, the management parking, the back lots where the parade floats were stored and maintained, and so very much more. Lowryland had its own suite of generators, much like the carnivals where I'd whiled away my childhood summers, but built on a substantially grander scale. Lowryland had freezers packed with enough food to wait out a zombie apocalypse. People looking for survivalists always focused on the preppers. They should have been looking at the big theme parks, where the roller coasters would keep on rolling long after the lights of Miami had gone dark.

Sophie drove past the first three parking lots, all of which were distant enough from even the employee gates to have their own shuttle system, and around a large building blazoned with the smiling face of Monty Mule and Hilary Hinny, the lovable cartoon scamps upon whose backs Michael Lowry the First had constructed an empire. Her car slid into her reserved slot with what sounded like a satisfied purr, obscuring her name, which had been spray painted onto the concrete when she became important enough to warrant such prime parking.

She looked at me again, expression grim. "Stick to your story, Mel," she advised. "Once we're inside, I'm not your friend, I'm the person who has to make sure every employee represents the best face of the company. If you say or do anything that makes my superiors think you might have been there—"

"I won't let you down," I said.

Sophie nodded.

"Good," she said, and got out of the car, leaving me to trail along behind her like a lost duckling, looking for a way back to the safety of the pond.

The air-conditioning inside the Public Relations building was like a punch to the face after the growing heat outdoors. It didn't help that PR, out of every department associated with Lowryland, had to "live the Lowry life," decorating everything in corporate iconography. Gone were the tasteful photographs and colors of the hiring office, replaced by aggressively bright primary shades and even brighter posters blazing out advertisements for the company's most iconic properties.

It could have been interesting, under the right circumstances, to wander through the halls and see the evolution of Lowry's style across the decades, from the white-and-gold minimalism of *Goldtree and Silvertree* to the lush pre-Raphaelite jewel tones of *Goblin Market*, all the way up to the stark green and silver of *Thistle* and the gilded pastels of *Mooncake*.

The three people waiting for us in the lobby sort of killed that idea. They were dressed like PR wonks the world over, in suit jackets, pressed slacks, and pencil skirts (all following strict gender lines, sadly; at least mixing it up a little would have made things interesting). Their accessories were in gaudier colors than the norm, allowing them to blend better with their surroundings, but a bright red pocket square or a chunky green necklace couldn't change the fact that they were the hard hand of strict formality trying to enforce itself on a fairy-tale wonderland.

There was no sign of Fern. I looked anxiously around, like she might be crammed into a corner somewhere, and clutched my duffel bag against my chest. It was part true concern, part distraction. I couldn't disguise myself, not with Sophie right there, knowing what I really looked like. But these people didn't know me. If I wanted to act like I was easily confused and frightened of losing my job, they couldn't call my bluff.

"Mr. Knighton," said Sophie, stepping toward the central of the three PR reps, hand already outstretched. He looked at her coolly before reaching out and slipping his hand into hers.

He looked more like a funeral director than someone who had any business working in Lowryland. When he switched his attention from Sophie to me, it was all I could do not to recoil. Megan was an *actual* reptile, and her gaze wasn't that reptilian. It was a crude, mammal-centric way of looking at things, and yet I couldn't help myself, because it was also true. He looked at me like he was trying to figure out the best way to take me apart.

"You must be Melody West," he said.

I had never been so grateful to be at Lowryland under an assumed name. If he'd said my real name in that voice, that hollowed-out, sepulcher tone, I would have been compelled to stab him. There are bogeymen who never manage to sound that much like they belong under a rock.

"Yes, sir," I said.

"Your friend assures me she was alone during last night's unfortunate incident," he said. "We have some security footage that would seem to contradict that. Can you tell me what happened?"

Why PR was asking this and not Park Security was sadly easy to understand. Park Security didn't care. Unless they had reason to suspect me of being the person who did the stabbing, their attention was needed elsewhere. But PR . . .

PR made sure people kept repeating that old canard about how no one had ever died on either Disney or Lowry property, because they spun and kept on spinning, turning straw into gold, turning rumors into reality. PR swept in when one of the studio's teenybopper TV stars got wasted in Goblin Market's supposedly adults-only wine bar, turning it into stomach flu and teenage hijinks and concealing the public drunkenness faster than a six-year-old can cover themselves in glitter. PR did the heavy lifting, keeping the Lowry brand bright and shiny and buffing out all the dings. They were the true predators of the Park ecosystem, the lords of this particular veldt, and I had good reason to be afraid of them. They'd tear me limb from limb if that was what they thought Lowry required.

They were loyal. Lowry kept them well-fed. They still scared the crap out of me, and I'd fought actual monsters that were trying to kill me with teeth and claws and other nice, normal things.

"Fern and I were roller skating after closing," I said, careful to keep my voice meek and my tone from wavering. If I oversold this, I'd end up setting off their bullshit detection systems, and then things would get ugly. "She knew I was supposed to open this morning, while she had the afternoon shift, so when I said I was getting tired, she told me to go ahead and go home. We do that sometimes."

"That seems like a great deal of trouble to go to for less than five minutes of enjoyment," said one of the two women. They were flanking Mr. Knighton like lionesses, and seemed just as friendly when it came to outsiders. I decided not to like them. Not that there had been much chance of *that*.

"It's part of how we stay close as roommates, and prevent fights in the apartment," I said. "Megan doesn't skate with us, but she always comes to watch, and she thinks it's funny."

"That would be Miss Rodriguez, would it not?" asked the other woman.

I concealed my wince at having been the first one to bring my second roommate into the conversation, and nodded. "Yes, it would," I said. "She's a resident at the hospital. She was at the ice cream shop while we were skating."

"Lowryland frowns on activities such as skating in the Park," said Mr. Knighton.

"We've spoken to Security, and they said as long as we wear protective gear and don't try to sue the Park if we bang our elbows, they have better things to worry about," I said. That wasn't *exactly* what they'd said, but it was the gist of it. We did a lot of things by "the gist of it" at Lowryland. Disney was probably more formal. Disney also had a lot more rules, a lot more moving parts, and a lot more overhead. Honestly, if this was the life I had to lead, I was glad I'd landed where I had. Disney would probably have ended with me stabbing some asshole in a Mickey Mouse costume in the throat for implying that I wasn't showing the proper attitude.

"Miss West is correct," said Sophie, smoothly interjecting herself back into the conversation. "While we don't *encourage* after-hours activities on Park property, we've shown time and time again that part of what gives the Lowry family our ability to stand together against adversity is the off-hours bonding we do of our own free will and without coercion. As Miss West and Miss Conway were not damaging Park property, and were wearing safety equipment, their activities are not under review at this time."

Her eyes said *drop it* loudly enough that it might as well have been verbal. To my surprise, the PR team frowned but didn't object.

Sophie looked to me. "How long do your skating sessions usually last?"

"Can be five minutes, can be three hours, depending on when we're scheduled to work the next day and how we're feeling." I shrugged. "I'll be honest—"

"Please," said Mr. Knighton.

I did my best to ignore him. "—sometimes knowing I'll get to have some fun in the Park before I go home is what makes it possible for me to keep smiling for our guests. I know work is work and play is play, but they have fun all day long, and I just want my turn. Is that weird?"

Mr. Knighton looked like he was grinding his teeth as he said, "It's perfectly normal."

Score one for the little liar. I gave him my best wavering smile, the one I used to use on teachers who wanted explanations for my bruises, and asked, "Is Fern okay? Can I see her?"

"Emily will take you to your friend," said Mr. Knighton. One of the two PR women—the one in the chunky green necklace and the impeccable eyeliner, winged back like she was about to go to war—took a half-step forward, identifying herself. He turned to Sophie. "Miss Vargas, if you would?"

Sophie walked over to join him and they strolled away down the hall, the second PR woman following them, and just like that, I was dismissed. I turned to Emily, strengthening my smile against whatever obstacle I was going to slam it up against next.

"Hi," I began. "I'm—"

"You stink like ghost, little girl," she said, an open sneer in her cultured tones. "Something's been haunting you. What have you been doing that you shouldn't have been?"

Six

"Being right is never as important as staying alive."

–Evelyn Baker

Inside the Lowryland Public Relations building, trying not to panic

I FROZE. My fingers heated instantly, so fast that I didn't have time to ball them into my palms before they brushed against the nylon strap of my duffel bag. The smell of singed plastic filled the air. I prayed Emily wouldn't notice.

Emily noticed. Her lips curved into a knowing smile. "Oh," she said. "So *that's* the way it is, hmm? I should have guessed. So what are you? Ambulomancer? Train-spotter? We've had a few of them infiltrate the Park. They say the monorail and the roller coasters do enough to keep them going. Or are you an umbramancer? We haven't had one of those in *ages*."

"I don't even know what that last one is," I said, my voice barely reaching the status of a squeak. "I mean . . ."

"You've got some balls on you, kid," said Emily. "Big brass balls. Or should that be big crystal ones?" She barked brief laughter at her own joke. The sound was utterly humorless.

"I have no idea what's happening right now, and I would like to leave," I said, in the prim, tight voice of an unhappy child. I heard that voice a hundred times a day from children who wanted to sit down, or go to the bathroom, or do *anything* that would allow them to feel like they had some influence over their own lives while in a place that was supposedly designed to cater to their every whim. Sometimes I thought their shrill demands for the latest Princess Thistle loom or Princess Laura storybook were born less out of greed and more out of the need to assert that they were still people who walked in the world; they were something other than the projection of their parents' desires for a perfect vacation scrapbook and "making memories."

"Then maybe you shouldn't have wandered into a crime scene," said Emily, making the suggestion sound almost amiable. "Look, I get it. You're stressed out, you're afraid I'm getting ready to blow the whistle on you, and you're apparently setting things on fire, which is a *nice* trick. Let me set your mind at ease." Her hand dipped into the pocket of her blazer. When she pulled it out again, she was holding a deck of cards. She held them out to me, fingers easing them into a fan.

Emily smiled. It didn't reach her eyes. It barely reached her lips.

"Pick a card," she said.

Something in her tone told me this wasn't a request. Hesitantly, I reached out and pulled a card from the middle of the fan.

"Show it to me," she said.

"I thought you were supposed to guess," I replied. I was stalling for time, hoping Sophie would come back or Fern would wander out of whatever room they were holding her in. Anything that could get me away from this cold statue of a woman, with her card tricks and her freezing eyes.

She would have been lovely, if it hadn't been for the chill coming off her in waves. She had the sculpted bone structure and porcelain coloring of an original edition Emma Frost—and all the good humor and friendliness that went with that particular comparison, which was to say, none at all. Her blazer and skirt fit so well that they had to be bespoke, and her shoes were black leather kitten heels, elegant and subtle and not so high as to leave her unable to keep up with someone moving at a brisk pace. Whether she'd shaped herself to the environment or whether the environment had shaped itself to her didn't matter. She was here, she was flawless, and she was poised to kill.

Meekly, I showed her my card. This time, her smile was more obvious, and far easier to read.

"The three of hearts," she said. "You're a sorcerer. Not a sorceress. There's no need to gender power. Power simply *is*, and it does what it will. But you haven't been trained, have you? No, barely at all—wait." She plucked the card from my hand, making it disappear. "That's why you reek of ghost. It's all about the bloodline."

My own blood felt like it was burning and freezing at the same time. My fingertips were as hot as they had ever been. If I'd touched the duffel bag now, it wouldn't have been scorched: it would have been engulfed in flame. "I don't know what you're talking about."

"Sorcerers and routewitches have one thing in common," she said. The rest of the cards followed the three of hearts, slipped back into her pocket and out of sight. "They run in families. Where you find one, you're likely to find a line of them, stretching all the way back to caveman days. Something in the genes. You're being haunted by someone who's trying to make you understand what you can do before you burn down the world, aren't you?"

Slowly, I forced myself to straighten, forced the tension out of my shoulders and the terror out of my eyes. I couldn't force the fire from my fingers. Like she said, it was in the blood, and right now, my blood was singing, stinging, demanding that I let it defend me and, by extension, itself.

So I stopped trying. I let the heat rise until she could feel it from where she stood, keeping my fingers well away from anything I might accidentally ignite. "She's my grandmother," I said coolly. Making Mary a blood relative was the best way to deflect suspicion, and my actual grandmother wouldn't mind. Better to make it seem like I was the last of my line. "She knew the last person in our family who had my little . . . problem, and she's been trying to help. She can't help. Not really. Now it's your turn. Who the hell are you, and how did you know about her?"

"Routewitches always know," she said, and smirked like this was some sort of amazing revelation. Which I guess it would have been, if she hadn't decided to treat me like a cat toy first.

My head throbbed. Fern was still somewhere in this building, possibly without a clean shirt, definitely without a clean pair of undies. Every minute that passed was another minute where I wasn't working, and even if there wasn't going to be a black mark on my record that anyone could see, everything has consequences in a place like Lowryland. It didn't matter how many times management said my absence had been forgiven: management wasn't a jury of my peers. The people I was supposed to have been sharing my shift with wouldn't necessarily remember all the times I'd covered their butts, but they'd sure remember the day I didn't bother to show up. I'd be paying for this for months. The fire in my fingers wasn't backing down, and for maybe the first time since I'd retreated into the comfortable identity of Melody West, former high school cheerleader and woman in hiding, neither was I.

"That's swell," I snarled, and was rewarded by her smirk fading, just a little, as she remembered that in the hierarchy of humans who can bend the forces of nature to their will, she was well below me. Or would have been, if I'd had any actual training.

Still, I could burn this building down around our ears if I felt threatened enough. That was something.

Routewitches are the most common kind of human magic-user, and they're tricky. Most of their powers have to do with distance and the road. Somehow—don't ask me why—this also translates into a certain amount of access to the afterlife, which they call "the twilight." They can talk to ghosts. Some of them can bend ghosts to their will, or ban them from areas. They do what they do and they do it well. It's just that what they do is limited to parlor tricks, compared to what a true magic-user can accomplish.

Taking Emily's fear as a sign to continue, I asked, "Why are you telling me this? I thought protocol was that we nod to each other and continue on without making a fuss. Sorcerers and routewitches don't fight over territory."

"No, they don't; that's true," she said. "Will you please come with me, so I can show you I mean you no harm? That I only want to help you?"

I eyed her warily. "I'm going to need a second."

"Of course."

I took a step back, putting some distance between me and Emily, before I closed my eyes and tried to focus on happy, soothing thoughts. Thoughts that didn't make me want to burn down the building, and fry myself along with it.

Me, and Sam, and the flying trapeze. He was relaxed, in his furry, fūri form, and he was holding onto the bar with his feet, reaching for me with his hands, primed to snatch me out of the air. My own bar was swinging high, and when I let go, I wasn't falling; I was flying, soaring across the tent toward him—

The fire in my fingers guttered and died, extinguished by the memory of better times. I opened my eyes.

"All right," I said. "Show me."

Emily smiled.

There was no sign of Sophie or the rest of the PR team as we moved deeper into the building, past posters, playbills, and framed cels that were worth more money than I'd ever seen in my life. Emily saw me looking and raised an eyebrow.

"I wouldn't have taken you for a true believer, with the way you were carrying on back there," she said. "This building is a priceless trove of Lowry artifacts." *That you were threatening to burn down,* came the silent accusation.

"Then you shouldn't have been threatening me in it," I said coolly. It was getting easier to maintain my reserve now that I was past the initial shock of confrontation. All I had to do was pretend Emily was my older sister and I could match every scrap of her smugness with a sneer. Better yet, my fingers were staying cool. Today's bout of wild magic was apparently finished, and not a second too soon.

"I suppose that's fair," conceded Emily. She kept walking, leading me through candy-colored halls toward what might well be my doom.

All the bright paint and childish posters aside, the building where Lowry housed their PR team could have belonged to any corporation in the world. We walked past offices, kitchenettes, and open floor plan work areas where clerical staffers typed, answered calls, and illicitly checked their email on company time. The air-conditioning and dehumidifiers were working overtime, so that even though it was a hot Florida morning outside, some of the people in here were wearing sweaters. Living the American dream of heavy-duty climate control that someone else has to pay for.

And I'd come within a panic attack of killing them all. My fingers stayed cool, but my cheeks grew hot as blood rushed to my face. I ducked my head, turning slightly away. If I hadn't been able to get my fire under control—

This had to stop eventually. It *had* to. Grandpa Thomas didn't leave a trail of char and embers behind him during his journey from England to Michigan, and according to his diaries—at least the ones I had access to—he'd never had a dependable instructor. He'd put most of the rules of what he was and what he was capable of together on his own, and if he could do it, so could I. I refused to consider any other option.

Emily stopped in front of an unmarked white door, pulling a key from her pocket. Really, the existence of pockets in such an artfully tailored skirt was more impressive than her card trick.

"I'll make sure your management knows you were with me; that will carry more weight than any excuses Ms. Vargas-Jackson may have offered," she said, sliding the key into the slot and turning it hard to the left. The air crackled with the sudden taste of ozone, like I was biting down on tin foil. Emily turned the key back to its original position. "I'll also send you with a book of free time slips for your shift mates. It wouldn't do to damage your social standing simply because you had the bad luck to find a corpse."

"I wasn't there when Fern found it," I said automatically.

Emily shot me an amused smile. "Please," she said. "Lies between us would be pointless and petty." She pushed the door open, gesturing for me to walk through.

There was a choice here. I could do what she wanted. I'd already come this far. Or I could do the smart thing for once, and *not* allow the creepy, overly secretive routewitch to get me into a room I didn't know the dimensions of.

But she knew what I was. She knew I wasn't trained. She wasn't family: if she said she could help me, the Covenant couldn't use her to track me down. If I didn't get myself under control soon, I was going to do some serious damage—the sort of thing that couldn't be covered up by lighting a candle or spraying some Febreze.

I stepped through the door.

The room on the other side was a small, featureless white square. Emily stepped through after me, pulling the door gently closed. "Five," she said. "Four, three, two, one."

"Because *that's* not the sort of thing that freaks people out," I said flatly.

She gave me a small cat that ate the canary smile and turned back to the door, producing another key. When she opened the door *this* time, it revealed, not the colorful hallway of the PR building, but a set of industrial chrome stairs descending into the dark of a basement that Florida's high water table should have rendered functionally impossible.

(Dig a hole in a place with a high water table, the water comes in to say howdy. All of Lowryland's underground ride structures are equipped with an incredible assortment of pumps, barricades, and dehumidifiers. That's part of why the Park has such a robust generator system. If the power ever went completely out for a substantial period of time, the flooding damage would be measured in the millions.)

I must have made a sound to register my disbelief. Emily's canary-eating smile widened.

"It's safe," she said. "You have my word. I swear by the Ocean Lady that no harm will come to you while you are in my company."

I didn't know what that meant, but it sounded pretentious, and when dealing with routewitches, that's usually enough for me. They tend to be the Hot Topic sort, fond of catchphrases and ritual weirdness. I can't really blame them. When magic introduces itself into the world in the form of a highway deciding to strike up a conversation, it's probably natural to go full-on mall Goth as a response.

Emily would have made an excellent mall Goth in her teen years. She had the bone structure for red eyeliner and glitter lipstick. Picturing her that way made her less terrifying, and I held tight to the image as I stepped through the door, down onto the impossible steps.

They held. They might be impossible, but that was no excuse for them to be structurally unsound. The walls were concrete, and the handrails had been bolted solidly into place, preventing accidents. The stairs themselves were gridded metal, the kind I'd encountered in a hundred gyms and auditoriums, and walking down them was dismayingly like walking back into my own past, descending the risers at some unfamiliar school's athletic field, ready to throw myself back into the fray.

Emily's steps echoed behind me, delicate tap, tap, taps as her heels impacted with the metal. I'd seen dozens of teen queens and derby spectators get their heels caught in stairs like these, sending them sprawling and suddenly shoeless, like Cinderella fleeing from the ball. Thinking of Emily eating stair was even better than the mall Goth thing, at least where it came to keeping me from freaking out. And keeping me from freaking out was *essential*. I wasn't sure how real this basement was, but I was damn sure I didn't want to be in it if it suddenly decided that being on fire was more fun than the alternative.

The stairs went on for a hell of a lot longer than was safe or possible in Florida, until they ended at a door. I looked over my shoulder to Emily. She nodded, smiling encouragingly, which was terrifying. Once again, it occurred to me that maybe going into a strange, potentially nonexistent room with a routewitch I didn't know was a terrible idea.

That didn't matter. It was go with Emily or run from Lowryland, and I was so tired of running. Sitting still was killing me, a little bit at a time, but my family didn't raise me to run. I was a Price. I needed ground. I needed someplace to stand.

I opened the door.

There was a shock when my fingers closed around the doorknob, like static arcing through the metal. It wasn't enough to hurt, barely enough to sting, and when it passed, I was looking at a conference room. Not just any conference room: judging by the view out the wide picture window, a conference room on one of the top floors of a building. Maybe the one I'd started out in. Maybe not. A large oak table dominated the room, and a buffet was set up along one wall, the smell of food earning a growl from my under-served stomach. I ignored it. I had bigger things to worry about.

Like oh, say, the people. Four of them were sitting around the conference table and one was standing at the end, next to the sort of bar graph that absolutely meant we were interrupting something. All of them had turned to look at the door when it opened, which meant all five were now looking directly at me. I had never felt so small, or so grubby, in my life.

Emily planted her hands between my shoulders and pushed me into the room. "Look what I found," she said, voice loud enough to carry all the way to the man with the bar graph. I didn't recognize him. I didn't recognize *any* of these people. I could see that they were all management, or whatever comes after management, the people who manage the managers. To them, I was nothing, an utterly replaceable gear in their perfect clockwork.

Or at least I had been, right up until now. They turned

the full force of their regard on me as I stumbled into their conference room, and I'd never wished for anonymity so much in my life.

"Emily?" The man next to the bar graph put his pointer down on the table with a soft tap. "Who's this?"

"Her name is Melody West, and she's a junior cast member, mostly working in the Fairyland zone," said Emily. "She's been trained for all zones of the Park, shows a marked preference for themed retail, and does not enjoy working in Lowry's Welcoming World. Of the five guest complaints she's received since starting her tenure, three were received in the Welcoming World."

"Five?" asked one of the women. "That seems excessive."

It wasn't excessive. Guests come to Lowryland for a magical experience that doesn't cost as much as Disney World, and some of them are primed to complain from the second they reach the Park and realize they're not miraculously going to have the whole place to themselves. Guests who've gone into full entitlement mode will make complaints against cast members because we didn't throw everyone else out of the store to give them the full princess experience they've been dreaming of since they were five. Honestly, the only reason we didn't all receive a hundred complaints a day was because making a complaint required going to see Guest Relations in the Hall of Records, and that took effort. People who want to complain about the color of the pavement aren't usually into making an effort.

"It's not," said Emily. "It's actually below the average for someone of her tenure and temperament."

"Have you brought her here to have her memory erased?" asked the man by the bar graph. I looked at him again, more alarmed this time. He looked calmly back at me. "Did you see something you shouldn't have seen, Miss West?"

"No one's erasing anyone's memory, thanks," I said. The fire was trying to surge back into my fingertips. I folded them against my palms, trying to stop the heat from spreading. "I don't know who you are or what you're doing, and I'm happy to keep things that way, so if you'll excuse me, I'll be on my way."

One of the women was sitting up straighter, her eyes fixed on my hands. Shit. "I can see fire through your fingers," she said. "Sorcerer. Emily, you've found us a sorcerer."

"It's not polite to trespass on someone else's territory," said the man, picking up his pointer again. That tap when he had put it down: that had been wood touching wood, not metal. His pointer was made of polished, old-fashioned wood. There's a word for a pointer made of wood, in some circles.

People call them wands.

I took a step backward, narrowly missing a collision with Emily. "I didn't mean to trespass on anyone's territory, and I'm not here looking for trouble," I said quickly. The door we'd come in through was clearly magical, and going back through it might not take me anywhere near where I'd started. Someone might even close it while I was inside, stranding me in that liminal room full of concrete and stairs. "I just needed a job. Lowryland seemed like a good fit for my skills."

"She's untrained," said Emily triumphantly. "Powerful, yes, but with no idea how to use it. She's been getting lessons from a ghost."

All five of them looked at me again. I squirmed, torn between the desire to explain myself and the desire to flee.

Based on the view out the window, we were at least seven floors away from the ground. Fleeing was not going to end well for me. "She knew the last member of our family to have any magic at all," I said, making my voice curt and hard, like I was getting ready to fight with my sister. "She didn't have any of her own, but she can at least tell me how he managed not to set everything on fire all the time."

"Fascinating." Another of the men stood, walking carefully toward me. "What was your name again?"

"Melody West." I'd been Melody for eight hours a day, every day, for four years, and longer on practice and game days, when I had sometimes been Melody for twelve to sixteen hours at a stretch. I tried to summon the smell of freshly-cut grass and sweat, the sound of the crowds roaring for our football team, which was never the best in our school district, but tried really hard, every day. I was Melody because I had been Melody long enough for her to belong to me, body and soul.

The man frowned, tilting his head and squinting. "That's not the only name you've used, but it belongs to you," he said.

"And you're a trainspotter," I said, recognizing the way he was looking at me, like someone nearsighted trying to read a schedule board. "How the hell is a route-witch working with a trainspotter and a sorcerer," I nodded toward the man with the pointer, "in a Lowryland conference room? This feels like the setup to a bad joke."

"In a way, it is," said the sorcerer. He pointed his wand at me. "Welcome to the Lowryland cabal. Please tell me, in small words, why I should let you live."

Seven

"Ain't no party like a pity party, because a
pity party only ends when you bury the bas-
tards who made you feel sorry for yourself."
—Frances Brown

*In an unknown location in Lowryland, surrounded by
magical assholes*

I STARED AT HIM. He smirked back.
   I burst out laughing.

This did not appear to be the reaction he'd been expecting. His smirk melted into a confused frown, and his
confusion melted into irritation, until he was glaring at
me, making no effort to conceal his anger.

"What?" he demanded. "What is so funny?"

"I'm sorry!" I said. "I'm sorry, that was just the most
'welcome to the X-Men, hope you survive blah, blah,
blah' moment I've ever had in my life. Like, I wish I'd had
a camera running, because I want to relive that sentence
over and over again forever. You have a wand. An actual
wand. Harry Potter Land is in Orlando, you know."

His glare deepened. "This is no laughing matter.
You've trespassed."

"No, I haven't. There's no posted sign saying 'sorcerers not allowed without an engraved invitation.' I applied for a job. I got a job. I do my job well. I do my job
every day, because I don't want to get fired. Which, by
the way, you're keeping me from right now—I was supposed to be at work over an hour ago."

"You're a sorcerer," said the man with the wand. "You shouldn't need to be told."

"I'm sorry," I said. "Can you please show me the super-secret sorcerer bulletin board? Is it an Internet forum, maybe? I don't have a logon. I wouldn't have been here if I'd known I wasn't allowed."

Emily stepped up next to me. "Let's not be hasty," she said.

"No, let's be hasty," I said. "I didn't ask for this. I'd like to leave, if you don't mind. This isn't really my scene."

"But it ought to be," she said. Turning to the others, she continued, "Melody is almost entirely untrained, and has spent no time working with anyone else of her kind. She's strong enough that I could feel the heat coming off her from feet away. This kind of power can do a great deal of damage—or a great deal of good."

Heads started nodding all around the table. I glanced at Emily, alarmed, and took a step to the side, putting some distance between us. It was mostly symbolic, given how close our quarters were, but it was a start.

"No," I said. "No, and no, and *hell* no. I'm not looking for my own personal Emma Frost, thanks."

"What?" she asked blankly.

"She's the headmistress of the Massachusetts Aca—you know what? Never mind. Just assume that I'll talk about comic books when I'm nervous, and you won't be wrong, which means you won't need to understand what I'm talking about." I focused on Wand Guy. He seemed to be the one in charge. "I'm not looking to be recruited."

"Most neophytes aren't," he said. His glare was fading, replaced by a cool satisfaction that was actually substantially more unnerving. "Let's see. Your hands started getting hot some time ago. It was slight enough at first that you dismissed it, and then flammable things—paper, cotton, even hair—started to char when you touched them, until you set your first fire. It may have happened while you were sleeping. Many of our kind wake to ruined sheets and fire alarms blaring."

I said nothing.

"Perhaps you've made a few small objects float, or

have moved something from one place to another. Perhaps you think you have things under control, that you can walk in the world as a living violation of the laws of physics and the world will be forgiving. I am here to tell you that you're wrong. There are people who hunt those like us. They call themselves 'the Covenant of St. George,' and they'll cut you down as a monster as soon as they'll look at you."

That wasn't entirely true. The Covenant has always had a tradition of captive magic-users, people like me and Grandpa Thomas who've been bent to the goal of making the world safe for a very specific idea of what it means to be human. I still did my best to look shocked and horrified, widening my eyes and slackening my jaw just that fraction that people usually read as sincerity.

"So why are we here?" I asked. "If there's people hunting us, we shouldn't all be together."

"Oh, she's adorable," said a woman in an orange jacket. "I want to swallow her whole."

"No, thank you," I said quickly.

The woman laughed as Wand Guy shook his head. "We're safe here," he said soothingly. "Lowryland is under our protection. We keep the Park healthy and thriving in the face of all the challenges thrown up by the entertainment industry, and in exchange, it provides us with the psychic and magical cover we need to remain hidden. You knew, didn't you, that placing yourself amongst so many people would keep you from being detected?"

"It even kept you from being detected by us," said Emily. "That's a bug in the system."

"My ghost said that if I went where there were lots of people, it would be harder to track me," I said carefully. I needed to avoid lies. The trainspotter would hear it if I lied. I didn't know how charged he was, but there were sufficient trains in and around Lowryland that I had to assume he was running at full power. That made him more dangerous than a polygraph, and a hell of a lot more effective.

"Your ghost. How quaint." Wand Guy smirked. "Your ghost was correct. People confuse the universe. All that thinking, all those changes to their ideas about the world. People can power anything, if you allow them the room to do it. You could stay here for a hundred years and the Covenant would never find you."

"A hundred years. Got it, thanks. Can I go back to work now?"

Wand Guy looked at Emily. "Is she not very bright, or is she damaged in some way?"

"I just met her," protested Emily. "I brought her to you because you needed a say in what was done with her, and because I *had* her. I didn't want to come up with an excuse to get my hands on her again."

"Wait," I said, holding my hands up in front of me. My fingertips were hot again. I realized all six of the people in the room were watching me intently. Some of them looked downright nervous. They knew what I might be capable of, maybe even better than I did. "Let's stop, okay?"

"Stop what?" asked Wand Guy.

"Stop preening and flexing and pretending we're all bad-asses. I sell souvenirs for a living. I'm ... really not sure what you people do up here, but I'm betting it's above my pay grade. Why am I here? What do you want from me?"

"It's simple," said Wand Guy. "You're here because I want to teach you how to be a better version of what you already are."

I stared at him, and for once in my life, I didn't have anything to say.

Magic is real. Call it physics we don't quite understand or *really* complicated math or an annoying way to cheat the rules—those descriptions come from Grandpa Thomas' notes, my cousin Sarah, and me, by the way—but it doesn't matter how it's described, because changing the description doesn't make it go away. Magic is real, magic has always been real, and some people can do magic.

Not all people, sadly. It's like having brown eyes or being left-handed: most forms of magic use are genetic, and people are either born with it or not. Routewitches can be made according to my Aunt Rose, but she's always really cagey about how that can happen (and to be honest, none of us have ever wanted to press the issue). Everything else runs in families, which means cases like mine, where the person who should have been doing the training is sadly unavailable, are more common than anyone wants them to be.

Without someone to teach me, I'd keep setting things on fire and bumbling through, becoming an increasing danger to myself and others, until I finally got caught. Whether I was caught by normal policemen who thought I was a dangerous arsonist or the Covenant didn't really matter, because the end result would be the same: imprisonment, and probably death.

A teacher would fix everything. A teacher would change my life, and make my future a hell of a lot brighter, since my other option was joining my grandmother on her endless quest for my probably-dead grandfather.

But a teacher would also know me better than I wanted anyone outside the family to know me, ever, and on the rare occasions when I'd considered looking for someone, I certainly hadn't been thinking about a man who looked like the ADA of the week on one of the *Law & Order* clones.

"Teach me," I said carefully. "You're a sorcerer."

"The nineteenth of my line," he said, with the kind of pride that always leaves a bad taste in my mouth. Most people who take that much pride in being the nineteenth *anything* in their family are the kind of folks who look down on girls like Fern and Megan for having the audacity to be born inhuman, and on girls like me for being common.

Trust me. If girls like me were common, we'd have a totally different class of problems. "What's the wand for? I thought sorcerers didn't use wands."

A few of the others exchanged looks, like I'd just committed the ultimate faux pas. Wand Guy stood straighter, narrowing his eyes.

"It's a focusing tool," he said. "You may find a wand

of use once your studies have progressed beyond brute force. My offer is simple: let me train you. Work with us for the betterment of ourselves and of Lowryland. Refuse, and I'm afraid your employment will need to come to an end. We can't have untrained sorcerers running around the property. It's untidy."

Two things were immediately clear. First, that he really, really wanted me to agree to let him train me. All of them were looking at me with avarice in their eyes, like dogs considering a platter of steaks on the way to the barbecue. They were a cabal of grown adults with control over their powers, and for some reason, adding an untrained baby magic-user to their ranks was the best idea any of them could come up with. That unnerved me.

The second thing was even more unnerving. Specifically, that there were five of them—six if I was counting Emily—and only one of me, and Florida is a state rich with swamps and alligators, aka, "Nature's body disposal service." If I refused them, my employment might not be all that was terminated.

"What do I have to do?" I asked.

Wand Guy smiled.

Fern sat in the corner of a small, unwelcoming room. The walls were painted electric yellow, and there was a vending machine packed with Lowry-branded snack offerings next to her chair, but those were the only concessions to the location: the room itself could have been part of any DMV or government office in the country. It was the sort of featureless, windowless place where people were sent to be forgotten about.

Her head snapped up when the door opened, and her whole face brightened when she saw that it was me. Then it closed off, leaving her wary and displeased. "An—Melody!" she said, barely catching herself in time. "I told you that you didn't need to come."

I winced at the first syllable of my real name, resisting the urge to look over my shoulder and check Emily's expression. If she didn't realize Fern had been starting to call me something else, I might get out of here without any more awkward conversations. That would be a nice change.

"Of course I came," I said, and held up the bag I'd been carrying since leaving the house. "I have my post-shift change of clothes if you want to borrow them. Also, I have a hairbrush."

"You are my favorite," said Fern, and lunged for the bag. She was exhausted from being up all night: when she moved, it was with the odd floating quality that only really kicked in when she'd started lowering her density to keep herself from falling down.

"I try." This time I did look over my shoulder at Emily. "Is this an okay place for my roommate to change, or should we head for a bathroom?"

"I'll be outside," said Emily. "Ms. Vargas-Jackson will be giving both of you a ride the rest of the way to the Park, and I'll get those time slips for you."

"Thanks," I said, with all the sincerity I could muster. It was more than half a mile from here to the employee entrance to Lowryland—even the backstage areas were enormous, thanks to the scope of the Park they supported. Getting a ride rather than catching a tram would probably shave half an hour off the trip.

(We weren't lazy. Lazy people don't work at Lowryland. But we *were* about to go and spend what remained of our shifts on our feet, and there was a non-zero chance our respective managers would ask us to stay late and make up what we'd missed, official note from the PR department or no. Any walking we didn't have to do was a good thing.)

Fern was staring at Emily, eyes wide and as wonder-struck as those of the children who came to see her every day in all her princess glory. "Time slips? Really?"

"Really," said Emily, with the sort of smug, patronizing smile that I'd come to expect from Lowryland management. "I'm sure if you ask Melody, she'll share." Then she was out, shutting the door behind herself as she left us alone.

Fern looked at me. I shook my head. This space looked empty, but that didn't make it safe. Cameras can be small. Listening devices can be smaller. Was I being paranoid? Sure. That didn't mean that I was wrong.

"They're giving me a whole booklet of time slips to apologize for pulling me off my shift this morning," I said, finally surrendering the bag to Fern's questing hands. She retreated back to her seat, hauling the bag open and starting to strip in essentially the same motion. I leaned up against the wall. We'd been on the same roller derby team. Our bodies held no secrets.

No visible ones, anyway. Fern didn't know about my little magical problem. It had seemed like a step too far. "Hi, having me as your roommate might bring the Covenant of St. George down on your head, and oh, by the way, sometimes I set things on fire without meaning to?" No. That wasn't a conversation I'd been willing to have.

I was going to need to have it now.

"Can I have some?" she asked, shedding her old bra and rubbing a deodorant stick under her arms and breasts before starting to put the new bra on.

"Of course," I said. "I don't know whether they're going to be fours or sixes, but I can give you a couple either way." Time slips were one of the many ways Lowryland management pitted us against each other, like we were fighting chickens in the farmyard of life. Each piece of carefully watermarked and uncopiable paper was good for two, four, or six hours of vacation time, and they trumped even mandatory attendance policies. A whole book of time slips was a great big slice of freedom pie.

On some level, I wanted to keep the whole book for myself. I'm only human, after all, and time slips could buy that most precious of commodities, free time during Park hours, when the stores off-property would actually be open. I could go to Target. I could shop for groceries, rather than trusting Megan and her idiosyncratic ideas about vegetables—specifically, that they were what food eats, and not food themselves—to fill the fridge.

But training with Colin, aka "Wand Guy," was likely to mean some changes to my work shifts, and my coworkers already didn't like me much. Spending my time slips on keeping the peace was probably for the best, even if I would prefer not to.

Fern, who would need to do her hair and makeup in the dressing room where her full costume waited for her, had already finished dressing. She looked at me expectantly.

"Have you eaten?" I asked.

"They had bagels in the room where they were going over my story," she said.

"Okay. Are you ready to get out of here?"

Fern nodded firmly.

If there had been any question of whether we were being monitored, that answered it. As soon as Fern nodded, the door swung open, and there was Emily, now with Sophie standing behind her. Sophie looked confused, even slightly concerned, which was something of a relief. She wasn't a part of this secret cabal that seemed to be in charge of the place: she was just someone I'd gone to high school with who happened to have been in the right place to help me when I needed her. I wasn't sure my heart could have handled finding out that Sophie had been lying to me all this time.

Sure, I'd been lying to her since the day we met, but I've never claimed not to have a hypocrite heart.

"I assume you're both ready to go?" asked Emily.

We nodded. She turned to Sophie.

"Miss West has been very helpful," said Emily. "We appreciate your bringing her here to review last night's events. We've found no wrongdoing on the part of either employee, and they're both well aware of the injunctions preventing them from speaking to either members of the press or the general public. Everyone's a blogger these days. Even the six-year-olds could be tiny public relations disasters in princess dresses and pigtails."

That was probably aimed at me. With one thing and another, I hadn't actually been given the "don't talk to anybody" lecture like I was supposed to have been. At least I had common sense enough to know better without anyone telling me.

"We appreciate your taking the time," said Sophie.

"I know," said Emily. Her hands moved too fast to follow, and like another card trick, she was suddenly holding two books of time slips, one stamped with a four and the other with the all-powerful, endlessly coveted six. She held them out, the four toward Fern, the six toward me. "As promised."

It was hard not to feel like I was being bribed, and even harder to care. I took the booklet, fighting hard not to snatch it out of her hand, and tucked it into my front pocket, where I wouldn't lose it. "We're ready to go if you are."

"I can still make my afternoon shift," said Fern, making her book—her bribe, since it had never been promised to her, and we were both smart enough to see it for what it was—disappear.

"Great," said Sophie, clapping her hands in a way that made me want to fall into a starting cheer position. "Let's get you two to work!"

"See you soon, Melody," said Emily sweetly.

I didn't say anything. I just followed Sophie away from that unkind little room, Fern at my heels.

Sophie was silent until we were out of the building, across the sidewalk, and in her car with the doors closed. Only then did she look at me and ask, "Are you all right?"

"I'm fine," I said, leaning back in my seat so I could see Fern in the rearview mirror. She looked tired but alert. She'd be fine. Roller derby teaches many important lessons about sleep deprivation and why it is sometimes just one more obstacle to wave at as you skate on by. We'd both sleep like rocks tonight, and the world would keep on spinning.

"That was Emily Doyle."

"Okay."

"She's a shark. Don't trust her. She shows up every time something happens, and she gets the credit suspiciously often."

Of course she did. She was a routewitch, and what were the paths and trails through Lowryland, if not roads? She might lack the power of her peers who drew their strength from highways and urban thoroughfares—but then again, she might not. Thousands of feet traversed the smallest of Lowryland's trails every day. That much presence, that much power, had to go somewhere, and Emily was as good a vessel as any.

"She just wanted to review my side of the story and make absolutely sure Fern and I were in agreement," I said. "We were. She had me sign a statement, promised me the time slips, and we were done. Where did you go?"

"To view the video footage. Nothing contradicts what either of you have been saying." She glanced at Fern in the rearview mirror. "As long as it stays that way, there shouldn't be any lasting effects."

"Except on the dead guy," I said.

Sophie sighed. "Except on the dead guy," she agreed. "Mel . . . you're not going to go all Nancy Drew and try to figure out what happened to him, are you? We have our own security. Lowryland is not the place to play out your high school dreams of cracking the case."

"Since I'm under the age of sixty, I'd actually be going all Veronica Mars, and no," I said. "I'm not a mystery solver. I do not yearn for the feeling of closure as the clues all come together. I mostly just want to get to work before I wind up getting docked a vacation day."

"You won't be docked a vacation day," said Sophie. "I updated your file with the reasons behind today's tardiness myself. You're *fine*."

"Except for the dead guy," chirped Fern.

Sophie sighed, seeming to deflate. I could still see my high school cheer captain in her, but for the first time, I could also see the adult woman who'd kicked and spat and clawed her way up the corporate ladder. We were the same age. Her birthday was less than a month before mine. In that moment, she looked like she was ten years my senior, something she usually concealed beneath makeup and careful hair and attitude.

"Except for the dead guy," she said, and while it was remarkably close to what she'd said after my last prompt, she hadn't sounded so damn defeated then. "Be careful, all right? Both of you. You've done nothing wrong, and I understand that, but you've been noticed. Having the eyes of Lowryland upon you is not always all it's cracked up to be."

"Understood," I said. She had pulled up in front of the gate that would take us past the boundary of the Park and into the endless warren of tunnels, offices, and locker rooms that would allow us to do our jobs. I flashed her a smile. "Thanks for the ride."

"Any time," she said.

Sophie sat there, hands resting lightly on the wheel, and watched as Fern and I walked down the sidewalk to the gate. I glanced back at her. She raised one hand in a small wave. I returned the wave, and we stepped through the gate, and we were gone.

Eight

"Performance isn't all sequins and bright lights and knowing when it's done. Sometimes performance is what drags you through a day when nothing else will stick around to finish the job."

–Frances Brown

Lowryland, subject to the judgment of coworkers, because that's fun

ARRIVING FOR MY SHIFT three and a half hours late was about as well-received as I'd expected. My cushy duty attending on the princesses was gone, handed off to someone who actually got to work on time, and I was back in retail hell. Whee. Sharp glances and casual glares greeted me when I stepped onto the floor of the Fine and Fair Gift Shop. Having anticipated this, I'd tucked my book of time slips into the pocket of my apron, and responded to the most acidic glares by pulling it out just enough to let my adversaries see the big golden "6" on the cover. Their eyes went wide, and judging by the speed with which the negative looks turned into friendly, open-faced smiles, the rumor mill was making sure everyone knew I was in the possession of a truly excellent Get Out of Snubbing Free card.

I was folding and stocking shirts when someone sidled up next to me, approach announced by the rustle of their long uniform jacket. "Hi, Mel," said a sweet voice.

I closed my eyes, counting silently to five before opening them again. Of course. I might be working in the same area every day this week, but that didn't mean anyone else was. Even Fern was doing a shift as Princess Aspen in one of the private "dining experience" restaurants, rather than hanging out in the main meet-and-greet.

"Hello, Robin," I said, glancing meaningfully at my nametag and its prominently displayed "Melody" as I turned to face her. "What can I do for you?"

She dimpled at me. "I was just wondering if you might need some help with the folding. Looks like there's a lot."

I glanced around. There were no guests nearby. The shop was in the middle of one of those odd, unpredictable lulls that came and went on even the busiest days, when the aisles would seem to empty out for no apparent reason, leaving us with the chance to catch our breath and repair all the damage the last wave of guests had done.

Naturally, that also gave us time to bother each other—or more specifically, it gave Robin the time to bother *me*. "I'm good, thanks," I said. "It's just the normal number of shirts."

"You shouldn't have to take care of all that on your own," she protested, and made a grab for the shirt I was holding, pouting at me when I moved it out of her reach. "You know, we could be really good friends if you'd only learn to play the game the way the rest of us do. A little give, a little take, a little yes, a little no. You're not willing to let anyone *in*, Mel, and we worry about you."

"Right." I put the shirt down and straightened, turning to face her fully. Crossing my arms where guests might see me was frowned upon: I joined my hands behind my back instead, which had the helpful side effect of preventing me from setting her on fire if she continued pissing me off. "And this sudden urge toward camaraderie, it has nothing to do with the book of time slips in my pocket, right?"

She could grab them, if she wanted to. She could make this physical. If she did, I'd be within my rights to get our shift supervisor involved. I could see by the way she hesitated that Robin knew it, too.

In the end, she took a half-step back, removing herself from temptation, and offered a toothy smile. "If I was hoping you'd share something you'd been so blatantly flaunting, can you really blame me?"

"No," I said. Her smile broadened. "But that doesn't mean I was planning to share with *you*." That same smile froze, while her eyes screamed silent confusion. I offered a smile of my own. "You're a bully. You're mean to people you don't need to be mean to, and you push people around whenever it suits you. You can't even get my name right. I was given these so I could offer them to my shift mates as apology for any inconvenience my absence caused them, but see, I know you, and I *know* my absence didn't cause you any inconvenience. Any extra work that tried to land on your shoulders would have been shunted off to whoever didn't dodge fast enough."

Robin's smile finally flickered and died. "You little b—"

"Excuse me, but do you have this in my size?" The guest appeared at my elbow like she'd come from out of nowhere, probably because she had. Ghosts aren't always good about following the rules of linear reality.

Robin jumped, squeaking in surprise. I turned. There was Mary, back in her Hot Topic shirt and jeans. I guess once a ghost figures out the right outfit for a haunting, they like to stick with it. She was holding one of the newer Laura and Lizzie designs in one hand, having probably snatched it off a shelf at random.

I offered her a bland, corporate-approved smile. "Let's go check," I said, and walked deeper into the store, away from Robin, who stared after me like I'd just drowned her puppy in the well.

Mary waited until we were well clear of my coworkers before dropping her voice and asking, "Where were you this morning?"

"Home, then I had to stop off at one of the admin buildings for a while, and then here. Why? Were you waiting for me?"

"No, I . . ." Mary paused, waving her free hand in frustration as she tried to toe the line between what she knew and what she was allowed to say to one of the living. I looked at her and forced myself to wait patiently. It wasn't always easy.

Having ghosts in the family means knowing the afterlife is absolutely, no question, real. Some people stick around after they die, continuing to interact with the living world—although how much interaction is normal is sort of up in the air, since our ghosts have been with the family since Buckley, where Mary and Rose both died, and the average man on the street is a lot less likely to believe in a haunting than we are.

Having ghosts in the family also means knowing that someone is probably always looking out for you—literally, in the "I can see it when you touch yourself" sense. When I was a kid and Mary was my babysitter, I used to be convinced that she was secretly Santa Claus. The white hair helped.

In the present, Mary finished her attempt to put a sentence together and said, "I don't always know where you are, but I always know *that* you are. I know when a member of my family dies."

"We're not blood relations."

"That doesn't matter. If it did, people couldn't haunt their spouses. Your family is who you tell the twilight belongs to you, and I told the twilight—and the crossroads—that I was a Price-Healy. You're mine. I'm yours."

I frowned. "If you know whenever one of us dies—"

Mary held her hand up. "Don't ask. I know what you're thinking about asking me, and I'm telling you, don't. You're not allowed to know. Not unless you want to take this to the crossroads."

Of course, it couldn't be that easy. If it was, Grandma Alice would have asked Mary years ago whether or not Grandpa Thomas was alive, and we wouldn't be in our current mess. Either we'd have them both back, or we'd have a whole different Grandma Alice-shaped mess to deal with.

"Sorry," I said. "You were saying?"

"I was saying that for about an hour and a half today, you were gone. You weren't alive. I didn't feel you die, but that didn't necessarily mean anything." Mary gave me a worried look. "You scared me."

I took a quick look around, making sure that none of my coworkers were lurking to try to score something they could use to blackmail me into giving up my time slips. Then I leaned closer and said, "You need to come to the apartment tonight. Something happened."

It was clear from her expression that she wanted to ask for details. It was equally clear that she knew better. Mary nodded, handed me the shirt she had been holding, and disappeared. Her timing was good, as always: immediately after she shuffled off her visitor's pass to this mortal coil, my supervisor came around the corner, looking uncomfortable as only a grown man in a wine-colored velvet vest could look.

"Melody," he said, striding toward me. "Robin has made a complaint against you."

"Has she, now?" I folded the shirt Mary had handed to me and returned it to the nearest shelf. "What a coincidence. I was just trying to decide whether I should make a complaint against her."

My supervisor raised his eyebrows, looking at me expectantly.

No one liked Robin, except for the people who liked her *too* much, the ones who scurried along at her heels and agreed with everything she said. It wasn't hard to decide what I should do:

I told him everything.

Oh, not *everything*-everything. I didn't mention magic-users, or routewitches, or being with Fern when she found the body. But I told him about going to the PR building to help my roommate, and how I'd been given a ride by my hiring manager, who wanted to encourage me to show the real Lowry spirit even if she had to haul me by the hand every step of the way. I pulled the book of time slips out of my pocket, showing him the six and the fact that all the coupons were still in place.

"I'm supposed to share these with the people my absence inconvenienced, to avoid hard feelings that might impact our ability to do our jobs," I said. "I didn't want to do it until our shift ended, because distracting other workers to make myself feel better isn't right. Robin came over and tried to strong-arm some of them out of me."

"She says you called her a bully."

"Only after she tried to bully me." I looked at him calmly. "Did she tell you she called me a bitch? If we're playing the name game, I think she wins, which means she loses."

He frowned . . . but his eyes were still on the book of time slips in my hand. Right. "You know I'm supposed to pass all formal complaints along to management."

"But in this case, given the circumstances, you'd be willing to let it slide as long as I gave you one of these, huh?" I tugged one of the slips free. The paper was heavy, slick, and ridged in places with the careful swirls and indents of the watermarking. It felt rich. I offered it to him.

He made it disappear. "I'll tell Robin I can pass her complaint along, but that doing so would require me to pass yours along at the same time. I expect she'll change her mind. Is there anything I can say that might help to mend the bridge between you two?"

"No," I said. He blinked. I shrugged. "She's awful to me. She always has been. I have something she wants right now, but that's not going to be true forever, or even for very long. I could give her the whole book and she'd still be awful to me as soon as she realized I didn't have a second one. You can tell her my name is Melody, not 'Mel.' That might mend *my* bridges."

"All right." He started to step away. Then he hesitated, and said, "You should take your lunch."

"I just got—"

"I'll see you in an hour."

He walked away, leaving me staring after him and wondering what I'd missed.

One application of my employee discount later, I was sitting in one of the outdoor break areas, protected from the rest of Fairyland by a tall, comforting wall. Our side of it was bare wood occasionally blazoned with signs reminding us to wash our hands, smile, and embody the Lowryland spirit. The Park-facing side was a lush maze of thorny tangles and artificial branches, making it look like an extension of the deep dark wood that ran all through Fairyland, helping to create the illusion of isolation that allowed us to exist separately from the rest of the Park.

My salad, a limp, dressing-soaked concoction from Mustardseed's, was about as appealing as eating cardboard. But it had calories, and nutrients, and I needed both those things if I wanted to survive the rest of my shift, especially since taking my lunch so early meant that I wasn't going to get another break today. I picked up my fork. I took a bite. Mustardseed's and their ability to ruin anything with too much vinaigrette came through again: it was like filling my mouth with someone's faintly bitter perfume. Apparently, "dressing on the side" was a concept they had never heard of. I chewed, swallowed, and repeated the action, trying to put my body on autopilot before I threw down my salad in disgust.

There was a distant bang. Someone screamed.

I threw down my salad, not in disgust, but in my hurry to jump to my feet and run toward the sound. As I ran, I spared a thought for the fact that my parents raised me to be the first one dead in any horror movie—the girl who runs *toward* danger is a hell of a lot less likely to survive than the girl who gets the hell out of the situation.

The thought that yes, good, something was happening, something I could potentially hit . . . that was a lot stronger, and accompanied by a sudden, triumphant heat in my hands, like the fire lurking in my blood wanted to be invited to this party as much as the rest of me did. I kept running, finding a little extra speed in my legs and applying it to the sprint. I might not have been doing my job recently—my real job, that is—being too busy hiding to seek out and get to know the local cryptid community, but I'd been staying in shape, laying in reserves against the inevitable day when the Covenant found me and decided it was time to bring me to justice. When that happened, I'd do no one any good if I wasn't in top form.

The screaming continued, getting higher and shriller, until it had almost become a keen. Before, it had been the shocked sound of someone being hurt. Now it was the shriek of someone in an intense amount of pain. I whipped around the corner—

—and stumbled, nearly toppling over as I took in the scene in front of me.

The woman who was careening around, trying to reach for her face, was wearing a Fairyland zone uniform: she must have been like me, on her break during the lull, going to grab a snack or a drink to tide her over until the next time she got a moment to herself. Unlike me, she had walked behind the Hill and Dale Fried Chicken Shop.

One of the fryers had exploded. I didn't know how that was possible. There should have been a thousand safety precautions to keep that sort of thing from happening, and to keep it contained inside the shop if it happened anyway. Fire extinguishers and sprinkler systems and foam baffles should have come into play. And they hadn't. Everything that could have gone wrong had gone wrong, resulting in a jet of boiling oil being forced through the thin back wall of the shop, where it had doused this poor woman from head to toe in heat.

Her hair was on fire. So was the back of the shop, and the nearby wall. Her hair seemed like the biggest problem at the moment. A few other cast members were hovering around the edges, some pointing, some shouting, at least one with their cellphone out, hopefully calling 911 or Park Security—Security would get to us faster—but none of them were *helping* her.

I recovered my balance and kept running, whipping off my apron. The flames on her head were small. That was the only good thing about this situation. She was more than half-coated in sizzling oil: if those flames reached the edge of the stain, she'd go up like a candle. This was going to hurt her. I was pretty sure being on fire would hurt her more.

When I was close enough, I whipped my apron onto her head, smothering the flames. She screamed again, agonized and confused. The fire in my hands surged, responding to the heat and the horror of the moment. I pulled the fire back as hard as I could, reining it in.

This was no time for hesitation. I hesitated all the same. If I could pull the fire already in my hands into myself and damp it out, why couldn't I pull more than that? I had no training. I had no preparation. I had to try.

Still using the apron to smother the flames on her head, I pulled harder, focusing on the way it felt to smother my own nascent fire in my own flesh. It was difficult to push and pull at the same time, like the old joke about rubbing your belly and patting your head, but I narrowed my eyes and bullied on through, refusing to allow for the idea of failure.

If it gets hot enough here, the second oil boiler will go, I thought, and pulled.

If I don't get the heat out of her skin, she's going to keep cooking under the weight of all this oil, I thought, and pulled.

If this place really catches, we're all going to die, and I refuse to die like this, I thought, and *yanked*, feeling the thermal energy around me surge and flow, finally obedient, into my waiting hands. There was too much of it. I yelped and dropped my apron, dancing back from the still-smoking, still-keening woman. My hands felt like they were on fire. Not literal fire, the way they sometimes were: so much heat that they were cooking. I could see blisters forming on my fingers. I waved them wildly, trying to make the heat disperse. I couldn't swallow any more of it, not without igniting, going up like the back of the fry shop, all fire and ash and—

Someone grabbed my hands and bore down hard, so that I felt my blisters burst. I turned a startled glance toward the face of the Emma Frost lookalike who was squeezing my fingers.

"Give it to me," she hissed.

I let the heat go.

Emily's hair frizzed out around the edges, blown upward by the heat, but her skin didn't redden, and her hands remained cool against my singed fingers. The only sign that this was any sort of challenge for her was in her eyes, which narrowed incrementally. The whole process only took a few seconds. Then she was letting me go, turning toward the injured woman, and shouting, "Somebody go tell the EMTs where to go! And for the love of God, someone get a flash mob going!"

Half the other cast members dispersed, seeming relieved to have clear instructions. I could hear murmurs on the edge of my awareness; guests, clustering outside the wall, trying to find the source of the screaming. Give them one of the biggest playgrounds in the world and they would still go looking for the things that they weren't supposed to see.

The woman who'd been injured wasn't screaming anymore. She was sobbing, her hands occasionally fluttering toward her face, but stopping shy of touching it, like she was afraid feeling the damage would make it real. Her burns were so bad that she was unrecognizable. I'd probably shared shifts with her for months, but I didn't know who she was.

I was struck by the sudden, terrible thought that this might be my fault. My magic, such as it was, was entirely uncontrolled, and responded to my anger. That boiler shouldn't have exploded. If this was Robin . . .

No. Her undamaged nametag said her name was Cathy. I hadn't done this. The realization allowed me to relax fractionally—which caused the pain in my hands to come surging back, as bright and electric as it had been when I was burning myself. I yelped and blew on them, trying to soothe the damaged skin and seared tissues.

A hand touched my shoulder. I stopped blowing and turned. Emily looked at me sternly.

"You'll need to see the EMTs," she said. "That was very brave and very foolish, what you just did. Sticking your hands into the fire to extinguish her hair? You're a credit to the Lowry name."

Her voice was a little too loud and a little too cadenced, like she was making sure that when people thought of this moment, it would be her version of events that they remembered.

Assuming anyone was even paying attention. The

flames were lower and sparser than I remembered, slowed down by my sudden, violent removal of so much heat from the area, but they were still climbing, and they'd started to grow again. Outside the wall, I heard the sudden blast of a bugle. The Wild Hunt was going to ride through the Park early today, hurrying the guests away from the area, allowing the fire department to get access without shutting all of Lowryland down. Safety first, but if safety could be accomplished without actually losing any money, that would always be the preferred option.

Someone shouted, and a team of Lowry EMTs in bright jumpsuits came running into the area, surrounding the unfortunate Cathy even as security staffers rushed in behind them with extinguishers in their hands. I wobbled. It felt like these people were shamefully late, but I knew the feeling was lying to me: I knew that it had only been a few seconds, a minute at most, since I had heard the screaming.

Emily's hands were a welcome pressure on my arm, holding me up. My booklet of time slips was on the ground, oily and now getting spattered with drops of fire retardant. Emily followed my gaze to the booklet, and sighed.

"I'll get you another," she said. "Truly, it's the least we can do after your heroic intervention."

Well, that, and bribing me didn't do much good if I didn't hold onto the bribe. That was fine. I didn't want to try bending my fingers right now anyway.

"How did you get here so fast?" I asked, blinking slowly at Emily. The EMTs were all busy with Cathy. It would be a few minutes before they got to me. The shock was starting to set in, unwilling to wait. Burns *hurt*.

"Just lucky, I suppose," said Emily, with another glance at Cathy. "I'll inform your supervisor that you won't be returning today, and put in for a commendation for your quick thinking and flexible response to the situation. Lowryland thanks you."

"Cool," I said, and stayed where I was as she walked away, leaving me surrounded by shouting, flames, and the smell of burning wood.

This day was not getting any better.

Nine

"Oh, isn't that special. Honey, go tell your
father we're going to need a bigger chain-
saw."

–Enid Healy

A *shitty company apartment five miles outside of Lakeland, Florida*

I WOKE UP TO the sound of the front door slamming and
Fern shouting, "Annie? Annie!"

"'S not my name," I mumbled, and automatically
moved to shove my hair out of my face, only to stop
when the bandages on my hand scratched my skin. The
sensation was followed by pain in my fingers as even that
slight pressure reminded my body that I was wounded.

"Annie!"

I sat up, lowering my hands, and called, "My room,
Fern."

The door was shoved open a second later, and there
was Fern, makeup still covering her face, hair still matted
from its time beneath her wig. She paused only long
enough to be sure that I was in one piece. Then she flung
herself across the room, flinging her arms around my
shoulders and bursting into tears all at the same time.

"Shhh," I said, fighting the urge to pat her on the
shoulder. I wasn't going to help her by showing obvious
signs of how much pain I was in. "It's okay. See? I'm fine.
I just got a little scorched. No big deal."

"No big deal?!" She pushed herself back, eyes terribly
wide in her pale face. "You got *burned*! I saw the dam-

age! The chicken stand is all burned out inside, and the walls are so messed up that they're probably going to have to close that section of Fairyland for *months*!"

"It was an accident," I said, still trying to be soothing. "Something broke when it shouldn't have broken, and someone got hurt."

"You got hurt."

"I got hurt because I was trying to help the woman who was right behind the boiler when it blew." I was grateful for the painkillers the EMTs had pressed upon me before sending me home to sleep. They had kept me from having any unwanted dreams. I was pretty sure Cathy's melted face was going to be a recurring feature in my nightmares for the foreseeable future.

"I can't . . . I can't be upset that you did that." Fern sniffled. "I know you'll always do that if you feel like you have to, and if you didn't feel like you had to, I guess you wouldn't be you."

"Exactly," I said, with as much of a smile as I could muster. It was dark in my room. The sun must have gone down while I was sleeping. That was a good thing. If it was dark, Fern couldn't see how much my smile was shaking. "Now, speaking of being me . . ."

"I'm sorry!" Fern clapped a hand over her mouth before repeating, through her fingers, "I'm sorry. I was so scared for you I didn't even think."

"It's okay," I said, trying to be reassuring. "There was no one else here."

Megan knew "Melody" wasn't my real name. She'd made a few comments about how the next time I got to decide what to call myself, I should pick something that didn't start with an "M," to cut down on confusion in the mornings. Nothing pointed enough that I'd been forced to respond to it, and it wasn't like I was worried about her spilling all my secrets—she had plenty of secrets of her own that needed keeping, and she was too good-natured to go in for mutually assured destruction—but her message had been clear. When I was ready to tell her who I really was, she was going to be ready to listen.

There'd been times when I was tempted. Her parents

were back in Ohio. My brother had been in Ohio when he'd been working with a colony of Pliny's gorgons, and while I wasn't absolutely sure Megan was one of theirs, I had my suspicions. It would have been nice to have one more possible exit strategy on the table.

But Alex was still in touch with the gorgons in Ohio because Alex is still in touch with everyone he's ever met. Alex still writes thank-you notes to his college professors, which he has to mail from a different *state*. If Megan found out I was Antimony Price, sister to Alexander Price, the chance that her parents would know where I was inside of the week, and my brother would know where I was inside of the month, was just too big of a risk for me to take.

Life was a constant game of risk assessments, and I didn't enjoy it one little bit.

Fern wiped her eyes with the back of her hand. "I wish it wasn't always you," she said miserably. "This is the most time we've ever had together, and I don't want it to be you."

"I grew up knowing it was always going to be me," I said, tone apologetic. "My hands will be fine in a day or two, and in the meantime, how about you make me a sandwich? I'm not sure I could hold a knife right now if I wanted to."

Before Fern could answer, there was a clatter from the kitchen. We exchanged a look.

"Megan isn't here," she said, voice going suddenly low. "Her shift at the hospital doesn't end for hours."

"Okay," I said. "Stay behind me."

Maybe that was the wrong thing to say. I could barely bend my fingers. I didn't have a gun, and I wouldn't have been able to pull the trigger if I had. But Fern still nodded obediently and stepped behind me as I got out of the bed. Together, we made our way toward the bedroom door.

The apartment was dark. Fern hadn't bothered to stop and turn the lights on during her charge toward my bedroom. That might work in our favor. My hands weren't good for fine motor control, but they could still grip, and I paused to grab a chunky ceramic vase off the table in the hall. Fern had brought it home from a swap meet, saying she thought it was pretty, and the thing was a magnet for the weird translucent lizards that kept getting in. We dumped the things out on the porch at least twice a week.

Well, they could find a new lizard motel, because I was about to smash this one over somebody's head. We inched our way down the hall toward the kitchen. We were almost there when I paused, sniffing the air.

"Is that chicken?"

"Good, you're up," said Mary, a beat before the kitchen lights clicked on. There was my old babysitter, white hair braided back to keep it away from her face, Lowry-branded attire traded for her more customary faded jeans and white peasant top. A red-and-white bucket that smelled strongly of fried chicken, clogged arteries, and good life choices rested on the counter in front of her, along with several smaller containers of side dishes—corn and gravy and potatoes.

Fern squeaked. Mary's attention switched to her.

"Fern, right?" she said. "From the Slasher Chicks. I've seen you skate. You're really good." Mary's outline wavered. A Slasher Chicks tank top replaced her peasant blouse, black and red and skin tight.

I sighed. "I hate it when you do that."

"But you love me, and you've done something horrible to your hands, which you're not going to let me tell your parents about, so I think we're even," said Mary.

Fern was gripping my left arm hard enough that it hurt. "She's a *ghost*!" she exclaimed.

"And you're adorable," said Mary.

"Okay, let's not," I said. "Fern, this is Mary Dunlavy, my childhood babysitter and adopted aunt. She's been keeping an eye on me so that my family doesn't burn down the world trying to find me and bring me home. Mary, this is Fern Conway, my roommate and teammate and easily startled friend. Please don't torture her for fun."

"I do everything for fun," said Mary. "It's a pleasure

to finally meet you, Fern. You've been a good friend to Annie. She doesn't have many of those."

"How are you a ghost?" asked Fern.

"I died, I wasn't ready to move on, I decided to haunt the living for a while, I wound up babysitting this one's grandmother," Mary hooked a thumb toward me, "and somehow that turned into haunting their family in specific. As long as there are Prices, I'm going to be around to change their diapers, wipe their noses, and try to keep them from getting swallowed by unspeakable creatures that they've brought home and named 'Fluffy.'"

"But you had to die?" asked Fern anxiously.

Mary gave her a sad, sympathetic look. "It's all right," she said. "Everything dies. One day, you'll die, and when you do, you'll find someone like me waiting to give you your options and docent you all the way into whatever you decide to do next."

"Right now, what I'd like to do is know why you're in my kitchen," I said.

"Because you told me to be," said Mary.

I paused. "Oh," I said finally. "Crap. I totally forgot."

"Because of your hands?"

"Because of my hands." I held them up. "One of the quick service restaurants had an accident. A deep fryer blew up, doused this poor woman in hot oil. I tried to help, and I burned my hands." That wasn't the whole story. From the look on her face, Mary knew it. But Fern didn't know about my little problem, and she was freaking out badly enough over Mary that I didn't want to drop any more surprises on her.

(It can be easy to forget, in a world where humans are the dominant species and human cultures are dominant no matter where you go, that all thinking creatures will have their own cultural ideas, opinions, and hang-ups. I didn't know what sylphs thought of people who could set things on fire with a touch, and I didn't want to find out by making myself homeless.)

"Did you get actual medical assistance, or did you just wrap them in gauze and call it a night? Because I can call your mother—"

"Please don't." I lowered my hands. "The Lowryland EMTs patched me up. It's only minor damage. I've got light duty for the next two days while I heal, and then I should be all better."

"Your mother will resurrect me just so she can kill me if I let something happen to you, and she scares me." Mary folded her arms. "She married in, remember? She doesn't have that automatic 'do what Mary says' programming that blood family gets. If I let you burn your fingers off, or whatever, she'll have me stuffed into a spirit jar before I can say 'it wasn't my fault.'"

"I won't burn my fingers off," I said. The smell of fried chicken was starting to make my mouth water, as my body remembered that I hadn't eaten anything since a few bites of bad salad. "Can you fix me a plate? I think I can hold a fork, if I'm careful about it."

"Of course," said Mary. She opened a cupboard and took down two plates. "Fern? Chicken? I'm assuming you're not a vegetarian, unless tofu bacon has gotten *much* more convincing."

"Please," said Fern.

"Now while I'm doing this, Annie, how about you tell me why you ceased to exist this morning, and what was so important that I needed to come to your apartment to find out about it?" Mary's tone was pleasant, but it concealed a razor's edge of tension and threat.

I swallowed a groan. Between the pain and the chicken, I had forgotten *why* I'd told Mary to come and see me—and now I had a problem. "It's nothing, really," I said, with a meaningful glance at Fern.

Mary narrowed her eyes. "Liar," she said.

"Wait." Fern looked between us. "Do you not want to talk because I'm here? Is that it? Don't you trust me? I thought you trusted me."

"I do trust you," I said. "I just . . ." I paused, and sighed. "I've sort of been keeping something a secret, and I don't want you to stop being my friend when you find out what it is. That's all."

"Oh." Fern frowned. "Is this about how you set things on fire when you're asleep? Because I know about that.

I think it's sort of cute. Are you sure you're not part djinn? Because that would explain the fire. Except I don't think they're cross-fertile with humans, and I know you're mostly human. Um. Except for the fire thing."

I stared at her. Mary stared at her. Fern shrugged, looking sheepish.

"You've set off the fire alarm a couple of times," she said. "Megan thinks it's faulty. I know you like her, but I figured it was sort of your thing to tell her about."

"Why didn't you tell me you knew?" I was reeling—more from the idea that I'd been able to sleep through the fire alarm than from the surprise of learning that Fern knew about my little problem. I was supposed to be able to wake up and move at a moment's notice.

Working a real job was taking more out of me than I'd realized. It didn't help that, with the exception of the knives in my room—which I had to keep hidden, in case of a surprise inspection, and which I couldn't take to work with me ever—I was living alone and unarmed, without even a colony of Aeslin mice to reassure me that I was going to get through this. On some level, I'd already given up. Sleeping through the fire alarm was one more sign that it was getting bad.

Fern shrugged. "I figured once you wanted me to know, you'd tell me yourself. In the meantime, I wanted you to be comfortable here. I know this has been hard on you. I've been helping as best as I could."

"Okay. Um. Wow." I took a deep breath. "Yes, this is about the fire thing. I'm entirely human, as far as I know, but my grandfather was a magic-user, and it seems I am, too. My hands get hot sometimes. Hot enough to start fires."

"What happened today—"

"I didn't do it." I couldn't even be angry that she had sort of asked. I would have asked, too, if our positions had been reversed. "I was having lunch when I heard the screams and went to see what was going on. The explosion had already happened. I burned my hands when I started pulling the heat out of her to try and reduce her injuries." My fingers throbbed in sympathy with the memory. I grimaced. "I'm hoping I don't need to do *that* again for a really long time. This hurts."

"Doing the right thing often does," said Mary. She looked at Fern. "Your roommate's a sorceress and I'm her dead aunt. Is that okay? Have we covered the situation? Because I'd like to move on before the other roommate gets home."

"We have about three hours," I said.

"I'm fine," said Fern. "This is sort of a lot? But I've already been through sort of a lot, so I guess it's more for the pile."

"Cryptid therapists must make so much money," I said.

Fern's expression was grim. "You have no idea."

"Here." Mary thrust a plate of chicken and the associated sides at me. "Take. Eat. Explain. Or I swear to God, I will haunt you so hard that you will never sleep, shower, or have sex again."

"I don't seem to be doing enough of any of those things at the moment, so I'm not feeling the threat, but I'll explain." I took the plate, moving down the counter before putting it down and clumsily picking up my fork. Bending my fingers even that much hurt. I still needed to eat, and I didn't want Mary deciding that it was time to bring the airplane out of retirement.

(Virtually everyone has to deal with people who knew them when they were babies, and will bring up awkward things like "hey, remember when you ran through the dinner party naked?" or "hey, remember how I used to pretend your fork was an airplane when you didn't want to eat your beets?" But most people understand that age is a real thing that happens to everyone. Mary . . . doesn't, so much. She knows the kids she cares for eventually turn into adults and have children of their own, and intellectually, she understands that this means we're not her charges anymore. Emotionally, she's been a sixteen-year-old girl since the day she died, and she'll stay that way until she moves on to whatever comes next for dead babysitters who serve the spirits at the crossroads. For her, we will always be children, and we will always need her to tuck us into bed and turn off our bedroom lights. There's something soothing about that. There's also something really sad. In my family, the two often go hand in hand.)

Fern got her own plate and came to stand beside me, expression expectant, like she'd been waiting for this particular iteration of story time for years. I put my plate on the counter and took a deep breath.

"Lowryland is secretly being controlled by a cabal of witches and magic-users, and they want to train me so that I'll be less of a danger to myself and others," I said.

"Huh?" said Fern.

Mary's eyes narrowed. "What *kind* of witches and magic-users?"

"There's at least one routewitch and one trainspotter, and there's a man with a wand who says he can teach me how to control whatever the hell it is I have going on, so I'm assuming he's a sorcerer like Grandpa was." I took a bite of mashed potatoes, since they didn't require chewing, swallowed, and said, "I'm going to let him teach me. I don't see where I have much of a choice."

"Neither do I," said Mary.

Fern was looking back and forth between us, seeming increasingly dismayed. "What do you mean, you don't have a choice?" she squeaked. "You don't know these people! What if they get too interested in you, and find out about Megan and me?"

"They already know," said Mary wearily.

Fern and I both turned to stare at her.

Mary shook her head. "People like that . . . you called them a cabal. That's not a word I hear you use all that often. Did they use it first?"

I nodded.

"There you go. People who call themselves a 'cabal' are usually very interested in keeping an eye on the territory they've decided to stake out as their own. In this case, Lowryland. There's no way they don't know about any nonhumans who live or work here. They probably know about the ones who just come to the Park to spend a day with their kids."

Fern looked ill. "They know? We have to warn people."

"Why?" Fern turned to look at me. I did my best to sound reassuring as I said, "If they know, they could have done something about it a long time ago. I know route-witches can ward against ghosts, but Mary can visit me here and at work. They probably have at least some influence over hiring decisions, and you still got your job, and Megan still got her residency. The Covenant hunts witches, too, when they can find them. These people aren't the same as you, but maybe they're not the enemy either."

"And if they are, learning how not to burn the building down is still a good thing," said Mary. "You said they had a trainspotter. How strong?"

"He's drawing power from the roller coasters, so . . . probably pretty strong? He couldn't pick up my real name by looking at me. I've spent too many years as Melody for that to be a quick trick."

"Well, it's best if you try to avoid him, and any other trainspotters they have, just to be sure."

Fern frowned. "What's a trainspotter?"

"Do you know what a routewitch is?" asked Mary.

"No."

"Okay. Trainspotters are a sort of routewitch. Route-witches draw power from travel, usually on the highway, but any form of travel will do. They're the most powerful of the journey magicians in general. Trainspotters only get power from trains. They need to be surrounded by a shell of manmade machine that someone else controls for them to tap into whatever the universe is trying to tell them. Interestingly, this makes them better at scrying, at picking apart the threads of reality and seeing what's true and underneath them. If the Covenant knew how to work with trainspotters without killing them, we'd all be in trouble."

Fern looked at me. I shrugged. "You can't keep a trainspotter captive without breaking their connection to the rails," I said. "The Covenant has their magic-users, but as far as I know, they've never managed to catch a road witch of any sort, and certainly not a trainspotter."

"They've had a few umbramancers, and those are

technically journey magicians," said Mary. "That's neither here nor there. Annie, if you're going to work with these people, you have to avoid the trainspotter."

"That shouldn't be too hard." Privately, I wasn't so sure. I had no idea how their structure worked.

But that woman nearly died today, and she was going to need years of surgery and physical therapy before she could recover, assuming she ever truly would. If I'd been better able to control the fire, I might have spared her at least some of that suffering. I definitely wouldn't have burned my hands. Whether it was a good idea or not, I needed the training, and these were the only people who were offering it to me.

"They must have some powerful wards on their headquarters," said Mary. "That would explain why you blinked out like that. As soon as you were on their home ground, you were hidden from everyone who might be looking for you. Even me."

"And you're a family ghost," I said, with a frown. "This is good, though. If you can't find me, the Covenant can't find me."

"You can't hide in their space forever."

"No, but it's good to know that I have someplace to run where the Covenant won't be able to stick a pin in me." I took a bite of chicken, actually chewing this time before I said, "I'm going to let him train me. The fire is getting stronger, and I'm having more and more trouble keeping it under control. I'll be a danger to myself and others if I don't figure this out soon."

"I'm not going to stop you," said Mary. "But I have three requests, and none of them are negotiable."

"Okay," I said. "Shoot."

"First, you call for me immediately after every session you have. I may not always be able to come. I'll hear you, and I'll know that you're all right."

"Deal."

"Second, if you wind up alone with that trainspotter—with any trainspotter, at any point—you run. I don't care if you have to abandon everything you own, you run. There's too much about you that no one needs to know."

I looked at her and nodded silently. Mary will protect me to the ends of the Earth and beyond. I've always known that about her. But if it's a choice between just me and the rest of the family, she's going to take the option that saves the most of us. She has the luxury of knowing that death is not the end. If she had to leave me in the path of a moving truck to pull both my siblings to safety, she'd just get to spend a few years teaching me how to be a better ghost. Not the worst thing that's ever happened.

"Third . . ." Mary took a deep, unnecessary breath, held it for a moment, and let it out before saying, "You don't have enough backup. You need more. You need to let me tell Sam where to find you."

"Absolutely not," I said. "Out of the question. I ran away from him so he wouldn't be in danger."

"Oh, and not because you were afraid that Antimony Price, the Ice Queen, might be starting to thaw?"

Fern put her hand up. "Who's Sam?"

"A friend," I said, as Mary said, "Annie's boyfriend." We stopped and glared at each other across the counter, which wasn't doing nearly enough to provide either one of us with cover.

Fern blinked. "Annie has a boyfriend?"

"Yes," said Mary, and "No," I said, again at the same time, again followed by glaring.

"Huh," said Fern. She paused before asking, more delicately, "Has he actually met you when you were being you, or did he only ever meet you when you were pretending to be somebody else? Because you can be really sweet when you're pretending to be somebody else."

I threw a biscuit at her.

Fern laughed as she dodged. "You're only angry because it's true."

"No, it's not; I was myself the whole time I knew Sam." Or at least a version of myself. A version who didn't have anything to worry about beyond the borders of a carnival, and a boy who might have loved her, if he'd only been given the time. "And we're not calling him here. It's not safe."

"It isn't safe for anyone," said Mary. "Not Fern, not me, and certainly not you. Why should it be any different for Sam?"

"Because . . ." I hesitated. "Because he didn't ask for any of this."

Mary's smile was small, and sad. "Oh, peaches," she said. "You think any of us did?"

The phone rang. We all turned to look at it.

It was a small idiosyncrasy in the Lowryland housing rules that every household had to include a fixed landline. We could all have cellphones—we were expected to, and those of us who lived on-property but had bad or absent credit could finance them through Lowry, Inc.—but we had to keep a landline, in case of emergencies. That way, no matter what happened, the company could say they had at the very least made a good-faith effort to contact us.

"You're closest," said Fern meekly.

I was also the one with the wrapped-up hands. I decided not to mention that as I turned and pawed the receiver off the wall, managing finally to get it wedged between my cheek and shoulder.

"Hello?" I said.

"There's a ghost in your apartment," said Emily.

I glanced at Mary, who was looking at me with both eyebrows raised. "Yes," I said.

"Do you want it there?"

The question was casual, but the many things it meant were anything but. Emily was a routewitch. She could ward my home against Mary in a heartbeat. I didn't know whether she could do it from a distance. I had to assume yes. Routewitches are all about distance, and this one was short enough to be effectively null.

"Yes," I said firmly. "It's the relative I told you about."

Mary's eyebrows climbed higher.

"Do you know what *kind* of ghost it is?"

There was the five-million-dollar question. If the Lowryland cabal was on my side, my answer wouldn't change anything: a dead aunt was a dead aunt, even if I was pretending she was a dead grandmother, and all dead relatives were worth preserving. If they were secretly the bad guys, having access to a crossroads ghost would be a temptation too far.

"Road ghost," I said. "That's all she's ever been willing to tell us. She died on the road, and now she's a road ghost."

"Ah," said Emily. "Colin was very displeased to hear that you'd been injured. Your shifts for tomorrow have been cancelled due to medical reasons. He expects you at his office by nine AM."

The line went dead. I hung the phone up gingerly, turning to fully face the others.

"Guess I've got class in the morning," I said.

"Guess I'm going to talk to a man about a monkey," said Mary, and disappeared.

My eyes went wide and my fingers went hot. "Mary?" I squawked. "Mary!"

She didn't reappear.

I covered my face with my hands. Fern patted me awkwardly on the shoulder.

"Don't worry," she said. "Maybe he won't come."

I groaned.

Ten

"Believe me, I want to be here even less than you do. Now, are we going to fight like civilized people, or am I going to stand here and taunt you?"

–Jane Harrington-Price

The Public Relations building of Lowryland, at way too goddamn early in the morning

EITHER COLIN DIDN'T TRUST me or he didn't trust the Lowryland train system, because when I opened my apartment door at eight-thirty, there was a sleek black car idling at the curb. Fern and Megan clustered in the doorway behind me, staring.

Megan made a clucking noise with her tongue. "Whoever he is, marry him and keep us in the style to which we'd like to become accustomed."

"He works in Public Relations."

"Whoever he is, murder him and make it look like an accident, but make sure you get away with his wallet," Megan amended.

"Thanks for the vote of murder-confidence," I said.

She flashed me a bright, toothy smile. "I always have faith in you when it comes to murder."

Fern tugged on my arm. When I turned to face her, she reached up and pulled me into a hug with suddenly heavy arms, effectively trapping me long enough for her to whisper, "Be careful," in my ear.

She let me go. I nodded, trying to show that I understood, before I stepped into the humid morning air and walked down the path toward the waiting car. The sky was bruised black along the horizon, speaking of a storm to come. When I opened the car's rear door, a blast of air-conditioning nearly rocked me back on my heels.

"Hello," I said. "I'm Melody West. Are you here for me?"

"Get in," said the driver gruffly.

I got in.

The car's interior was real leather, and smelled buttery and rich, like I was wrapped in a cocoon made of nothing but the idea of money. I sank into it, trying not to do the math on how long this car could have paid for my groceries, and failing.

My family isn't poor. We do a lot of work for the cryptid community, and while they may not all pay in money as humans understand it, the barter system can turn into money easily enough, and we have really good accountants who truly understand the process of making our income look believable. But my parents believe we should know how to be hungry, because things like that can be a disorienting shock to the system otherwise. I could balance a budget by the time I was sixteen, and I'd spent enough summers eating elbow macaroni and stewed tomatoes with the Campbell Family Carnival to genuinely respect how much easier money made things.

This car wasn't just about being expensive or being easier than the cheaper alternatives: it was about making sure people *knew* the owner had money, enough to burn it on all-leather interiors and the latest bells and whistles. There was even a bottle of water in the holder between the seats, cold enough for beads of moisture to be forming on the outside.

"You're late," said the driver gruffly.

"It's eight-thirty," I said. "My lessons don't begin until nine."

"Which means being there at nine," he said. "You should have come out three minutes ago. Buckle your seatbelt."

I fastened my seatbelt—that's never been the kind of instruction I needed to receive twice—but I was still surprised when he rammed his foot down on the gas and sent us racing out of the apartment complex, heading for the nearest highway at a speed that seemed designed to attract the attention of the local police and make us even later. That was, until he reached under the dashboard and produced a blue bubble light, which he set in front of the steering wheel. It flashed rhythmically, and the traffic melted away in front of us.

"You're a cop?" I asked warily.

"Lowryland Security," he replied.

"Huh," I said.

We weren't on Park property. It was questionable whether we were even on Lowry property. They owned a disturbing amount of the land around here, including pieces that no one would expect, neighborhoods filled with single-family homes, strip malls, even supposedly public parks. No one associated those places with Lowry, but look deep enough and the trails of ownership were clear. That didn't give Park Security any authority there.

The flashing blue light was setting my teeth on edge. I tried to focus on it, and found that I couldn't; my eyes skittered away from the moment of the flash. Something about it wasn't right.

But it sure did make the drive easier. We pulled up to the backlot gates with eight minutes to spare, and my driver even stopped the car when we reached the PR building. I reached for the handle. The door was locked.

I was considering whether or not to get worried when the door opened from the outside, revealing my driver. "We're here," he said.

"Great." I unfastened my belt and slid out. The man was close to seven feet tall, and built like a wide receiver from the NFL. "Anybody ever tell you that you're incredibly tall?"

He didn't even crack a smile. "Get inside," he said.

"Yes, sir," I said, and turned, walking away as quickly as my little feet would carry me. The man wasn't as unsettling as his little blue light, but something about him made me think that lingering in his presence wouldn't be a good idea.

The air-conditioning inside the PR building was

turned up even higher than it had been in the car. Emily was waiting for me in the lobby. She wrinkled her nose at the sight of my yoga pants and tank top, and asked, "Don't you own any *real* clothing?"

"I'm a minimum wage Park employee," I said. "If I can't get it for a discount at the company store, I don't own it."

"We're going to have to fix that," she said, and sniffed, like the mere sight of synthetic fibers offended her. "Come on. You don't want to be late." She spun on one perfectly shaped heel and stalked down the hall toward the elevator, leaving me to hurry after her.

At least it didn't look like we were taking the magical stairway to absolutely nowhere this morning. "I'm getting that idea," I said, once I had managed to catch up. "Do you have any idea what's going to happen today?"

"You're going to earn our faith in you." Emily stopped in front of the elevator and pressed the button. It lit up. She pressed it three more times anyway, doing an impatient little jig with her knees. "We don't get much new blood around here."

"Bad reputation?"

She rolled her eyes. "Please. We offer a *health plan*. We have the best reputation of any cabal this side of the Mississippi River—and did you see that bullshit the LA folks pulled on live television last year? Right now, I think we're the best regarded cabal in the country."

"Then why?"

"Because there isn't much new blood to get." For the first time, the muscles around Emily's eyes relaxed, her gaze softening, becoming less predatory and more wistful. "You don't know how much you've missed."

The elevator doors opened with a ding before I could say anything, and the moment passed: Emily's mask of cool disdain snapped right back into place as she waved imperiously for me to get into the tiny, featureless box. The urge to balk was high. There's a word for people who follow strangers into places with no clear escape route, and it's not "survivor."

But there was fire in my fingers and inertia at my

heels: I didn't want to run again, or try starting over in a place where luck might not be on my side. And luck *had* been on my side since choosing to come to Lowryland. How else could I explain just happening to stumble across my old high school cheer captain—or even having the Melody West ID in my go bag, when I was supposed to have buried her years ago? The cabal was big and scary and unknown. They were also offering to help me get myself under control before someone got seriously hurt. My lucky streak hadn't failed me yet.

It was going to. Lucky streaks always do. For the moment, I needed to let my bets ride, and roll the dice again.

Emily smirked as I joined her in the elevator. That seemed to be her default expression. "Timid, new girl?"

"You know, you should be played by Natalie Dormer in the movie," I replied flatly. "You have the right mix of mean and murderous."

"I'll take that as a compliment," she said. She pressed a button. The doors slid shut. "Let's go over the rules for today."

"Since you haven't told me what they are, can you really expect me to go over them?"

Emily rolled her eyes. "I hate new girls," she said. "You always think you're so clever, and you're so very wrong. Rule one: do as you're told. Colin knows what he's doing and you don't, so if he's giving you an instruction, he has a good reason. You can ask questions—in fact, asking questions is rule two—but you need to listen."

"Got it," I said.

"No, you don't, but I believe you'll try, and that's honestly more than some of us are expecting from you. Rule three is going to be harder. You need to remember that you are a guest here, in our space and in Lowryland, and comport yourself accordingly."

"Got it. Use my manners."

"Lady of the Underpass preserve me," muttered Emily. The elevator doors opened, revealing a large, empty room that wouldn't have looked out of place in a suburban dojo or dance studio. One wall was mirrored; another was clear glass, showing what felt like all of Florida from a seemingly impossible height. I was suddenly very glad never to have suffered from vertigo.

Once again, Emily placed her hand between my shoulders and shoved, pushing me out of the elevator and into the wide, empty room.

"Have fun," she said. The elevator doors closed on her smirking face, and she was gone.

The room seemed even larger without the safety of the elevator behind me. I took a few hesitant steps forward, wishing I had a knife, or better yet, twenty knives, or better *yet*, twenty knives and a brick of C-4. Plastic explosives are a strange and dangerous security blanket, but they tend to make whatever's scaring me go away quickly, so I'm in favor.

My reflection looked small and scared and frazzled, nothing like the image of myself that I've always tried to project. I stopped, looking critically at myself. My hair was good. Megan didn't have hair of her own—again, snakes—and consequentially viewed me and Fern as life-sized versions of her childhood Barbie dolls. When she'd learned I used henna to keep my hair closer to red than brown, she'd actually squealed and demanded I let her take over the process. Since I hadn't been doing my own henna since high school, I'd gladly handed her the reins.

I needed to eat more. My collarbones were showing too clearly through my skin, and that has never been a good look for me, or a goal of mine. My sister is a dancer and always will be, whether she's doing it professionally or not. For her, weight management is a part of her career. I, on the other hand, skate to kill and set things on fire with the power of my mind. The trapeze requires a certain awareness of size, but that's as much about knowing the strength of your partner as it is the size of your pants. Sam had been perfectly happy to sling me around the big tent—boobs, hips, and all—and he had never once suggested I needed to cut back on the sandwiches in anything other than jest.

Lowryland hadn't been as kind. I was still eating, but my meals were more like the one I'd failed to consume yesterday for the most part: Park food, scarfed down fast, assuming it made it past my lips at all. Nutrition and the food pyramid were no longer my friends.

"Hello?"

No response.

"I'm assuming you're watching me right now, since it wouldn't make sense for you not to be—not when I'm in your nice training room and all. So if you're watching me, you must be testing me in some way." I was talking partially to hear myself talk, and partially to see whether anything in the room reacted. Nothing did. "I do better on tests when I know what I'm supposed to be accomplishing. Just an FYI."

Still no response. This would get irritating fast if I allowed it to do so, which was probably what my new teacher was counting on: the more annoyed I was, the more likely I was to set something on fire without meaning to. I didn't know whether this was intended to gauge how much power I could generate or give them a baseline of how easy I was to annoy, and—honestly—I didn't care. They were playing games. I could play games, too.

"I wish I had my skates. This is a nice smooth floor like the ones I used to train on, not like the bumpy paths in Lowryland. I could build up a real head of steam here." I walked to the middle of the room, dropped my bag, and kept walking until I came to the bar in front of the mirror, where I kicked off my shoes. Verity would already have been practicing her ballet form. I had something similar in mind.

My hands hurt less than they had immediately after being burned. My fingers still felt thick and clumsy, slow to obey my commands and slower still to clamp down, but that was okay; what I had in mind didn't require fine motor manipulation. Bending forward, I rested my forearms against the floor, putting the bulk of my weight on my elbows. I held that position for a moment, letting my spine lengthen into the pose, before lifting up onto my toes, clenching the muscles at my core, and slowly, carefully lifting my legs into the air.

As always, there was a moment where it felt like I was going to overbalance, sending myself crashing to the floor. The moment passed, and then my toes were lightly tapping the surface of the mirror, reassuring me that gravity was working the way it was supposed to.

Trampoline and the trapeze are all about core strength. Without it, you'll never get off the floor. Funny thing: cheerleading and being a roller derby jammer work the same muscle groups. I may not be the fastest thing on two feet—although give me a pair of skates and I'll give damn near anyone a run for their money—and I may not have the best aim in my family, but I can hang upside down like a bat for *hours*. It's actually pretty soothing. Even blood needs a vacation every now and then, and I enjoy sending mine to visit my brain.

Closing my eyes, I focused on my breathing, letting every inhale fill my entire body, letting every exhale root me deeper in my pose. The pain in my hands receded, driven away by the meditative focus on being exactly who and what and where I was.

A door clicked shut somewhere behind me. I didn't open my eyes.

"Miss West, may I ask what in the world you're doing?"

The voice belonged to Wand Guy. Nice to know I'd been right about who was keeping an eye on me. Still not opening my eyes, I said, "I figured you'd gotten stuck in a meeting or something, and wanted me to entertain myself. I'm meditating."

"You're inverted."

"Not quite. I can't trust my hands, and there's no hang bar on the ceiling anyway."

"Please remember what it means to be right-side up, and turn to look at me while I'm talking to you." He didn't sound angry. More confused, with a healthy side order of amusement.

That was something I could work with. I tapped my toes against the mirror one last time before lowering my legs toward the ground, pushing myself farther up onto my elbows at the same time, until I was drawing a horizontal line with my body. This accomplished, I lowered my legs the rest of the way down and opened my eyes, meeting my own gaze in the mirror.

There was Wand Guy, standing behind me and about eight feet back, his wand in his hand. He was wearing a suit—big surprise there—and a quizzical expression.

"Yoga?" he inquired.

"Among other things." I pushed myself to my feet, dusting off my knees before I turned to face him. "It helps to keep me calm."

The corner of his mouth quirked upward. I'd guessed correctly about the idea behind putting me in this room by myself, then. "I see," he said.

I offered him my biggest, brightest smile. "So what's the plan? How are you going to teach me to avoid going full Carrie?"

"How much do you know about other sorcerers in your family line?"

The question was mild, but that didn't mean it wouldn't have teeth. It's always hard to know how people will react to the name "Price." Some of them think we're still with the Covenant, which makes us monsters. Others think we've long since sold the human race out in favor of the cryptid communities of the world, which also makes us monsters. And regardless of how he responded, telling him who I really was would compromise that whole "hiding" thing I had going on. So I kept smiling, and I lied.

"Not much." So far so good. "It was my grandfather, according to our family ghost, and she didn't see too much of what he could do—just knew that he could do it. He didn't leave behind any instruction manuals. Unfortunately, he didn't have any other family, so it wasn't like we could go talk to them when I started smoking."

"How much does your grandmother know? Having a family ghost is unusual enough that she must be aware of *something*."

This was where I'd need to start treading carefully. So far as I knew, magic-users can't detect falsehood any more than, say, routewitches, or babysitters. They can learn to read people, but they can't hear a lie the way a trainspotter would. So I could tell Colin lies and be okay, as long as I constructed a chain that made logical sense and wasn't likely to trip me up later. It was just that if he asked me to repeat any of this in front of the trainspotter, I was going to go down in flames.

Oh, well. I'd come too far to let one more possible disaster keep me from learning what I needed to know. "I didn't know she was my grandmother when I was little. I thought she was my imaginary friend," I said glibly. "She would appear after my parents turned the lights out. She told me bedtime stories and chased the monsters out of my closet before she went away. When I asked my mom about her, she always said there was no girl in my room after bedtime. Every kid has their own version of normal, you know? When other kids talked about their imaginary friends, I thought they could see them the way I could see mine."

"I . . . see," said Colin.

In for a penny, in for a pound. "She went away when I was nine. That was the year I found out Santa Claus wasn't real, and neither were imaginary friends. She came back five years later, when I had a bad dream and set my pillow on fire. She's been with me ever since."

"And she couldn't tell you anything else about your grandfather?"

"Just that he'd been an immigrant, so if he had any relatives, they were very far away, and he never liked to talk about them." I looked at Colin, all wide eyes and innocence. If I'd had a bow to clip in my hair, I would have. Anything to make me look less like a potential threat. "I really hope you can help me. I'm so tired of being afraid everything is going to burn."

"That isn't a fear you'll need to harbor for much longer," said Colin. "Have you ever listened to a baby's cry?"

I blinked. "Um, yeah. I'm a human being who works at Lowryland. My days are filled with crying babies."

"Infants scream without concern for the damage they may do to themselves in the process. Their little throats are forever raw from the strain of howling their

indignation to an uncaring world. As they grow older,
they learn to use their voices for other things. They learn
to speak, in some cases to sing, to modulate themselves.
Would you say that speech is a better use for the voice
than primal howls?"

"I guess . . ."

"That's what I'm here to do for you," said Colin, with
more than a trace of smugness. "Right now, you are an
infant. A powerful one, yes, but capable of nothing more
complex than the magical equivalent of screaming because you want your diaper changed. You are a danger
to yourself and others. As you learn to control what you
can do—to speak, in a magical sense—you won't be able
to scream as loudly. Your body will learn its limits, and
refuse to allow you to endanger yourself unless your life
is on the line."

I brightened. "No more fires?"

"Not unless you intend to cast them, and even then,
they'll require substantially more work than they do
now." He shook his head. "The Covenant of St. George
has much to answer for. They've been the end of so many
magical bloodlines—very nearly including yours, I'd wa-
ger. There's no other reason for an adult sorcerer to
leave his territory and move someplace where he'd have
neither family nor familiarity to protect him."

In a way, the Covenant *had* been responsible for the
death of all my grandfather's blood relatives. They had
sent them, one after the other, into the face of danger,
and when danger swallowed them whole, the Covenant
had turned its eyes to other families, and other opportunities. The Price family was small now, but we were doing
worlds better than Grandpa Thomas had been, back
when he'd been the last branch of a dying family tree.

"All right," I said. "Where do we begin?"

We began with concentration exercises. Colin would
show me flash cards, asking me to memorize their contents in a matter of seconds, and hold them at the fore-

front of my mind as he asked me dozens of unrelated questions. He would recite poetry, only to stop and demand that I echo it back to him. He wouldn't repeat a single word.

I drew circles and chanted riddles and focused and concentrated, and at the end of our three-hour session, I felt like I'd been running laps for the entire time. My head ached, my skin was too tight, and I was deeply aware of every ache in my ass from spending most of the lesson sitting on the hardwood floor.

Colin smiled at me. "How are your hands?" he asked.

I paused. "Cool," I said finally.

"Good," he said. "Your lessons start in earnest tomorrow." Then he stood and walked away, into the window, into nothingness, and was gone, leaving me to stare after him.

Okay. This was going to be interesting.

Eleven

"You can't do this alone. Nobody can. Nobody should have to."

–Alice Healy

*Lowryland, three weeks and eighteen lessons later,
trying to stay awake*

My BREAK FROM WORK only lasted for three days—
paid, of course, since I'd been wounded in the
course of trying to show the "true Lowry spirit," and
since my new mentor held some undisclosed but apparently terrifying position in the corporate hierarchy—
before I was shoved back into the workforce, hands still
bandaged to keep the healing damage from freaking out
the paying guests.

(I was doing better than poor Cathy. Lowry, Inc. was
covering her medical bills, since it was their deep fryer
that had experienced a mechanical fault at the exact
wrong time. That was the least of her problems. She was
going to have a long road to recovery, one that would
involve multiple skin grafts to rebuild her face. Every
time someone mentioned her in my presence, it was all I
could do not to blurt out the location of the last Caladrius-
run hospital I knew of in North America. The avian cryptids can heal almost anything, given sufficient time and
resources. They could put Cathy's face back together, or
at least back into a shape that wouldn't hurt every time
she tried to open her eyes. Some secrets must be kept.
That doesn't make keeping them any less painful.)

Every morning I got up and went to the PR building,

where I spent hours with Colin, studying, reciting, and working my way through the long, slow process of learning to control the gifts I'd never asked my genes to give me. When I was done with *that*, I would shower, change, and get a ride to the employee gate, usually arriving just in time for my shift to start. Not exactly the sort of schedule that leaves a lot of time for a social life.

Not that my time mattered. I'd been assigned to Fairyland on a permanent basis after telling Emily it was my preference within the Park. Having friends in high places paid some useful dividends, even if half the people I worked with now looked at me like I was a corporate spy, while the other half scurried around in silent terror, having somehow convinced themselves that I'd shoved the unfortunate Cathy into the fryer under the mistaken assumption that she was Robin.

I had never been popular at work, but this was rapidly approaching ridiculous.

And yet.

I hadn't started a single fire, intentionally or otherwise, since I'd started working with Colin. He'd asked me to pull the heat out of several candles and a handful of bright, spitting sparklers, turning fire into smoke into nothing at all, and I was starting to feel like that was the sort of thing I could learn to enjoy, the point where my body somehow converted the kinetic potential of the world into a beautiful sort of stillness.

If I really tried, I could hold that same stillness under my breastbone, comforting and soothing me when my coworkers left me standing by myself in the middle of a guest-clogged store. I was clinging to that stillness now, as the afternoon parade floated majestically by outside the gift shop. The *Goblin Market* float was parallel to our window, and Princesses Laura and Lizzie ran wildly from one side to the other, dodging marauding goblins. Every time the music hit a crescendo they would grab one of the large plastic vines that had been provided for their use and swing themselves out over the adoring crowd, waving and blowing kisses before they turned around and did it all again.

Other floats had other princesses and other routines, which meant that Fern was probably enjoying her lunch right about now. The princesses in the parade weren't the ones who did the meet-and-greets with the guests: their costumes were usually sparklier, less screen-accurate, and designed for a different range of motion. Since only one iteration of each character could be loose in the Park at any given time, the photo princesses were getting a well-deserved break.

The same could be said for those of us working along the parade route. The sidewalks and walkways were clogged with gaping guests, making it virtually impossible for anyone to get into or out of the store. It was probably a safety hazard. As long as it gave us time to fold all these damn shirts, I didn't care.

That's what I was doing when the engine blew. I was folding shirts, hands working on autopilot while my mind reviewed Colin's most recent set of training exercises, my back to the street. There was a loud banging noise, like a nail gun going off, and someone screamed. That first scream was the bellwether for quite a few more. In a matter of seconds, the world was made entirely of screaming.

I dropped the shirt, fingers suddenly nerveless, hands refusing to close. There was no heat, but I whipped around all the same, running toward the window. Half my coworkers were already there. No one shoved or jockeyed for position. We just stood, frozen, terrified, as the *Goblin Market* float toppled sideways, falling onto the crowded sidewalk.

Several screams cut off abruptly, like the screamers were no longer available for comment. That was enough to break the spell my shock had cast. I ran for the door, pausing only long enough to lean over the counter and grab the first aid kit we kept there for the inevitable staff accidents. I didn't think individually packaged aspirin and mini-bandages were going to help much, but I had to do *something*.

The street outside had devolved into pure chaos. People were still screaming, scattering away from the fallen float like it was a giant grenade chucked into their midst.

The sound was somehow muted, unable to live up to the impact of that first, ear-splitting cacophony. Babies and young children wailed, clinging to their parents or—more chillingly—sitting abandoned on the curb, with no caretakers in sight.

The float itself was on its side, completely obscuring a long stretch of sidewalk, burying whatever had been there under more than a ton of plastic, papier-mâché, and metal rebar. A red pool was forming along the float's edge, and despite the theme of the area, I knew it hadn't come from a pomegranate, full and fine.

One of the curling blackberry vines the actresses playing Laura and Lizzie usually used as handholds while they raced around their float was on fire. I ran toward it, trying to feel the heat, to focus my training on pulling it out of the world. A burning float was one of the only things I could think of that would make this already bad situation genuinely worse.

My hands stayed cold and calm. They were just hands. I stopped in the middle of the street, buffeted on all sides by guests fleeing from the accident, and stared at them. There was no heat. I could feel what was coming off the float, feel it getting stronger as the fire began to spread, but it was all external fire. There was nothing inside me.

Colin's words about babies and the way they screamed, hurting themselves because they didn't know any better, flashed through my mind. I knew better now. I knew hurting myself didn't do me any long-term good. But dammit, I could have done with that lesson kicking in a little later.

"Fuck," I muttered—a firing offense if any of the fleeing guests felt like reporting me for swearing while wearing an official Lowryland uniform—and started running again, heading for the center of the chaos.

The actress playing Lizzie had been flung free when the float went down. She was sprawled on the concrete about ten feet away from the wheels, one arm bent at an angle that spoke clearly of a bad break, the sort of thing that would require more than just a cast to repair. I stopped next to her, crouching down and feeling for a pulse. She moaned when my fingers pressed against her throat. That was a good sign. Dead people don't usually make a lot of noise.

"You need to be as still as possible," I said. Most of the crowd was already past this point, fleeing for places that weren't at risk of being on fire; the injured actress's chances of being trampled were low. "You fell hard, and you could have a spinal injury."

She moaned again. It was difficult to tell for sure whether she could hear me. If she couldn't, she was unlikely to move, and if she could, she would hopefully listen. I shoved myself back to my feet and ran on toward the float, hissing, "*Mary*," under my breath.

"Mary" is a pretty common name. My dead aunt doesn't appear every time I say it, which is a good thing, given how many Marys I've met through cheerleading, roller derby, and being a physical meat creature who walks in the world and has to deal with the consequences of uninspired parents. But she *hears* it every time a member of the family says her name, and she can choose to come and see what we're going on about. I ran, and suddenly a white-haired woman was running next to me, her steps making no sound.

"What the hell?" she demanded.

"Float fell," I replied. There were sirens in the distance, the sound of Lowryland's emergency teams racing toward us. There'd be no effort to cover this one up. This wasn't some behind the scenes accident where no guests had been injured. This was a full-on disaster, and everyone was going to get involved.

The trouble with something like this—apart from the loss of life and the therapy that all these children were going to need—came from Lowryland's design. Like most Florida theme parks, real estate was at a premium, and a space that wasn't somehow interactive or eye-catching or otherwise keeping our guests engaged was a waste of money. That meant there were very few straight roads within the Park itself. Security staff could come through the backlot and the tunnels, but the emergency vehicles? Those had to travel along one of a limited number of routes, and at this time of day, with the rest of the parade still clogging the street and screaming guests fleeing everywhere, getting through to us was going to be just this side of impossible.

"What do you want me to do?" demanded Mary.

I looked quickly around. No one was looking at us. Anything that happened now was likely to be written off as shock, a hallucinatory aftereffect of seeing something this horrible happen in a place that was supposed to be all about happiness and joy.

"Go under the float," I said. "See how many dead we're dealing with. If there are any ghosts, see if you can convince them to go away. I'm going to take care of the kids."

Mary nodded and was gone. I kept running until I reached the sidewalk and the first of the sobbing, somehow left behind children.

Please, you were with an older sibling who forgot about you, I thought desperately, picking up a weeping little girl with one arm and grabbing a baby carrier with the other. The girl wailed and buried her face against my shoulder. I was a stranger, sure, but I was a stranger in a Goblin Market costume. She was wearing a sparkly Princess Laura dress. Having someone from what was probably her favorite movie come to rescue her must have been the only thing that made sense right now.

There was blood on the lacy edge of her dress. *Please think it's jam,* I thought, and ran until I reached a bench, where I plopped both child and carrier down.

The little girl didn't go easily. She grabbed for me as soon as it became apparent what I was trying to do, making a keening noise in the back of her throat, like a distressed puppy. I offered her my brightest Lowryland smile.

"Hi," I said. "I'm Melody. What's your name?"

"Ginger," she sniffled.

"Is this baby with you, Ginger?"

She shook her head.

"Okay. I have a big job for you, princess. Do you think you can do a big job for me?"

"I want my mommy," she whispered.

I understood the sentiment better than I'd ever thought I would as an adult. I wanted my own mommy so badly that it hurt. "I know, princess," I said, smoothing Ginger's hair back from her face. "But I need to help some more people before we can go find your mom, and I need you to be brave and strong like Laura, and watch this baby for me, okay? I can't take a carrier with me while I make sure everyone else is okay."

Everyone else was *not* okay. There was too much blood for that, and too much screaming, even now that most of the guests had fled. A lot of people were never going to be okay again. I kept looking at Ginger and kept smiling, listening to the sirens getting closer and the wailing of the wounded.

Finally, sniffling, she said, "Okay," and leaned against the baby carrier. The pressure of her body caused it to rock, and the wailing infant stopped, apparently startled into silence.

"I'll be right back," I said solemnly, before turning on my heel and sprinting back into the chaos.

Mary was there, her hair standing out like a banner against the blood and smoke. Sometimes I thought she had someone with her, but whenever I tried to look closer, they were gone, fading back into the landscape. She was gathering ghosts, the newly-dead who were still too close to the twilight to be visible to the living. That was . . . that was not great. I mean, it was great in the sense that Lowryland might not wind up more haunted than it already was, and yet. It would have been nice if no one had died.

It would have been *wonderful.*

I plucked four more children off the sidewalks and ran them back to Ginger, who was taking enthusiastically to her new role as "person who was keeping an eye on everyone else." I would drop them off and run again as she started to explain the situation, that I was one of Princess Laura's helpers, and I was going to find all their mommies and daddies just as soon as I was finished finding everyone. She made it sound like a game. That was probably at least half shock speaking, keeping her from fully understanding what was going on.

A little shock would have been nice. A little shock would have been *great*, as I moved aside a sheet of fallen plastic to reveal the actress who played Laura. *Had* played Laura. She wasn't going to be playing any roles after this one, save perhaps—after the mortician finished working on her—the role of beautiful corpse. Lizzie's actress had gotten off easy with her broken arm. Laura's actress had a broken neck, and a wide swath of skin had been scraped off the side of her face, exposing muscle and bone.

"I'm so sorry," I whispered, and placed the plastic gently back across her body, so none of the remaining guests would accidentally see her and realize what had happened.

She wasn't the only casualty. She wasn't even the worst of them. I was trying to convince a weeping man to let go of his boyfriend's hand and move away from a structurally unsound piece of the float when the sirens suddenly got much closer, and I turned to see the full Lowryland security team rounding the corner. A knot in my chest let go, allowing me to breathe again. They were here. I wasn't alone anymore. I wasn't alone.

A glance at the flower clock next to the gift shop told me that it had been less than ten minutes since the float collapsed. It felt like it had been so much longer. I straightened, trying to shake off the feeling that time was broken, that something had somehow gone horribly wrong and caused everything to stretch out like taffy.

A child was crying. An adult was still screaming. The Lowryland security team was running for the float, while the handlers they'd brought with them were working to clear the remaining guests away.

A hand touched my elbow. I flinched and whipped around. There was Mary, now wearing the uniform of a Fairyland staffer. It made sense. She didn't do it often, for fear of attracting the wrong kind of attention from management, but with the chaos around us, no one was going to be pointing fingers at a single unfamiliar face.

"Come on," she said, getting a firmer grip on my arm and tugging me backward, toward her, away from the chaos. "You need to stop staring and come on."

I looked at her blankly, not resisting, but not helping her either. That shock I'd been wishing for felt like it was finally settling in. Yay. "What? Why?"

"Because people are snapping out of it, and they're taking pictures, and you've been behind smoke or behind ghosts until now, but the number of cameras is about to skyrocket, and I can't keep your ugly mug off the news forever." Mary looked at me grimly. "Run or get outed to the world."

I chose "run."

Mary slung an arm around my shoulders as I hunched slightly forward, trying to give the impression that I was feeling poorly and needed to get to a toilet before I tossed my cookies all over the bloody pavement. People behind us were shouting and clearing the sidewalks, and no one was paying attention to two seemingly uninjured workers.

We made it through the employee door and into a quiet stretch of the backlot before my knees went weak and I nearly toppled forward. Mary was there to grab me and keep me from going over—mostly. She was still sweet sixteen, and a skinny sixteen to boot. I was more than a foot taller, and easily fifty pounds heavier. She managed to slow my descent, but in the end, she couldn't keep my knees from hitting the concrete.

The crunching sound they made was familiar from a thousand roller derby practices, and oddly soothing. The world was turning itself merrily upside down. I could still feel pain, and still pay for the choices I made.

"Hey." Mary knelt in front of me, brushing my hair away from my eyes. Her own eyes were a thousand miles of empty highway, a color that wasn't really a color and was more a state of despair. They shouldn't have been soothing. I've been looking at them for almost my entire life, and they were something familiar I could cling to. "Stay with me now. Don't you go wherever it is you want to go."

"I want to go *home*," I whispered, and my voice had so much in common with little Ginger that it hurt to hear.

"You could."

"I can't."

"I know." Mary offered a small, half-pained smile. "But you're with me now. Breathe. Keep breathing. I'm going to go get you something to bring your blood sugar back up. You should be safe here. Do you feel like you'll be safe here?"

I nodded, closing my eyes. Despite the bone-deep weariness that was settling over me now that the adrenaline was leaving my body, I wasn't hurt; I wasn't even scratched, unless I wanted to count my aching knees. I was just *tired*. This was so like what I had trained for, and so unlike it at the same time, that I didn't have the coping mechanisms I needed.

"Okay. I'll be right back. Don't go anywhere."

There was the faintest of sounds, like air rushing back into the space where she'd been, and I was alone. I kept my eyes closed, inhaling through my nose and exhaling through my mouth, looking for that quiet core of serenity that Colin had been helping me to find.

The fire hadn't been there when I needed it. After so many accidents and one notable save—it's hard to top burning down the big tent while I was still in it for the needlessly dramatic, even if that alone hadn't been enough to save the carnival—the fire hadn't been there. I was learning to speak, and losing the ability to scream. That was unnerving on a level that I didn't really have the words for. If turning me into a better sorcerer meant I wasn't going to be able to defend myself, was it really worth it?

(Did I even *want* to be a sorcerer? I didn't have a choice about being a magic-user. It's in my genes, a gift from a distant grandfather who disappeared long before I was born, and I can't reject it any more than I can change the color of my eyes. But there's a big difference between having a talent and training it in a specific way. If I kept working with Colin, one day his way wouldn't just be the right way: it would be the *only* way, and I wouldn't understand why I'd ever thought differently. There was only so much of a window for stopping this, and it was getting narrower by the day.)

"Miss West." The voice was Emily's. The fact that it hadn't been accompanied by footsteps was somehow unsurprising. Routewitches aren't heard when they don't want to be. "Why am I not surprised to find you in the midst of another crisis?"

"I didn't do it," I said, not opening my eyes. I *hadn't* done it. The fact that I'd been nearby both times was just a terrible coincidence.

Wasn't it?

"I know. I do believe we may need to have a conversation, however, about why you run away whenever it seems your picture might be taken. You can open your eyes, by the way. It's just the two of us here." I could hear the smile in her voice. It had teeth. "Your little ghost isn't going to be able to come back until I decide to let her. It seemed like a good time to remind her that she's a guest in our home."

Crap. I opened my eyes and tilted my head, looking up at her. "You knew she was here?"

"I know whenever a ghost steps foot on Lowryland property. Most of them are tourists even among the guests. You'd be surprised by how many people have 'ride the Midsummer Night's Scream one last time' as their unfinished business. Well, that, and the Re-Entry. I'm not sure why it's the roller coasters that bring back the dead. Maybe it's something about wanting to feel afraid enough to be alive again." Emily shook her head, looking unperturbed by the lack of a clear explanation. "I know every time she visits. I just didn't know why she was showing up here. Now I do, and I can find her whenever I want."

"Right." My stomach sank. After more than fifty years, was I going to be the one who doomed Mary to a routewitch's spirit jar, all because I wound up choosing the wrong theme park? They probably didn't have these problems at Disney World.

"Get up." Emily offered her hand. I took it, letting her pull me to my feet. She looked at me critically. "You have blood in your hair and on your collar. That's going to be difficult to get out of the fabric."

"I'm good with blood."

Emily raised an eyebrow. "As you say. I'm going to be recommending all damages due to this incident be waived on the cast member level. We don't want to discourage people from playing Good Samaritan when things like this happen—which, God forbid, is sometimes unavoidable. We run a fairly tight ship here. Accidents are still going to slip through."

My fingers itched, not with fire, but with the urge to slap her. "Princess Laura's face came off on the pavement," I said quietly. "This wasn't an accident. This was a tragedy."

Ginger was probably still waiting for me to come back. No. No. I couldn't think like that. Ginger's mother was fine. She wasn't one of the people crushed under the bulk of the float. She was *fine*. She was probably with her daughter right now, helping to get the other children back to their families. Ginger would be the darling of the people looking for a positive human interest story to pluck out of this disaster, the little girl in the Princess Laura dress who'd stepped up and somehow organized her own little nursery school.

I was happy to let her have the limelight. She might get something good out of it. All I would get was pain.

"Of course, it's a tragedy," said Emily. "What do you take me for? I'm not a monster, Melody. But this Park is my world, and it's your world , at least for now. Whether you intend to stay with us forever or not, you need to consider Lowryland in everything you do."

"Her face," I repeated.

"Yes. Security is coordinating the EMTs now, and we have firetrucks and engineering en route, ready to remove the float and find out what caused the failure. This is a public relations nightmare. We'll be dealing with the repercussions for a year or more. Disney will laugh all the way to the bank. And you helped. You ran into the danger when there was no reason to. You're a very lucky girl." Emily reached out and took my chin between her thumb and forefinger, looking at me critically. "*Very* lucky."

I took a step back when she let me go. It was automatic, unavoidable. She didn't look surprised.

"Go home, Melody," she said. "We're closing early today."

Then she turned and walked away, leaving me utterly, achingly alone.

Twelve

"There are a lot of ways to be haunted.
Some of them are even good ones, if you're
up for it."

–Mary Dunlavy

Lowryland, backstage, walking slow

MARY DIDN'T COME BACK.
I stayed where I was for a good ten minutes,
counting the seconds, listening as the sounds outside the
wall moved from quick urgency to slow, methodical dili-
gence. They weren't trying to triage the wounded or rescue the trapped anymore: they were trying to evacuate
the remaining guests before they began unearthing the
dead. The actress who played Laura in the parades would
probably be one of the first bodies removed, since she
was only covered by a thin sheet of plastic. I couldn't
even figure out what part of the float it had been, before
everything went to pieces.

And Mary didn't come back.

When I couldn't put it off any longer—not without
risking a return appearance of Emily, or worse, the rest
of the employees from my shift, who had all seen me
running for the float—I turned and trudged toward the
door that would take me into the tunnels. Once I was
there, I could walk back to the locker room, change out
of my uniform, and get my things. I needed to be out of
here. I needed to go *home*.

The tunnels were dim and smelled like boiled laundry.
That was a constant. On hot days, they were actually

cooler than the rest of Lowryland, thanks to that easy darkness. Someone could have told me there was an entire colony of bogeymen living peacefully under the Park, and I would have believed them. Given how I was feeling, I would probably have asked for directions. Tea with a quiet, accepting bogey community was about all I was feeling up for.

People hurried past me, none of them stopping to ask how I was or why there was blood in my hair. I couldn't blame them. They all looked about as shaken as I felt, and doubtless with far better reason—at least I'd been trained for this sort of thing. They were ordinary people, going about their ordinary business, and now here we were. Everything was falling apart.

I didn't realize I had turned away from my own locker room until I was standing in the doorway of a nearly-identical room, looking blankly at a group of women who were encircling one of their own. The one in the middle was sobbing like her heart was broken. Maybe it was. I took a step back.

My heel hit hard against the concrete floor. Several of the women looked around. One was still wearing Princess Lizzie's dress, although she had removed the wig, revealing a clean blonde crewcut. Another, in street clothes, raised a hand and pointed at me.

"You," she said. "You were corralling the kids after the parade crash. I *saw* you."

The other women started looking around, murmuring. I spotted Fern at the back of the group, and some of the tension left my spine. She was all right. She was *here*. I wasn't alone anymore.

The Princess Lizzie was looking at me expectantly, clinging to the hand of the woman who had pointed me out. I forced myself to nod, and said, "Yeah, that was me. I was working in the gift shop when . . . when whatever happened, happened. Please don't ask what went wrong with the float. I don't know. I just knew I had to do something."

"Andrea and Marissa," said the princess. "Are they all right?"

I looked at her blankly. She looked back, impatient, until she realized that I wasn't being dense: I didn't know who she meant.

"They play Laura and Lizzie on the float," she said. "Marissa borrowed my wig." There was a wealth of concern in that sentence, making it clear that she wasn't just asking after her misplaced possession: she was asking after her friends, the way I would have asked after Fern or Megan if I thought they'd been in the path of danger. The fact that she didn't have the words to frame her question didn't change the size of it, or its terrible weight.

"Oh," I breathed. The room held its breath. "I . . . Marissa plays Lizzie?"

She nodded.

"I'm pretty sure she has a broken arm, so they're probably taking her to the hospital. She didn't look like she had any other injuries. She was thrown clear when it went down." *Please don't ask about Andrea. Please. Please don't ask—*

"What about Andrea?" asked another princess.

Dammit. "I'm sorry," I said.

The whole group stared at me for a frozen second before they began to wail and keen. It was an unearthly sound, too alien to have come from human throats. I took a step backward, suddenly afraid that they were going to blame me for the whole incident.

"Come on."

Fern was at my elbow in eerie parody of Mary's earlier appearance. She had managed to change out of her velvet gown while the other princesses were interrogating me, and had it stuffed into a garment bag over her arm. The makeup still smeared on her face was generic enough that no one who saw us would peg her immediately for a fleeing Princess Aspen.

Her eyes were wide. She looked worried. I shared the sentiment.

Not trusting my voice and not wanting to attract more attention from the grieving gaggle of actresses, I nodded and took another step back before I turned and fled, alongside Fern, into the relative safety of the tunnel system. Anyone we encountered here would be as focused on getting out of Lowryland as we were.

Fern knew me well enough to see how upset I was, and didn't say anything as we walked toward the locker room where my own clothes waited. I flexed my fingers reflexively, chasing away a heat that wasn't there. It's not that I *enjoyed* setting things unpredictably on fire. I didn't. It was just that it was familiar, something I had grown accustomed to dealing with, and I missed it now that it was gone, the way I sometimes missed a really bad bruise after it had finally finished healing. Yes, a bruise is a bad thing to have. There's still something soothing about poking it.

When the door to my locker room came into view ahead of us, I stopped, turning to Fern. "This is the second time something awful has happened while I was right there."

"Yeah," said Fern softly.

"We need to talk."

She winced, and I knew I was on the right track. "Yeah," she said again. "Okay."

I nodded, satisfied with that answer, and the two of us walked the rest of the way to the locker room, where all the other employees from my shift appeared to have already come and gone. The air smelled of sweat and hairspray, and while no one would be foolish enough to damage Lowry property—not if they wanted to keep their jobs—there was a distinct aura of "we grabbed and we ran" about the place, some indefinable quality to the slammed lockers and off-kilter benches that spoke of swift abandonment.

Fern followed me to my locker, where I stripped out of my smoke-scented, bloodstained uniform. Each piece was like a weight being lifted off my shoulders, taking a slice of the accident away with it. The smell still lingered in my hair. A quick shampoo would deal with that, and I would smell like strawberries and artificial cotton candy instead of a disaster. I couldn't wait.

It wasn't until I tugged my shirt on and reached for my jeans that Fern spoke. "Please don't be mad at me," she said.

I gave her a sidelong look. "Did you do something I should be mad about?"

"Yes," she said. "No. I don't know. But even if I did, please don't be mad. You're my best friend. I don't want you to be mad at me."

I paused. There were tears in her eyes, heavy and threatening to fall. She looked small and scared and very young—almost as young as she had on the day I'd joined the Slasher Chicks, when she'd looked at me and seen one more human to stand between her and the rest of the world. I hadn't seen her smile until the day when I'd asked, in my usual sledgehammer way, whether she knew what a sylph was. She'd been sticking to me like glue ever since, going where I went, doing what I did. Being my friend.

"Are you the reason I'm in Florida?" I asked, keeping my tone light.

She shook her head. "No," she said. "But you're probably the reason I'm here."

I looked quickly around. Lowry always *said* they didn't have cameras or listening devices in the locker rooms, and enough of us were trained to tattle that it made sense the way people who shoplifted or actually violated Lowry policy always seemed to get caught the second they stepped backstage. But that didn't prove the cameras weren't there. They could easily be hidden behind the mirrors, or built into the walls. We weren't safe.

"Later," I said.

Fern nodded. "I already called for a ride."

"A ride?" I frowned. "Megan's still on shift, isn't she?"

"I didn't call Megan." Fern looked at me earnestly. "Will you come? I can explain everything, if you'll come."

We lived together. We worked together. Even so, it was surprising how often we were apart. Our shifts didn't always coincide. Now that I was training with Colin, I was often out in the mornings, and even before that, there had been a lot of days when I'd get home and Fern would be off doing something else, something outside the house that didn't involve me. I'd never asked, because I hadn't wanted to pry.

Maybe I should have pried.

"I'll come," I said, and finished getting dressed in silence, running a brush through my hair to chase the worst of the smoky smell away before I stuffed my costume into my backpack for washing and turned to face Fern.

"I'm ready," I said.

She nodded, and stood, and led me out of Lowryland.

The tunnels ran all the way back to the employee lot, and beneath it, keeping workers safe during tropical storms and hurricanes—as long as they didn't flood, anyway. If the tunnels ever lost structural integrity, we could find ourselves with a whole new set of problems. Fern led the way, her hair pale enough to almost serve as a flag through the dim-lit underground space, and I followed, too weary and beat down to question what I was doing. She would lead me to safety, or she would lead me to my doom. Either way, I wouldn't stop seeing the dead Princess Laura sprawled in the middle of the Lowryland street.

Being a theme park princess doesn't come with special powers. It doesn't even come with special privileges, if Fern was anything to go by. They're people in pretty dresses, trying to be a huggable face for a beloved childhood character, and no one cares that those dresses weren't designed to be worn in the Florida heat, or that there are really ten people wearing that same costume over the course of the day, in parades, meet-and-greets, waiting backstage for the current title holder to go on break. The tiara isn't magic. It still felt wrong for one of the princesses to die on duty, like a compact had been broken.

Fern walked past the doors we usually used to exit for the tram stops or the train, until we were heading down a narrow stretch of tunnel that I'd never seen before. The ceiling was dismayingly low, and the walls smelled of rust. I paused, frowning, and looked back. Yup. The light was definitely dimmer here.

"Fern . . ."

"It's okay. These are still official tunnels. They just don't get used much since the tram went in. People used to have to walk all the way to the train whenever they wanted to go home. Can you imagine?"

It *felt* like we were walking all the way to the train. "Yes," I said flatly. Then I paused. "Wait. Didn't they move the train station when they put the trams in?"

"They did," said Fern, and pushed open a narrow, unmarked door, revealing a slice of Florida sky. It was still light, but it wouldn't be for much longer; the sun was riding low, casting everything in that shade of gold that hundreds of horror movies set in middle America have conditioned me to think of as the color of apocalypse.

There was a car idling next to the sidewalk, the sort of hefty American muscle car that looked like it could drive through a wall and not really notice. It was painted avocado green, which had to be intended as ironic, since I refused to believe there had ever been a time when someone would find that attractive. Fern trotted toward it, leaving me with no choice but to follow if I wanted all of this to start making sense.

The window rolled down as we approached, and a familiar face appeared in the opening. She looked a lot like Fern, but with the color balance adjusted until she seemed less like she had spent the last twenty years hiding in a basement from the terror of the sun. Her skin was slightly less pale, accented both by a spray of freckles across the nose and the sort of artful smoky eye that has no business existing outside of a music video. Her hair was dark blonde, and her smile was achingly sad, like she'd been waiting for this moment for a while.

"Hi," said Cylia. "You might as well get in."

I stared.

Here is a thing I have learned, after spending my life surrounded by ghosts and talking mice and the ever-present threat that some people my great-great-grandparents pissed off will show up and go all Montagues and Capulets on my ass: there is no such thing as a coincidence. Things that look coincidental are almost always tricks or traps, or some combination of the two. When Cylia told me to get in, I took a big step backward, wishing I had a weapon, wishing I hadn't allowed Colin to extinguish the fire in my fingers, wishing I had *anything* that could help me out of this.

"You're here," I said.

"Yes," said Cylia.

"You're in Florida."

"Yes," said Cylia again, and looked at me with a mixture of fondness and frustration. "Do you really want to do this on the sidewalk?"

I did not. Then again, I didn't really want to do it anywhere. I wanted to return this entire day to the factory and get a replacement, one with less fire and screaming and unexpected death. "No," I admitted sullenly.

"Then get in the car, and we'll do this at the warehouse." Cylia Mackie, captain of the Wilsonville Rose Petals, shook her head. "I haven't killed you up until now. Why would I start?"

"There are so many reasons I can't even list them all," I muttered darkly, and got into the back. A car this old wouldn't have child locks, and if I was going to bail while the car was in motion, I preferred to do it out the back, where I'd have more opportunity to roll away before she could swerve to hit me.

Cylia sighed as Fern got into the front passenger seat. "Were you this suspicious of Fern?"

". . . no," I admitted, after a lengthy pause.

"Maybe you should've been. She's from Portland, too, after all. Wasn't it a big *coincidence* that she wound up here right about the same time you did?" Cylia hit the gas. The big muscle car rumbled to life, waking like the beast it was, and rolled down the street. "The air-conditioning doesn't work, but you won't be able to hear a damn thing we say if you roll down the windows. It's your call."

"Right." This was getting confusing. I didn't like it. "Nice, uh. Nice car."

"Isn't it? Bought it on Craigslist the day I hit town. Well, bought most of it. Poor thing didn't run. It was missing an ultra-rare engine piece that hasn't been manufactured since the dawn of the dinosaurs, and it was basically just sucking down garage space for this kid who'd inherited it from his grandfather. And wouldn't you know it, some collector who didn't know what he had put that same engine piece on eBay the very next day." Cylia laughed, less amused than keeping up appearances. "Funny how the world works sometimes."

"Yeah," I said. "Funny."

Cylia Mackie. Roller derby captain. Personal assistant, of the sort who does all their work over the phone and via email, which meant that her job, at least, could come with her to Florida. And jink. Which meant she could be ally, threat, or both at the same time.

The jink is a hominid cryptid of unknown evolutionary origin. We know they're closely related to the mara, and that's about where our cheat sheets run out. We know that my honorary uncle Al, in Vegas, is a jink, which is why my family's scant available information is viewed as being incredibly detailed and complete by people who don't have access to an actual jink. Like many of the more human-appearing cryptids, they've survived through secrecy, isolation, and luck. In the case of the jinks, that luck has been more active than it's been for most. Because jinks?

Jinks manipulate luck.

No one's sure how they do it, and that includes the jinks themselves, who usually describe the process by shrugging, waving their hands, and asking pointed questions like "How do you breathe?" and "What is the process by which your body turns food into energy?" In short, it's inborn and indescribable, and after my training with Colin, I had a lot more sympathy for that sort of thing. I couldn't explain the exact mechanism by which I'd been setting things on fire, and now that I wasn't doing it anymore, I couldn't explain the exact thing that had caused me to stop.

The trouble is, when I set something on fire, I wasn't removing fire from somewhere else in the world. Fire was an infinitely expanding resource. The same can't be said for luck. When a jink tweaks their own luck to be better, there's always bad luck down the line. If that same jink tries to stave off the consequences of their own actions by stealing good luck from someone else, that person will get to enjoy all the karmic balancing of something they never did in the first place.

Cylia met my eyes in the rearview mirror and said, with perfect calm, "I didn't."

"Didn't what?"

Her laugh was low, throaty, and bitter. "Don't, okay? I've been a jink my whole life, and I've been around humans my whole life, and I've seen the way people look at me when they think I'm getting something I don't deserve. If your luck's too good, everyone thinks you stole it. If your luck's too bad, everyone thinks you earned it. So don't. I didn't steal your luck. I'm not the reason you're here. But you're the reason I'm here, so if you could stop looking at me like that, I'd really appreciate it."

I blinked, sinking back in my seat. "I wasn't," I said, and my voice sounded weak and unsure to my own ears, and I had no idea where we were going, but I knew it was going to be a long drive.

It was clear Cylia knew Lakeland from the way she drove: not with the brash aggression of a tourist or the timidity of a newcomer, but with the calm, assertive speed of someone who'd memorized the location of the speed traps and dangerous intersections. Her great beast of a car cornered like a dream, which was impressive in and of itself, given how big the thing was. The fact that it was ugly couldn't possibly have impacted its speed, but it felt like it should have, like anything this hideous should have crept along, not raced.

In short order, the lights of Lowryland were so far behind us that they were barely a smudge on the horizon, and Cylia was pulling into an unfamiliar parking lot, in front of a building that was equally unfamiliar but still felt like coming home. It was a big warehouse, the sort that made sense when America did all its own manufacturing— the sort that have been sitting empty or finding new uses over the last thirty years. Some of them turn into storage, or office space, or live-work lofts. Some of them wind up in the hands of dragons looking for a place to start a Nest, or filled with communities of mixed cryptids who'd rather shut the doors with humanity on the outside for a change.

And some of them, the ones that are too oddly shaped or awkwardly located to be good for anything else, wind up getting turned into roller derby venues. A banner stretched across the front of the structure informed anyone who drove by that this was the home of the Lakeland Ladies. A smaller banner underneath gave their website and suggested roller derby would make a fun night out for the family looking for something to do after they'd exhausted the joys of licensed theme parks.

The thought of some of the families I saw wandering through Lowryland stopping in for a night of roller derby was almost enough to bring a smile to my face.

"There's no practice tonight, but I have a key," said Cylia, parking right in front of the warehouse. "Either of you got your skates?"

"No," I said, as "Yes," said Fern. I turned to look at her. She shrugged, sheepish. "I always have my skates, and I usually have yours too, just in case," she said. "I hoped you'd want to skate tonight."

"Thanks," I said. The word wasn't enough. The thought of a real track under my wheels was intensely appealing, enough to make my eyes burn with the beginning of tears. I was so tired. Having something normal would be . . . it would be the world.

But it wouldn't change the fact that Cylia was here, and shouldn't have been. I gave her a sidelong look. "How come you have a key?"

"This area is technically zoned as residential. There are two crappy little apartments above the warehouse, and as long as they're being rented, the space we use for our track is a really big 'community room,' and we don't get torn down by the people who think we're making a mockery of the tourist trade. Right now, I'm renting one of the apartments." Cylia's smile was quick and wry. "I've gone from team captain to alternate junior jammer, but hey, at least I have a place to sleep. Sometimes life works out like that."

"Especially for people who can influence probability," I said, and promptly regretted it.

Cylia shrugged. "We work with what we have," she said, and unlocked the door, slipping through it into the dark warehouse on the other side.

Even the *smell* of Lakeland Ladies warehouse was familiar, sweat and wood oil and WD-40 and bleach and dried beer. I paused at the threshold to take a deep breath, allowing my spine to straighten. Aromatherapy works. It's just that not everyone finds lavender and roses to be the most soothing things the universe has to offer. Some of us have a different definition of "smells like home."

There was a clunking sound, and the high overhead lights began flickering on in stages, staggered to reduce their draw on the local power grid. I stayed where I was, watching the familiar, unfamiliar landscape reveal itself one piece at a time.

There was the track, polished wood flat against the ground, more than half-cupped by the bleachers, which were all on rollers in case they needed to be moved in a hurry. The rest of the trackside space was reserved for standing-room tickets, which cost less, and kept the space fluid. There were the closed-up food stalls, probably connected to a makeshift kitchen, where snacks and beer would be peddled during the games themselves—and yes, there was the almost obligate disco ball, dangling from the ceiling like an invitation to better times ahead.

Cylia walked back to where Fern and I waited, and offered me a slightly off-kilter smile, asking, "Are you done being suspicious? Can I get a hug?"

"No, and yes," I said, and hugged her. "I have no idea why you're here, but it's good to see you."

"She's here because of me," said Fern.

I let Cylia go and turned, blinking. "Excuse me?"

Fern looked uncomfortable but held her ground, looking at me levelly as she said, "After you went away, I asked Elsie if she'd tell me if anything happened to you. I was so scared, and no one would really say where you'd gone, and I wanted to help. If there was any possible way, I wanted to help. You're my best friend."

"Okay . . ."

"Um." Fern paused. "Don't be mad at her, okay?"

"People keep asking me not to be mad." I pinched the bridge of my nose. "It's starting to piss me off."

"Elsie called me when you didn't come home and she said you'd run away because the Covenant of St. George was trying to find you and it wasn't safe and she was sorry but she didn't know where you were and maybe you needed a miracle," said Fern, rapid-fire.

I lowered my hand and stared at her. "What?"

"I knew I had to find you. I knew you'd try to do everything alone if I didn't, and I knew you'd get hurt. Probably really, really hurt. You're just human, Annie. You can't save the world without help." Fern looked at me earnestly. "Don't be mad."

"I . . . but you . . . how did you *find* me?"

"That would be me." Cylia raised her left hand. The overhead lights glittered off her wedding ring. "She told me what she needed. She needed you to be safe. She needed to be able to be where you were, and to be in a position to help. As for me, I needed a change and I had an excess of bad built up, so I cashed in my chips and moved across the country to help a friend. I've done more for less."

"An excess of—" I caught myself mid-sentence, but not fast enough to see Cylia's smile go tight around the edges. Damn. "I'm so sorry for your loss."

"Me, too," she said. Her hand dropped back down to her side. "It was a heart attack. Tav was older than me — not quite cradle robbing, but close enough to make some people uncomfortable. That's how it has to be when your species is on the way out the door, you know? You meet somebody you think you could be happy with, and you grab on with both hands, because there's every chance in the world that you're not going to get a second shot at being happy like that. He loved me. God, he loved me. He never let me be the one to spend the luck to keep us safe. He never told me how much he was spending, either. I guess it turned out to be too much, because he was walking out the door, heading for work, and then he was gone—dead before he hit the ground. The sort of big, catastrophic failure that ends everything. But he left me his life insurance, and no debts, and the memory of being loved by someone who cared so much that he was willing to use his heart as collateral against the future. How do you get mad at somebody like that? You don't."

All of this must have happened after I'd left for the Covenant. I remembered Cylia's husband as a smiling figure in the stands on the nights when the Slasher Chicks had skated against the Rose Petals. He'd always worn his wife's team colors, proud in pink and glorious in green, and he'd cheered louder than anyone when the Rose Petals had pulled off a particularly clever bit of skating. I'd never actually met the man, but he'd seemed like a nice guy, and Cylia had clearly loved him.

Fern looked between us, timid as I'd ever seen her, and said, "After Elsie told me you were in trouble, I asked Cylia if she could find you. If she could take me where you were. She said . . ."

"I said the luck doesn't work that way, because it doesn't, but that I could get us to where we'd be able to do you the most good, even if it used up most of what the world owed me for taking Tav away." Cylia shrugged again, less expansively this time, like she was talking about something easier and more everyday than the death of a spouse. "I grabbed. I twisted. And for the next three days, every channel I got was showing a Lowry film, even the ones like CNN, and when I threw my map of the USA across the room, it fell open to Lakeland. So I figured we needed to be here. We got here, this place was open, Lowryland needed a Princess Aspen . . . the luck knew where it wanted us."

"How did the Covenant *ever* find you?" I blurted. I felt bad about it immediately, but I didn't try to take the question back.

Cylia shook her head. "People think we're thieves. People are always happy to tell the authorities about thieves, even when they don't trust the authorities either. I don't steal good luck from people. I can lure free range luck toward myself, but there are consequences. Look at what happened to Tav."

"Yeah," I said uncomfortably.

"So someone told the Covenant 'hey, those people over there, I think they're witches,' and one of us got cut open, and someone figured out we weren't absolutely, perfectly human, and suddenly we were on the public enemy number one list, along with all the other species whose camouflage was too good." Cylia looked at me with cold, flat eyes. I suddenly wondered how much of my situation she knew about—and how much of it she was planning to hold against me. "If you look human and you're not human, you're worse than a manticore. At least a manticore isn't going to seduce a good Covenant soldier away from the path of righteousness."

"My family's human, and we do that all the time," I said weakly.

"The jury's still out on that," said Cylia.

Right. We were getting too far afield from the original topic, and I was getting more and more uncomfortable: it was time to get back to basics. "Fern, you said we needed to talk when I asked you why bad things kept happening near me," I said. "Why?"

Fern looked at Cylia. Cylia looked back, raising one eyebrow, and shook her head. Fern sighed and turned back to me.

Having watched this little interplay with increasing dubiousness, I asked warily, "What?"

"It's aftershocks," said Fern.

"Of what?"

"Of me spending a whole lot of luck so we'd all wind up in the best possible position," said Cylia.

I stared at her, slow fury building in my gut. "You mean this is . . . you *caused* this?"

"No," said Cylia immediately. "This was going to happen, no matter what, just like you were already heading for Florida by the time Fern told me we needed to get you. The accidents have nothing to do with me. But when I bent your luck to put you into proximity of *good* things—us—that had to be balanced, and the universe is balancing it by putting you into proximity of *bad* things. It's only because I started with so much good luck that you're winding up close enough to help without getting seriously injured. The aftershocks won't last forever. They're the cascade effect that always follows a major adjustment. And this isn't your fault, and it isn't mine."

Colin could be an aftershock. Having a teacher drop into my lap when I was in a position to learn and leave, rather than being tied to him for the rest of my life, was almost the definition of luck. Still . . . "Is this going to cost me anything?"

"No." Cylia looked at me. "I already paid."

The blankness in her voice made me want to apologize for the world, for things I'd never done and would never dream of doing. I swallowed the impulse, and asked instead, "Do you both skate here?"

"I don't have *time* to be on a team, and I don't want to skate if you're not skating with me," said Fern. "We're the best. Slasher Chicks forever."

"I don't have that sort of misplaced loyalty, and a girl needs something to do with her free time," said Cylia. "I've been working on Fern."

"I am an uncrackable fortress," said Fern serenely.

I looked at the track. It looked just like every other regulation flat track in the world, smooth and polished and beckoning, and I was so tired. So damn tired. My life kept flipping upside down, and no matter how hard I tried, I couldn't seem to make it stop.

"Let's skate," I said.

Fern smiled.

The track was smooth as silk beneath my wheels, with none of the cracks or irregularities that could turn skating at Lowryland into the bad kind of adventure. Falling would still hurt, but it would be the good, clean hurt of an impact well earned, and not the slightly offensive hurt of a fall I shouldn't have taken.

(It's funny, but pain seems worse when it's unreasonable. When I broke three ribs falling from the top of a pyramid during cheer practice, I was totally cool with that, but when I broke an arm falling into one of my own pit traps, I was a lot less sanguine.)

Fern, as always, skated like it was an excuse to play keep-away with the laws of physics. There was no one here to put on a show for, and so she was varying her density as she whipped around the track, bleeding it off when she was on the straight stretches, pulling it on when she was zipping around a corner and needed to keep herself from overbalancing. If I hadn't known what she was doing, I probably wouldn't have jumped directly to "density manipulation," but it was easy to tell that she was doing *something*, which was why she skated straight when we were in the middle of an actual bout.

Cylia was a better skater in many ways. She knew the track. She knew her body and its capabilities. She was taller than Fern, but when the sylph wasn't tinkering with her mass to gain momentum, Cylia was actually faster, because Cylia knew how to position her body to reduce wind drag. She'd never been in a position to cheat the way Fern could. Her potential cheating was of a more subtle sort—and she *never* did it on the track. Luck changing without warning was the way derby girls got hurt.

I fell somewhere between them, skill-wise. I had to work harder than Fern, which meant I had a better idea of the actual techniques a good skater used. I couldn't make myself lighter to avoid a fall, or heavier to keep someone from knocking me over. But Cylia had been skating for a lot longer than I had, and once you get past the base levels of a person's natural athleticism, practice is what makes perfect. Back home in Portland, we were both jammers, and she was one of the ones I had to look out for when we were skating against each other.

There was no competition on the track tonight. Just three people circling, doing all the stupid and impulsive shit that could get somebody seriously injured during an actual game. I couldn't remember the last time I'd felt this removed from my troubles, or this close to the girl

I'd been for most of my life. I missed her. Almost as much as I missed my mice, and my family, and Sam.

There had been a night—after Verity had returned from her first season on *Dance or Die*, before she'd left for New York—when I'd come downstairs to make myself a midnight sandwich and found her sitting with Alex at the kitchen table, both holding mugs of cocoa, talking quietly. My older siblings had always been closer to each other than they were to me, capable of opening up when they were alone in a way that enthralled and frightened me. I liked being the baby, but there had been times when I wished my parents would decide to have another baby, so I could be somebody's Alex, so I could have the kind of friend my siblings seemed to effortlessly be for one another.

"I felt like I was forgetting myself," Verity had said, eyes on the marshmallows melting in her cocoa, shoulders hunched. She's been shorter than me since I was twelve, but in that moment, she hadn't looked short. She'd looked *small*, beaten down and human, and for the first time, I'd realized that my sister was as mortal as I was.

Alex hadn't said anything. His eyes had darted toward the stairs, and I'd held my breath, willing him not to notice me. Either he hadn't, or he'd decided this was something I should hear, because he still hadn't said anything. He'd just looked back to Verity.

"Being Valerie was *easy*," she'd said, spitting the word out like it was bitter. "All I had to do was dance. Valerie didn't care about anything else, and for me to be her, I had to stop caring, too. It was easy, and it was tempting, and if I'd won . . ."

"You didn't."

"But *if I'd won*, I would have kept on being her, because it was easy, and it was fun, and I wasn't scared. Nothing was trying to eat me. I got to just . . . exist."

Alex had reached across the table then, putting a hand on her wrist and smiling. "Hey," he'd said. "You're always a winner to me, and I like Verity better than Valerie."

She had raised her head and smiled back, and I had crept back up the stairs to my room without my midnight snack, but with a head full of things that wouldn't let me go to sleep for hours.

Here, now, skating circles with two people I actually trusted, who actually knew me, I finally understood what Verity had been talking about. I was always Antimony Price, and I always would be. I was also Timpani Brown, Covenant recruit, who had wanted nothing more than to kill the monsters that had killed her family, until she'd found a new carnival, and fallen halfway in love while she was trying not to fall off the trapeze. And I was Melody West, former cheerleader on the run, current employee of Lowryland, sorcerer in training.

Timpani and Melody didn't have to keep track of who they were. They *knew* who they were, because they were only one person each. I was all three, under the pressure of remembering who I really was, of holding fast to the core of identity that belonged to me and me alone. It would have been easier if I'd had my mice. Mice never let anybody forget who they really are.

We skated, and the world was simple.

The trouble was going to come when we had to stop.

Thirteen

"Your family, your real family, will always
welcome you home with open arms. Anyone who says you can lose their love isn't
really family, no matter what blood says."

–Evelyn Baker

A shitty company apartment five miles outside of Lakeland, Florida

FERN AND I CREPT through the apartment door and into
the darkened living room sometime after midnight,
shoes in our hands, trying to be quiet enough not to
wake Megan. We were almost to the hall when a voice
spoke from the couch.

"Nice to know that you're not dead."

We froze, me grimacing, Fern pressing closer to me,
like she thought I was going to protect her. Which, let's be
honest, I would have happily done if this had been some
dangerous monster or supernatural threat. Sadly, it wasn't.
It was our roommate, and she did *not* sound happy.

"Hi, Megan," I said weakly, turning toward the voice.
I couldn't see her, not even an outline, but I had no doubt
that she could see me. Gorgons have excellent night vision. "How was your shift?"

"Eight fatalities—*fatalities*—from an accident inside
the Park, in the area I know you were working today."
The light next to the couch clicked on, revealing Megan.
She was glaring behind the smoked lenses of her glasses,
and if it had been possible for sheer anger to make her
gaze more powerful, I would have been petrified before

I had a chance to blink. "You want to tell me where the hell you've been?"

Looking at her, even as a friend and ally, it was easy to understand why the Covenant had taken one look at the gorgons and gone "we need to kill those in a hurry." The snakes surrounding her face had picked up her anger and transformed it into something out of a horror movie, rising until they formed a sort of hood of scales and fangs and potential pain. They were all pulled into striking positions, flattening their heads slightly to make themselves look bigger. I knew Megan didn't have conscious control of what they did, and that was a good thing, because if she *had* been able to tell them what to do, I would have had to assume she'd ordered them to scare the pants off me.

"Skating," said Fern, in a meek voice. She stayed pressed close at my side. She was scared, too.

We keep frightening each other. Whether we mean to or not, we just keep frightening each other. "Neither of us was hurt when the float collapsed, but I was right there," I said. "I was technically one of the first responders because I beat the security team and the EMTs to the wounded." Andrea who had played Laura, her face gone. Ginger, parents missing and eyes bright with tears. "I . . . it messed me up pretty bad."

"So I took her skating," said Fern, picking up the essential shape of the narrative. She stepped forward, putting herself between me and Megan. Scared as she was, she knew I didn't share her immunity to a gorgon's gaze. "I'm sorry I didn't text. I knew you were working."

Megan held her glare for a moment before thawing and saying, "It's okay. I had my hands full all night. I didn't even start really worrying about you until I got home and you weren't here. Neither of you was hurt?"

"We're fine," I said. "Eight people died?"

"And about fifty were injured. What *happened*?"

I opened my mouth to reply. Then I hesitated.

Cylia hadn't done this. She said she was innocent, and I believed her. Jinks don't create luck, just move it around, and if she hadn't been spending her luck since reaching Florida, the accident couldn't be her fault. My proximity to it was on her—and it was exactly what I would have asked for, if she'd told me this was coming. Because I'd been close, I'd been able to help. Because I'd been able to help, maybe things had been less terrible.

"I don't know," I said finally. "I was in the shop when something went bang, and by the time I made it outside, the float was on the ground and people were running everywhere. I don't think it was something somebody did on purpose."

"Why not?"

"Because . . ." I hesitated again, this time to review my memory of the crowd. There had been a few people standing frozen in their shock and terror, but that was normal. Drop an alien monster into a tour group and it'll have plenty to eat, because not everyone will be able to recover in time to run away. "Because there wasn't anyone who seemed overly happy about what was happening. It could have been sabotage, I guess, if someone was looking to hurt the company, or reduce competition for another theme park, but that seems extreme. I think we'd have seen signs before this."

"So what? Mechanical failure?" Megan frowned. "I thought they'd have safeguards against that sort of thing."

"All the safeguards in the world won't stop something that really wants to break." I rubbed my forehead with one hand. The skating had cleared away the fog, making it easier for me to think. That didn't make any of this comfortable. "It doesn't feel like intentional sabotage. It was too big, without having any convenient gloating."

"That's terrifying." Megan wrapped her arms around herself. "I'd almost rather this be something somebody had done."

"It's easier to fight a person than an accident," I said. It was hard to stop replaying the scene over and over in my mind. Now that Megan had caused me to knock the mental scab off, it was like all the infection that had built up behind it was leaking out, coating the world in a thin veneer of screams, blood, and burning.

There was still no fire in my fingers. I never would have

thought I'd miss it this much. It had been with me for so long that it felt like a normal response to trauma or stress, and now that it was gone I felt almost numb, like something essential had been taken away. I could feel it burning deep down, when I forced my attention inward and *looked*, but it refused to come, no matter how hard I called. Part of that might have been the proximity of my roommates. Fern knew about my semi-controlled magic. Megan didn't. Neither of them had actually *seen* me play pyromaniac with a touch. It was only reasonable that I'd be holding back in their presence.

(And I could tell myself that as much as I wanted. The fire still wouldn't come when I was alone, no matter how hard I begged, because it hadn't come last night, and it hadn't come when it could have helped me. I wasn't an infant anymore, where magic was concerned. My body was forgetting how to scream.)

"Do you have a shift in the morning?" Fern asked.

Megan nodded. "I start at nine, and I'm on the clock until nine tomorrow night, at the absolute earliest. You should probably figure on not seeing me for a few days. That's part of why I decided to sit up tonight. I wanted to know that you were okay."

"I don't have an email from scheduling yet," said Fern.

I glanced at her, startled. I hadn't even thought to check. Then again, I was the one with the cheap phone that was *only* a phone and couldn't receive anything more complex than a text message. I was used to getting my shift information at the start of the week, and not having any updates until the end. The float disaster changed things. The whole Park, or at least the Fairyland section, could very well be closed.

"I'm going to go check my email," I said, and took a step toward the hall.

The doorbell rang.

All three of us froze—more than three, if I counted the sudden stillness of the snakes on Megan's head. With the living room light on, it was impossible to pretend nobody was home. Indeed, the thought had barely managed to form when the doorbell rang again. This time, the person outside leaned into the act, sending the tone belling loud and clear through the apartment. They were going to wake our neighbors if they didn't stop.

Megan bolted to her feet and ran for her bedroom, where she kept the wigs. Fern didn't move.

Right. I didn't have a weapon and I didn't have fire in my fingers and I didn't have a clue, but I didn't want our neighbors reporting us to corporate, either. Taking a deep breath, I straightened my spine until it creaked. That helped. I always feel better about walking toward my certain death when I do it with good posture. I shot a reassuring glance at Fern and started for the door, intending to answer it before our unexpected guest could ring the bell a third time.

I opened the door. Sam's hand was raised, finger poised to press the bell again. He froze. I froze. We stood together yet apart, two statues staring at each other across a gulf of less than two feet.

I knew what he was seeing: sweat-caked hair plastered to my neck and shoulders, tattered secondhand tank top and yoga pants, skin that bore a sheen of sunscreen and the omnipresent glitter that coats everything in Lowryland. The urge to slam the door, run to the shower, and come back when I was presentable was almost overwhelming, and yet he looked at me like I was candy, cake, and Christmas all rolled into one. A girl could get used to being looked at that way.

As for me, I was looking at a tall, brown-skinned man of mixed Chinese and European descent, broad-shouldered in that way that comes with spending too much time on the flying trapeze, floppy-haired in front and close-cropped in the back. His ears stuck out a bit too far and his hands were a bit too big for the rest of his frame, but I liked those things about him. They proved he was real. Actually, I liked everything about him, and had since he'd stopped glowering at me and started smiling instead.

He wasn't smiling now. He looked stunned, like he couldn't believe this was actually happening. I understood the sentiment.

When we finally started moving again, he was faster.

He's always been faster than I am, a blessing of biology enhanced and improved by training. He closed the distance between us in a single step, his hands coming up to cup the sides of my face, and his lips tasted like bad coffee, diner pie, and terrible decisions, and none of that mattered one damn bit. Sam was *here*. Sam was *kissing me*. Everything else, good, bad, or yet to be determined, could wait.

The heat coming off of his skin was intense. As a fūri, Sam runs hotter than a human man, even when he's in his seemingly-human form. It was a comforting piece of proof that this was really him, enough so that I leaned even closer, his hands holding my face like an anchor, my body seeking his in the open, liminal space of the doorway.

The doorway. We were standing in the doorway. The doorway to the apartment, which meant the *door* was open, which meant anyone who looked would see me standing there, kissing a strange man who most definitely did *not* work for Lowry Entertainment, Inc.

I broke the kiss. Sam looked at me, wide-eyed and betrayed. And adorable. God, he was adorable. Had he always been this adorable?

Fucking hormones, I thought, before grabbing his shirt, growling, "Inside," and yanking him into the apartment. He had the presence of mind to catch and slam the door behind himself. He even used one of his hands to do it. The boy was staying human until he had the full lay of the land. That pleased me, although I couldn't say I'd expected anything else. I'd been maybe-dating him for less than a month. He'd been a therianthrope for his entire life.

Fern, still standing next to the couch, was gaping at us, open-mouthed and shocked-looking. "Are you going to do a murder in our living room?" she squeaked.

"What?" asked Sam.

"No," I said firmly. "No one is getting murdered." I hesitated before amending, "Right now. Murder is always on the table for later."

Fern looked reassured. Sam did not. That was fine: Sam was about to become a lot less reassured about everything. I whirled on him, finger pointed at his chest.

"You," I said, voice low. "What are you doing here?"

Sam blinked. "Uh," he said. "Hello to you, too. Gosh, I missed you. No, don't worry about it, I'd love to come into your apartment and have this conversation in front of a total stranger. That sounds like a bucket of fun. Everybody loves a bucket of fun."

"I *live* here," said Fern, sounding squeakily affronted. She folded her arms and narrowed her eyes, which for Fern was the equivalent of a full-on glare. It was adorable. Telling her that probably wouldn't have been a good idea. "Who are you? Why were you kissing—" Then she stopped, glare transforming into a look of stricken confusion as she realized she didn't know what to call me in front of him.

I laughed. I couldn't stop myself. Fern looked hurt, and I laughed even harder, which was rude of me, but after the day I'd had, I thought I was owed a brief moment of healing hysteria. Sometimes the rational, reasonable thing isn't the thing to do after all.

Sam sighed heavily. "You broke her," he accused, looking at Fern. "I left her alone for six months, and you broke her. This probably voids the warranty."

"Lowry Security will have you out of here so fast that you'll leave behind those gross flip-flops like you're in a cartoon," said Fern.

I glanced at Sam's feet. He was, in fact, wearing flip-flops, which seemed like the best possible compromise between his natural disdain for footwear and the human world's tendency to insist that people without shoes on are not to be trusted. They looked like they'd been stolen from a resort pool. The urge to start laughing again rose in my throat. I swallowed it down. Healing hysteria might be nice, but if I spent too much time indulging myself, I wasn't going to get anything done.

"No calling Security," I said. "Fern, this is Sam Taylor, my . . ." I trailed off. We'd never formalized anything. I'd been too busy running away before the Covenant could use me as an excuse to kill Sam and everyone he'd ever cared about.

"I'm her boyfriend," said Sam gruffly.

"Boyfriend," I concluded. My stomach did a flip that

had nothing to do with the trouble I might or might not be in, and everything to do with the way Sam kept glancing at me, quick, sharp-edged looks, like he was cataloging every inch. My hands itched, not with heat, but with the desire to touch him and keep touching, tactilely reassuring myself that he was really here, that this wasn't some sort of cruel dream cooked up by my overstimulated subconscious. "Sam, this is Fern. She's one of my roommates."

"Wait," said Fern, eyes going wide again. "This is the boyfriend? *This*?" She waved her hands, encompassing the whole of him. "I didn't think this was your type."

Sam raised an eyebrow. "Meaning what, exactly?" he asked, in a dangerous tone.

"Hobo," said Fern.

"Uh, have you met her?" Sam pointed to me. "Hobo is precisely her type. Especially since last time I checked, she was running away from everyone in the world who cared about what happened to her. Dating someone like me just means she's sticking with her theme."

Listening to the two of them avoid using my name was already getting old. "Sam, Fern knew me before I went undercover. Fern, Sam knows my real name, remember?"

"Wait, you told her about me?" Sam looked obscurely pleased.

"You were serious about that?" asked Fern.

"I was." I looked between the two of them. Normally, I'm against revealing cryptids, even to each other. That sort of thing is private. Normally, they're not both standing in my living room, eyeing each other with anger and mistrust. This was my fault. I needed to fix it. "He also knows what I do for a living. I mean he *understands*."

That was about as broadly as I was willing to hint. Fern's eyes narrowed, studying Sam with a new intensity. Sam took a half-step back.

"Is she going to turn inside out and start waving weird tendrils of flesh at me?" he asked.

"What?" I said. "No. Fern's not . . . I don't think I know of anything that does that. Have you seen something that does that? Where?" I shook my head. "No, don't tell me. We're getting off-topic."

"Annie, is your boyfriend human?" Fern's tone was icy. "I think you should have to tell me if he isn't."

This was escalating quickly. I glanced at Sam. He nodded. Looking back to Fern, I said, with some relief, "No. He's not."

"I didn't think so." Fern returned her attention to Sam. "He stands wrong for a human."

"I do not," said Sam. "I stand perfectly fine."

"You don't," said Fern. "But that's okay. I don't stand right either. I'm a sylph."

"I thought you might be." Sam smiled—a quick, relieved expression. "We had a couple of sylphs with the carnival when I was a kid. When they did the flying silks, nobody could even come close."

"So if we're all done glaring at each other, can we get back to me figuring out how pissed I am?" I asked. "Sam, what are you *doing* here?"

"Mary found me." He didn't even have the grace to look contrite. "She said you were in trouble. I came running."

"Mary?" asked Fern. "Your dead aunt really went looking for your hobo boyfriend because a parade fell on people? Because I thought she was kidding."

"She knows about Mary?" asked Sam. "Wait—a *parade* fell on people? How does that even happen?"

His questions, while valid, were more than I felt like answering right now. I was tired, and I wanted to go to bed and sleep for a year, and I wanted to throw myself into his arms and enjoy the feeling of having someone I could hold onto, someone who wouldn't push me away, no matter how much I encouraged them to. I couldn't do either of those things. I rubbed my face instead.

"Mary told you I needed you," I said wearily.

Sam nodded. "She said things were getting really weird for you, and she wanted someone on the ground who was allowed to help and was faster than you are. I think it helps that I'm not, you know, actually one of your relatives."

"Family can't come here," I agreed. "Blood. Too easy to trace."

"I'm here." Fern sounded hurt. "I'll help you if you need me."

"But I'm still faster than you are." Sam stepped out of his flip-flops.

I knew what came next, and so I watched Fern instead of Sam as he transformed, marking the way her jaw tightened and her eyes went wide. Her shoulders seemed to lift a few inches higher, signaling a decrease in her personal density. That was an instinctive flight response in sylphs. As it wasn't followed by screaming, jumping into the air, or running away, I guessed it was probably okay.

I looked back to Sam. He was recognizably the same person, only . . . not . . . at the same time. His hair had shifted from black to a dark brown ticked with blond undertones, while also spreading down his cheeks in what would have been sideburns, if they hadn't been so clearly made of fur. His features were broader, more simian in some ways, and entirely alien in others, and his arms were longer, fingers resting slightly below his knees rather than at mid-thigh. The biggest changes were his feet, which now looked more like a second pair of hands, and his tail, which was long and curved behind him in what I had come to recognize as a relaxed position. All of him looked more relaxed this way. Maintaining his human-esque form was a matter of effort and concentration, and he was only truly comfortable when he could stop and be himself.

"You're a *fūri*," said Fern, in a tone that couldn't make up its mind between wonder and irritation. It would have been impressive, if she hadn't been directing it at Sam. "Why didn't you say you were a fūri? I thought you were extinct!"

"I get that a lot." Sam rubbed the back of his neck with one hand. "I didn't say it because it's not the sort of thing I go around saying to the lady at the Starbucks, you know? But I really am faster than you. I'm faster than just about anyone."

"Are you faster than I can take off my glasses?"

The voice was Megan's. All of us turned. She was at

the mouth of the hall, her wig in her hand, the snakes covering her head rising into silent strike positions, their eyes fixed on Sam. Her other hand rested on the arm of her glasses, ready to whip them off.

I sighed. I couldn't help myself. "Please," I said. "Please, can we all just accept that we're friends here, or at least not enemies, and stop threatening each other? This is starting to feel like a bad comedy routine."

"Whoa," said Sam. "Gorgon."

"Pliny's gorgon," said Megan. I could have used her voice to chill my drink. "I live here. Who are you?"

"Megan, this is my boyfriend, Sam Taylor," I said. "He's a fūri, which is a kind of yōkai. Sam, this is Megan, my other roommate. She's a resident at the local hospital. Megan, please don't paralyze Sam. Sam, please don't get paralyzed."

"What, I don't even get to fight back in this scenario?"

"She can look at you faster than you can throw something at her." That's what makes gorgons, of all types, so dangerous. I rubbed my face again. "Can we talk about all this after we've had some sleep? My head is spinning."

"Is he staying the night?" asked Megan.

"Yes. No. I don't know." I looked at Sam. "Are you?"

"Only if you want me to," he said, and smiled uncertainly.

"He's staying." I turned back to my roommates. "Please. Sleep, relax, and know that I absolutely vouch for him. I trust him with my life."

"That's good, because you're trusting him with ours," said Megan.

She turned and walked back down the hall to her room. Fern followed, pausing to pat my arm and lean toward me.

"He's cute," she whispered, sotto voce, and was gone, leaving me and Sam alone.

I looked at him. He looked at me.

"Hey," I said.

"Hey," he answered. His tail, which sometimes seemed to have a mind of its own, wrapped itself around his left leg, pulling tight in clear anxiety. He looked down at it and scowled. "Sometimes I wonder why I don't keep this thing put away."

"Because it would be uncomfortable for no good reason," I said, and took a step toward him. The urge to touch him again, to reassure myself that he was really here, really real, was almost overwhelming. I was angry, yes, but not at him. All my anger was reserved for Mary. When I looked at Sam, all I felt was . . .

Was relief. I was so relieved to have him here that I could have cried.

"Yeah, see, I want to believe you care about that sort of thing, but you know what's uncomfortable for no good reason? Lying there bleeding on everything while your asshole girlfriend walks away to 'protect you.'" Sam gave me a sharp look, anger and recrimination in his eyes. "I would have come with you. You didn't have to do this—any of this—alone."

"I know you would have," I whispered. "That's why I couldn't let you."

Leonard Cunningham, presumptive heir to the modern Covenant of St. George, had been there when one of his underlings had put a bullet in Sam's head. He'd been there when the bullet ricocheted against bone, unable to deal with fūri skeletal density. That meant that—if it happened again—he'd be packing something with more power. The Covenant watches. The Covenant listens. The Covenant, slow and hidebound as it seems, *learns*. Leonard would kill Sam as soon as look at him. Sooner, if he had a sniper available.

Sam shook his head. "That wasn't just your choice."

"Your grandmother needed you."

"You needed someone."

"I had Mary."

"I've done some research since we split up. Having Mary isn't much better than being on your own."

I didn't say anything.

Every kind of ghost has its own limitations. For Mary, those limitations take the form of her connection to the crossroads. I couldn't *ask* her for much of anything, because the crossroads might interpret that as my starting to offer a bargain—and while the crossroads ghosts act on the side of the people who go down to make deals, the crossroads themselves are a lot less charitable. They would chew me up and spit me out, and laugh the whole time. As the youngest member of the current generation, I was the one she had the most leeway around, because she was still, until I passed her to someone else, my babysitter. As soon as Verity or Shelby got pregnant, I'd lose that rarified status, and I'd see Mary as often as anyone else did, which wasn't nearly often enough.

Sam sighed. "I just wish you hadn't gone. And I wish you were happy to see me."

"What?" I blinked at him. "Sam . . . I'm so happy to see you I don't know how to put it into words."

"Really? Because you sure aren't acting like—"

Whatever else he'd been about to say was lost as I did the only thing that made sense: I stepped closer and kissed him again. This time, I was the one pressing my hands against the sides of his face, tangling my fingers in the short hair that limned the edges of his cheekbones, making them easier to find. This time, I was the one pressing myself forward, trying to close all the distance between us, to render it irrelevant.

Something snaked around my waist: his tail, grabbing me and pulling me closer still. I didn't resist. He was holding me, and I was holding him, and for a moment, the world almost made sense. This was something I could do. This was something I could understand.

He broke away, hands still on my shoulders and tail still around my waist, and asked, in a tone that broke my heart a little, "Does this mean I can stay?"

I forced myself to smile. "It means I may never let you go," I said, and kissed him again, and prayed—yes, prayed—that I wasn't about to fuck this up.

Fourteen

"Love is love. If anybody tries to tell you your love's not worth having, shoot them in the kneecaps a couple of times. It won't change their minds, but it'll make you feel better."

–Frances Brown

The smaller of two bedrooms in a shitty company apartment five miles outside of Lakeland, Florida

SAM DIDN'T UNTWINE HIS tail from around my waist until we were standing in my bedroom with the door soundly shut behind us. Only then did he let me go, take a quick, assessing look around, and sit down on the bed, folding his hands in his lap and looking at me gravely. My heart did an odd stuttering sidestep, leaving me frozen.

"Mary said I needed to come because you wouldn't let her call for me," he said. "She said you didn't ask, and that meant there was no obligation, but that she was worried about you. Why was she worried about you?"

I couldn't guess from looking at him how much Mary had—or hadn't—elected to share. He might be testing me, making sure I'd tell him the truth. Or he might be offering me an out. I could downplay the cabal and the accidents, make it sound like Mary was just worried about how isolated I was, and . . .

And I'd be lying to him. I didn't want to lie to him. I wanted to hold him and let him tell me it was all going to be okay, even if we both knew it wasn't going to be. I wanted *him* to be the one who lied to *me*.

"Remember how I sometimes set things on fire by touching them, even when I don't mean to?" I asked.

Sam nodded stiffly. The last thing he'd seen me set on fire was the big tent at his family's carnival.

"I can't do that anymore."

"What?" He frowned. "Why not?"

"Because it turns out it's not good for me. I could hurt myself channeling magic that way. I met a cabal of people who know how to use magic safely, and they're teaching me. I mean, I guess they're teaching me. I haven't actually *learned* much yet, except for how not to set things on fire all the time."

"I thought you wanted to stop setting things on fire."

"I did! I do. I just . . ." I shook my head. "It feels like something's missing. It's weird. I understand why random pyrotechnics aren't a good thing. I guess I assumed that if I gave that up, I'd get something else in return. Maybe that comes later."

"So why did Mary tell me you needed me here?"

"She's been around a long time. She knew my grandfather. He was a magic-user. I inherited it from him. I guess she worries. She doesn't want these people to take advantage of me, and she wanted me to have some backup." I took a deep breath. "That's not necessarily a bad thing. Weird shit's been happening in the Park lately."

Sam tilted his head. "Weird shit? Like what?"

"Like a deep fryer exploded and nearly burned a woman to death. Like a parade float collapsed today, and a bunch of people actually died." Again, the image of Andrea and her missing face flashed behind my eyes. I shuddered. "It's not good. It's not *right*. Lowryland is obsessive about safety. If they get a reputation for hurting people, they'll wind up shutting down. I don't even know if they'll be open tomorrow. Something's wrong."

"Then we'll fix it." Sam stood, putting his hands on my upper arms and looking at me solemnly. "I'm here now. I'm not leaving again. You don't get to send me away."

"I could run." I tried to make my voice seem light, casual even. I failed.

Sam wasn't buying it. His expression darkened, and

he said, "You got one freebie. You already used it up. If you run away from me again, I'm tracking you down and looking at you sadly until you agree to stop."

"What, not shaking me?"

"We both know that wouldn't be cool, and it'd just give you an excuse to try to kick my ass. I have better things to do with my girlfriend than have superhero fights." Sam paused before adding thoughtfully, "Although that could be cool. We should put that on the list for later."

"There's going to be a later?"

The corner of Sam's mouth curled upward. "I sure hope so," he said, and kissed me.

I was filthy, sticky with sweat and smoke and residue from the parade fire, which had smelled chemical and foul thanks to the burning plastic of the artificial trees. None of that mattered. Sam kissed me like he'd been starving since I'd walked away from him and I was the first meal he'd been offered in all that time. His hands moved to cup my ass, fingers splayed to give him the best possible grip.

I pulled away. He looked hurt.

"Did I—"

I shook my head. "No," I said, and was relieved to watch the glimmers of worry disappear from his eyes. "These clothes are gross. Mind if I take them off?"

Sam looked surprised for a moment. Then he grinned. "Not if you don't," he said.

We stripped quickly, both of us, and there was nothing erotic or enticing about it: we were two people getting naked as fast as we could. Sam got out of his jeans while I was still untying my shoes, and "helped" by unfastening my bra with his tail, looking innocent all the while. I was laughing too hard to say anything about it, and kept laughing as I stepped out of my shoes and yoga pants. Then I straightened, laughter stilling, and looked at him. He looked back.

It was strange seeing him without a canvas sky behind him, without the sounds of the midway jangling quietly in the distance. He was a beautiful man. He always had been, although it had taken me a while to see it. When we'd first met, I'd been the stranger in his family's carnival, the threat to his way of life, and he'd reacted accordingly. I knew now that he was just a protective person. He'd been taking care of his own. Somehow, somewhere along the line, I had joined that list, and I was so grateful, and so afraid of everything that could imply.

He stepped closer, raising one hand to rest his fingertips against my cheek. The heat coming off his skin made me shiver, but in a good way.

"We don't have to do this," he said. "I didn't come here because I wanted to get laid."

"I know," I said, and kissed him again, and conversation was over for a while.

The first time—the only time—we'd been together like this, we'd been standing at the edge of the end of the world, and we had gone in knowing we might not get another shot: that we were attempting to put paid to everything our relationship was and might have been in a single hour. There hadn't been *time* to slow down or to explore. There hadn't been time to admire. We had that time now, with morning miles away and both of us carnival-trained into silence, which meant my overprotective roommates wouldn't come charging in to save me.

For the first time in a long time, there was nothing I felt like I needed to be saved from. I was exactly where I wanted to be.

Sam looked me up and down, appreciation and eagerness in his eyes, and I didn't move, giving him the opportunity to change his mind. After a moment, he paused, and frowned.

"Annie? You okay?" A faint blush spread across the visible part of his cheeks. "Is it the furry thing? I can . . . y'know, stop . . ."

"You'd be dead if you were human," I said, and stepped toward him, closing the last little gap between us. There was a fine sheen of fur on his chest, where a human man would have had wiry hair, and it tickled pleasantly, making me press myself even closer. I reached up and traced the whisper-thin outline of the scar on his forehead. It was barely visible. Sadly for me, I knew exactly where to look. "Pow, right in the head, and you'd be dead. No more Sam. No more asshole monkey throwing me around the flying trapeze. The furry thing didn't bother me before you got shot. Now? I wouldn't care if you never stopped again. All I want you to do is stay alive."

"I could say the same thing to you," he whispered, tail snaking around my waist and pulling tight. There was no way for me to get away without hurting him.

I didn't want to get away. "So keep me alive," I said, and kissed him hard.

He responded by grabbing my ass again, this time using the combined leverage of tail and palms to boost me up off the floor. I wrapped my legs around him, holding myself in place, and stayed there as we fell onto the bed, kissing each other hard all the while.

The kissing went on for quite some time, accompanied by a certain measure of groping as we got familiar with one another again—and in some cases, for the first time, since we didn't need to worry about a Covenant strike team or Sam's grandmother bursting in at any moment. Heavy petting with someone who essentially had four hands was a whole new experience for me. For most people, I would imagine.

Sam pulled away slightly, and asked, "Condom?"

I blinked at him, dazed and slightly out of synch with myself, before I replied, "In the bedside table. For emergencies." Not that I'd been counting on anything like this happening, but the best way to wind up in a bad situation is to be unprepared for all eventualities.

"Cool," he said, and kissed me again, and we toppled past the point of no return.

When I was a kid, on the rare occasions when Verity had treated me like a sister, instead of like some sort of weird stranger who lived in her house for some reason, we'd had a few slumber parties. Just her and me and my cousin Elsie, and later, when she'd started feeling secure enough

in her ability not to read random minds to travel, my
cousin Sarah. We'd all sit up all night eating popcorn and
watching scary movies and talking about whatever
seemed important—which was, quite frequently, sex.

I'll never forget those nights, the four of us and the
occasional mouse sitting in the dark living room, talking
about things that were too adult for me, but which I'd
wanted to hear anyway. I'd wanted to hear everything, to
devour it all and make it a part of me. I'd never said
much. There wasn't really anything for me to contribute,
and I hadn't wanted to remind Verity of how young I
was, or give her a good reason to send me away.

"Sex with therianthropes must be *amazing*," Verity
had sighed, sweet sixteen and dreaming constantly of
being kissed, and I'd been thirteen, already inclined to
hate her, but yearning for her approval all the same. It
was a weird, toxic brew that I shared with younger siblings all over the world, and the only antidote was time.

Elsie, who had been the most experienced of the lot of
us, having actually kissed a girl before the end of the
school year, had looked at her blankly and asked, "Why?"

"Because the stamina they need to change forms
without suffering from multiple organ failure has just got
to translate to bed," Verity had replied, attempting what
might charitably be called a leer.

"You're a pervert," Elise had said, in a prim tone, and
I had thrown my allegiance in with her on the spot.

Now, years and miles and a thousand bad decisions
later, I lay curled against Sam in the cocoon of my sheets,
the hot Florida air pressing down on us and covering our
exposed skin in a sheen of sweat, and thought Verity had
been onto something, in her usual blunt instrument man-
ner. It wasn't the stamina, or the potential for shapeshifting. It was that the therianthrope in question was Sam
Taylor. I didn't love him. He didn't love me. But as his tail
tightened around my waist, drawing me closer in his
sleep, keeping me anchored, I realized two things:

If he didn't leave soon, I was going to wind up loving
him, whether I wanted to or not.

And I didn't want him to go.

I pressed a kiss to the skin of his cheek, just above the furry line of his cheekbone, nestled my head against his shoulder, and closed my eyes. I was hot and sticky and needed a shower more than ever. Between the parade accident, the roller skating, and the remarkably acrobatic sex, I was sore in places that I hadn't been consciously aware of before. There was no way I was going to fall asleep. No way.

What felt like seconds later, I opened my eyes again, and I was alone in the bed. Sunlight slanted under the edge of the curtain, filling my room with an eerie *Twilight Zone* glow. I sat bolt upright, the muscles in my back and thighs protesting, looking wildly around for any sign that Sam's sudden appearance on the doorstep hadn't been an oddly sexual wish fulfillment dream.

There wasn't one. My clothes were strewn around the floor, but that happened regardless of whether I had company. Back at home, a messy room had been a solid defense mechanism. Once my siblings figured out that they couldn't tell where I'd spilled the caltrops just by looking, they'd gotten a lot more careful about sneaking into my room to steal my shit. Here, it was a comforting reminder that this wasn't forever: one day, I would shove all my secondhand Lowry tank tops and worn-out yoga pants into a bag and go back to the loving arms of my family, where I didn't have to be frightened all the time. Better yet, I'd leave it all behind, and drop a match on it as I walked away.

I slid slowly out of the bed and grabbed my yoga pants off the floor, yanking them on before casting around for a shirt that didn't smell like blood, sweat, or diesel fuel. It was harder than it should have been, but in short enough order I was dressed and creeping out into the hall, shoulders hunched, listening for signs of danger.

Instead, I heard laughter, and the distinctive pop of frying bacon. The smell of pancakes hit me a moment later. I straightened up. There's only one person who would come into my apartment and start making breakfast—and as a hint, it's not one of my roommates. Fern can't cook to save her life. Megan *can* cook. It's just that most of the things she produces are dangerous to the human esophagus.

I walked briskly down the hall to the small "dining nook" attached to the kitchen, separated by a Formica island that should have been remodeled sometime in the late seventies. Our battered secondhand kitchen table was occupied for a change, by Fern, sipping a mixed berry smoothie out of a reusable 7-11 cup . . . and Sam, who had a cup of coffee in his right hand and another held firmly in his tail, in case someone tried to take it away.

Mary was in the kitchen, flipping pancakes with the ease of a long-time diner cook. She turned at the sound of my footsteps—or maybe at the sound of my heartbeat, ghosts can be creepy sometimes—and flashed me a grin. She was dressed in her customary seventies hippie gear, peasant blouse and bell-bottomed jeans, and there were daisies braided in her hair.

"You left your phone in your gym bag," she said. "Fairyland is closed today, and all workers who witnessed the accident—that would be you—have been given a shift off, with pay, probably so you won't sue. And, um, someone named Colin texted you and said that under the circumstances, you didn't need to come see him this morning. So you're free. There's bacon, and pancakes will be up in a moment."

I stayed where I was, blinking, trying to tamp down the lingering remnants of panic and replace them with something verging on comprehension. It didn't help that Sam wasn't wearing a shirt. Combining a higher than human body temperature with our unreliable air-conditioning probably made that a bad idea. He offered me a sideways, almost hesitant smile.

"You were out cold," he said. "I didn't want to wake you. Especially not once Mary said you didn't need to work."

"I wouldn't have let him wake you anyway," said Mary. "You don't sleep nearly enough. You need to work on that."

"You're dead," I said. "You sleep forever. Where's Megan?"

"She had to go to the hospital for her shift," said Fern around a mouthful of bacon. The reason for her relative quiet was obvious when I looked at her plate: she was doing her best to show Sam that size didn't matter when it came to putting away breakfast foods. "She said to tell you she doesn't care if your boyfriend stays over, but if he drinks her cherimoya juice, she'll let her hair bite him."

"Sam, don't drink Megan's cherimoya juice," I said, heading for the kitchen. The lure of pancakes was too great to resist any longer.

"What's a cherimoya?" he asked.

"It's a fruit," I said. Mary handed me a plate. I began piling pancakes and bacon onto it. "They're from Colombia, I think. Incredibly tasty, unless you eat the seeds, which will kill the crap out of you. Really interesting neurotoxins. Megan puts her cherimoya into the juicer whole."

Sam frowned. "Meaning . . . ?"

"Meaning the juice is full of crushed neurotoxic seeds, and if you drank it, you'd probably be dead before you hit the floor, so don't drink it." I walked back to the table. The seat next to him was open. I hesitated like a kid in a high school cafeteria before sinking into it, and was rewarded for my bravery with a quick, shy grin.

Fern rolled her eyes. "Get a room."

"I have a room," I said. "I just came out of my room."

"I spent the night in her room," said Sam with the faintest hint of smugness. He took a sip of his coffee—first one mug, and then the other. "No work today. That's good, right?"

"Good and bad." I leaned across the table to snag the milk. When you have hobbies like mine, healthy bones aren't just a good idea, they're a necessary investment in not becoming a smear on the track. "Good, I didn't oversleep and get myself in trouble. Bad, I don't know what I'm going to do with myself."

"Says the girl with her boyfriend, who she hasn't seen in six months, sitting next to her," said Mary.

I shot her a glare that would probably have been a lot more effective if it had contained any actual heat. "I told you not to bring him here."

"I didn't," said Mary. "I just told him where to find you, and that you needed him if you wanted to stay alive."

"It's not like I was doing anything," said Sam.

Fern fixed him with a stern look. In that moment, she seemed to be channeling my mother. I choked on my milk, barely managing to keep it from coming out of my nose.

"What *do* you do?" she asked.

"Well, ma'am," he said, with sudden politeness, "I'm normally a trapeze artist with my family's carnival, and I do a lot of administrative tasks for my grandmother, who owns the show. Unfortunately, we had a little issue with fire damage—"

"Meaning Annie burned the whole damn place to the ground to keep the Covenant from tracking them all down and killing them deader than I am," said Mary blithely.

Sam continued, unruffled, "—and had to shut down for the rest of the season. The insurance money is coming through, and we've rented a training facility in Indiana, so everybody's staying in shape. This will probably be good for the show in the long run. New rides, new equipment, time to work on our routines without needing to worry about keeping our bellies full—honestly, it's a blessing."

"I hear a 'but' coming on," said Mary.

"But it's boring," said Sam. "But there are humans around like, *all the time*, talking to my grandmother, or running more tests on the residue from the fire, or doing one more interview before they sign off on the latest report. And we're sharing space with another carnival, and they're all nice people, but they have their own way of doing things, and some of them are sort of naïve when it comes to remembering that humans don't own the whole world, just most of it. So I have to stay human unless I'm in my room or in a closed rehearsal."

Fern frowned. "So?"

"Imagine trying to hold in a sneeze when you really need to pee," said Sam. "Now imagine doing that *forever*."

Fern's frown melted into a look of horror. She looked to me for confirmation.

"He means it," I said, nodding. "Fūri aren't like chupacabra. They actually have a default form, and it's not the one that looks like me."

One of the other jammers with the league back in Portland, Princess Leya-you-out, is a chupacabra. For her, standing on two legs is exactly as natural and comfortable as wandering around on four. She doesn't change forms when she sleeps, because whichever form she's in is her "real" one. Sam, like all fūri, works slightly differently. For him, humanity is an effort, a disguise he puts on, rather than a shape he shifts out of.

"Wow," said Fern. Then, almost shyly, she said, "When we're kids, sylphs don't have a stable density. That's why we don't really live in big family groups anymore. Sometimes children float away, and that's not safe, so we all have to take precautions."

"What kind?" asked Sam.

"Um. Well, usually, people have babies and then give them to crèche workers to raise. We have, you know, a few of them left. Around the country. Big houses in the middle of nowhere, where kids can grow up until they're old enough to know what density their body ought to be. Then you practice every day, until you can stay the same always."

I frowned. "When do your parents come back for you?"

"Oh. They don't. We're all adopted." Fern was suddenly very interested in her bacon. "Once you settle, a family that has a space for a kid will come and get you, and then you're theirs. My family was really nice. They had dropped off a daughter about my age, so maybe I was even related to them."

Sam's frown joined mine. "How do you, you know," he asked. "Not wind up sleeping with your brother by mistake?"

"People who aren't good to sleep with smell wrong when you're in estrus," said Fern blithely. "Like you wouldn't smell right, so I wouldn't sleep with you, because you're not the same species as me."

"Huh," said Sam, while I stuffed a bite of pancake into my mouth to stop myself from asking any more questions. This was fascinating to me, and that was the problem. If I let myself, I could turn this into an all-day biology lesson, and I couldn't even write anything down. Until I made it home, back to my mice and my notebooks and the safety of the family compound, I had to view every space as compromised, all the time, and that meant never leaving a written record.

"I have to work today," said Fern, and stood, saving me from myself. "They only closed Fairyland, and that's going to channel extra traffic into all the rest of the Park."

"Even though bad things happened?" asked Sam.

"Remember the carnival after I found the dead body?" I speared another piece of pancake. "People love a tragedy, as long as they feel like they're seeing it from a safe distance. Ticket sales are probably up for the day."

Complaints would be up, too. People who'd decided to come to Lowryland hoping for a glimpse of charred pavement or damaged landscaping would nonetheless be furious when they realized that a whole section of the Park was closed down. The managers would be working double time to soothe the shouters and the tantrum-throwers, leaving their poor underlings to handle the wolves. It was going to be a fun, fun day, and while I wouldn't say that a day off was worth it, I was grateful not to need to go into the fray.

Not as an employee, anyway. I paused thoughtfully before I turned to Sam, grinned, and asked, "How'd you like to go to Lowryland?"

Fifteen

"There's a place for everything, and everything has its place. It just so happens that this knife belongs in your spleen."

–Enid Healy

The front gates of Lowryland

A S AN EMPLOYEE OF Lowryland, I got free access to the Park and its guest facilities when I wasn't working. Better yet, I was allowed to bring people with me. Not every day, but twice a month, which was twice more than I'd been asking anyone to come up until now. I hadn't even known that Cylia was in town, and without her, who was I going to invite? Nobody, that was who.

Nobody until now. Sam tilted his head back, features impeccably human, eyes shaded by a Monty Mule baseball cap that Fern had dug out of the front closet before running for the tram, and squinted at the façade above the gates. It was an impressive piece of wrought iron filigree, rendered all the more eye-catching by the fact that its elegant whorls and delicate traceries actually etched out the faces of Lowry's most famous cartoon characters.

"I never thought I'd get to see a Monty Mule head bigger than I am tall," he said, in a hushed tone.

I shot him a sidelong glance. "Don't tell me you're a true believer."

"What?" He shrugged broadly. "I grew up in a carnival caravan. Until I was old enough to actually *do* stuff, videos kept me from driving Grandma up the wall. I've seen everything Lowry's ever done. Most of it twice."

"Only twice?" I asked.

"No," he said. "I'm lying so I'll still seem cool and macho and awesome, and like I'm not internally screaming about the idea of getting to meet Laura and Lizzie."

"You won't today." The line inched forward, tourists digging their tickets out of their fanny packs while sneering locals flashed their annual passes like the ability to fork over way too much money for a piece of character-branded plastic somehow granted them a measure of moral superiority. Both groups were accompanied by overexcited, overstimulated children, the girls in puffy princess dresses, the boys waving plastic swords and bellowing at one another.

(Occasionally we'd get a girl with a sword—we got plenty of girls who looked at the swords with raw avarice in their eyes, like they'd never seen anything so beautiful before and never would, ever again—or a boy with a princess crown, but sadly, the parents were the ones paying, and the parents were often not in the mood to listen to what their kids *wanted*. If I ever had kids, they were all going to have dresses, and swords, and tiny siege engines, if that was what it took to make them happy.)

Sam looked at me, hurt. "Why not? Do you need kids to meet the princesses?"

The brief image of him bribing families to let him borrow their kids was as charming as it was likely to involve Park Security. I shook my head. "No, but Fairyland is closed, remember? They do their meet-and-greets in Fairyland."

"So who's that?" Sam pointed past the ticket takers and the lines. I looked.

There, in the front plaza, in front of the majestic Rainbow Fountain that ticked off the hours of Lowry's dreamland, were two princesses in wine-dark jewel tones, surrounded by children squalling for their turn at a picture. I blinked, nonplussed.

"I guess they moved the girls for the day." It made sense—Laura and Lizzie were two of Lowry's most popular princesses, buoyed by their soft feminist message and striking color palette. They weren't pastel, which made them popular with girls who'd been sold the message of "not being like other girls," and their movie actually wasn't awful, which meant they stayed popular with teenagers. Maybe I was biased, working in their section of the Park and all, but I should have realized that management would relocate the princesses rather than disappoint that many kids.

The line moved again. We reached the front, and I showed the ticket taker my cast ID, letting her run it through the scanner. When it brought up the record indicating that I was an active employee who hadn't brought in any guests this period, she handed Sam a ticket to use if he needed to leave and come back again before waving us both into the Park, not even bothering to tell us to dream big—the standard greeting.

I didn't mind, but this was Sam's first time, and it bothered me a little, at least until I saw him making a beeline for the two actresses in their princess gear, a determined look on his face. I laughed and chased after him. No one needed to tell us to dream big. Sam was going to do it without any prompting.

It took half an hour to get through the queue around the princesses and snap a few pictures of Sam, using his phone to do the dirty deed. He looked almost bashful, sandwiched between the two girls with his hat shading his eyes and a shy grin on his face. When he was done, he came bounding back to me, snatching the phone out of my hand and checking the pictures like he couldn't believe they were really there.

"Wow," he said. "Oh, wow. Look at that. There I am."

"So did you come looking for me because you missed me, or because you heard I might be able to get you into Lowryland?"

The question was asked in jest: I was laughing by the time I finished. The look Sam gave me was pure seriousness.

"I'm here for you," he said, tucking his phone into his pocket. "I just. You know. Wanted to meet them."

"Hey, and I'm cool with that," I assured him. "Come on. Let me show you where I work."

I offered him my hand. He took it without hesitation, and we strolled, together, like a couple of tourists, out of the entry plaza and onto the long small town stretch of Lowry's Welcoming World.

Some people like to say that Lowryland is nothing more than an expensive Disneyland knockoff, planned for Florida before Michael Lowry learned about Disney's Florida Project, by which time it was too late to change the construction plans. Nowhere is that comparison more apt than in the Welcoming World. It was designed in conjunction with a couple of comic artists who'd done work for the sci-fi pulps back in the fifties, and it's like what would happen if Main Street, USA, got rebuilt by Martians using nothing but a book of postcards. The overall effect is cartoonish and strange, like something out of a dream. Even the landscaping is designed to enhance the idea that everyone who goes there has somehow been transported to another planet, someplace where the ordinary rules of an ordinary world couldn't quite apply.

Kids love it, except for the occasional hyper-aware ones who look around themselves with wide, almost terrified eyes before bursting into betrayed tears, unable to resolve what they expect to see with what's actually in front of them. Adults, have a lot more years of inherent visual assumptions to claw through, mostly don't notice the architectural oddities, or dismiss them as "quaint" and "old-fashioned," dragging their sometimes weeping children through the last standing remnants of someone else's idea of occupied Mars.

Sam clutched my hand a little tighter as he gawked shamelessly, taking in every inch. We walked straight down the middle of the street toward the center hub, the Park rising around us like a mountain range. The Welcoming World ended, not at anything so gauche as a castle or a roller coaster, but with a huge central plaza contained inside a gigantic artificial geode. Crystals sparkled from the walls, lit from within by soft LED bulbs that gave everything a twinkling, glimmering effect. A tilted bronze map of Lowryland stood on a small dais, separated from everything around it and surrounded by tourists snapping photos, chattering all the while.

"Fairyland is closed today, but that still leaves us with Chapter and Verse, Deep-Down, Candyland, and Metropolis," I said, pointing to the relevant areas on the map. "If you want to watch the fireworks tonight, the best viewing area is lakeside in Deep-Down. I think we have an aquatic-themed area that isn't a water park mostly *because* of the fireworks. It's way harder to accidentally set things on fire when they're wet."

"I want to see *everything*," said Sam.

I laughed. "That's not going to happen in one day. The Park was designed to make it as close to impossible as they could, because they want people to come back over and over again. But we can see a lot."

Sam turned to give me a hopeful look. "And then we can come back?"

"On my next day off, sure." Megan and Fern had sign-in privileges, too, and as far as I knew, had never really used them. We could get Sam good and sick of Lowryland.

The thought was oddly appealing. While he was here, I knew I had someone in a position to watch my back. Fern was a good friend, but she was currently in the Enchanted Grove over in Chapter and Verse, smiling for the camera. She wouldn't be able to come if I called. Whereas Sam, for all that he was looking around himself like a kid in a candy store, seemed inclined to stick to my side for as long as I'd let him.

I was starting to suspect that it would be a long, long time.

Now he was looking at the "geode" wall. "I would love to climb that," he said thoughtfully.

"The Park used to allow it."

He shot me a startled glance. "Really?"

"Yup. Twice a year, as part of a Park-wide field day thing. You could sign up for the half-marathon, for swimming laps in the Kraken's Lagoon, or for free-climbing on the geode wall. They still do the half-marathon, although the rest of the activities have been discontinued for safety reasons. Which really sucks. I'd love to climb it, too."

"Did someone fall?"

"No, but there was a concern that someone *would*." I shrugged. "The people who climbed during the field day were volunteers who'd signed up and filled out forms promising not to sue the Park if they fell for any reason other than the wall collapsing. There were cushions and athletic gear and trained climbing instructors and you know how many people noticed those details when they looked at the pictures?"

"I'm going to go out on a limb and say 'not many,'" said Sam.

I nodded. "Incidents of people who hadn't filled out any of that paperwork trying to sneakily climb the wall spiked after every field day. When parents started boosting their kids up to the wall so they could get a 'cool rock-climbing picture,' the Park shut the whole thing down."

"People are why we can't have nice things."

"Pretty much." I gestured to the map again. "Where do you want to start?"

Lowryland is set up in a wheel-like shape, making it possible to walk from one zone to the next in a neverending loop. All zones connect to the hub, which was going to be important today: with Fairyland closed off, the hub was the only way between Candyland and Deep-Down.

Sam looked at the map for a moment before pointing to Chapter and Verse, which was the first zone to the left of the hub. "There."

"There it is," I said. Taking his hand again, I started for the wall. He came without any resistance, letting me lead while he goggled in wide-eyed delight at everything around us.

"Chapter and Verse is technically the literary-themed zone, but really it's where they stick everything that doesn't work somewhere else," I said. "Aspen and Elm are usually there, and sometimes you can catch Little Red Riding Hood and the Wolf in the mornings, although they move around more. They spend a lot of time in the Welcoming World." Because what a kid who was afraid of the angles of the architecture needed was an anthropomorphic Big Bad Wolf popping around the corner to say howdy.

Sometimes I wonder how anyone loves these places at all. The roller coasters are nice, sure, but the atmospheric trappings that make the theme parks so successful also turn them into nightmare factories.

Sam grinned at me. "We're gonna see *everything*," he said, and we plunged on, through the gateway to Chapter and Verse—stylized to look like it was made of frozen ink and flying manuscript pages—and into the true body of the Park.

My first "date" with Sam had been at his family's carnival. That should have prepared me, at least a little, for the sheer degree of enthusiasm that he would bring to a theme park. What is a theme park, after all, if not a carnival that has grown up and put down roots? Even Disneyland had gained in popularity with the addition of several displays that had debuted at the World's Fair. Michael Lowry hadn't had that early boost, but by the time he'd broken ground in Florida, Disney had already provided the world with a handy roadmap of what *not* to do in putting an immersive environment together. Lowryland was a masterpiece of the carnival arts, and Sam knew how to appreciate them.

Sam dragged me up one side of Chapter and Verse and down the other, exploring every nook and cranny, pulling me into line for every ride, even the ones most adult guests would sniff at and dismiss as designed for kids. As long as he could fit in the seats, he was riding the ride, and if he was riding the ride, I was riding the ride. We got our picture taken with Aspen and Elm (Fern giggling behind her hand and fighting not to break character the whole time). We bought corndogs from the Monty Mule's Mealtime Melody cart near the exit from the *Mooncake*-themed River of Stars roller coaster.

Sam grinned the whole time, only letting go of my

hand when it was absolutely necessary. Even then, he kept an eye on me, like he was afraid I would melt into the crowd and disappear. It should have been annoying—I've never liked being hovered over, which is why it's funny that I wound up being the kid who kept our phantom babysitter—but it was sweet, in a weird way. He didn't want me to go away again. As long as he relaxed once he figured out that disappearing wasn't my favorite trick, we'd be fine.

Chapter and Verse is the most eclectic zone, thanks to serving as a dumping ground for every property that doesn't fit cleanly somewhere else, and it only took a few hours for us to exhaust its many wonders and move on to Candyland, where everything is pink and green and smells like sugar. Sam paused at the threshold, sniffing the air.

"How . . . ?"

"Scent dispersal units hidden in the bushes." It helped that—with the exception of a few fruit trees—Candyland is the one zone without natural greenery. Almost everything there is crafted from plastic, steel, and glowing bulbs, creating an atmosphere that would have been called Wonka-esque, if that wouldn't have been stepping on someone else's copyright. "There's a petition every year or two to take them out. Allergies."

"Huh."

"Ironically, it's never the people with the allergies who want the scent dispersal shut down. It's usually folks getting offended on their behalf." Mostly parents at that. "We offer gluten-free gingerbread in this part of the Park, though, and that means there's a powerful lobby to keep Candyland exactly as it is."

"There's a lot more politics involved with running a theme park than there is with running a carnival," said Sam ruefully.

"Yeah, but we also have Hansel and Gretel and a house made out of gingerbread." I leaned in impulsively, planting a kiss upon his cheek. "Come on. Let's go see if the bakery is open."

The bakery was open, and selling all four of the

standard flavors of gingerbread—original, chocolate, cinnamon-spice, and gluten-free original. We got a sampling platter and settled under the shade of a waffle cone-shaped umbrella to watch the people come and go, kids dragging their parents toward the confections, or toward the waiting meet-and-greet with the Candy Witch, who was in prime sugarcoated form. Sam scooted his chair a bit closer to mine, and we sat there, eating gingerbread, existing. Not running away from anything or anyone. Not in fear for our lives. Just *being*.

It couldn't last. Sam gave me a sidelong look and asked, "How are your hands?"

"Cold." I raised one of them, looking at it critically. "The more I learn, the less I can do."

"Does it scare you?"

I lowered my hand, thinking about his question for a long moment before I said, "Yes. What if it never comes back? What if I trade being actually useful for knowing all the things I *could* do, if only I hadn't put the fire away? But it makes me hopeful, too. I didn't always set things on fire without meaning to. I used to be pretty much normal. I could probably adapt to being normal again. I'd spend less on burn cream, anyway."

Sam bumped my shoulder with his. "This is a bad time to start lying to me."

"Come again?"

"I've met you. You've never been normal, *Melody*."

I wrinkled my nose at him. He'd been given strict instructions to use my alias throughout the day, and he hadn't slipped once—dating a cryptid meant dating someone who knew what it was to keep a secret or pay the price—but he kept saying my "name" like it was some sort of complicated joke he was hoping I'd understand. Sam grinned at me.

"So this is what you do now?" he asked, changing the topic. "You wander around somebody else's playground, keeping kids from trying to eat the décor?"

"Most of the time, I'm in Fairyland, not Candyland," I said. "But yes. I spend my days trying to keep kids from tearing the Park apart, and making sure all of these people will think of us before they think of anyone else when it's time to plan their next family vacation."

"Do you like it?"

I paused. Finally, I said, "That's sort of a hard question for me. I'm pretty good at my job. I don't mind the rules, management does their best to be fair, and I like being allowed to run around the Park when I'm not on duty. It gives me something to focus on. I appreciate that. There are a lot of moving pieces in Lowryland. I could work here for twenty years and not know everything."

Sam looked perplexed. "Do you *want* to work here for twenty years?"

"Oh, hell, no." I didn't have to think about that answer. "I want to go home. I miss my family. I want to know what's going *on*. Exile may be fun for a little while, but as a long-term plan? It's terrible. I have no concept of where we stand with . . ." I dropped my voice. "You know."

Was I being paranoid, thinking that a member of the Covenant of St. George might have decided to bring their children for a pleasant vacation in Lowryland? Yes. But much like Fern hadn't been able to reveal herself to the dragons without fear of causing trouble, I couldn't run the risk of the Covenant hearing me.

It was funny. We were in a cathedral built to honor and uplift fairy tales. Everything about this place was a story, carefully crafted and orchestrated to instill a sense of awe and wonder in the guests around us. I could have stood up and started explaining, loudly, how a ghost had been my primary babysitter since I was born, how she had sung me doo-wop songs in my cradle and organized my family's colony of talking mice into backup choruses, and no one would have batted an eye. Lowryland was where you went to be a little left of the norm.

That didn't change the fact that if I used proper names, called Mary a crossroads ghost or called the mice an Aeslin colony, I'd be running the risk of attracting the wrong kind of attention. Stories are universal. Details, though . . . details can get you killed.

"When do you think it'll be safe to go home?"

"I don't know." I sighed. "It's not like I have an exit

strategy here. I'm sort of hoping that once I know enough about my magic, I'll be able to shield myself from anyone who comes looking. I could go home if I just knew I wouldn't be followed."

"Can't Mary—"

"No." The word came out sharper than I meant for it to. I stood, picking up our empty plates, and said, "There are some serious limits to what Mary can and can't do for me. Actually teaching me is off the table. So is doing that sort of a favor. I'd need to make a bargain for that."

Sam pulled a face. Interesting. I had never asked whether the füri had a tradition of crossroads bargains. Looked like they did.

"No," he said. "Let's not do that."

"Agreed. Let's not." I started down the path, which had been stylized to look like it was made from frosting, flanked by springy gumdrops. Too much time in Candyland could make me feel like I needed to eat the entire world. "We can't cut through Fairyland, so it's back to the hub from here, and then on to the Deep-Down. I think you'll like the mermaids, and the Drowned World coaster is supposed to be one of the better ones in Florida. It's definitely the only one with actual sharks as part of the ride environment—"

I chattered as I walked, trusting Sam to follow me. We were doing this for him, after all. I liked the Park, but with Fairyland off the menu, I would already have been in the Deep-Down, hanging out with the phantom pirates and eating endless buckets of chicken at Mother Carey's Seaside Barbecue. Sam was the one who wanted to see absolutely everything that Lowryland had to offer, and I was merely his willing guide.

I was so focused on telling him about our next steps that I didn't hear the cracking until it turned into a splintering roar, followed by the sound of children screaming. I whipped around. The top of one of the taffy-flower trees—a plastic-and-steel rebar brainchild of Lowry's engineering division—had snapped off, and was plummeting toward a pair of kids holding plates of gingerbread. They couldn't have been more than seven, and they were watching the tree fall with the dull-eyed resignation of the walking dead. They knew this was how they ended.

A brown blur slammed into them from the side, knocking them out of the way before the tree could crush them. Their screams turned into the open-throated sobs of frightened children everywhere. Sam—because it could only have been Sam; no one and nothing else moved that fast—didn't stop or slow down. He kept moving, into the shadows of the artificial forest.

By the time he popped out again, I knew what he was about to do, and I was braced. Dropping our plates into the trash bin, I raised my arms, like I was preparing to be caught on the trapeze. He grabbed onto me with surprising delicacy, wrapping one arm around my torso and his tail around my waist, and I was borne up, away from the ground, into the distant spires of Lowry's closed and smoke-singed Fairyland.

Sixteen

"One of these days, something is going to
go right. But probably not today."
—Jane Harrington-Price

Lowryland, about to have a very unpleasant afternoon

SAM DIDN'T STOP RUNNING until we were well away
from the crowds and standing under the awning of
the Midsummer Night's Scream waiting area. The small,
bus stop-like structure was intended for use by families
of riders, people whose health wasn't good enough or
height wasn't great enough to endure the multiple drops
and inversions.

He let go of me, stepping away. "Cameras?" he asked,
huffing and puffing all the while.

"What?" I blinked at him for a moment before I
realized—with horror and dawning dismay—that he
hadn't shifted back to his faux-human form. He was still
simian, clearly fūri. "Sam, change back."

"Are there cameras here?" He leaned forward, putting his hands on his knees. It wasn't nearly as pro-
nounced a lean as it would have been for a human his
height and build. Still struggling to get his breath back,
he asked, "Is anyone recording this?"

Something was wrong. I looked frantically around,
comparing the angles of the roof to the known locations
of the surrounding cameras, before I said, "No. We
passed at least six getting here, but there aren't any cameras focused on this spot."

"Good." He straightened up, wheezing a little, and said, "Get me out of here."

"Can you—"

"No."

The word was simple, direct, and changed everything. I looked around again, mentally comparing what I knew of the Park layout to what I knew of the camera array. Fern and I had spent a cheerful week learning the location of most of the hidden cameras before we'd started skating in the Park, using that as a guide to where she could and couldn't play games with density.

Like all major theme parks, Lowryland is incredibly focused on guest safety and security, and figured out long ago that cameras were both cheaper and less distracting than security patrols. If you're in a public area, or more importantly, on a ride, someone is watching. It keeps graffiti and shoplifting under control, and prevents people from doing things they shouldn't while the rides are in motion. But there are blind spots. Even the most comprehensive camera array in the world can't be everywhere.

Most of the rides had cameras on the areas people were able to access easily, preventing kids from slipping under barricades and falling into the artificial deep-sea vents in the Deep-Down, or climbing the conveyor system in Metropolis. But that was as far as they went. Putting cameras on an entire outdoor ride environment didn't make fiscal sense, and there was no way a guest could get to, say, the back of the Midsummer Night's Scream without tripping a few of the exterior cameras.

Unless they could go straight up to avoid the ground cameras entirely, that was.

"All right," I said. "Can you pick me up again?"

Sam didn't say anything. Only nodded.

"Okay. See that tree?" I pointed. "Look at the fourth branch up. That's the only camera aimed at the waiting area. It may not even be on, since the zone is closed, but we don't want to count on that. I need you to jump from here to the branch right below the camera. That should take us through the blind spot. Can you do that?"

"I hope so." Sam sounded uncertain. That was enough

to give me pause . . . but when he held out his hand, I still took it, letting him gather me in something that was between a bridal carry and the beginnings of a Fastball Special. He took a step backward, looking assessingly at the branch, and then he *leaped*.

Nothing human could have made that jump. Humans can be strong, swift, and athletic, but we don't have the raw muscle power of our simian cousins. Sam had the strength. Even then, he might not have been able to hit his mark, if he hadn't spent his entire life training for the trapeze. Everything we are in any given moment is the sum of our experiences and choices up until then, and as we flew through the air with me clinging to his arms, I was temporarily glad that the fire in my fingers had fled. My nerves were so frayed that I would definitely have burned him otherwise.

He landed on the branch so lightly it barely rocked. I pressed a finger to my lips, signaling him to silence, and pointed to a point on the roller coaster's environmental shell that was just outside the range of what guests were assumed to be able to reach.

Florida's weather, while generally warm, is unpredictable enough that building fully outdoor roller coasters is a gamble. Sure, they look impressive, but there's always a chance a storm will roll in and shut them down during the busy season, and any exposed track is likely to require triple the maintenance. The Midsummer Night's Scream was constructed almost entirely inside a plastic and fiberglass "mountain" covered with real soil and real plants, including a blackberry tangle wide and wild enough that it had to be cut back weekly to keep it from getting out of control. The coaster train only emerged into the open air three times during the ride, twice in plain sight of the viewing area. That was enough to keep families mollified, and the controlled ride environment inside the mountain made it substantially easier to control the overall experience. Everyone walked away happy.

Right now, the mountain was serving a different purpose: cover. Sam leaped from the branch to the point I'd indicated, and then again when I pointed for the second time, into the heart of the blackberry snarl. The landscaping team had a private entrance there, right where the vines grew thickest. They used it for pruning the bushes without affecting what guests saw, since management wanted the Midsummer Night's Scream to look like an untouchable fairy wilderness.

That was working in our favor. If there was one place in Lowryland where I *knew* there wasn't a camera, it was here.

Sam put me down as soon as we landed, huffing and puffing again. I took a step backward to give him room, stopping when the briars behind me poked my shoulder. His tail curled and uncurled around his ankle, betraying his anxiety more clearly than anything else about him.

"What's wrong?" I demanded.

"I don't *know*." He gave me a half-panicked look. "I keep trying to go back, and I can't. It's like that part of my brain isn't working anymore."

"Okay. We can deal with this. We're out of range of the cameras, we're—"

"How are we going to deal with this?" he snapped. "You can't even start a fire!"

I gave him a hurt look. "Sam, I'm trying to help. Please don't yell at me."

"Sorry. I'm—I'm sorry. I just don't know what to do." He rubbed his face with one hand. "This has never happened to me before."

"Getting stuck?"

He nodded, face still covered. I realized that he hadn't looked directly at me since we'd landed here, not even when he was snapping at me.

Stepping slightly forward—we were in close quarters, but he'd still managed to put distance between us when he put me down—I gently gripped his wrist and tugged. He was stronger than I was. He could have resisted me. He didn't. Instead, he let me lower his arm, revealing the anxious, almost trapped expression in his eyes.

"Hey." I didn't let go of his wrist. "We'll fix this."

"What if we don't? What if this is something that *happens* to fūri eventually, and nobody told me, because my

dad is off in China somewhere, and my mom didn't leave a forwarding address or instructions on where to find him? What if I was supposed to start hiding from people months ago, to keep from being surrounded when the switch snapped?"

"Okay, breathe. If fūri got stuck in one shape or another, it would have been in my family's records, and it's not. Grandpa Thomas wrote about visiting a whole neighborhood of fūri in Hong Kong before he settled in Michigan, and he didn't say 'but the grandparents never changed shapes, so I guess they couldn't,' and that's not the sort of detail he would have missed. This isn't just something that happens."

"Then why is it happening *now*?"

"I don't know," I said. "Why can't I set things on fire? Something's wrong. But Sam, if you were going to get stuck, this is the best place in the world to do it. All we have to do is avoid Security. Any guests who see you will think you're with one of the shows."

Sam didn't look impressed by my logic. He twisted his wrist out of my grip and I let him go, although not without regret. His body language was hunched, closed down, and the anxiety in his eyes was quickly mounting toward a full-blown panic. I had never regretted the difference in our species more. Maybe if I'd been a fūri, I would have known what to do, what the little, difficult to articulate touches were that would let me unlock the door to his fear and let the shadows out.

Or maybe I did know. I'd been scared for a long time about someone discovering the fire in my fingers, alternately wishing it away and wishing it on everyone else, wishing for an X-Men world where we'd all have weird powers and no one would be different.

(And knowing that it wouldn't have changed a damn thing, because we already *do* live in an X-Men world. Artie is an empath with pheromones that make him endlessly attractive to anyone who likes guys and isn't a close relative, which is why he spends all his time locked in his basement. Elsie is a persuasive telepath, and her blood makes people horny and possessive. Sarah is ...

Sarah is Sarah. Add in the dead aunts and the dimension-hopping grandmother and we're already a comic book, and it's never made anything easier. Not for a second.)

"Sam." I reached for him again, this time resting the back of my fingers against his cheek. He closed his eyes, leaning into the touch. Thankfully. I don't know what I would have done if he'd recoiled from me. "We'll figure it out."

"And if you can't?"

"Then we'll figure out a way to get you safely back to Indiana, and I'll come for you as soon as I can."

His eyes snapped open. "What?"

He looked so startled that I actually laughed, which could have been the exact wrong thing to do. I hesitated. He didn't pull away. I risked a smile.

"What, you think you can get rid of me just because you stopped shaving? Please. My cousin Artie is one of my best friends, and he hasn't seen the sky without coercion in years. Literally years. If you took him outside at noon and didn't slather him in sunscreen, he'd probably burst into flames." I kept smiling. "I've never asked you to stay human before I would kiss you, have I? It'll mean spending a little more time apart, but whatever. It's not like we don't know how to do that. I think it's most of what we've done so far."

Relief flooded over Sam's face. His tail wrapped tight around my waist and he pulled me toward him, virtually yanking me into an embrace. I didn't resist, not then, and not when he started kissing me, hands against the sides of my face, tail tightening as if to make absolutely sure that I knew better than to try going anywhere.

When he finally pulled back, he rested his forehead against mine and said, "Thank you."

"It's okay," I assured him. "We've been through enough. I'm not letting you go over something this small."

"You call this 'small'?" He held up one long-fingered hand. "This is all of me."

"That's what I said." I grinned briefly before sobering. "But it's all of you that we need to get out of here. Lowryland doesn't allow adults to wear costumes."

Sam snorted. "Good thing I'm not wearing a costume, huh?"

"Yeah." I turned to look thoughtfully at the maintenance door. "I have an idea. Ever seen *Alien*?"

Sam blinked.

It's technically a violation of, oh, several dozen Lowry Entertainment, Inc. rules to take non-employees into the tunnels under the Park. Punishable by immediate termination, fines, black mark on your record, yadda, yadda, everything is awful. But at the end of the day, they'd have to catch me before they could do anything about it.

The tunnels leading to Fairyland were largely deserted, since maintenance still happened at night, even when there were closures on Park property. The process of restoring the street to its pre-accident condition would be swift, efficient, and most of all, unseen. Anything that could break the illusion that Lowryland was a magical kingdom where nothing ever went wrong would be concealed from the eyes of our paying guests, because without them, the Park might as well burn.

I inched in first, looking around to be sure I was alone before beckoning for Sam to join me. The sound of the door closing behind him seemed impossibly loud. I winced, waiting for footsteps to come running in our direction. When they didn't, I relaxed marginally and pointed upward, indicating the supports and pipes running across the ceiling.

"Most of those should hold your weight," I whispered. "If something seems unstable, move on to the next one, and keep moving. As long as you don't fall . . ."

"You'd make a hot space marine," he said, and kissed my cheek before jumping nimbly up to the ceiling, catching hold of the pipes with hands, feet, and tail. He had to pull himself into what was virtually a crawl, rather than dangling with bent knees, but once he was done, he was far enough up that no one was going to see him by mistake. I hoped.

I blew him a kiss and started walking.

This wasn't a tunnel section I was familiar with, but the people in charge of Lowryland's subterranean layout learned long ago that getting employees lost wasn't good for anybody. All the thoroughfares are constructed along as simple and straightforward a pattern as possible, and while there aren't any maps, there are little architectural quirks that can be used for orientation if necessary.

(As for why there are no maps, well, if a guest *did* somehow manage to get into the tunnels, we *wanted* them to get lost. Not permanently, "open a missing persons case" levels of lost, but lost enough that they'd think twice before going through any more forbidden doors. We got one or two kids in the tunnels every season, usually people who'd read about them online and couldn't wait to see the secret side of Lowryland for themselves. They forgot that some things are secret for a reason.)

Sam moved like a shadow on the ceiling above me, making my joking *Alien* comparison a little more unnerving. Every time I caught a glimpse of his tail from the corner of my eye, I would stiffen momentarily, until I remembered it was my boyfriend and not a murderous xenomorph.

"Definitely a Halloween costume to keep in mind," I muttered.

There isn't much cell signal in the tunnels. Phone calls were right out, but text messages could generally get through. I pulled out my phone as I walked, keying in Cylia's number before texting a quick request for her to come and pick up me plus a guest—and to bring something with a hood. Hopefully, she'd be curious enough to actually show up, and compassionate enough to bring what I'd asked for. If she wasn't there when we emerged, we'd figure something out. Figuring something out is sort of what it means to be a Price.

The unfamiliar tunnels gave way to more familiar ones, and I kept walking. The sound of conversation from up ahead drifted back to greet us. I tensed and kept going as a Metropolis food service crew passed, some of them nodding genially in my direction. I didn't recognize any of their faces. That didn't matter. If I was down here, moving with purpose, I was a cast member, and if I was a cast member, I was family. We didn't all like each other. We still had to stand together against the endless tide of tourists and demands.

Once they were out of sight behind me, I glanced at the ceiling and flashed Sam a thumbs-up. He returned the gesture, looking relieved. Maybe this was going to work after all.

"Well, well, well," said a voice. "If it isn't Princess Melody. Slumming, your highness?"

"Hello, Robin," I said, turning to face her. *Don't let her look up,* I thought. *Distract her so she doesn't look up.* "What are you doing down here?"

"Unlike some people, I still have to work for a living," she snapped. She was in the paper doll primary colors of Chapter and Verse, the exaggerated stitches on the sleeves dyed yellow, which meant she was working somewhere near Aspen and Elm. She wasn't one of their handmaids. That was a much more flattering costume. That mattered; she knew I lived with Fern, and I wouldn't have wanted to wind her up before sending her off to spend a shift with my roommate.

"Oh, right. You weren't in Fairyland yesterday, since they stopped scheduling us together after we reached the mutually assured destruction stage. I got the day off because I wound up covered in blood after I ran to help our guests—helping people. That's not something you'd know much about, is it?" I offered her a sugary smile. "I earned this break. Sorry you didn't."

"Seems like you just happen to 'earn' everything good, and I don't earn anything." Robin took a step forward, back suddenly straight, shoulders suddenly hunched. She wasn't taller than I am—few women are—but she was a pretty sizable girl. She could do some damage, if she decided she wanted to.

On some level, I wanted her to try. I hadn't been in a proper brawl in months. At least when I'd been with the Covenant, and then with the carnival, I'd been able to keep myself in shape, sparring with people and bouncing off the walls. Since coming to Lakeland, I'd been taking my training where I could find it—and where I could find it came with a shameful lack of punching things.

Plus I knew I could put her down in under a minute if I had to. That was the problem. No matter what the movies say, knocking someone unconscious is a dangerous game. I'd either need to crack her skull without breaking it, or cut off the blood supply to her brain without doing permanent damage. One slip, and I could kill her. Not something to do lightly, and not something to do when I was trying to sneak Sam out unseen. I couldn't forget the fact that he was clinging to the ceiling above me, and *would* get involved if he felt he needed to.

Quick and clean. That was the plan.

"Maybe if you were nicer to people, people would be nicer to you," I said.

"Who're you to talk? You don't *have* any friends, except for the little blonde bubble girl. What, did you steal her from a cult somewhere?"

"Don't talk about Fern like that."

"I'll talk about Fern any way I damn well please, and you won't stop me." Robin peeled her lips back in a sneer. "She's a freak, and so are you. Good, honest people shouldn't have to look at your kind when we're in a place like Lowryland."

"Pretty sure Michael Lowry would say we were the ones he built it for. The ones who needed it, and not the ones who wanted it."

"Pretty sure Michael Lowry's dead," said Robin, and swung for my face.

By the time her fist was there, I wasn't anymore. She overswung and stopped, looking puzzled.

"Come back here," she snapped.

"What, so you can hit me? I don't think so."

She swung again. I dodged again. It would have been funny, if she hadn't been getting so much more progressively frustrated. It was like sparring with one of my parents, back when I'd been an eight-year-old ball of rage and ambitions, with reflexes that couldn't quite keep up with what I wanted them to do. They'd always given me a few easy ones to evade before they started really trying to hit me, letting me find my rhythm, letting me feel like I could win.

Only here, there was no "letting" about what Robin was doing. She was pulling out her best moves, and had no idea why I was evading them with such ease. There were tears in her eyes when she made her third swing, again missing me by a country mile. That seemed to be the last straw: she stopped attacking and stood there, glaring daggers at me.

"What are you?" she demanded.

"A former cheerleader," I replied. "We learn to dodge."

Robin shook her head in disgust. "You're *never* going to be a Lowry girl. Never. You'll always be an outsider, and we're never going to let you in."

"I don't need you to," I said. "I've got friends, and I've got plans, and right now, I've got places to be. Leave me alone, all right? That's all I've ever wanted you to do."

Robin sniffed, and for a moment, I thought she was going to do something else—apologize, maybe, or attack me again. It could have gone either way, and either way had the potential to be interesting, because either way had the potential to change things.

Instead, she sneered, "I have a shift," and walked on down the tunnel, heading for Chapter and Verse. I waited until her footsteps had faded before glancing up.

Sam wasn't there.

Panic had time to grip my chest, acid-bright and electric, before he stuck his head out of one of the electrical vents on the ceiling and said, in a loud whisper, "You could fit a whole squad of boy scouts in this thing."

"Sam, what . . . ?"

"If you put her on the floor, I didn't want her to look up and think she was hallucinating the giant monkey." He pulled himself out of the vent, dangling by his arms for a moment before he got feet and tail wrapped back around their respective grips and had recovered his previous flat position. "Besides, it let me rest my arms for a second. Are all your coworkers that sweet?"

"She's the sweetest," I said. I started walking again. Above me, Sam matched my stride, moving with an inhumanly fluid ease. "I keep to myself, and I don't play social games. For some people, that makes me weird, and possibly a threat. As long as they don't start putting poison in my bag lunches, I don't care."

"You don't like people much."

"Neither do you."

Sam laughed darkly. "I guess that's why we like each other."

I smiled, keeping my head down, and kept walking.

We reached the narrow, near-abandoned tunnel that Fern had shown me after the accident. After we had turned the first corner, out of view of the main passageway and well clear of anyone else looking to get to work, I glanced up.

"You can come down now," I said. "It should be safe."

"Thank God." Sam dropped to floor level, landing in a crouch before straightening up and beginning to massage his hands. "I thought I was going to get a cramp."

"On the plus side, your position on this season of *American Ninja Gladiator* is pretty much secure."

"You don't think they'll call the tail cheating?"

"They may want you to tie a weight to it or something."

"Fun for the whole family." He looked at me sidelong, and smiled, almost shyly. "Thanks again for helping me out of here."

"That's what I'm here for." I could feel my cheeks getting red. People being consistently glad to see me was a weird enough experience these days to be a little weird and embarrassing. I was going to have to get used to it if Sam was going to stick around—and I wanted Sam to stick around. I wanted it more than I would ever have been able to admit to myself two days ago.

"Not just that," he said, wrapping his tail loosely around my left wrist while he kept rubbing his hands. I flashed him a smile. We walked on.

At the end of the tunnel, I gently unwound his tail from around my wrist and turned to face him. "Okay, this is what happens next," I said. "I'm going to go out and see if my friend Cylia brought you that hoodie. If she's there, and if she did, we're in the clear. If either of those things is missing, we'll figure it out. Either way, we're not on Lowry property anymore, so things should get a little easier."

"Who's Cylia?" Sam asked warily.

Crap. That was the step I'd forgotten. "She's someone I skate with back at home," I said. "She's trustworthy, I promise."

He relaxed. "So she's not human, but you don't want to say she's not human because that's her business, not mine," he said. "Cool. I mean, you kind of have to tell her right now, me being furry and everything, but you don't gotta tell me until she's comfortable with it."

"Exactly." I kissed his cheek—quick and light—and opened the door, letting the summer sunlight come slanting in. It was brighter than I expected, almost blinding after the dimness of the tunnels. I squinted.

There was an avocado-colored muscle car parked at the curb.

Silently thanking every deity I could come up with for Cylia's lack of a local social life, I trotted over the dusty ground between me and the street. The window was already down when I reached the car. I leaned inside. Cylia gave me a look split evenly between worry and curiosity.

"Everything okay?" she asked.

"Did you bring the hoodie?" I asked.

She nodded before leaning into the back seat and pulling out a cloak. An actual *cloak*, the sort of thing Alex used to wear when he was going off to war with his SCA buddies. (Because pretending to go to war on the weekend was absolutely a fun thing when there was always the chance of the Covenant of St. George bringing the war home to us. Yes. Fun, and not weird and a little questionable. Really.)

"We have some pre-game shtick involving Merlin and the tree and it's a long story, but will this work?" She thrust the cloak at me. I took it.

It was easily six feet long, and while the fabric was

heavy enough to cause heat stroke if worn for long in this climate, Sam wasn't going to be wearing it for long. "It's perfect," I said. "I'll be right back."

I turned then, running back across the ground to the tunnel opening. The door was cracked slightly, and I could see Sam peeping out. When I was close enough, I grabbed it, hauled it open, and thrust the cloak at him.

"Put this on," I commanded.

"What the—whoa. You have friends with wizard cloaks in their closets? Just like, lying around?" He looked at it for a moment, bewildered, before swinging it around himself and fastening the clasp. "I am *super nerd*," he breathed, with actual reverence. Then he pulled the hood up.

It couldn't conceal the fact that his features weren't quite human, but it blunted the effect enough that if we didn't stop for burgers, we'd be fine. "You are super nerd," I agreed warmly, and pushed the door open. "There's the car."

"Got it," he said, and took off running.

Sam's speed wasn't as much of a factor on flat ground—he was a leaper, not a sprinter—but it was still impressive to watch him running full-tilt toward Cylia's waiting car. I followed, pausing only long enough to be sure that the door was latched and wasn't going to swing open again as soon as we were gone. The last thing I wanted to add to today's pile of troubles was a reprimand for leaving one of the exits open. Then I turned, and I ran.

Sam reached the car at least fifteen feet ahead of me, grabbing the back door and throwing himself bodily inside. I put on a little extra speed, slowing only when I reached the car. I slammed the back door before opening the front and sliding myself into the seat next to Cylia. Sam was a fabric-swaddled lump in the back, the hood pulled down until it covered his face completely. Cylia was looking at him with curiosity, and not asking. The sound of her not asking was almost loud enough to fill the car.

"Okay," I said. "We're clear. Sam, this is Cylia, the friend I told you about. Cylia, this is Sam, my boyfriend."

"You finally got a boyfriend? Damn." Cylia's tone

was light, but her face remained worried. "Elmira's going to owe me so much money when we get home."

"Miracles happen. Sam? It's okay to pull the hood back a little. I promise Cylia won't freak, and I don't want you to suffocate."

"I got the air-conditioning fixed yesterday, on a hunch, but this is still Florida," said Cylia.

"Okay . . ." said Sam warily, and pulled the hood back, enough to show Cylia the shape of his features, the furry streaks along his cheekbones.

Cylia gasped.

Sam had time to look hurt—and I had time to question the wisdom of being in this car—before she shook her head, putting her hands up, palms outward, one toward me and one toward him.

"So you're a fūri, that's fine, good for you, and Annie, good for you, too, you found a boyfriend with bones that are really hard to break, I'm babbling, sorry, I just . . . what *happened* to you?"

"Not sure what you're talking about, not sure I want to sit here while you explain it to me," said Sam darkly.

"It's not the fūri thing, I swear!" protested Cylia. "It's your luck."

"What about his luck?" I asked.

Something in my voice must have told Cylia that she was treading on thin ice. She looked at me and shook her head.

"It's gone," she said. "His luck is *gone*."

Seventeen

"The thing to remember about allies is that they want you to be an ally right back. If you're not a friend to your friends, you're going to be an enemy eventually."

–Alice Healy

Lakeland, Florida, at the warehouse home of the Lakeland Ladies

WE ARRIVED AT THE warehouse to find the Lakeland Ladies in the middle of practice, circling the track with a familiar rattle of wheels and exchange of breathless, amiable insults. Walking into that wall of sound was like a short, sharp slap. For a moment—only a moment—I was back in Portland, watching my own team get ready for a bout, and all I needed to do was strap on my skates and the world would start making sense again.

The moment passed. The skaters were strangers. The team banners on the wall were unfamiliar, local logos and local colors and nothing that belonged to me. Most importantly of all, Sam was holding my hand, fingers so tight that my own fingers throbbed a little from the lack of circulation. I didn't pull away or ask him to lighten up. He was scared, confused, and in the company of a woman he didn't know—Cylia, who was leading us across the warehouse, toward the stairs. If he needed to squeeze my hand a little too tight to get through this, I was going to let him.

A few of the skaters noticed us, and waved. Cylia waved back. "Just passing through!" she called. "Need to deal with some personal shit!"

"Did you bring us fresh meat?" asked one of the derby girls. She was looking at me assessingly, studying me with an expression that bordered on avarice. "She ever skate before?"

"Yes, she skates, and no, she's not here to try out," said Cylia. She didn't slow down, and so Sam and I didn't either. We needed to get out of this open, human-filled space before his lack of luck caused his cloak to snag on something and get pulled aside. "She's an old friend, and we gotta go."

"Aw," chorused a couple of the derby girls.

"Come back soon, fresh meat," called another.

"Why do they keep calling you that?" whispered Sam. He sounded half freaked-out and half annoyed, which was sort of endearing. It had been a long time since anyone had wanted to defend my honor.

"That's what new derby girls are always called," I said. "I haven't been fresh meat for years. I'm old and tough and sort of spoiled now."

"Best description of you I've ever heard," said Cylia.

We climbed the stairs to her small apartment, which was standing unlocked. I gave her a curious look. She shrugged.

"I leave it open during practice. I know none of the girls would steal anything—I don't have anything worth stealing except for my laptop, and if that went missing, the team captains would move Heaven, Earth, and Purgatory to get it back—and this way they have access to my shower if they need it. That's always been the policy with the overhead apartments, which is part of why they try to only rent to derby family. No one wants to lose access to a hot shower."

All that made sense to me. "Right," I said.

From the look on Sam's face, none of it made sense to him. He was smart enough not to argue. Under the circumstances, we didn't have that luxury.

Cylia's apartment was small enough to be compact, cozy, or cramped, depending on living preferences. The living room was about the size of my bedroom back home, with doors leading off it to the kitchen and even smaller bedroom. Everything was decorated in early thrift store, with a comfortable-looking, overstuffed couch given pride of place in front of the ancient television. It reminded me, in its piecemeal way, of home.

"Bathroom's through there," said Cylia, indicating the bedroom door. She closed the door, thumbed the deadbolt, and turned to Sam. "All right. Drop the cloak. Let me get a look at you."

Sam shot me an uncertain glance. I nodded, trying to project encouraging vibes, and he unfastened the cloak, letting it fall from his shoulders.

Cylia frowned, scanning him up and down before looking him dead in the eyes and saying, "My name is Cylia Mackie. I am a jink, which means I'm as inhuman as you are, just slightly better at hiding it. I won't say you can trust me, because I don't know you well enough to make that kind of promise. I will tell you that Annie trusts me, and you wouldn't be standing here, with her, if she didn't believe I could help. Will you let me try to help?"

"Sure," said Sam, uncomfortably.

I didn't say anything. Cylia was right that we wouldn't have been here if I hadn't trusted her—although being trapped in Lowryland with no car and a boyfriend who had suddenly lost the ability to change shapes had made my definition of "trust" a lot more flexible. Cylia was nonhuman and could drive. Right now, that made her the most trustworthy person I knew.

Cylia stepped toward Sam, reaching toward him like she was approaching a skittish animal. At the last moment before she would have actually pressed her hand against his chest, she stopped reaching and swept her fingers downward, through the air a bare inch or so from his skin. She stepped back again, frowning, and stuck her index and middle fingers in her mouth.

"This is weird," said Sam.

"Life is weird," I said.

"It's *gone*," said Cylia, around her fingers. She pulled them out of her mouth, scowling, and said, "Your luck is *gone*."

"That's what you said in the car," said Sam. "You

didn't explain what it meant then, and you're not explaining what it means now."

"I mean . . . oh, hell." Cylia scowled for a moment before she said, "Neither of you is a jink, so neither of you can see luck. That means there's going to be a certain amount of 'take my word for it' in what I'm about to say. Can you do that for me?"

"We can try," I said.

"Okay. This sort of thing goes better when you have something to do with your hands. Follow me." She turned and walked into the kitchen, where a card table was shoved up against the wall. There were three folding chairs already waiting there. Had this been anyone but Cylia, I might have thought she'd planned our visit. As it was, I knew that she'd just gotten lucky.

I settled with my back to the wall. Sam sat in the chair on the long edge of the table. After a moment, he scooted it around so that he was next to me, both of us crammed into a space that was barely big enough for one. I patted his knee reassuringly, and he responded by wrapping his tail around my ankle, holding me in place, keeping me where he was. I made no attempt to pull away.

Cylia went to the fridge and returned with a Tupperware pitcher filled with distressingly pink liquid and three matching glasses. "Hibiscus lemonade," she said, putting the glasses down and filling them. "Drink. The sugar will help."

"Can I get that in writing to show my grandmother?" Sam asked, taking one of the glasses. "She likes to say that having a grandson who can literally climb on the ceiling justifies keeping the sugar levels low in our house."

"The sugar will help you regenerate your luck," Cylia said. "I can't speak to hyperactivity."

"Oh."

I took one of the glasses. The lemonade was toothachingly sweet, but tasty all the same. "What do you mean, the sugar will help regenerate his luck?"

"All right." Cylia sat. "This is where we get into things that you're going to have to take my word for, because you literally don't have the senses to understand them."

"Huh?" said Sam.

"Jinks and mara—their cousins—have an extra organ in their brains," I said. "It's sort of like the electroreceptor organs you find in sharks. It lets them see things that are invisible to the rest of us."

"Like luck?" asked Sam dubiously. "That doesn't sound like a real thing."

"If everything that didn't sound real would have the decency to stop existing, the world would be reduced to what could be reasonably detected by a jellyfish, and I wouldn't need to pay my water bill," said Cylia. "Jinks see luck. It's everywhere, on everything. It . . . accretes like dust, sticking to whatever it touches until it rubs off, or gets used up, or blows away. Luck isn't a thing you earn. It's a thing you have."

"Isn't that distracting?" asked Sam.

"Is color vision distracting? Because there are people who don't have that, and they probably think the rest of us are weird, the way we run around seeing red and green all the time. How about depth perception? Or any of the other things that vision can do? I was born seeing the luck, and so it's normal to me. If you took it away, *that* would become distracting." Cylia laughed uncomfortably. "Right now, *you're* distracting. Looking at you is like looking at . . . like looking at a hole. There's no good, there's no bad, there's no nothing."

"How does that happen?" I asked.

"Before I can go into that, you need to understand a little more about how luck *works*," said Cylia. "Like I said, it sticks to you. Like attracts like, luck attracts luck, so someone whose innate luck is mostly good will get more good luck, and someone whose innate luck is mostly bad will get more bad luck. It isn't fair, but there it is. Babies are born with a thin sheen of their mother's luck on them. In jink communities, it's customary to visit an expectant mother every day and take away any bad luck that's managed to stick to her, so the baby can have the best seed luck possible. It doesn't always work. If the community's overall luck has turned bad, the best they can do is try to minimize the damage."

"Where does luck go?" asked Sam.

"You spend it," said Cylia. "Everyone does. It's a little more intentional for jinks, because we know what we're doing, but everyone does it. Say you're running for the bus, and you *know* you should be late, but you're *hoping*, so hard, that something will have slowed the bus down just a few seconds, so that you can catch it before it pulls away. If you have enough good luck banked up, it may burn off, and there's your bus. Lucky you."

"So why isn't everyone winning the lottery every day?" asked Sam.

I liked this. He was asking questions; he was involved. Better yet, I, as the sole human at this table, wasn't the one asking things that could be viewed as potentially invasive. Being a cryptozoologist is like being a zoologist crossed with an anthropologist, and knowing that there's always a chance your subjects will get offended and kick you out for something that seemed like it should have been perfectly innocuous.

Nothing is perfectly innocuous once a multi-century genocide gets involved. Nor should it be.

"Because when you burn good luck, the amount of good luck you have goes down, which makes it more likely that bad luck will come to fill the gap, and because people who aren't jinks burn luck without meaning to," said Cylia. "If you followed me for a week, you'd think I wasn't a very lucky person. I don't get the good parking or find the mislabeled pack of top sirloin in the discount bin. I don't score amazing dresses in just my size on the clearance rack. The little lucks that haunt normal life don't haunt mine, because I don't choose them. I save what I have, and I use it when I know that I have enough good luck to cover what I want *and* keep me from turning into a bad luck magnet."

"Huh," said Sam. "I . . . okay, I think I followed that. You only spend a dollar when you know you have five more."

"Basically," said Cylia. "Actually, that's a great way of looking at it. Most people don't know how much money they have in their pockets. If they find a dollar, they spend it. Jinks know how much we've got. We can make good choices about when to save and when to spend. And sometimes we spend even knowing it's going to get us hurt. Sometimes we say 'I have a lot of good luck, I'm going to spend it all at once, I'm going to break the world.'"

This time, I didn't say anything because I knew all too well what she was talking about.

My family picks up allies and claims them as relatives, in part because there are so few of us, and in part because making someone an honorary aunt or uncle marks them as ours—as protected—to the rest of the world. My Uncle Al in Las Vegas is like that. He's originally from a jink community that got hit by a Covenant purge. The adults spent every scrap of good luck they had managed to save over the course of their lifetimes in the cause of getting the kids out of there safely. All the kids got away. All the kids found new homes, new lives, and a second chance.

All the adults died. There was too much bad luck, too much backlash, and not a single one of them was able to get lucky enough to run.

"One of the reasons people don't always like jinks, no matter how hard we try to be good neighbors, is because we *can* see luck, which means we can *move* it. Say I looked at Annie and thought 'wow, she has so much good luck, she doesn't need all of that,' and thought I could make better choices with her luck than she could. I could take it." Cylia shrugged. "If I were being kind, I could take a little bit, and luck isn't only dollars: it's pennies, too. If I steal a penny from every person I see over the course of a day, I'll wind up with plenty, and none of them will notice the difference. An ethical jink will never damage the community around them."

"What about an unethical one?" asked Sam.

"An unethical jink could rip away every scrap of good luck you have and leave you with nothing but bad," said Cylia. "Like attracts like, which means more bad luck would come, and you'd probably catch that bus you were running for when it ran you over."

"So are you saying an unethical jink stole Sam's luck?" I asked.

"I wish I were," said Cylia. "We could deal with that.

Look, if I took your good luck, I'd leave the bad behind, and vice-versa. If I tried to take *both*, at the same time, it would be more than I could hold. I'd start bleeding back onto you. It is *impossible* for a jink to take all your luck, good and bad, at the same time—and even if a team decided to play some sort of fucked-up luck con on you, there'd be dust on you by the time they were done. Luck is a natural force of the universe, like gravity. It's everywhere. It's in the *air*. And you, my friend, have been scrubbed as clean as ... I don't even know. As clean as something very, very clean."

"Okay, hang on," I said carefully, while Sam was still gaping at her. "Can we fix this? Because not having *any* luck sounds like a bad thing."

"It's not a bad thing. It's not a good thing. It's a perfectly neutral thing, which is why it's going to turn into a bad thing."

Now both of us looked at her blankly. Cylia sighed.

"Okay. Say you open a door that has a fifty-fifty chance of triggering a booby-trap. Good luck, it doesn't happen. Bad luck, it does. Well, Sam is currently a third variable. He opens the door, nothing happens, not because he got lucky, but because the trap has somehow failed to register his presence. Which sounds like good luck, sure ... until someone with mostly bad luck comes into the building and all the traps go off at once. Or someone with mostly good luck comes into the building and the trap goes off, with Sam between it and its potential target. He's not even an inanimate object right now. He's a null spot. Other peoples' luck is going to use that."

"My head hurts," complained Sam. "How does this explain why I can't change back to looking human?"

"I have no idea, but I'm betting it has something to do with your luck being gone," said Cylia. "Good luck would have shielded you from the negative effects of whatever you were exposed to. Bad luck would have made you shift back to your normal form at the worst possible time. The fact that you were able to get out of Lowryland without an angry mob in close pursuit tells me that it's not a matter of the second."

"I changed to keep a couple of kids from getting hurt, and then I realized I was stuck," said Sam slowly. "I don't *know* that anyone saw me."

"Neutral situation," said Cylia.

"Okay," I said. "So why is this a bad thing?"

"Because we don't know why it happened, for one," said Cylia. "Because it's not natural. Everyone has luck, like everyone has gravity. Suddenly losing one of the basic concepts of the universe? Probably not a good thing. Most of all, because right now, he's clean, but luck collects on everything, and bad luck is more common, as a free-floating element, than good luck. People hoard good luck and do their best to let go of the bad. So statistically, whatever luck he rebuilds from here is more likely to be the bad kind. If you hadn't come to see me, I'd say he would have been a total bad luck bear inside of the week."

I stared at her.

Sam recovered first. "So how do we fix this?"

"Seed luck. I can spare a little. Annie ..." Cylia squinted at me. "She can spare a little less, maybe, but still, she can spare some. It's the difference between a worm in her apple and no worm in her apple."

"Which is the bad one?" asked Sam.

Cylia shrugged. "I don't judge. Anyway, if we give you some seed luck, you should be able to start rebuilding it on your own. Hell, you may wind up luckier than you started, since you'll be starting with mostly good luck."

Sam blinked. "What do you mean, 'mostly'?"

"No luck is pure."

"Okay," I said. "I'm happy to give some luck to the cause of Sam not getting creamed by a bus. What I want to know is, why does not having luck stop him from shifting shape?"

"Maybe it does, maybe it doesn't. We'll deal with that next." Cylia licked her finger, leaned over the table, and wiped it on Sam's bare arm. He made a disgusted noise, recoiling, and she answered it with a sunny smile. "Suck it up, buttercup. That's some luck for you. Good luck, high-octane stuff. Enjoy."

"Did it have to come with spit?" Sam demanded.

"Yes." Cylia turned to me, licking her finger again. "Give me your arm."

Wrinkling my nose, I did as I was told. "Soap," I said. "Soap and hot water and ew."

"You people are such babies," said Cylia, and swiped her finger down my arm—or started to, anyway. Midway through the motion she froze, eyes widening and face paling, until she looked like something out of an amateur theater company's haunted house.

"Cylia?" I asked warily.

She made a pained whimpering noise.

Right. That's the sort of thing that has never meant anything good. I yanked my arm back, breaking the connection between us. She slumped backward in her chair, breathing heavily through her nose.

"Cylia?" I asked again. "You okay?"

"Fuck *me*," she said. Her voice was huskier than it had been before, pitched so low in her throat that it was almost a rumble. She reached for her glass of lemonade, hand shaking so badly that she nearly knocked it over in the process of getting a grip on it.

Sam and I watched in silence as she lifted the glass, took a deep drink, and closed her eyes, her breathing slowly returning to normal. After more than a minute had passed, she put her glass down and opened her eyes, looking at us gravely.

"It's you," she said, jerking her chin toward me. "You're the reason he can't shift back."

"What?" I asked, and "*What*?" Sam demanded, and neither of us moved, and I was so grateful for that that I could have cried. If he had jerked away from me, I would have understood the reasons—how could he not want to pull away, if his current condition was my fault? How could he want to be anywhere near me?—but I would never have been able to forget that it had happened. I would never be able to let it go.

"Okay." Cylia moved her first two fingers to her temples, rubbing briskly. "Okay. I . . . okay. Luck is not the only thing that exists and is invisible and intangible and moves around the world. You can't bottle gravity. Okay?"

"Okay," I said numbly.

"But if you do things right, if you set things up correctly, you can steal gravity. Make it weaker in one spot because you've made it stronger somewhere else. It's like moving luck, only harder, because luck is free-floating, while gravity is internally generated."

"I don't think that's how physics works," I said.

Cylia shot me a wry look. "Yeah, well, I didn't get a degree from metaphor school, all right? I had the luck stuff prepared. Tav and I wanted kids someday, and we knew I'd have to be able to explain it to them. This is uncharted ground for all of us."

"Sorry," I said.

"Don't worry about it," she said, with a quick shake of her head. "We're sticking with luck and gravity, because I don't feel like dealing with anything else. If you take all of someone's luck, they're screwed. They won't make more. They'll have to walk around luckless until enough of it sticks to them to give them a baseline again. If you take all of someone's gravity, on the other hand, or even *most* of someone's gravity, they'll make more, and they'll keep making more, which means you can harvest more. You can pull their gravity away again and again and again, because they'll always generate another batch. It's a renewable resource."

"What does this have to do with me not being able to switch back to human?" Sam demanded.

"Someone's harvesting her gravity." Cylia switched her attention to him, which felt like nothing so much as mercy. She was giving me space to absorb what I was about to hear. "When you lost your luck, you lost your barrier against whatever's funneling away her gravity—or something. I don't know what they're taking, but they're taking *something*, and whatever it is, it's similar enough to the energy you use to transform that when it felt you, it took that too. The good news is that it's an energy you generate on your own. If you stop touching her, it'll grow back."

"How long?" asked Sam gruffly.

Cylia shook her head. "I don't know."

"Sam, let go of my ankle." He turned to look at me,

eyes going wide. I smiled wanly. "Your tail. It's wrapped around my ankle. You need to let go. You're still touching me."

"But . . ." He stopped, catching himself, and unwound his tail, whisking it out of my reach.

I felt suddenly unmoored. I leaned away, pressing myself against the wall. If Sam hadn't been between me and the rest of the kitchen, I would have gotten up and started pacing. "Cylia, why did you react like that when you touched my arm?"

"Because whatever's sapping your energy and his energy tried to take mine. Only I pulled back, and it didn't know how to deal with it. It was tug-of-war with something I don't know and couldn't see, and I did *not* like it." Cylia shook her head. "Not one damn bit. Whatever trouble you're in this time, I don't know where it came from and I don't know how to fix it."

"But—"

"I'm a jink. If you break your luck, I can help. If you press your luck, I can at the very least point and laugh before the great gray cloud of karma settles around your head and devours you whole. I don't do weird unseen mystery energy-sucking bullshit, which is what this is." Cylia leaned back in her chair, a little farther away from me. "You need help. Not from me."

"Wait." Sam looked deeply frustrated. We both turned to him. He looked at me, then at Cylia. "I want to be sure I have this right. You're saying someone . . . someone *did* something to Annie that makes her some sort of energy vampire?"

"Yes, and no," said Cylia. "She's not the one who's sapping energy, and she's not *keeping* it either. She's more like . . . like a funnel attached to a vacuum cleaner than the vacuum cleaner itself. All the energy is passing through her and going somewhere else."

"And losing my luck is why this started happening now when it wasn't happening to me before?"

Cylia nodded. "Luck is like the body's ozone layer. It protects us from a lot of the ambient energies in the world. This . . . funnel, it's inside Annie, under her luck, sapping her energy. It couldn't reach you until your luck was gone. That's part of why jinks are dangerous. If someone could take all the world's luck away, we'd just be ghosts walking around in bodies we hadn't figured out how to put down yet."

Ghosts . . . I sat up a little straighter. "Can ghosts see luck?"

"Jink ghosts can," said Cylia. "They are *nasty* when they decide to haunt somebody. Human ghosts can't."

"So Mary wouldn't have noticed Sam's luck going away," I said. "It could have disappeared last night."

"No, it couldn't have," said Cylia.

This time, Sam and I turned to look at her. She shrugged.

"He's too clean, or was, until I flicked some of my own luck onto him. Whatever took his luck took it *all*, and took it within the last few hours. After that, it would only have been a matter of time before the energy that fuels his transformations ran out, if he was touching you."

Sam had been touching me all day, from the time we got to Lowryland until he'd swept those kids out of the path of yet another collapse. I was starting to think Lowryland had an infrastructure problem. . . .

Or maybe it had a luck problem.

"Do inanimate things have luck?" I asked.

"I told you, it's like dust. It sticks to everything. You'd think a table wouldn't have much cause for being lucky, but everything wants to exist. Everything wants to be treated well, to be remembered, to *endure*, even if the wanting isn't what we'd recognize as conscious. This glass isn't alive." She held up her drink. "That doesn't mean breaking would be good for it. So on some level, the glass 'wants' to be unbroken. If it has good luck, when I drop it, it'll land on the carpet—and if it misses and hits the linoleum, and *I* have good luck, I won't step on any of the shards."

"Luck is a lot more complicated than I expected it to be," I complained.

Cylia gave me a look that was half sympathetic, half entertained. "We tell jink kids luck is like math. You start by learning to add the good and subtract the bad, and then you learn how to keep the sums from ever getting too negative or too positive, and then you start doing calculus."

"I should introduce you to my cousin Sarah," I said, slumping in my chair. "She thinks the world is made of math, too."

"Because it is," said Cylia. "Yes, things have luck. Why?"

"We've been having weird equipment failures at Lowryland lately," I said. "There was the parade that Fern and I told you about. There was the deep fryer that blew. And the reason Sam shifted forms was to save some kids from getting squished when one of the fake trees collapsed. Those things are supposed to be unbreakable. If something's messing with the luck . . ."

"Pulling enough luck off of the inanimate could make it vulnerable," said Cylia thoughtfully. "Or it could be the sinkhole effect."

"Please don't use fancy terms like you think we're supposed to know them," said Sam sourly. "I just met you. I'm not hugely comfortable with *any* of this, and I really don't want to need a phrasebook to know what the hell you're talking about."

Cylia sighed, putting her glass down. "Okay. Something stripped all your luck away. We're agreed on that, right?"

"Yes," I said, before Sam could say anything else. He was in a bad mood, and I couldn't blame him. I was in a pretty rotten mood myself. But I'd known Cylia long enough to trust her, and he hadn't. Right now, that was making all the difference in the world.

I missed the feeling of his tail around my ankle and his hand in mine. I would have felt a little less unmoored, I thought, if something had been holding me down. I also missed the fire in my fingers. If anything should have brought it surging back, it was this . . . but it wasn't coming because it wasn't there. Because someone had been stealing it away from me.

If that someone was Colin, or anyone else from his little magical nursery school, I was going to show him that there was more than one way to set somebody on fire.

"When luck is removed, it creates ... Zeus, I don't have the words for this shit. It creates a blank spot. And for a little while, the *shock* of the removal will keep that blank spot blank. Hence you still being effectively a null-luck zone when you got here. Your body hadn't had the time to recover and start gathering luck again. With me?"

"Sure," said Sam. "Why the fuck not?"

Cylia didn't look like she appreciated his answer, but she pressed on. I silently vowed to buy her ice cream or something. "Once the shock wears off, the system will panic and begin gathering luck from any place that it can find it."

"Which means bad luck, right?" I asked.

"Yes and no."

For a moment, Sam and I were united in glaring at her. Cylia grimaced.

"I told you this was complicated," she said. "Look, if you're talking free-range luck, the bad kind is infinitely more common, and hence infinitely easier to find. But someone who has *no* luck won't just suck up the free-range stuff, they'll start pulling it off things that can't fight back. Inanimate things."

"Hang on," I said. "So what you're saying is that if what happened to Sam has happened to other people, and those people went to Lowryland, they might have pulled the luck off of parts of the Park trying to rebuild their own?"

"If they stayed long enough, yes." Cylia looked grim. "Which would mean *those* things would start gathering free-range luck, since they'd lack the self-awareness to go looking for intentional replacement luck, and they'd wind up with a big load of badness."

I rubbed my face with one hand. "I need to go."

"Where?" asked Sam. "I still can't transform."

"I know," I said. "But I need to get back to Lowryland."

Eighteen

"Never gamble with anything you're not willing to lose. The house doesn't always win, but there are some chances not worth taking."

–Mary Dunlavy

Lakeland, Florida, at the warehouse home of the Lakeland Ladies

"NO," SAID CYLIA CALMLY, taking another swig of her lemonade. She swallowed, sighed, and added, "I wish like hell I could risk something stronger, but you know what they say about day drinking. Once you start, it's a hop, skip, and a jump to waking up one day as a bartender in some crappy coastal tourist resort, shaking your denim-clad rear for tips. I like bartenders. I like denim miniskirts. But wow, do I hate tourists."

Sam and I both stared at her blankly. Finally, in a hesitant tone, Sam said, "I don't think *anyone* says that. Like, ever. I don't even believe that you've said that before just now."

Cylia shrugged. "Yet here we are."

My temper was beginning to boil. I narrowed my eyes, looking down the length of my nose at her, and pictured how nice she would look on fire. "What do you mean, 'no'?"

"I mean 'no.'" Cylia looked back at me. "I will not drive you back to Lowryland. I will not tell you which bus to take to get to Lowryland. I will not let you run out of here and ditch me with your fuzzy boyfriend while you go and get yourself killed. This is not a good idea. This is a bad idea."

"What makes you so sure I'm going to go and get myself killed?"

Cylia rolled her eyes so hard that for a moment, they looked like they were going to pop out of her head and roll away across the floor. "Please. First, I've met you. Second, you're currently a weird energy sink, and third, you have some of the most bizarre luck I've ever seen. You could get yourself killed walking to the 7-11 for chocolate milk. If you run out of here without a plan, you're going to end up dead, and how am I supposed to explain that to Fern?"

"I'd be more worried about how you were going to explain it to me," said Sam dourly. "Annie, why do you want to go back to Lowryland? It sounds like whatever's going on started there and . . . crap. I just answered my own question, didn't I?"

"Yeah, you did." I looked at Cylia. "How much do you know about human magic-users?"

"Enough to know that I don't know jack," she said. "They make magic, they use magic, sometimes a lot of things wind up on fire because of their magic, and there's never been a jink who could do what they do."

"Makes sense," I said. "Humans can't see luck the way jinks can."

"Everyone can move luck, but only we can see it."

I paused. "Uh, Cylia?"

"Yes?"

"Are you cool with dead people?"

Cylia blinked. "There are about a hundred different ways I can interpret that question, and none of them actually make any sense," she said. "What do you mean, exactly?"

"Annie has dead aunts," said Sam.

"Somehow, not helping," said Cylia.

"I need to ask someone a question, and it probably isn't you," I said. "Are you cool with dead people?"

"You mean ghosts?" Cylia shrugged. "I guess. One of my second cousins stuck around being a ghost for a few years before he went off to do whatever comes after ghosting. He was a pretty chill guy. Used to help me sneak into the movies."

"Great." I clapped my hands, chanting, "Betelgeuse, Betelgeuse, *Betelgeuse*."

"How many times do I need to tell you, that's borderline offensive and not a good way to summon a ghooooo . . ." Mary trailed-off mid-word, suddenly realizing that she was in an unfamiliar kitchen, standing in front of a total stranger. "Uh."

"It's okay, Aunt Mary," I said. "Cylia's from my roller derby league."

"Technically, no, but what's a little intrastate rivalry between friends?" Cylia offered Mary a bright smile that was only slightly strained around the edges. "I didn't know I was going to be hosting a party today. I would have done some cleaning up if I had."

"I don't care if she's from your roller derby league, pumpkin. Being a derby girl doesn't make somebody cool with the dead." Mary glanced at Sam, only now seeming to see his furry condition. She frowned. "Okay, what the hell is going on?"

"That's a really long story and I promise you'll get the whole thing, probably with footnotes and I may need to draw some flowcharts to make sure *I* understand it, but can you please do me a huge favor?" I flashed my brightest, most hopeful smile in her direction. "Can you see if you can find Aunt Rose?"

"Why?" Mary's eyes narrowed. "Antimony Timpani Price, you will tell me what's going on *right now*, or so help me—"

"Something stole all of Sam's luck and something different is sapping my magic, which is why I can't set anything on fire, and when I touched him after his luck was gone, the thing that's been stealing my magic stole his . . . whatever the fuck it is that therianthropes use when they transform, so he's currently stuck all monkeyed-out, which means we can't *go* anywhere and he nearly got caught on camera by Lowry Security, so I need to talk to Aunt Rose and find out whether a routewitch could do any of this, because it's going to make a difference for what happens next."

The words poured out of me in a messy rush. Mary stared at me. So did Sam and Cylia. I shrugged, spreading my hands helplessly, and said nothing.

Mary turned her eyes heavenward. "Sometimes I wonder why I don't move on," she muttered, and vanished.

"All right, before the dead woman comes back to my apartment and *what* the *hell* is this day even *doing*, I want you to explain," snapped Cylia. "*Now*."

"Mary is a crossroads ghost," I said. "She always knows where her family is, and she's been with us for three generations now. She has a vested interest in me staying alive."

"Well, that's just dandy. Invite the crossroads over for coffee. Sounds great to me."

I shook my head. "She's a ghost, not a guardian. She doesn't set up the deals. She speaks on behalf of the person trying to make them, and tries to minimize the damage, if she's allowed. No member of my family has gone to the crossroads to make a deal since my grandfather." What had happened to Grandpa Thomas had been enough to make every member of the family since listened when Mary told us to be careful. We liked this dimension. We wanted to stay in it.

"Okay," said Cylia slowly. "And Rose is . . . ?"

"Rose Marshall."

Sam turned to stare at me. "Rose *Marshall*."

I nodded.

"The girl in the diner."

"They call her that in some places, sure."

"The girl in the green silk gown."

"I think that one's a little more common on the coasts these days. We don't have as many diners. But yes, that's her."

"The phantom—"

"—prom date," finished a new voice, as my Aunt Rose appeared in the middle of the kitchen, hands shoved into the back pockets of her faded jeans, head canted at a hard angle. Aunt Mary was a silent presence behind her, watching as Rose said, "Wow, Annie, you went and found a fellow who knew *all* the stories. Impressive. Did you notice the part where he's a monkey? Because I don't know about you, but that would make a bit of a difference for me."

"You're dating your car," I said, and smiled in sweet relief. "Hi, Aunt Rose."

"Hi, yourself," she said, and smiled back.

Like Mary, Rose died young. A lot of ghosts did, or at least look like they did: since their appearance is malleable, the dead tend to settle at whatever age they felt most comfortable when they were alive. A ghost who looks sixteen might have died at sixteen, or might have died at sixty-five. It's hard to say. But they can't look older than they were when they died, because they never wore that face, never lived inside that skin. For Rose and Mary both, the clock stopped before high school ended, and they'll never look old enough to drink.

Unlike Mary, with her long white hair and her empty highway eyes, Rose still looks like the kind of girl you might see down at the corner store, drinking a soda and sticking her thumb out for a ride. She usually wears whatever's "in" with people who actually are the age she appears to be, cycling effortlessly through the fashion spectrum, coming back time and time again to a sort of Bruce Springsteen greaser chic, in jeans, white tank top, and sneakers. And jacket, of course. Rose is a hitchhiking ghost, eternally wandering the highways and byways of America, looking for the ride that will get her where she needs to go. She'll never find it—that ride doesn't exist—but she'll have a good time while she tries.

They call her the girl in the green silk gown because she died on her way to the prom, back in the 1950s, and when things get bad, she appears in the dress she was wearing when her car ran off the road. Seeing her in jeans meant things weren't as bad as they could be.

Rose has no obligation to help our family. But she's an honorary aunt for a reason, and she does what she can to keep us out of trouble, when we call. Which isn't often, by mutual agreement. She'll always try to come. She'll always do her best. And we'll always remember that when we call her away from the road, we're calling her away from an afterlife that doesn't have anything to do with us—not yet—where she's needed, and valued, and has shit to do.

"Aunt Rose, this my friend Cylia Mackie, and my . . ." I hesitated. Was I ready to take this step with a family member? More importantly, with a family member who didn't share Mary's inclination toward keeping her cards close to her chest? If Mary was a lockbox, Rose was a loudspeaker, and anything I told her today would wind up getting broadcast to the rest of the family as soon as she saw them.

Good. Maybe they'd feel better if they knew I wasn't all by myself, and Sam looked somewhere between wary and miserable, like he'd been waiting for me to repudiate him since the moment he'd realized he could no longer pass for human. Fuck. That.

"This is my boyfriend, Sam Taylor," I said firmly. "He's a fūri."

"Half," said Sam. "Uh, hi, second dead aunt."

Rose stuck her pinky in her ear and swiveled it exaggeratedly around. "I'm sorry. I could have sworn you just said 'my boyfriend,' which would imply that you, Annie, have a boyfriend, and means a bunch of people have probably lost bets."

"Shut up," I said genially.

Sam frowned. "Is this because I'm not human, or . . . ?"

"Oh, no, honey, I don't give two shakes of a dead dog's dick about *that*, and neither will anyone else worth knowing," said Rose. "We have all sorts of people in the family, living and dead. You'll fit right in. It's mostly the idea of Annie dating at all. She always said it was a waste of time."

"We've only managed to have three dates," I protested. "One was at the carnival, one was at a roller derby game, and one was at Lowryland."

"So you found a boyfriend who likes to do the shit you like to do? Miracles never cease. Now." Rose sobered.

The air in the room seemed to chill. Her hands were still shoved into her back pockets, but she suddenly looked much older than her apparent sixteen years, and there were shadows in her eyes I didn't want to challenge. "Why did you send her," she hooked a thumb toward Mary, "to drag me off the ghostroads and into whatever you living people are trying to do to each other this time? I've got shit to do, little Annie, and my thumb didn't bring me here."

"I need to ask you about routewitches."

Rose went still.

Routewitches are common, as humans with magic go. That's a very qualified statement. Maybe one person in a thousand has the potential to become a routewitch, and most will lose or bury that potential before they hit their teens. I don't know what the actual numbers are, but if more than one person in ten thousand can actually hear the highways sing, I'll eat my skates.

It's commonly understood that most, if not all, road ghosts—ghosts like Rose—were or could have become routewitches when they were alive. Not only that, their natural habitat brings them into regular contact with the routewitches, whether they want it to or not. Routewitches and road ghosts represent one of the frontiers where the living and the dead collide, no matter how hard they try to keep themselves separate . . . and quite honestly, most of them don't seem to try at all.

"I don't know what you're expecting me to tell you," said Rose stiffly. "I'm not a routewitch. Even if I could have been, once, that kind of magic belongs to the living. I haven't been among the living in a long, long time."

"I know," I said. I glanced to Cylia before looking back to Rose, and saying, in a careful tone, "Someone is siphoning off my magic, Aunt Rose. I can't start fires. I can barely *feel* the fire. It's being drained away. And someone stole Sam's luck, which meant that when I touched him, the siphon took the energy that lets him transform."

"I gave him some luck back, but when I tried to take a slice from Annie to supplement it, whatever's been draining her—wait, what?" Cylia's head snapped around as she stared at me. "What do you mean, magic?"

"I'm a sorcerer," I said with a shrug. "Surprise."

"She sets shit on fire. It's pretty sexy," said Sam.

"Too much information, monkey-man," said Mary.

Rose blinked. Rose snorted. And then, without further ado, Rose burst out laughing. She pulled her hands out of her pockets and put them over her eyes, bending slowly forward until her elbows were resting on her knees and her entire body was shaking with the effort of continuing to breathe. Which was honestly just dramatics, since she was *already dead*.

Sam leaned a little closer to me, careful to keep from touching my skin as he asked, quietly, "Is she okay?"

"Rose has a weird sense of humor," I replied, not bothering to lower my voice. I glared at my dead aunt instead. "Which is fine, except for the part where it gets in the way of her getting on with things and telling me what I need to know."

"Oh, man. Oh, Annie. Oh, jeez, I want to be there when your parents find out about this one." Rose straightened up, wiping phantom tears from her eyes. "If I promise not to tell them about him, will you promise to call me before you take him home to meet them? Please?"

"Yes, but I need you to tell me about routewitches," I said.

"Am I the only one upset by the idea of *her*," Cylia pointed at me, "having the power to set things on fire with her mind?"

Rose shrugged. "Matches are cheap. Setting fires is good for a parlor trick, but it's not as useful as it sounds. Are you asking whether a routewitch could steal your magic, Annie?"

"Yes," I said.

"No." Rose shook her head. "That's not how routewitches work. They couldn't steal your luck either. Those aren't road concepts. They can't take them."

"What *can* they take?" asked Sam.

"Excuse me?"

"You said luck and magic aren't road concepts, so

routewitches can't take them," said Sam. "That makes it sound like there's something they *can* take. What can they take?"

"Distance," said Rose. "Routewitches can steal distance."

I frowned. "Meaning what, exactly?"

"Distance is potential, and potential is power," said Rose. "If you walk a hundred miles, that's a hundred miles of power slathered all over your skin. A good routewitch can peel that away from you. It's the basic driving force of the snake cults, only less scaly, and less stupid."

"I knew that part," I said. "I've heard of routewitches *using* distance—it's the main power behind most of their spells—but I've never heard of them stealing it before."

"That's because ethical routewitches won't," said Rose firmly. "Apple won't let them."

Sam put up a hand. "Who's Apple?" he asked, with the air of a man who had gone wading in the shallows, only to discover that there was a whole deep ocean waiting to devour him.

"She's the current Queen of the Routewitches. She holds court on the Ocean Lady, and she'll kick your ass from here to Tuesday morning if she thinks you're breaking her rules. Not a nice woman, necessarily, but a fair one, and a reasonably kind one, when it comes to that. The routewitches have done worse." Rose shook her head. "Stealing distance is like stealing anything: it's a violation. They'd have to rip it off of a person, unless they could make it a trade somehow, and even that would be . . . difficult. The road thrives on fair exchange."

"Meaning . . ." I prompted.

"Meaning I get flesh from the loan of a coat, and a phantom rider gets freedom from the length of a road, and everything balances. If a routewitch wants distance from the living, they would normally need to make it part of a barter. I'll give you this if you give me that. It's hard to do that accidentally."

A cold feeling appeared in the pit of my stomach. I felt myself go very still, the hair on my arms standing on end. "Sam," I said, and turned to face him, *only* him, focusing on the lines of his face until I couldn't see anyone else, not even in my peripheral vision. It needed to be only him, because this was my fault. "Can I see your ticket?"

Sam blinked. Understanding bloomed in his eyes, spreading to cover his entire expression, wiping everything else away. "Yeah," he said, and dipped his hand into his pocket.

He put the ticket on the table like it was a dead rat, something to be dropped as quickly and as cleanly as possible. He pulled his fingers away almost instantly, as if he was afraid lingering would give me the opportunity to touch him again. That hurt. Not as much as the realization of what must have happened, but . . . it still hurt.

I picked up the ticket, turning it over. The fine print on the back was as dense and tight-packed as I remembered. Turning my body toward Rose, I read aloud, " 'This ticket is provided under the auspices of Lowry Entertainment, Inc., and cannot be transferred or re-sold once activated. Acceptance of this ticket constitutes agreement to be filmed, photographed, and interviewed for future marketing purposes while on Lowry property. Acceptance of this ticket is perpetual and binding. All clauses can and will be exercised at the discretion of Lowry Entertainment, Inc. No refunds or returns will be entertained.' " My mouth was dry. I paused and swallowed, resisting the urge to close my eyes. "There's a quote under that, from one of the early Monty Mule cartoons. 'If you're lucky enough to be lucky, share the luck around.' "

Rose snapped her fingers. "And there it is."

"Oh, my sweet Zeus." Cylia put her head on the table. "I think I'm going to be sick."

Sam looked between us, and scowled. "Now's where someone explains this to me in small words, or I get pissed."

"When you took the ticket, you gave Lowry permission to take your luck." Rose stepped forward and snatched the ticket out of my hand—or tried to, anyway.

In the absence of a coat, her fingers passed straight through the paper. She scowled. "Mary!"

"I'm not your maid," said Mary. She moved to stand next to Rose, gesturing for me to hand over the ticket. I did. Rose transferred her scowl to the other ghost.

They're both dead, but the rules governing them are very different, and while I wouldn't want to be the one to say that one was better off than the other, watching Rose struggle to interact with the living world when she didn't have a coat was sometimes a strong vote in Mary's favor. Although unlike Mary, Rose doesn't answer to a malicious and sometimes predatory force of the universe. Checks and balances in all things, I suppose.

"Is that going to take Mary's luck now?" asked Sam.

"No; the ticket's nontransferable," said Rose, sounding distracted. She leaned forward, scowling at the words for a moment before straightening, shaking her head, and announcing, "You work for assholes. You know that, right, Timmy?"

"'Timmy'?" asked Cylia.

"My full name's 'Antimony,'" I said, frowning at Rose. "I sort of know that, but why do you say so?"

"Because taking one of their theme park tickets grants them unlimited consent to take your luck whenever you're on Lowry property. Do you know how much shit Lowry *owns*? They're no Disney, but I'm pretty sure they own an *airport*. You're fucked. You take one of these and stuff it in your wallet as a pretty souvenir and it doesn't matter if it's six years later, they can activate it and steal whatever they want from you." Rose shook her head. She looked disgusted. She also looked distantly impressed, like she was fighting her own desire to admire their work. "A routewitch didn't write this, but a routewitch helped. It's very close to the standard distance exchange. I give you this, you give me that, everybody walks away happy."

I put my head in my hands. "When Sam took the ticket, he agreed to the fine print, and now Lowry gets to take his luck."

"Not if we burn the ticket," said Mary calmly.

I lifted my head and peered at her. "Aren't you worried about *your* luck?"

"It's nontransferable, and I'm dead," she said. "I have a different kind of luck now. Isn't that right, Cylia?" She turned her open highway eyes toward our hostess.

Cylia sucked in a startled breath, sitting up a little straighter. "Yes, ma'am," she said. Any incongruity in a woman nearly ten years my senior addressing a teenager as "ma'am" was washed away by the empty roads of Mary's eyes. "No living jink can touch ghost luck. Dead ones can touch living luck, but we don't talk about them much."

"You shouldn't," Mary agreed. "If you did, even the people who ought to be your allies would join the Covenant in hunting you down. Some power shouldn't belong to anybody. Annie?"

"Yes, Aunt Mary?"

"You need to get the hell away from Lowryland. Whatever these people are doing, it's not right, it's not good, and it's going to get a lot more people hurt than it already has."

"You're right," I said. "But I'm not going."

Everyone stopped. In the case of Mary and Rose, they stopped so perfectly, so completely, that they might as well have been pictures painted on the air. Sam and Cylia just froze. They were still alive, and I took comfort in that fact. Sometimes it can be awkward, being the only living person in a room.

Sam recovered first. "If I were allowed to touch you right now, I'd be slinging you over my shoulder and running for the door," he growled. "Why the hell don't you want to leave?"

"Because you're not allowed to touch me right now," I said.

He looked at me blankly. So did the others. I sighed.

"The luck-theft doesn't target employees," I said. "We don't get tickets like guests do. We have our passes, and we're supposed to keep our ID badges on us at all times. I'm willing to bet that there's some kind of a counter-charm built into the plastic to keep us from being affected if we *do* pick up a ticket for some reason, or we'd be dealing with a rash of dead janitors." They couldn't be stealing luck from employees. There was no way they'd have been able to cover for that many accidents.

"So?" said Sam.

"So employees are getting hurt. It started recently, and it's getting worse. People died in the parade collapse." I took a deep breath. "This began when Fern found the dead man outside the Midsummer Night's Scream. The people who would know said that . . . they said he'd been unlucky. The cut that killed him was a fluke. So call him a possible consequence of the normal luck theft. He got his luck swiped, and then he got into a fight, and what should have been a pretty standard tussle turned into murder."

"This isn't explaining why you need to stay, sweetie," said Mary, sounding more like my babysitter than she had in years. "If anything, this is explaining why you need to *go*."

"Because it was after that man died that the cabal running Lowryland found out I existed," I said. "They're stealing my magic. They said they would train me, and instead, they've been using me like a battery. Employees didn't start getting hurt until I waltzed in and dropped an untrained, uneducated magic-user in their laps. They're using me to boost their effects, and people are dying. We can't leave until I figure out how to stop them and get my magic back."

I had lived for years without fire in my fingers, and when it had started to develop, I'd wished it gone with everything I had. Now I finally had someone willing to take it away from me, and all they wanted in exchange was more than anyone had the right to ask me to give.

Lowryland owed a lot of people a lot of luck, and I was going to make sure the bills were paid. I owed the dead that much. They had been hurt, however inadvertently, because of me.

Mary sighed. "Why the hell did I instill a sense of responsibility in you? Biggest mistake I ever made."

"You wanted me to be the best that I could be," I said.

"Well, the best you can be is a pain in my ass," she said.

I turned to Cylia. "Can Sam stay here? Until his strength comes back and he can shift again?"

"Yes, of course," said Cylia, and "Fuck that idea," said Sam, at the same time, so their words piled on top of each other in a complicated heap.

I frowned at him. "You can't be near me until your luck comes back."

"No, I can't be near you *and* human until you stop being a magical energy vacuum cleaner, but you keep saying you don't need me to be human, so who the fuck cares?" Sam gave me a pointed look. "Unless you were lying."

I didn't hesitate. I leaned forward and kissed him, deeply enough to get my point across. Sam kissed me back, and I would have been a fool not to feel the relief in the action, or the way his shoulders relaxed, letting his body settle a little deeper into his chair, making a space for me to fall into.

Mary cleared her throat. "I'd say 'get a room,' but you might," she said. "Can we focus?"

"Sorry," I said, sitting up.

Sam beamed at her. "Not sorry," he said.

"Didn't think you were," said Mary. "Sam, you understand that it's not safe—"

"If it's not safe for me, it's not safe for her," he said. "I don't have to go out in public. Both her roommates know I'm not human. I can sleep on the couch if I need to, give my luck time to grow back and shield me from the sucking. Whatever. What I *can't* do is walk away and leave her alone again. Don't ask me to."

"And this way you don't have to feel bad about not calling my parents," I said. "I'll have backup. Cylia can even drive us back to the apartment. Maybe Megan and Fern will have some luck to spare."

"Saints preserve me from the living," said Mary, rolling her eyes ceiling-ward. "All right. Since it seems like you've thought of everything, can you just promise me that you'll be careful?"

"Nope," I said. "When a Price promises to be careful, that's when we get dead."

"Speaking of dead," said Rose. "It's been fun seeing you again, Timmy. Good luck defeating the evil luck-sucker empire, but if this is routewitch doing, I'm not sticking around to find out what they'll do to a girl like me."

It was the sensible thing to do. Rose has been a hitch-hiking ghost for so long that she's crossed the continent dozens, if not hundreds, of times, and the spells she'd fuel would be terrifying. I smiled wanly.

"Thanks for coming, Aunt Rose," I said.

"Anytime, squirt," she said, and was gone, vanishing from the world as easily as she'd appeared.

Something wrapped around my ankle. I didn't need to look down to know that it was Sam's tail.

"All right," I said. "Let's fix this."

Nineteen

"You don't owe the world anything. That's why you should try to make it better no matter what. A lack of obligation does not mean a lack of mercy."

–Evelyn Baker

A shitty company apartment five miles outside of Lakeland, Florida, getting ready for a war

EXPLAINING THE SITUATION TO Fern and Megan had been easier than I'd expected. Maybe it was showing up with a fūri who couldn't transform, or maybe it was the dead woman offering to draw flow charts. Mostly, I think, it was Cylia, who looked human and wasn't human and hadn't asked for anything they could measure or perceive.

I sat on the couch with my hands tucked between my knees, wondering how I could have been foolish enough to think I could get something for nothing—that a little training would be enough to stop the fire from consuming everything around me, and that all I'd have to pay for it would be my time. It had been a beautiful promise and a perfectly tailored trap, and I had walked into it with my eyes wide open.

The cushion beside me barely dented as Fern sat down. On the other side of the room, Cylia was taking a finger-scoop of good luck from Megan and wiping it on Sam, who bore it with furry, put-upon dignity.

"You okay?" asked Fern, bumping my shoulder with hers.

I wanted to tell her to be careful. I wanted to tell her

that there was a hole in my heart pulling away the energy of the people around me. I didn't. She already knew that—it had been a part of the explanation of the situation—and unlike Sam, she hadn't had her luck ripped away. She was safe from me, as long as she was employed by Lowryland.

Instead, I ducked my head, offering her a weary smile, and said, "I've been better."

"You don't look like you've eaten in, oh, hours," she said.

"Probably because I haven't. Cylia gave us some lemonade." I leaned back on the couch. Megan was wiping the spit off her forearm. Sam was flexing his hands, looking around the room like he was trying to decide where to go without risking bumping into me.

Having him here and not being able to touch him was almost worse than not having him here at all. Only almost. Being able to see him, to know that he was . . . well, not okay, but at least alive, at least breathing, that was better than anything as simple as physical contact.

"Lemonade isn't food," said Fern disapprovingly. "We could order pizza."

"Pizza is food," I agreed.

Fern took that as consent. She turned to the rest of the room. "Anybody up for pizza?" she called.

"Better make that two," said Cylia. "Sam's body is trying to rebuild luck and energy at the same time. He's going to eat like a teenager."

"I already eat like a teenager," said Sam. "I'm a growing monkey."

"Don't grow too much more, or you'll be morally obligated to climb the Empire State Building," said Megan, looking him up and down.

He waved it off with a sweep of his hand. "Nah. I don't like blondes." The look he shot in my direction made it very clear that brunettes were another matter.

My cheeks reddened, but I held to my dignity, sitting up a little straighter and saying, "We need to figure out what we're doing about this cabal, and about the luck thefts."

"They don't have a jink working for them, so you don't need me," said Cylia. "If you sneak me into the Park *without* expecting me to touch one of those tickets, I can try to rebalance the luck of anyone who's been affected, but that's about as far as I can go."

"It's better than nothing," I said. "Thank you for being willing to help."

"There's some self-interest here," she said. "If the Covenant ever heard there had been issues with inexplicably missing luck in Florida, they'd probably come for another purge. I couldn't live with myself if I'd been in a position to prevent that, and had chosen to do nothing."

I couldn't stop a small, grim chuckle. "You've just described the motivation of everything my family has done in the last hundred years," I said.

"Then I understand you a little better," she said. Producing her phone from her pocket, she said, "I'll go order the pizza," and retreated into the hall.

Megan looked at me, expression calm, snakes hissing wildly all around her face.

"We must practically seem like statues to you," I blurted.

She blinked, painted-on eyebrows rising, before she smiled in sudden understanding. "It was the source of a lot of early cultural confusion," she admitted. "Our 'hair' always gives our feelings away, unless we cover it, and for a gorgon to cover their heads in private is a grave insult. We didn't understand that humans could stand there with their heads uncovered, and tell us lies, and be believed."

"That makes sense," I said softly.

"I treated the wounded, after the parade collapsed. I held hands. I listened to people asking if we'd seen their children. I'm just a resident. I shouldn't have been doing half the things I was doing, but the hospital was overwhelmed, and we had to take care of everyone. Whoever's using you to boost their luck-theft, they're killing people now. I'm in this until it's over. You should know that." Megan's voice remained calm, and her snakes grew more and more agitated. "Whatever I can do, I'll do."

"Me, too," said Fern.

"Me, three," said Sam. He flexed his hands again, before scowling. "I still can't change, but I feel like I'll be able to soon. It *itches*."

"Well, don't touch me again until your luck's grown back enough to protect you," I said. He looked hurt. I shook my head. "We need you at your best. That means fast and sturdy *and* capable of blending into a crowd. Right now, you're not blending anywhere outside of a comic book convention."

"I've never been to one of those."

"Then when all this is over, I'll take you to one."

"When all this is over . . ." He paused, looking at me seriously. "Are you gonna go home when this is over?"

I slumped into the couch. "I can't." Sam looked like he was going to protest. I raised my hand, cutting him off. "Not 'I don't want to,' Sam, I *can't*. The problem that has me running hasn't gone away yet. I just ran into a different problem. Lowryland is being controlled by unethical human magic-users who're harvesting luck from their guests because who the fuck knows why. Because they're power-hungry assholes. But they're not the Covenant. If we beat them, that doesn't magically make the Covenant go away, and it doesn't magically make it safe for me to go back to my family. It just means I find another place to run."

"I always wanted to be a member of the A-Team," said Sam philosophically.

I blinked at him. "What?"

"If you're still running, I'm coming with you," he said. "No offense, but this 'I can do it on my own, just watch' bullshit hasn't worked out too well, so I figure it's time we try a little 'we have vigorous sex in every cheap motel between here and Maine' bullshit. At least that'll be more fun."

"I'm coming, too," said Fern. "Not for the sex part. I have headphones."

"I'm not," said Megan. "No offense, Annie. I didn't go to medical school and put my family in debt to run off and play medic for your weird fugitive adventures. I just

want to survive whatever the hell is going on at Lowryland and make it home to my parents. You being a Price
makes sense—sweet Medusa, does it ever—but it doesn't
exactly encourage me to stay around you. Even if you
might be able to get me your brother's autograph."

"No offense taken," I said. I stood. "I need weapons."

"Be still my heart," said Sam.

I wrinkled my nose at him as I walked out of the living room, into the hall, and past Cylia—still on her
phone—to my bedroom.

When I'd fled from the burning carnival, I'd been as
close to devoid of weaponry as any Price ever got. I'd
been running virtually naked for the better part of a
year. Back home, I would have had an arsenal at my disposal, all the knives, guns, and more esoteric weaponry
that a girl could want. Having a family obsessed with
combat techniques and staying alive, and a grandmother
whose idea of an appropriate gift for a little girl was a
box of caltrops, had done a lot to distort my idea of what
"normal" levels of weaponry were.

Working at Lowryland meant no weapons, ever, because normal people don't feel the need to hide twenty
throwing knives in their clothing before they leave the
house. Staff didn't have to go through the metal detectors, but accidents happen—lord, do accidents happen—
and I had no faith in my ability not to stab someone who
got overly aggressive, which happened sometimes on
days when the rides weren't behaving, and the weather
wasn't behaving, and the tourists felt like they needed
somebody to complain to. So I'd taken to keeping most
of my paltry supply of weaponry in a box under the bed,
where I could reach it if I needed it, but otherwise
wouldn't be tempted to start carrying it again.

I knelt. I pulled the box out. I looked at the heap of
throwing knives—two full sets, one provided by the Covenant as part of my cover story for the carnival, one provided by the carnival once I had started working there—and
other, slightly more makeshift weaponry, marbles and
sharpened jacks and hand-braided wire garrotes. I took a
deep breath. That didn't seem like enough, so I took

another, focusing on the homecoming those knives represented.

No more Timpani Brown, Covenant trainee. No more Melody West, ex-cheerleader and Lowryland employee. Just Antimony Price, Annie, the girl I had been born to be, the girl with fire in her fingers and no real sense of where she stood in the structure of a family that had an heir and a spare and her, youngest child who didn't know who or what she should grow up to be.

Or maybe I wasn't that Annie anymore either. I knew who I wanted to grow up to be. I was going to protect my family, and I was going to protect my friends, and I was going to learn how to use what I'd inherited from my grandfather, even if it meant joining my grandmother in her endless, quixotic quest to bring him home. I had a purpose now. Maybe it wasn't the purpose I'd been expecting, but . . . it was mine. That made it more than good enough.

One by one, the knives vanished into my clothing, settling against my skin in the old, familiar patterns, made new again by time and distance from the last time I'd been allowed to strap them on. I wrapped the garrote around my wrist like a friendship bracelet and filled my pockets with problems for other people to deal with. When I was done, I was fifteen pounds heavier and felt a hundred pounds lighter, like I had borrowed Fern's shifting relationship with density.

The last thing I did was pull the knife from under my pillow and slide it into my sock, and I was back. I was myself again.

The others turned to look at me when I returned to the living room. I held up my hands, turning them back and forth to show that they were empty.

"Nothing up my sleeves," I said. A flick of my wrists and I was holding a pair of throwing knives, balanced between my thumbs and forefingers. We live in a world where magic is real and monsters lurk under more than a few beds, but there will always be a place for sleight of hand.

Sam grinned. "Does this mean you're ready to get angry?"

"I guess it does," I said. The knives disappeared back into my clothing. "I guess it's time for all of us to get angry."

The doorbell rang. Megan sat on the couch, picking up the towel she kept there and wrapping it around her head in a quick, practiced motion. The snakes, apparently conditioned to keep still in the dark, coiled and stopped moving, which was good, since otherwise the towel would have been pulsing like something out of a horror movie.

"Actually, it's time for us to eat pizza," said Cylia, walking calmly past me to the door. Sam got up and darted down the hall to my bedroom, out of sight.

I offered Fern a quick, tight smile, and went to the kitchen for plates.

The thing about riding gallantly into battle is that unless something is actively trying to kill you *right now*, it's probably a good idea to eat first. We fell upon those two pizzas like we were starving—which, to be honest, several of us were. It had been a long time since our gingerbread at Lowryland, and baked goods do not a balanced diet make.

Megan, despite having mouse-eating snakes attached to her head, is a vegetarian; out of respect for her dietary needs, one of the pizzas was a virtual garden of plants that can be baked in an oven without turning completely disgusting. The other pizza was a meat-lover's special. Megan ate the first, Fern ate the second, and I slapped two pieces together to form a perfectly balanced sandwich, a trick which Sam and Cylia quickly emulated.

(Cylia had also been smart enough to order several two-liter bottles of Mountain Dew to go with the food. Cylia was rapidly approaching the status of "my favorite.")

For a little while, there was no room for conversation: there was only room for chewing, something that's universal across all species, no matter what their diets entail. Megan stole bits of sausage from the meat-lover's pizza and fed it to her hair while chewing on her own veggie-enriched slice; Sam double-fisted his pizza slice sandwiches, eating with a speed and efficiency which I frankly admired, even as I kept a hand free for my drink.

The pizzas were nearly gone when Sam paused, hiccupped, and turned human again. We all blinked at him.

"Huh," said Cylia, who had only seen him in his fūri form. "You're actually kinda cute."

"Thanks?" said Sam.

"I think he's cute both ways," I said, earning myself a quick grin.

"Does this mean my luck's back to normal?" asked Sam.

"Not quite," said Cylia. "I know you're going to glare at me, but if I were you, I'd avoid touching Annie for a while longer. Give it a day. Most of the luck I lathered onto you was good, because why the hell bother starting someone out with a big load of bad—seems to me you've got enough bad going already—and now you're starting to pick up ambient luck, which is more mixed. Once your shell gets back to normal, you'll be safe to do whatever you want."

"By then, hopefully I won't suck as hard," I said.

Fern choked on her pizza.

I blinked at her before I felt myself turn bright red. "Oh, my *God*, you have a *filthy* mind," I squawked, and threw a napkin at her.

That was the trigger. We were tired, we were tense, and we were about to go into a fight against people whose abilities we didn't fully know or understand. People get weird when they're looking down the barrel of something like that. Fern batted the napkin away and threw her pizza crust at me. I snatched it out of the air and threw it back, only to be hit in the side of the face by a pillow flung by Megan. She was laughing, and her snakes seemed to be doing the same, their mouths gaping open in silent serpentine smiles.

Cylia grabbed another pillow, holding it in front of herself and doing an admirable job of compacting her long limbs into a complicated curl. "I'm fragile!" she yelped.

Sam hit her with an empty soda bottle.

The living room descended into chaos. Fern grabbed a pillow in each hand and bounded into the air, dropping her personal density until she was practically floating. Sam's tail wrapped tight around her ankle, and she yelped before she realized that he was swinging her at Megan. Her yelp transformed into a maniacal laugh, both pillows raised to strike. Megan ducked but still got a mouthful of upholstery for her trouble, Fern aiming low to avoid hitting her glasses.

I laughed too, dropping to the floor and beginning to chuck wadded-up napkins every which way, keeping the air full of projectiles, which Fern kept batting aside in her determined quest to smack Megan a second time. Cylia flicked her fingers every time it looked like my napkins were going to hit her, sending them careening in odd directions as some gust of wind from Fern's flight or other atmospheric disturbance knocked them out of true. My aim hadn't been that bad since I was a very small child, but I didn't manage to land a hit on her once.

It was fantastic. Play is an essential part of learning what the body is capable of, and while we were all just blowing off steam, I was learning more of what our group was tactically capable of than I could possibly have asked. The only factor that was missing was Megan's stony gaze, and even when Fern was hitting her with the pillows, she was being careful not to knock our resident gorgon's glasses off. Which mattered.

"Time-out!" I called.

Sam stopped swinging Fern. Robbed of her momentum, she drifted slowly down toward the floor. Cylia peeked out from behind her pillow.

"Truce?" she asked.

"Not quite," I said. "Megan, I know you can't paralyze Fern. What about Cylia and Sam?"

"I don't know," she said, blinking at me as she wiped a smear of tomato sauce off one cheek. Her hair writhed and settled, a few locks drawing back in curious curves. "I've never looked directly at a jink or a fūri before."

"Got it." I looked at Sam and Cylia. Cylia, who in her

own weird way knew more about the cryptid community than Sam did—he had been raised by his human grandmother, who had always done her best, but who had been missing some essential facts about his biology— grimaced.

"I don't know either," she said, in a tone which implied that she *really* wasn't looking forward to the next part. "I don't suppose we can say 'probably' and leave it at that?"

"Not the best plan," I said. "If we need to get you sunglasses, we should probably know that before things get messy."

"I won't turn you to stone unless I'm making an effort, and I promise not to make an effort," said Megan, in a tone that was probably meant to be reassuring, and missed the mark by about a mile.

Sam unwound his tail from Fern's ankle, suddenly seeming to realize what we were talking about. "Hold up a second here," he said. "I don't want to be turned to stone."

"Megan is a Pliny's gorgon," I said. "She can stun *or* petrify, depending on what she's trying to do, and whether or not her hair is uncovered."

"Can't petrify if the snakes can't bite you," said Megan cheerfully. "My wigs double as a safety measure. I'll be taking them off before I try to freeze the bad guys."

"This isn't helping," muttered Sam.

"Unless Megan's life is actively threatened, she's unlikely to be trying to turn anyone to stone," I said. "But we need to know if you need sunglasses, and whether she needs to be as careful around you as she is around me."

"My mother was human," said Sam. "If she can stun you, she can probably stun me."

"It might be tied to the form you're in," said Megan.

Sam opened his mouth to protest again. Then he closed it, sighed, and said, "You're going to do this no matter what I say, aren't you?"

"No," I said. "If you don't consent to her looking at you, she won't look at you."

He and Cylia both relaxed.

"But," I continued, "if you don't consent to her looking at you, you have to agree to stay here while I take her and Fern and go to face the cabal."

Sam's eyes narrowed. "No."

"Then she looks at you." I shook my head. "We need to know. You don't go into a fight without *all* the relevant information, and this is super-relevant."

"This feels a little bit like blackmail," Sam informed me.

I shrugged. "So it's a little bit like blackmail. I'm okay with that if it means you don't get stunned in the middle of a bad situation."

"It doesn't hurt," said Megan. "It's more like going to sleep and not dreaming for a little while. We can even stun each other, if we work at it." She glanced at me. "It's how we get around the lack of anesthesia in most of our hospitals."

Being a cryptozoologist sometimes means learning something new every day. I managed to keep the surprise out of my face as I nodded and said, "That makes sense."

"Fine," said Cylia. I turned to look at her. She shook her head. "I want to be involved with this fight about as much as I want to gargle a mouthful of spiders, but people are screwing with luck, and that sort of thing paints a big target on the jink community. Even if we don't have anything to do with it, this is going to get a bunch of us killed if it doesn't stop. So fine. Stun me."

"Sam, close your eyes," I said. "One at a time." I closed my own eyes, putting my hands over them for good measure.

"I'm taking off my glasses," warned Megan. There was a soft hissing sound from her hair, and then a thud as—presumably—Cylia hit the floor.

"She's out," reported Fern.

"Sam?" I asked.

There was a pause before he said, "I'm not letting you do this without me."

Several seconds ticked by. Nothing happened.

"Sam?" I asked again.

"Nothing," he said. "I'm going to try something." There was a faint stretching sound. I'd heard it before. It was the sound of fur retracting and muscles moving to fit a human's musculature, rather than a fūri's. It was followed by a much louder, more distinct sound: that of a body hitting the floor.

"He's out," reported Fern.

"I'm putting my glasses back on," said Megan. "It's safe."

I opened my eyes. Both Sam and Cylia were sprawled on the floor, unconscious. Sam was unconscious in his human form, which was strange enough to be unnerving. Since fūri was his default, he normally couldn't stay human when he wasn't awake.

"I think we need you as the anesthesiologist if we ever have to take him to a human hospital for some reason," I said.

Megan's smile was half-feral, and very full of teeth. "My rates are reasonable, and I'm not the only Pliny's gorgon working in the medical field."

"That's good to know." I stood, beginning to gather the wreckage from our pizza party. Fern got up and joined me. "How long are they going to be out?"

"No more than ten, maybe fifteen minutes," said Megan. She didn't get up to help us. Maybe she felt like she'd already done her part. Even her snakes seemed calmer, twining around themselves in a serpentine parody of a braid. "I didn't put a lot of oomph behind it."

"Can you modify the, ah, 'oomph' on the fly, or is this one of those things where you have to call your attacks before the GM rolls?" I asked.

Megan blinked at me slowly before she snorted. "Sometimes I forget how much of a nerd you are," she said. "I have to 'call my attacks,' as you put it, before my target's eyes are closed. So if you point me at someone and say they need to be *out*, make sure not to get in the way."

The thought of winding up a lawn ornament because I got in the path of one of my own allies wasn't appealing. I nodded. "Got it. Can human magic-users deflect your gaze?"

"Not so far as I know," said Megan. "My dad's pretty paranoid. I bet he would have told me."

"Awesome," I said.

Fern and I finished cleaning up while Sam and Cylia slept. Sparing them the physical labor seemed only fair, given that we were responsible for their current condition. Fern did pause to look at Cylia and sigh wistfully.

"I wish I wouldn't feel like a jerk for drawing all over them," she said.

I snorted.

"Anyone drawing on me is going to get a bucket of water dumped over their head when they least expect it," said Sam.

I started a little, surprised. "You're awake?" I glanced at the clock. It had been roughly six minutes since Megan knocked him out. Not quite the ten to fifteen she'd guessed, but that made sense: he hadn't gone down until he'd changed forms. He must still have a certain degree of resistance.

"Can't quite convince anything to move, but yeah," he said. "It feels like my whole body went to sleep."

"Can you change forms?"

"Not sure." Sam's brow furrowed. It was like watching someone try to shake off a shot of Novocain after a trip to the dentist. He relaxed again. "No. Which would be less upsetting if this hadn't _just_ happened."

"It's muscle control, not anything more serious," said Megan soothingly. I had never heard her break out the doctor voice before. She saw me staring and flashed me a thumbs-up. "As soon as the paralysis wears off a little more, you'll be fine. It's unusual for you to even be awake right now."

"I'm an unusual guy," said Sam, and opened his eyes. His lips twitched as he tried to frown. "Your ceiling is dull."

"So paint it," I said.

"So don't," said Fern. "Lowry doesn't allow employees to paint their company-owned living areas."

"So move," said Sam, and transformed, skin rippling and limbs lengthening, until the monkey-man I had come to see as the real him—the him that mattered, the him I was rapidly falling in love with—was stretched out on my floor. Immediately, he leaped to his feet, displaying a level of muscular control that was virtually unthinkable in a human athlete, and stretched, fingertips brushing the ceiling.

"Better," he said.

"Agreed," I said. Sam smiled at me, shyly again, and for a moment, I almost forgot that I wasn't allowed to touch him yet.

Fern cleared her throat. I jerked back.

"As soon as Cylia's awake, we can move," she said. "Is there a plan? Or were we just going to storm the castle? Because Lowryland has a lot of castles. I don't think we should go storming them all willy-nilly."

It felt like it should have been the middle of the night. A glance at the clock confirmed that it was only half past six. The media buildings would be closed. The cabal would still be there. Colin and Emily never seemed to leave before nine, and half the time my "lessons" had been held when the world was dark, on the days when I had morning shifts to deal with.

"Here's the plan: kick their asses." I looked at Cylia, sprawled on the floor like a dead thing. "Make them understand that they fucked with the wrong group of weirdoes. And then get the fuck out of here."

"Sounds good to me," said Sam, and cracked his knuckles with a sound like a small-caliber handgun going off. "Let's rock."

Twenty

"Sometimes leaving survivors isn't the kind
option. Sometimes it's a warning to others."
–Frances Brown

*Heading for the Lowryland Public Relations building,
ready to rock*

ROCKING HAD TO WAIT until Cylia was awake, for several reasons, the most important of which was that
we were going to be using her car. It was simple logistics:
Megan was driving a beat-up green Corolla that worked
great for getting three people to the Park, but really
wasn't equipped to ram a gate. Also, out of all of us, she
was the one planning to stay at Lowryland long enough
to finish her medical residency. Any pictures of our little
adventure needed to leave her out of it.

(We could get her to the admin center through the
time-honored method of "putting someone in the backseat, across the laps of everyone else there, under a blanket." Traffic cams are everywhere. I was going to be
wearing sunglasses and a big floppy hat, which should be
enough to keep me off the Covenant's radar, but if
Lowry Security decided to check the footage later, they
needed to count four people in the vehicle, not five.)

Fortunately, a gorgon's gaze isn't like a drug: once
somebody shakes it off and opens their eyes, they're basically ready to roll. Once Cylia was awake, we were five
minutes from hitting the road. We wouldn't even have
been that far if I hadn't wanted to give everyone one last
opportunity to change their minds.

No one did. Whatever else happened from here, it was going to be all of us.

So there we were, five people crammed into one mid-century American muscle car, Sam in the front seat and Cylia behind the wheel, while Fern and I—both in floppy hats that hid as much of our faces as possible—rode in the back, Megan stretched across our laps.

The gates to the admin complex were supposed to be locked at all times, requiring ID cards and verifications to get through. Even if that failed, the guards were supposed to be there, checking everyone against their computers before they allowed anybody to enter the secret fastness of the Lowry empire. It was their bad luck that when we pulled up to the gate, it was to discover that entire stretch of wall dark.

Cylia looked at the rearview mirror, directing her words to me: "Localized power outage. They're not uncommon around here, sadly. Sometimes it's rats chewing on the substation wires. Sometimes it's alligators chewing on the rats. Either way, we're in the clear."

"No, we're not," said Fern, and I could hear the frown in her voice. "This much good luck for us means bad luck for you later."

"Try to keep me alive," said Cylia. She got out of the car, walking around to the wooden barrier that was supposed to prevent intruders from just driving onto the property. It lifted easily when she pushed on it, apparently designed to be operated manually.

She got back into the car, and we drove on.

The power outage had been even more localized than I'd initially assumed: the streetlights scattered around the parking lot were on, casting every rock and remaining car into stark relief. Cylia chose a spot that was close to the Public Relations building, and also to the fence that separated it from the nearby swampland. She killed the engine, hands still resting on the wheel, and stared at the greenery on the other side of the chain-link.

"Anyone wants out, this is where you say so," she said.

"Does that mean you want out?" I asked.

"No." Her chuckle was utterly mirthless. "Tav would

tell me to run like hell, because the life of every jink in the world isn't worth my own. Let me be a species of one, if that's what it comes down to. But Tav left. I'm a widow, and I make my own choices, and I say these assholes need to pay for fucking with a force of nature that was never meant to be theirs."

No one else said anything. The moment stretched out until it seemed to fill the whole car with silence, until the whole world was silence. They were waiting on me.

I took a breath.

"All right," I said. "If things go south, scatter. Megan—"

"I'll hit the swamp," she said. "Nothing there can hurt me."

"I'm not leaving without you," said Sam, utterly calm, like he was talking about ordering another pizza. "So if things go south, I'm grabbing you, and heading for the highest ground I can find."

"Given where we are, that's in Lowryland," said Fern. "Regroup at the Midsummer Night's Scream? Fairyland's closed. It's the safest place to go."

The fact that she was talking about breaking into one of the largest theme parks in Florida like it was no big deal was as endearing as it was accurate. I nodded firmly.

"It's a plan," I said. "Let's go."

The night air outside the car was warm and humid, hot enough to have been an Oregon summer, even though the sun had been down for almost an hour. We walked across the parking lot to the Public Relations building, where the door, as always, was unlocked.

That was where the bad luck caught up with us. We stepped inside just as one of the conference room doors opened, and Emily emerged, followed by Sophie Vargas-Jackson. My old cheer captain. The woman who had believed, for all the time she'd known me, that I was a victim.

Emily froze, eyes going wide in surprise and shock. Sophie did no such thing. She took us all in with a single flick of her eyes, identifying Fern and Megan as Lowry employees and clearly filing Cylia under the same category—

no one could know everyone who worked for the Park, not and have room in their heads for anything else—before stalking toward us.

"You *bastard*," she hissed, and slapped Sam, hard, across his human-seeming cheek.

He took a step backward, more out of surprise than in response to the blow, and raised a hand to touch the spot where he'd been struck. "What the hell, lady?" he asked.

"You bring her here to make her resign?" she demanded, eyes fixed on Sam. "You think if you get her away from us, you make her yours again?" Her next sentence was in Spanish, venom dripping from every word, enough to make the language barrier almost inconsequential.

Sam blinked. "Uh. I think you have me confused for somebody else."

"Does she have you confused for someone who is *not* an employee of Lowry Entertainment, Inc., and thus has no business in this office?" Emily unfroze, taking a brisk step forward. "Miss West, what is the meaning of this intrusion?"

Her tone promised retribution. The last twenty-four hours of my life meant I didn't care. People who were trying to wreak retribution were almost always people I was allowed to punch, and I was really looking forward to that right about now.

"I need to see Colin," I said, and turned to Sophie. I wanted to take her hands. I wanted to thank her for everything she'd done for me, for trusting me, for giving me a place to lick my wounds and heal before the world remembered I existed and compelled me to start moving again. I couldn't do any of those things. She would never have been willing to leave if she'd understood what was happening, and I didn't dare touch her, not when I didn't know whether her luck was intact. With my luck, she'd secretly been a therianthrope this whole time, and touching her skin would strip her protections away and leave her vulnerable in ways I didn't even like to think about.

Instead, I said the thing I knew would make her feel better, without actually being a lie. "Sophie, this is Sam,"

I said. "I met him about six months ago, and I love him, and he would kill any man who hurt me. He's not the reason I had to run. If anything, he's the reason running broke my heart."

"Uh, hi," said Sam, looking a little dazed. "Nice to meet you."

"Melody loves you?" Sophie looked him up and down, cheeks reddening slightly. "Sorry I slapped you, then. But if you hurt her—"

"Ma'am, I am not intending to hurt her, and if I did, I promise you, I'd regret it." Sam managed a small smile. "Melody is the best thing that's happened to me in a very long time."

"I think I may be sick," said Emily. She pushed Sophie out of the way—literally pushed her, sending the other woman stumbling to the side—and moved so that she was standing directly in front of me, our noses only an inch or so apart. "Mr. Brightman is not currently available. As your employment is in question following this little . . . stunt . . . he may not be available in the future. Leave. Now. It might save your job."

"Ah, but will it save my soul?" I shrugged expansively. "Sorry, Emily, but I'm not here to save my job. I'm here to save Lowryland."

"What are you talking about?" asked Sophie.

I managed, barely, to suppress my wince. Sophie was a civilian, a human civilian—I was almost certain, like, ninety-five percent certain—and she didn't need to be here for what was about to happen.

Luckily, I wasn't the only one on the scene. "I can explain," said Megan, stepping forward and reaching for her glasses.

I closed my eyes, opening them only when I heard the soft sound of Sophie hitting the floor. She looked a bit like something discarded, lying there with her limbs akimbo and her face slack, artificially at peace.

Emily wasn't at peace. Emily was staring at Megan, eyes wide and mouth slightly open, hands raised in a complicated warding gesture.

"A *gorgon*," she breathed. "You brought a *gorgon* to

the Public Relations department. Are you insane, or just stupid?"

Megan pushed her glasses back up her nose, getting them seated firmly in place before she said primly, "My parents taught me not to sling around words like 'insane' as if they were insults, so fuck you very much, lady. And fuck your little ward, too. If I'd looked at you, you'd be on the floor."

"Sam?" I said tightly.

"On it," he replied, and scooped Sophie into his arms, carrying her to one of the plastic chairs in the corner. They were designed more for show than for any semblance of comfort, but at least she wasn't going to wake up on the ground. She'd probably have a raging headache, and no idea what had actually happened to her. Those were small things, when compared to the potential consequences of keeping her conscious.

"I need to see Colin, Emily," I said again, with as much dignity and patience as I could scrape from the bottom of my heart. There wasn't nearly as much as a good Lowry girl would have found. Being used did that to me. "I know he's here."

"How?"

"Because you're here, and you're too much of a company girl to waste resources on yourself alone." I took a step toward her, my flameless hands balled into fists at my sides, like that would somehow call the fire back. It wouldn't—I knew that—but it would sure make it easier to deck her. "You're a routewitch. Ask the road what you should do."

Emily's eyes widened fractionally, her gaze snapping to my companions, reading and assessing them as she tried to figure out how much trouble she was in. To her credit, she didn't accuse me of telling lies. She already knew Megan was a gorgon, and since none of us were passed out, having looked away or closed our eyes as necessary, it was clear that all of us knew, too. Whatever my companions were, they knew enough to know that routewitches were real.

"The road is not a toy, little girl," she said, in a

patiently withering tone. "You're interfering with matters so far beyond you that you might as well be an insect crawling on the pavement, struggling to understand things that have never been yours to know."

"Insect imagery," I said. "Nice." I unclenched my fists, slowly flexing my fingers to limber them up. "Do you read a lot of cold war spy novels, or does that sort of thing come naturally once you become an evil mastermind? Oh, wait. You're not the evil mastermind here. You're just the routewitch. Does the road even talk to you anymore? Or have you used up so much of what you should have been that this is all you get? Just the paths of Lowryland, and the charms you put on innocent guests to rip their luck away. . . ."

This time, Emma's flinch was visible. There was no way it wouldn't have been. "How do you know that?" she demanded.

"How can you *do* that?" I countered. I could see my allies out of the corner of my eye, falling into position behind me. Sam and Cylia were to my right, Fern and Megan were to my left, and this was all going to end so very, very poorly, and there was nothing else we could have done. Having a duty to the cryptid world means having a duty to the human race at the same time, and to the people who blur the line. People like Sam, who had one human parent and one yōkai parent. People like Emily, whose humanity was unquestioned, but whose abilities were preternatural at best.

People like me, who should have had fire in my fingers, instead of cold ashes.

Her eyes narrowed. "You have no idea what you're doing. You're throwing your future away."

"You used your magic to hurt people who never did anything to you. What right did you have? Luck isn't a toy."

"Don't you sound like the pious little killjoy?" Emily shook her head, giving our group one last look before she raised her hands to the level of her face, palms turned outward, showing us that they were empty. "I surrender."

I blinked. "What?"

"I said, I surrender. I give up. You win. I am your prisoner." Emily sounded almost bored, like she was reading a script someone else had written, and which she didn't think much of. "You can do with me as you like, and I'm assuming that what you'd like is for me to unlock the elevator and take you up to have a little chat with Mr. Brightman. Am I correct?"

"Uh, yeah," I said, exchanging a glance with Sam. Every alarm bell I had, and a few I would have said I didn't have, was ringing. But we needed to get to Colin. We needed to end this.

Sam nodded marginally. So did Fern. All right. I turned back to Emily.

"All right," I said. "Take us to your leader."

We left Sophie asleep in the lobby, where she'd hopefully wake up, assume she'd dozed off from overwork, and go home believing our entire encounter had been a surreal dream. It wouldn't help when the next day found me missing from the Lowry complex, but it would at least keep her from charging up the stairs, looking to stop whatever bizarre nonsense was going on. She didn't deserve to be hurt by this.

No one did. That was really the problem. No one who came to Lowryland, whether they were looking for a temporary escape or for a whole new life, deserved to be hurt by a group of irresponsible magic-users who thought that being able to do something most people couldn't somehow gave them the right to do whatever they wanted. Sometimes people did things that they deserved to suffer for, like licking bees or using poison ivy for toilet paper. The world is not infinitely merciful. But this place was supposed to be an escape. It was supposed to be a fantasy that anyone who could afford a ticket was allowed to be a part of, unjudged, unharmed, without fear. Emily, Colin, and their little cabal had taken that away.

Also, they had taken away my magic, and as soon as I got it back, I was going to set all their arrogant asses on fire. No matter how much I'd wished the flames away when they were making my life difficult, they were still *mine*, and no one got to take them from me. Ever.

The theme from *Mooncake* played in the elevator as we rode slowly through the length of the building, reduced to pastel blandness by whatever process is used to create ambient sound. I twitched, unable to calm my nerves. Emily didn't help. She studied her fingernails, ignoring the rest of us, calm and unruffled and perfect in her iced lilac business attire. She didn't look like she'd last five minutes in a fight. She didn't need to. She was a routewitch, and she had her own tricks.

Belatedly, it occurred to me that an elevator was its own form of transport, a box that moved like a ship on the sea. Could the cables pulling it along be considered a road, if I cocked my head and squinted? She'd already managed to twist her magic enough to use it as a weapon when it was never meant to be. Were we running along a road in the company of a routewitch?

As if she could hear my thoughts, Emily glanced my way and smiled, stretching her fingers straight before lowering her hand. "When this is over, remember that you asked for it," she said sweetly.

The elevator dinged. The doors opened on the large, mirrored room where Colin had conducted my first lessons. Emily motioned toward the opening.

"After you," she said.

Sam shoved her out of the elevator. She stumbled into the center of the room, stopped, and turned to blow us a kiss. That was all the warning we got. It wasn't enough.

The elevator doors slammed shut, and we fell.

Twenty-one

"Gravity doesn't play favorites."

–Enid Healy

Locked in an elevator, plummeting to our dooms, which was not exactly the plan

MEGAN SCREAMED. FERN'S FEET left the ground as she bled off density—the standard sylph response to unexpected stress—and she promptly slammed against the elevator roof. Cylia backed into the corner, pressing her hands flat against the walls and bracing herself. It wasn't hard to believe that if we hit the ground, she would be the only one of us to miraculously survive. Seeing all her friends die might even be enough bad luck to counterbalance her lack of injury.

Sam grabbed my wrist with fingers that were once again too long to be human and dusted with a thin covering of fur. I looked up at him, and despite the grim situation we were in, it was almost comforting to see his transformed face. It's amazing how quickly we can find a new normal.

"Annie," he said, voice tight. "What do we do?"

We were still falling. Physics said we shouldn't have still been falling. The Public Relations building was five stories from the outside, and the room where Colin had been doing my training had been at least fifteen stories up, and if either of those things were true for the elevator, we would already have hit the ground. Emily could be using routewitch magic to bend the distance the elevator traveled, giving us an extra amount of "down" and letting us gather more speed as we approached terminal velocity. The impact would hurt a lot more this way. But maybe it was a good thing. It gave us more than just farther to fall.

It gave us *time*.

"Boost me up," I commanded.

Sam didn't hesitate. He let go of my wrist and grabbed my waist, hoisting me to the ceiling where Fern bobbed like a frightened blonde balloon. I flashed her a quick, razor-thin smile.

"It'll be okay," I said, pulling two knives out of my shirt. "When I say 'push,' push."

Fern nodded mutely. The whites showed all the way around her irises, broadcasting her terror to anyone who cared to look. Megan was still screaming—and under it all, the faint, soothing theme from *Mooncake* continued to play. Right.

This wasn't the time for subtlety. Ramming the point of one knife into the lock on the hatch at the top of the elevator, I shoved the other under the edge, pulling it to the side until it nested against the latch that held the whole contraption in place. Most elevator access hatches aren't designed to prevent people from breaking into them, since most people aren't tall enough—or don't have a convenient trapeze-artist boyfriend to offer a boost. I slammed the heel of my hand against the wedged knife, and was rewarded with a popping sound. Grabbing the other knife more firmly, I twisted hard to the left. This time, the pop was louder, and accompanied by a snap.

"*Fern!*" I yelled. "Push!"

The sylph reached around me and shoved. When nothing happened—probably because she weighed virtually nothing, and thus had no leverage behind the motion—she took a breath, shoved again, and fell as she yanked all the density back into her bones.

I heard her hit the floor with a crunching thump, like a bowling ball dropped on hardwood. I couldn't look down to see whether she was hurt, or whether she had punched a hole straight through the bottom of the elevator. I was busy levering open the crack she'd created, using both my knives to pry the wood apart. Once the opening was large enough, the knives vanished back into my shirt and I gripped the edge of the hatch, pulling myself onto the top of the elevator.

It would be difficult to overstate how much more terrifying everything became once I was crouching on top of a metal box, plummeting through a gray-walled chasm, with braided metal cables whipping lightning-fast right next to my face. For a split second, I missed the comfortably mirrored walls of the elevator itself, and the distant, familiar sound of music drained of all power and passion.

The moment passed. Comfort isn't worth it when it gets you dead. Poking my head back around the hatch, I held my arms out. "Start passing them up!" I yelled.

Megan was first. She grabbed hold of the elevator roof until I was pulling Cylia up, and then moved to help me. The wind from our fall whipped her wig away, leaving her hissing, agitated snakes exposed. One of them snapped at my cheek, not quite making contact. I chose to focus on getting Cylia situated on the roof, then turned back to reach for Fern.

Sam was hoisting her up without visible effort—she had bled off her density again, which was probably a good thing, given the way her left leg was dangling and the visible pain in her face. I grimaced, and swallowed the apology that threatened to rise up and distract us all from the situation at hand. We were still falling. We wouldn't be falling for much longer. When there's a fall, there's always a stop at the end, and I wanted to avoid that if it was humanly possible.

Cylia gathered Fern to her side, and Sam hoisted himself out of the elevator, joining the rest of us on the roof. He shot me a quizzical look. I wanted to tell him that I didn't know, that I *couldn't* know, that this sort of thing wasn't what I *did*. I was supposed to be the useless youngest child, not some sort of messed-up action hero leading her personal A-Team through the gates of hell and into a crisis that didn't validate parking.

But this was where we were. This was what we had to do. I took a breath.

"Grab Megan and Cylia and jump," I said.

It wasn't a complicated plan. I could see Sam check it against our speed of descent, against the shaft around us, and find it flawed but feasible.

"I love you," he said, and grabbed Cylia and Megan, one with each hand, before leaping into the air.

There was an elevator landing bay every ten feet, ledges jutting out into the shaft. I didn't have time to wait and see whether he'd managed to grab one. I needed to trust him. I needed to trust *me*. I grabbed Fern by the waist. She barely weighed more than a sack of dried leaves, substantial but airy at the same time, her density all but gone. She slung her arms around my neck, holding on for dear life.

I jumped.

Sam had the kind of strength that my human legs could only dream of. He'd also been making his jump when we were almost ten feet higher in the elevator shaft. At her current weight, Fern wasn't dragging me down, but neither could she dump her density enough to become truly negative: she could float. She couldn't fly. My feet left the elevator roof, we curved upward in something between an arc and a prayer, and we were going to fail. We were going to fall again, this time without the elevator to catch us, and while Fern might survive, I was going to die. I was going to be the first Price in generations to end where the mice couldn't see, with no one to add my deeds to the family record.

Fern clung to me. I closed my eyes. "I'm sorry."

Something that felt like a rope—but wasn't—wrapped around my waist and jerked me to a stop at the apex of my small, human leap. The shock of the stop caused me to let go of Fern, who drifted downward more than she fell, finally grabbing hold of my leg and hanging there while she patiently waited for me to recover.

"Now I know how Gwen Stacy felt," I muttered, and looked up.

Sam was gripping the ledge of the nearest elevator bay with his hands, and holding Megan and Cylia with his remarkably prehensile feet, leaving his tail free to keep me from falling to my doom. He offered me a worried, toothy smile.

"Sorry," he said. "I don't date dead girls."

"Probably a good thing," I said. "My grandmother was worried about my grandfather dating Mary for a while, and that caused problems for *years*."

"Was he?"

"Hell, no. Mary doesn't date the living."

Megan looked between us, eyes wide and a little frantic. "Uh, hello? Hanging in an elevator shaft? Shouldn't you be getting us *out* of here?"

"Not yet," I said.

Sam shook his head.

Megan opened her mouth to object again. There was a terrible crashing, tearing sound below us, accompanied by a billowing wave of dust and smoke and metal particles that slammed upward at a terrifying rate. Sam yanked me closer to the wall. I grabbed hold, tucking my head against my chest and squeezing my eyes tightly closed. Just in time: the worst of the wave flowed over us, ruffling my hair, striking my skin in a dozen places, little stinging specks that would have been so much worse if I hadn't been prepared.

Silence followed. When the wave had passed, I cracked an eye open, looking down. Nothing moved. Fern, still clinging to my leg, offered me a wan smile.

"Is it over?" she asked.

"That part is," I said, and looked up. Sam was looking down at me, anxiously, his face showing signs of strain. "Fern, how bad is your leg?"

"I don't think it's broken," she said.

"If we pass you up to the ledge, can you stand long enough to pry the doors open?"

Fern hesitated before nodding. "I think so. But how are we going to get me up there?"

I smiled. I hoped she would find the expression encouraging. I knew she probably wouldn't. Oh, well. "I'm going to throw you."

Fern blinked slowly. The gloom in the elevator shaft was deep enough that I couldn't see the fine details of her expression, but I knew her well enough to piece them together in my mind. I waited for her to finish working through the idea, and was rewarded with a smile.

"Like a whip?" she asked.

"Like a whip," I said.

Her smile turned into a grin.

Thanks to a certain movie with Ellen Page and Drew Barrymore, the whip is probably the most famous roller derby move in the world, even though it's relatively infrequent and often ineffective on the track. It *looks* cool, and that made it the perfect concept to frame a movie around (since "learn to fucking skate, you look like roadkill" is not a good title). Basically, the smallest, lightest skater available—usually the jammer, since she's the one we need to speed up—joins hands with a line of her peers, who then use their momentum to "whip" her down the track, letting her get the sort of distance that would be otherwise impossible.

I looked up at Sam. "I need you to swing me," I said.

"What?" squeaked Megan. "No!"

"Are you doing a whip?" asked Cylia, who had been a derby girl longer than I had, and knew what this sort of setup looked like, even when it had become suddenly vertical.

I nodded.

"Cool," said Cylia, as if she weren't hanging from the foot of a therianthrope monkey in an elevator shaft. I decided I liked her more than I had realized.

I reached down with both hands. Fern reached up with one, and our hands met, her fingers clasping tight around mine. She let go of my leg with her other hand, and we were two for two, a line dangling down into the dark.

Sam began to swing his tail, haltingly, like it hurt him to do. It probably did. We were like Rapunzel's prince climbing up her hair, only we were two women hanging from a monkey's tail. There was a joke in there somewhere. I wasn't in the mood to go looking for it just yet. We swung, and I whipped Fern higher and higher, until I ran out of reach and let her go, sending her soaring toward the others. Cylia grabbed for her—

—and missed, the shorter blonde floating past unhindered. Megan made a panicked squeaking sound. Fern adjusted her density ever so slightly, and dropped back into Cylia's hands. The loss of momentum and altitude would have been deadly for someone like me, whose mass was fixed. For Fern, it was barely a pause before Cylia was whipping her up again.

This time, she flew straight and true, grabbing hold of the elevator ledge and hoisting herself up. She winced a little as she put pressure on her left foot, but it held her weight, and kept holding as that weight almost visibly increased, Fern settling deeper and deeper into her position. Once her density was high enough that she didn't have to worry about being whipped away by the faint wind still blowing from below, Fern wedged her fingers into the crack between the doors designed to keep people from falling into the elevator shaft and began to shove.

Strength is important. Strength can be the thing that turns the tide. But leverage is based as much on size as it is on strength, and Fern, for all that she was a dainty, delicate-looking little thing, was also a professional athlete, spending every minute she could strapped into her skates and going for the gold. If roller derby were played at the Olympic level, she would have been trying for the team. She would never have qualified—good as our little regional league was, there are other, better skaters out there—but she would have made it farther than most people expected. She was good. She was strong. And at the moment, she had the undeniable density of someone five times her size.

Fern pushed, and bit by bit, the elevator bay doors responded. They had never been intended to keep people *in*, after all, only to keep people from falling to their deaths. The doors inched farther and farther open, until she was standing between them, her hands pressed flat against their respective edges, refusing to let them close.

"Little help here?" she said.

"On it," said Sam, and pulled himself into a handstand with the sort of ease that I could only envy. Cylia and Megan, dangling from his feet, appeared to do a slow somersault above me. I was hanging from his tail, and simply found myself hoisted farther out of the hole. Enough farther that I could reach the lip of the ledge.

Careful not to dislodge Sam's tail from around my waist, I reached out and grabbed the ledge with both hands, getting a good grip before I angled my body downward. Sam glanced my way, saw what I was doing, and unwrapped his tail from around my waist with an expression of relieved gratitude. Gravity immediately kicked in, my lower body swinging down to slam against the wall in a half-controlled arc. I gritted my teeth, gripped the wall a little tighter, and waited for the impact to stop echoing in my bones. Then, deliberately, I began pulling myself up.

Megan and Cylia were already on their feet by the time I climbed up to join them. Sam was leaning against one of the elevator bay doors, while Fern leaned against the other. He had his left foot in his hands, and was massaging out the kinks with broad, firm strokes.

"Remind me not to do that again for at least a year," he said, grimacing. "I am going to be one big ache tomorrow."

"But we'll have a tomorrow, and that's what counts," I said. "Everyone okay?"

"That was better than zip lining," said Cylia.

"My hair threw up," said Megan.

I paused. Sadly, that did nothing to dispel the image her words had conjured. "Ew," I said, finally. "Come on." I started walking. The others, mercifully, followed, Fern limping.

Outside the elevator shaft was a standard Lowry corporate hallway: more brightly colored than, say, an accounting firm, with framed cartoon posters on the walls instead of actuarial tables, but otherwise as featureless and emotionless as any other business in the world. I looked around, frowning.

"I wish my cousin Sarah were here," I muttered. "She's our math guru."

"Meaning what?" said Cylia.

"Meaning the building tends to get taller when the people on top want it to, and my on-the-fly math skills aren't good enough to tell me how far we fell." According to the plaque next to the elevator, we were on the fifth floor. That should have been the top. We'd fallen a hell of a lot farther than that.

"Can we take the stairs?" asked Fern.

"They could be a hundred floors high," I said. Then I paused. "Wait. No, they can't."

"Please pick one, this is making my head hurt," said Megan.

"Emily's a routewitch. She's the one doing their distance work. Distance is a constant. How far we fell is how far we have to climb, and we didn't fall a hundred floors. We fell a long way, but not *that* long." I looked at the elevator shaft.

Sam followed my gaze, and shook his head. "No. I might be able to climb to the top. I could probably even carry one of you. But I can't carry everyone, and I'm not leaving all our backup behind. Not going to happen."

"I thought you were letting me lead this," I said.

"Only as long as I'm also keeping you alive," he replied firmly. "Keeping you alive is the most important thing I'm doing right now."

"I'm touched, really," said Cylia. Her tone was dry, but her expression was sympathetic. "Although I care more about my own skin than the monkey seems to, he's not entirely wrong. We're not doing anything that ups our chance of being slaughtered."

"Do they know we're still alive?" asked Megan. "If I'd dropped an elevator on somebody, I'd figure they were dead." Her snakes were standing on end, tongues flicking constantly. That, more than anything else, told me how much rage was behind her calm exterior. Megan was a medical resident who just happened to be a gorgon. She'd never been thrown down an elevator shaft before. She was *pissed*.

"Maybe," I said. "Maybe not."

Megan nodded. "Then we take the stairs." She looked around at the rest of us, neutral expression melting into a scowl that Medusa herself would have admired. "Nobody drops me down a hole."

I smiled.

Twenty-two

"Tired is for after the battle ends. Tired is
for winners. Losers get to sleep a lot longer,
and they don't wake up again."
—Jane Harrington-Price

Climbing up a lot of stairs

THE STAIRS DID NOT go on forever. That would have
been impossible. If routewitches had been able to
extend mundane stairways past the limit of the Earth's
gravity, like some *Phineas and Ferb* nightmare science
adventure, they would have found a way to boost the
space program decades ago. Roads crisscrossing the so-
lar system, distances that planet-bound routewitches
could only dream of . . . oh, they would never have let us
stay within the grasp of gravity. No matter how much
they enjoyed using it as a weapon.

The stairs did, however, go on for a long, long time.
Cylia, Fern, and I were all used to skating for hours, and
while we weren't exactly thrilled by the climb, we managed with relative ease once Fern figured out the exact
balance she needed to strike between density and injury.
I took point, a knife in each hand and fingers aching for
fire. Cylia was close behind me, ready to pull me out of
the way if something loomed.

Sam brought up the middle, Megan slung over his
shoulder like a sack of potatoes. She wasn't protesting.
The gorgon was in reasonably good shape, but she was
also a med grad student, and this sort of thing wasn't
part of her daily rounds at the hospital. Letting her walk

would have slowed us down considerably, and Sam didn't seem to have a problem carrying her.

Fern finished our procession, stepping light—so light that she frequently launched herself several feet into the air, landing on a higher step as gently as a feather drifting back to earth. She was moving slower than any of the rest of us but still keeping pace through the sheer dint of taking the steps so many at a time.

Every time we reached a landing we would stop, tensing, while I cracked the door open and looked through. For the past eight floors, what I'd seen on the other side was the same hallway. The *exact* same hallway. Emily could bend space and distort distance, but routewitches can't actually create what isn't there. The strange otherspace I had walked through the first time I'd come to this building had been the creation of one of the other magicusers. That was worrisome. Of the members of the Lowryland cabal, the only ones I was absolutely sure of were Emily, Colin the sorcerer, and Joshua the trainspotter. The others were a nebulous mass of faces and ill-defined abilities.

Belatedly, I realized that should have been another warning sign. Yes, I was Colin's student. Yes, it was reasonable that he was my primary contact with the rest of the cabal. But when I'd joined my roller derby team, there had been a big mixer for me and the rest of the fresh meat, so we could understand what we were getting ourselves into. When I'd joined the cheerleading squad, we had all gone out for pizza to get to know each other, because the people in charge understood that without the pom-poms and spirit fingers, most of us would never have been friends. Even my employment as a low-level Lowryland cast member had started with team building exercises.

If the cabal had really wanted me as a member of their team, they would have treated me like a member of the team, not shunted me into a corner where Colin could keep an eye on me. I had been so blinded by the possibility of getting myself under control that I hadn't paid attention to the parts of the narrative that didn't fit, the ones designed to keep me on the outside and out of the way.

Saying this was all my fault would have been sheer arrogance, untrue, and unhelpful. These people had been spinning their spells and doing their damage long before I'd come on the scene. But I'd made them stronger, whether I'd intended to or not, and I had been a part of the damage they'd done since I'd agreed to let them have access to me. I needed to fix this.

We were approaching another landing. I motioned for the others to stop, eased the door open, and peeked through the crack into the wood-and-mirrors training room. We were here. We were finally, after so many stairs, here.

I looked over my shoulder and nodded. Sam put Megan down. She stepped forward, joining Cylia at my back, and reached for her sunglasses. She didn't remove them—not yet—but with her hand on the frame, she was armed and dangerous.

No more waiting. No more walking. It was time to move.

I pushed the door open, and we stepped through.

The room where Colin had conducted the bulk of my training was empty. We moved to the center of the floor, which seemed the least likely location for a trapdoor, and stopped, looking carefully around.

Back home, I had a reputation for digging pit traps and otherwise making my siblings' lives difficult. I studied the walls and floor, looking for places where the woodgrain didn't line up the way it should have, or where an angle seemed ever so slightly wrong. I didn't find them. Either there were no traps in this room, or they were too well hidden for me to see them.

Or something else was going on. I looked at the mirror. Our reflections looked back at me, Megan still mercifully wearing her sunglasses. Stunning myself with friendly fire would have been one hell of a capper on an already lousy evening.

"Everyone, get ready," I said, drew a knife, and flung it as hard and as true as I could toward the dead center of the glass.

The sort of throwing knives we used at the carnival are light, designed for distance more than damage. They can travel a long way, but if you're aiming for something solid, you're more likely to blunt your blade than you are to actually break anything.

If you're aiming for something solid. My knife hit the glass and the mirror shattered, shards falling harmlessly to the ground to reveal a concrete box of a room, more basement than anything else, with a set of gridded steel stairs leading downward. My heart leaped into my throat. It was the room Emily had led me through on my first visit, and that meant those stairs ended in the conference room.

"We're almost there," I said, flexing my fingers again. There was still no fire, but the heat of my anger made up for it. "Mind the glass."

Shards of mirror crunched underfoot as I walked toward the opening I'd created, pausing only to retrieve my knife. When I reached the edge of the mirror, I paused, turned, and motioned for the others to stay back.

"Give me a second," I said. "Sam, be ready to pull me out."

He nodded. Megan looked confused.

"Pull her out?" she asked. "Why?"

"In case it's booby-trapped," said Fern cheerfully, like she was explaining a particularly clever derby maneuver. "It probably is. It would be if it were *my* dark creepy room behind a big glass sheet."

Megan's mouth dropped open. She looked to Cylia for support. Cylia shrugged.

"This is life outside a gated community," she said. "It gets weird."

We could banter for hours. That was nice—banter is comforting, which is probably why Spider-Man does it so much—but it wasn't getting us any closer to done. Sam was the fastest person I'd ever met, human or cryptid. If anyone could get me out of the way before some deathtrap slammed closed over my head, it was him. And I trusted him to do it. I trusted him completely.

Maybe this was what love felt like. Smiling despite myself, I turned to face front, took a deep breath, and stepped over the base of the broken mirror, into the dark basement.

Which promptly burst into super-heated flame around me.

I screamed. Much of my training focused on powering through sprains and even broken bones, learning how to walk on a twisted ankle without making a sound that might give away my position, but my parents—hard-nosed as they sometimes were in the pursuit of preparing us to survive in a world filled with dangers—had never actually set me on *fire*. I'd never even set *myself* on fire before, not really. I'd scalded my arms and blistered my palms, but I had never burned from head to toe. I had never been *consumed*.

I wasn't being consumed now. I couldn't be. The thought hit like a blow. If there was as much fire as I could feel around me, I wouldn't have had the *time* to scream. I would have been reduced to ashes in an instant, and I'd be either gone or a ghost—and ghosts don't burn. I looked at my arms, struggling to swallow the screams rising in my throat. They were untouched, perfectly smooth and fine. The heat felt real. The fire felt real. My skin did not agree.

I looked back. Sam was slapping at the flames in the opening, trying to get through the fire to get to me, fighting his own instincts. He wasn't calm enough to see that his hands were as untouched as mine—when he pulled them out of the illusion of the flame, it was only to shove them back in again, struggling to save me.

He was crying. He was fighting and he was crying, and I wondered what he saw when he looked at me. It couldn't be an anguished but intact woman, or he wouldn't be fighting so hard. We had both seen stranger than someone walking untouched through fire, and he'd seen me set myself alight more than once without ill-effects, although my fire could hurt me, and only danced when it was still connected to my skin . . .

To my skin. I turned back to the flames, looking at

them with wide eyes. The pain was receding. Either the nerves responsible for relaying sensation were giving up in the face of an enemy too great to be described, or the fire was changing.

The fire was recognizing me.

"Sam, can you hear me?" I called.

"Annie?" There was a clattering sound, followed by a hiss, and an anguished, "I can't reach you! Annie, are you all right?"

"What do you see, Sam?"

A hitching indrawn breath, and then a soft: "I can't reach you."

That answered the question of what he saw when he looked at me. "I'm fine, Sam. I was surprised, and I was in pain, but I'm not hurt. The fire isn't really burning me." Because the fire was mine, and once it had realized that, it had started pulling back.

It wasn't intelligent, as such. Fire knows how to burn, and not much more than that. But it belonged to me, it belonged *with* me, and it wanted to come home. I looked at the flames dancing all around me, licking at the air, and I knew they wanted to come home. I just didn't know how to let them.

"I'm sorry," I said, holding out my hands, fingers spread, palms toward the ceiling. The heat was entirely gone now, replaced by a pleasant coolness. Sam was still fighting the illusion of the fire, but not as hard; he could hear me. Even if he couldn't quite believe me, he knew I was at least intact enough to talk. "I thought I was learning to control you, and instead, I was letting someone take you away from me. I should never have done that. Can you forgive me?"

The flame burned blue, pressing in closer, until everything was fire, and there wasn't room in the world for anything else. I kept my eyes and hands open.

"I don't know how to take you back," I said softly. "If you know how to come back on your own, come home. If you don't, please, pull back. Let my friends help me, and we'll make the bastard who put you here put you back where you belong."

This room wasn't real. I'd known that the first time I'd stepped into it. The water table was too high and the walls were too thick. Magic had made this place, and magic was sustaining it, and it only made sense that they would put the pieces of my magic that they weren't using in what was effectively the largest bell jar they had available to them.

The flames froze for a single heart-stopping moment before they sank back into the floor and were gone. I could still feel them, the way I'd always been able to feel them lurking in my fingers, but . . . distant, like they and I were both swaddled in a whole roll of bubble wrap.

I didn't have time to think about what that meant, as Sam slammed into me from the side the instant the flames faded, literally sweeping me off my feet and carrying me easily four feet deeper into the room. Not a good idea, from a trap-avoidance standpoint, but then he was kissing me, and I had other things to worry about, like kissing him back while his tail wrapped around my waist and pulled me closer, until I was in danger of having the breath squeezed right out of me.

Cylia cleared her throat. "Excuse me," she said, sounding amused. "It's fun watching you two try to suck each other's faces off, and I am *very* aware of what danger does to the hormones, but do you think we could put this on the back burner until we're not supposedly using stealth to sneak up on the people who want to hurt us? Just as a thought? Because this is not what I want to die for."

"Speak for yourself," said Sam, and put me down.

Finally free to look around the room without fire or fūri getting in the way, I turned in a slow circle, studying my surroundings. The mirror had broken inward, covering the floor in shards of glass. There were scorch marks on the walls. Interesting. The fire hadn't harmed me or Sam, but it had been trying hard enough to get out at one point that it had been able to burn concrete.

The char was thickest on the wall around the mirror. My stomach turned. If the magic had flowed from me into this space, that would have been where it realized we were no longer together. It might be nothing but instinct and power. That hadn't stopped it from under-standing that something was wrong while I was running on intellect and denial. I shook my hands. My fingers were still cold.

They weren't going to stay cold for long.

"Follow me," I said, and started for the stairs.

Our descent was fast compared to everything else we'd already been through. In what seemed like not nearly long enough, I was in front of one last door. Megan was behind me, ready to remove her glasses, and Sam was behind her, out of the line of visual fire. I took a deep breath.

I opened the door.

The Lowryland cabal, seated around their conference table, dressed in their impeccable business clothes, turned and looked at us. Emily was the only one who looked even remotely worried. Colin, especially, seemed utterly and completely calm, as if this were the sort of thing he dealt with every day. As if he had been expecting it. Which he probably had. He was a sorcerer. He had to know that *eventually*, I would put two and two together.

I felt like a fool for letting it take this long. That feeling propelled me forward, over the doorframe, into the conference room. "You've stolen something of mine," I said coldly. "I want it back."

"Ditto," said Sam. He paused. "That sounded cooler in my head."

"Yes, by all means, impress us with your 'coolness,'" said Colin. He sneered on the last word, and he didn't stand. "I've stolen nothing from you, little apprentice. I've taken only a tutor's fee. Can I be blamed if you didn't read the fine print before you signed?"

"You people really love your fine print, don't you?" I flexed my fingers, this time not trying to call fire, just to relax them enough for the knives to come easily. "You're hurting the guests."

Emily's eyes widened. "Are you genuinely telling us you're here for *them*? Don't be ridiculous. They're mind-less tourists looking for a good time. They spend more money than some people make in a year just for the opportunity to touch a fictional princess and pretend that makes everything okay. They're sheep. We're farmers."

"One, that should be 'shepherds,'" I snapped. "Two, no you're not, and also ew, and what the fuck is wrong with you? People have been *killed*. This has to stop."

"Your power is settling down," said Colin, in what was probably intended as a soothing voice. I was not soothed. "Now that I know how to control it, we'll be able to adapt. The accidents were regrettable growing pains. I assure you, they won't happen again."

"Can I pull his head off?" asked Sam conversationally. "I bet it would be easy. Can I try? I think I'm gonna try."

"I'm fascinated by how quickly you were able to raise an army of monsters," said Joshua. He stood, and I had to fight the urge to take a step back, away from his prying, scrying eyes. "I wouldn't have expected it. None of these people are human, are they? Only you. Why is that?"

"She has unusually good taste in friends," said Cylia. She managed to sound nonchalant, which was no mean feat, given the situation. We were surrounded. Half these people were unarmed, and it didn't matter, because they *were* the weapons.

Joshua could look into our eyes and see every plan we'd ever sketched, whether we planned to act on it or not. He was a trainspotter at the height of his power, fully charged by the motion of the roller coasters and the monorails, and I didn't know enough about what he was capable of to be properly terrified. Colin might need a wand to access his magic—and maybe that had something to do with the kind of control he'd been trying to teach me, or maybe it was a statement on how limited his power would have been without the tools of his trade— but wand or no, he could certainly ruin our day. Emily had already shown her capability to steal luck and distance, both of which were key to getting out of this alive. The rest of them . . .

Stomach sinking, I realized how smoothly I had been played. Colin had taken me on as his apprentice, neatly isolating me from the rest of the cabal before I could even ask whether this was how things were normally done. Back home, we lived according to a complex and sometimes contradictory web of secrets, keeping them from everyone around us—even, sometimes, from each other. My parents didn't know about the fire in my fingers. I'd been afraid to tell them, afraid that they would judge, or worse, look at me differently. And now they were never going to look at me again.

When Colin had started keeping secrets, when he had started hiding the other members of the cabal behind carefully contradictory schedules and "need to know," it had seemed normal enough to me that I hadn't thought to question it. Secrecy was just normal. It kept us breathing.

"You need to get out of here," I said tightly. My eyes were on Colin, but my words were for the people who'd come with me to the top of this impossible tower. They didn't have my training. They didn't have my weapons. They had their native abilities, and those were good, those were incredibly useful, but they weren't the same as a knife, or a crowbar, or even a coherent plan.

I was a fool, and my friends were going to pay the cost.

"I still want to take his head off," said Sam.

"Also, no," said Cylia. "We don't run out on our own."

"That means you," said Fern.

Megan didn't say anything, but I heard the hissing of her hair, and knew that she was at my back with one hand on her glasses, ready to stun anyone who drew her attention.

I took a deep breath, looking for strength in the fact that I was not alone. I had never really been alone, because there were always people ready to have my back, if I was only willing to reach out and ask them. "I did not give you my magic when I allowed you to train me," I said. "I certainly didn't give you permission to use it against people who'd done nothing wrong. And you." I turned to Emily, who raised one eyebrow, mouth pursed in an amused moue. "This is beneath you. This isn't how a routewitch is supposed to behave."

"You're not one of us, so who are you to judge?"

asked Emily. She spread her hands, indicating first the sumptuous boardroom around us, then her perfectly tailored Egyptian cotton business suit. "You think I should have agreed to live like some sort of trailer trash hobo because the highway speaks to me? Because road magic is somehow more 'pure' when the people who practice it have *nothing*? Please. Times have changed. The world has changed. If routewitches want to find ways to use our natural talents for a profit, we should be allowed to do exactly that. In summation, little girl, screw you."

She moved her hand like she was throwing a ball. I realized what she was doing too late and flung my own hands up in a blocking motion, fingers spread, palms empty. There was no fire there to stop whatever she was casting. In that moment, it felt like there never had been.

A body slammed into mine from the left, rocking me to the side, and Cylia was there, her fingers moving fast, a complicated motion somewhere between macramé and braiding a friendship bracelet. The motion looked effortless, but the strain on her face gave her away.

"She's trying to offload her bad luck onto us," she said, through gritted teeth. "A little help, please?"

"If you think I'm looking at your gorgon, think again," said Emily. She sounded almost gleeful, like this was the most fun she'd had in years.

"Wasn't thinking that," I said, as brightly and blithely as I could. I moved my own hands. There was nothing magical about what followed, only skill and practice and good American steel flying through the air on a straight, true path, heading directly for Emily's shoulders.

A blast of fire from Colin's wand caught my knives mid-flight, knocking them off target and sending them clattering harmlessly against the window. The smell of hot metal and hotter glass filled the air.

Sam moved.

He was fast and fluid like the artist that he was, launching himself into the air and impacting with the conference table in almost the same movement. He grabbed a fistful of papers in each hand, flinging them into the air to create confusion. Several members of the cabal shouted.

One woman's eyes went black, and the air around her darkened for a moment before she abandoned the attempt. Turning the lights out wasn't going to hurt us any, and it might help us. After all, we were the ones with the target-rich environment.

"Witch," I shouted, putting the name to her powers. I didn't know how many of the others knew what it meant to be facing a witch, full stop, with no modifiers, although Cylia nodded, still braiding the air as quickly as her fingers would let her. "Sam! Get the wand!"

Colin whipped around, wand raised and already spitting fire. Sam wasn't there anymore. He had leaped for the ceiling and was hanging from the light fixture, his weight pulling heavy on the bolts. They would only hold for a few seconds. That would have to be enough.

I threw another knife. This one caught Colin in the back of the shoulder. His grip on the wand faltered, if only for a moment. That was all Sam needed. He snatched it from the air with one foot, tossing it up and catching it with his free hand.

"*Annie!*" he shouted, and flung the wand at me.

I snatched it from the air, too relieved to think about what he'd said. Touching the wood was like touching the fire that had been stolen from me. Colin was shouting something, but I was too focused on the wand to care. It was filled with fire. I wanted that fire. That fire wanted me. We wanted each other, so badly that it ached in the pit of my stomach, in the marrow of my bones.

Quickly, before I could change my mind, I snapped the wand in half. The resulting backlash flung me against the window, through the glass, and out into the seemingly endless night, where I fell.

Well, crap.

Twenty-three

"Mercy is for the winners. When you're losing, it's the last thing you can afford."
—Alice Healy

Falling

THE WORLD STUTTERED AROUND me as the space-warping spells on the interior met the reality of the outside world, finally settling on a compromise: my fall was not from as high as it should have been, given how far we'd climbed, but it was farther than it should have been, given that the window I'd crashed through was no longer there. Only the shards of glass falling in tandem with my body betrayed any sign that it had ever existed in the first place. I was going to hit the pavement in a spray of shards, a modern Tinkerbell who never really learned to fly.

An arm wrapped around my waist as something slammed into me from the side, and Sam and I crashed back into the building together, smashing through the nearest window. His body shielded me from the worst of the impact. When we landed, he turned me, so that I was looking into wide brown eyes set in a worried face.

"Are you all right?" asked Sam. "Did you know that was going to happen?"

"No," I said, and clung to him. Heat flickered in my fingertips, too weak to be called real fire, reminiscent of the way it had been when the flames first started curling through me, before they had been fanned into a bonfire. My magic was coming back. Not fast enough to save me, but still. At least I was going to die in one piece. "Where's everyone else?"

"Up," said Sam. He stood carefully, helping me to my feet at the same time. "Was that 'no' to 'are you all right,' or to the other thing?"

"The other thing." I grimaced as I rotated my shoulder, feeling the joint complain. "We need to get back to them."

"Uh, that's probably going to be easier said than done, since, you know—"

Whatever he was going to say was lost as something pounded hard against the door to our temporary sanctuary. Sam turned to me, clearly expecting me to know what to do next. It would have been touching, if not for the fact that we were trapped, with no weapons more useful than my knives, no exit, and no way to get back to our friends.

But we had a window. We were three floors up, maybe more, and the edge of the swamp was less than twenty feet away. There were no security cameras in the swamp. Alligators, yes, cameras, no. I pointed.

"Throw me," I said.

Sam stared. "What?"

"No time to argue!" Whoever had followed us down was still pounding on the door, and they'd be through in a moment. "Throw me!" He'd slung me almost twice that distance when we were in the tent back at his family's carnival, and he'd had a lot less motivation then. If he threw me hard enough, if I could shape my descent like this was just another trick on the trapeze, if I could hit the water at the right angle to prevent myself from slamming into an alligator, if, if, if . . . if we could manage all those things, we might be able to walk away from this and get back to our people. We might escape.

Sam looked, for an instant, like he was going to argue. Then he nodded and kissed me, before grabbing my waist with both hands. I went as limp as I could, trying to think of this as perfectly normal, the tent lights around us, the net below us, the world aligned to let us dazzle the crowd without hurting ourselves. We were going to be fine. We were going to be *fine*.

He flung me away from him so hard that I was going to have bruises on my ribs for a week, assuming I lived long enough for them to form. I curled myself into a tight ball, cutting down on wind resistance, feeling the air whisking by around me, as jagged as the broken glass I was leaving behind. When I judged that I'd flown far enough, I stretched out in the classic pose of the flying trapeze, legs pressed together like the shaft of an arrow, arms spread wide, like I thought I could will myself into becoming a bird.

Below me, the parking lot was a black, yawning chasm, ready to swallow me whole, to batter my body and break my bones, one more victim of Lowryland's stolen luck. Then the landscape changed, sliced in two by the knife's edge of the chain link fence, and I was flying over the swamp, green and brown and hungry. I was already losing momentum, beginning to drop, a superhero whose comic had been destined for cancellation from the very first panel.

I screwed my eyes tightly shut against the mud and muck, and let the water have me.

I've always hated swimming.

Alex loves it. He enjoys the freedom and weightlessness of the water, and anyway, it's easier to study frogs and alligators when he's on their level. Verity doesn't mind it. She prefers dancing, but swimming has enough in common with dance that she can find enjoyment in the activity. Me?

I knew the water wanted me dead long before I felt fire in my fingers. We were natural enemies, the water and I, and it didn't matter whether it was in a swimming pool or the Pacific Ocean, it would kill me if I gave it the opportunity. So I endured my swimming lessons exactly as long as my parents forced me to do so, learning enough that I was at a low risk of drowning—as long as I stayed conscious. As long as I wasn't plummeting blind into a swamp filled with alligators and unknown obstacles. As long as I had *some* common sense.

It really sucks how often my early training is no match for the world in which I live.

I hit the swamp hard enough to knock the air out of my lungs. I think I blacked out. It was hard to tell, since everything around me was darkness, leaving me functionally blind and unaware of danger. I drifted several feet in a state of shock, barely even able to muster up gratitude for the fact that I had managed to avoid slamming into either the ground or some unseen, even less yielding obstacle.

Something splashed to my left. I was not alone.

My brother Alex is the reptile expert, but that doesn't mean I'm ignorant. A noise like that in a place like this was likely to mean "alligator," aka "America's own prehistoric killing machine." The alligator is proof that once evolution gets something right, it stops screwing around with the details and lets it go on its merry, murderous way. Even a juvenile could kill me if it caught hold of me here, and I was much more likely to attract the attention of an adult, given my size, given the volume of my splash. I needed to move.

Too bad my body had other ideas. My lungs ached. My stomach did the same. It was like the water had punched me, right after Sam had flung me more than twenty feet across open space.

Sam. The thought was electric, shocking some of the strength back into my useless limbs. There hadn't been a second splash. He was more than strong enough to jump that distance, unless he'd decided to climb down the side of the building instead. As long as he hadn't tried to stay and make a stand, he should have been able to get away. Please, he was able to get away.

I rose out of the water with a gasp, trying to minimize my splashing as I stood, spat out the muddy taste of the swamp, and began moving away from the sound that had awakened me. Alligators, snakes, worse things, they were all out here with me. I needed to move. I needed to get away from them. I needed to get to Sam and the others.

My fumbling hands found solid ground. I pulled myself up onto the grassy bank, pulling knives from inside my shirt and getting a good grip on them. They were small—far too small to be effective against a hungry alligator—but they still made me feel better. We all have our security blankets in this world.

Once I was standing, it wasn't difficult to spot the Lowryland administrative complex. It was the big, bright square blazing with light, a clear contrast to the dark around me. Carefully, all too aware that I'd do myself no favors by putting a foot down wrong, I began making my way toward the light.

I was almost there when a dark shape moved in front of the fence. I stopped, keeping to the shadow.

"Annie?"

"Sam!" Relief chased caution away. I ran across the last stretch of swamp between me and him, hitting the chain link and pressing my hands against it, knives still held against my palms. There was Sam, back in his humanoid form. He smiled wearily at the sight of me.

"You're like a cockroach," he said. "I'm dating a cockroach. That's pretty cool."

I laughed. The sound had a little too much in common with a sob. "That's me," I said. "The unkillable girl."

"Good. I like your dead aunts, but I don't wanna date a ghost. I'd wind up feeling like a cradle robber when I kept aging and you didn't." Sam looked over his shoulder toward the admin building. "How do we get back up?"

If it hadn't been for the fence between us, I would have kissed him. "I don't know," I said. "We'll figure it out."

"Or not."

The voice belonged to Mary. I turned. There she was, glowing faintly against the dark. She looked sad. That wasn't unusual. Being dead seems to come with a lot of sorrow. She also looked scared. That was a little stranger.

"Hi, Annie," she said. She glanced past me. "Hi, Sam."

"Hi, Miss Mary," said Sam. "You're looking, you know. Spectral and sort of creepy tonight."

"Flatterer." Mary turned her eyes back to me. "You shouldn't go back in there."

"I have to. My friends—"

"Aren't in there anymore." She shook her head. "You broke a sorcerer's wand. Do you know what that does to the wards and enchantments on a place like this? Their ambulomancer shifted them away as soon as they realized what you'd done. The blast killed their witch and her trainee. They set their chained guards on the hunt for you, but those can't leave the building. Your former employers are out for blood now."

A strange calm settled over me, spreading out from the pit of my stomach until everything else was washed away. "And they have our friends."

Mary nodded. "Yes."

"Fern, Cylia, and Megan. The cabal has them."

"Yes," said Mary again. "They're lost, Annie, you must see that. Your magic has been almost entirely siphoned away, Sam is hurt—"

"Wait." I turned. "You're hurt?"

Sam shrugged, looking sheepish. He took his hand away from his side, revealing a torn shirt and skin that was ripped and red with blood. "It's just a little road rash," he said. "No big."

"Very big," I said firmly. "Any injury is *very* big as far as I'm concerned. Do you need to go back to the apartment? I won't be angry if you sit this out."

"Are you going to sit this out?"

I shook my head. "I can't."

"Then neither can I." Sam shook his head. "Where you go, I go. That's the rule. The only reason I let you walk away before was because I'd just been shot for the first time. I think I was allowed a little lapse in judgment."

I wanted to kiss him. I wanted to hug him. The damn fence was still in the way. "I love you," I informed him, and turned back to Mary. "Sorry, Aunt Mary. No can do on the leaving our friends to the tender mercies of people who think luck theft and magic siphoning is a fun thing to do. If you want to tell me where they are, we can get this over with quick. If not, I'll figure it out."

"You know what it would cost for me to give you

specific information," said Mary. There was a challenge
in her voice. "You think this is worth that?"

"It would be if I needed it," I said. "Luckily, I don't
need it, because I know where they are."

"You do?" asked Mary, with the ghost of a smile.

"You do?" asked Sam, sounding bemused.

I shifted so I could beam at both of them at the same
time, each out of one corner of my mouth. "We've damaged their power. They're going to go where the heart of
their empire lies. They're going to go to Lowryland."

The nice thing about old cars is how easy they are to
hotwire. Cylia was probably going to be pissed that I'd
cracked her steering column. I'd make it up to her. Not
being dead would be an awesome start.

Sam sat in the passenger seat, still in his human form,
clutching the grip above the door with white-knuckled
fervor. The gauze I'd found in the glove compartment
stood out starkly white where I'd covered his scrapes
and bruises. Mary was in the back, occasionally flickering
out of existence when I took a curve too fast, only to
reappear a second later, keeping easy pace with the car.
From the way Sam rolled his eyes at her, I guessed her
impermanence wasn't helping.

Oh, well. There'd be time to worry about my boyfriend's nerves later, when we weren't racing an unspo-
ken deadline for the lives of our loved ones. I kept my
foot down and tried not to think about how much I hate
driving, or how I didn't have a license, or how easy it
would be to crash into something big and solid and die
horribly. (Okay, I was failing at not thinking about any of
those things, but I could pretend. Boy, could I pretend.)
In what felt like no time at all, we were rocketing into
the virtually deserted employee parking lot, rolling past
the cars of security staff and janitorial workers to park
as close to the doors as I could get us.

Mary grimaced as soon as the engine died. "Bad news,

kiddo," she said, through gritted teeth. "I can't get out of the car."

"What?" I twisted in the driver's seat to frown at her. "Why not?"

"Your routewitch has apparently decided you don't get any more help tonight. She doesn't want me even this close to her territory, but this car has a lot of miles on it, and it's shielding me from her repulsion charms. At least a little. If I tried to get out, I'd find myself slammed back into the twilight before I could say 'boo.'"

"So don't get out," I said. "Stay here. I'll send anyone we find to the car, and if the charms collapse, you'll know we've managed to take Emily down."

"Annie ..." She paused, looking faintly ill before she said, "If it's a choice between the crossroads and the cemetery, you call for me. No routewitch can keep me out when there's a bargain to be made."

"It's not going to come to that," I assured her, got out of the car, and walked toward the gate.

Sam was close behind me. He pulled up by my side, matching his steps to mine, and asked, "Do you have a plan?"

"Not so much."

"Do you have enough knives?"

"Never."

"Do you mind if I ask you a question?"

I glanced at him. He looked earnest, faintly confused, and determined. I sighed. "Go ahead."

"What's with Mary? She told me what she could when she was keeping me updated on you, but ... I feel like there's a lot she had to leave out."

"You don't ask *small* questions, do you?" I exhaled. "Do you know what the crossroads are?"

"Yeah. You go down to the crossroads when you want to make a deal."

"Just like that. Only you don't normally need to go anywhere; the crossroads can find you, if they're interested enough. Some people go to the physical place where the crossroads are currently manifesting, and those are the people who *want*. Most folks stumble into a deal. Bad bargains, sold souls. The usual." I shook my head. "Not a good plan. I don't recommend it."

"I'm picking up on that. So Mary . . . ?"

"Was human, was dying, and made a deal with the crossroads to stay on as a ghost and serve them for as long as they want her. See, when you make a deal at the crossroads, it's sort of like an episode of *Law & Order*. You get the defense, and you get the prosecution. Mary's the defense. Mary's the one who tries to argue the crossroads into giving you what you *want*, instead of what you technically asked for. She's the good guy."

Sam frowned. "Even though she's working for them?"

"When you have a choice between Godzilla and Cthulhu, you take Godzilla every time. At least the King of Monsters isn't actively out to destroy humanity. Mary . . . Mary isn't cruel. She doesn't make bargains with family if she has any choice in the matter. She reminds us that while crossroad bargains may seem like a cheap and easy way out of a tight spot, there's always something else that can be done. And she makes brownies using my great-grandmother's recipe, which is pretty amazing."

There was a lot else I could have said, like how people like us have a tendency to trip and stumble up against the spirit world, and how having her around made sure we never did it by accident. How she'd been able to successfully keep any member of the family from calling on the crossroads since Grandpa Thomas—and how she never let us forget what he'd done, or what he'd paid for doing it. How much we needed her, and by extension, how much she needed us, because having a family to worry about kept her from falling into the trap that waits for all the world's ghosts. As long as she had us, she couldn't forget that she'd been one of the living, once. She couldn't forget that the living were small, and soft, and worth worrying about.

We were going to keep reminding her forever, if I had any say in the matter.

We had reached the gate to the Park. It was locked,

but that was no real barrier: not to people who'd trained on the trapeze and didn't care about getting busted. Sam formed a basket with his hands and I stepped into it, one knee pulled toward my chest in a classic cheerleading pose. If not for the humidity and the darkness and the fact that we were about to commit an act of breaking and entering, it would have felt just like old times. He boosted me up. I grabbed the top of the gate and hoisted myself over it, dropping down into the Park proper.

Sam appeared next to me a second later, having leaped over the gate. He offered me my backpack. I shook my head as I took it and slung it over my shoulder, smiling at him fondly.

"Show-off," I said.

"Hey, I have to keep you interested," he replied.

"Trust me; keeping me interested is not going to be the problem," I said. "Keeping me breathing may be, but so far you've been up to the challenge."

"Planning to stay that way," he said.

The Park was deserted, lit by the minimum number of bulbs and glowing fixtures. It would have made more sense to light the place up like midday for the sake of the janitorial staff, but that would also have attracted attention. Insomniacs and teenagers were attracted to Lowryland's rare midnight openings like moths to a flame, following the blazing lights of the complex across the freeways of Florida. Maintenance and cleanup happen in the dark, lest they be seen, lest they be noticed.

They're not the only things that happen in the dark. I shook my hands and felt the ghosts of flame in my fingers, still too drained and distant to reach. I breathed in the familiar, irreplaceable scent of Lowryland, that mixture of plastic reality, real sweat, fried sugar, and sunscreen, and felt regret welling up in my chest, stronger than the flames but fanning them at the same time. This was my last walk through the Park. By the time the sun came up, we'd be gone.

The skeleton twist of the Midsummer Night's Scream loomed ahead of us, rendered eerie and organic by the shadows surrounding it. I pointed.

"There," I said. "That area's been closed all day, so janitorial will be staying clear, and the maintenance should be done by now. That's where we're going." It felt right. It felt *true*. That was where we'd agreed to meet our people, and the cabal was running scared, drawing power from their routewitch and their ambulomancer, both of whom were tied to the narrative logic of the road. Add in the trainspotter, who would want to be someplace where he could recharge himself if the need arose, and it was the place in the Park that made the most sense.

That made me nervous. Things that make sense aren't necessarily unreal. What they are, frequently, are traps.

I glanced at Sam. He was moving easily enough, despite the blood on his shirt, and if he was doing this well while concentrating on looking human, he was probably close to top form in his natural shape. It was the "close" that was the problem. Every time we ran into each other, I seemed to put him in danger.

Except no. Except he'd known when he came looking for me that being in my presence was likely to mean bullets and bloodshed and the occasional bout of arson, and he'd shown up anyway. He'd made the choice this time, putting himself in harm's way for the sake of my company, and I'd be damned before I took that away from him. If Sam wanted to be here, then here was exactly where he belonged.

"The security cameras are on even at night, but once people start flinging impossibilities around, it should be okay," I said, voice low. "There's no way cryptids haven't been caught on film before. The folks who see them either say 'this is a hoax' or 'this is outside my pay grade,' and it doesn't get out. Lowryland isn't going to want to be associated with something that looks like a B-grade horror movie. They'll bury it."

"You seem pretty confident."

"My family's been doing this for a long time."

I felt, rather than saw, Sam's glance in my direction. "Do you miss them?"

"More than anything." I even missed the ones I don't like very much, like Verity. My family shares my context.

They know my education, my experiences, where the bone-deep bruises on my psyche are. We have secrets from each other—God, do we have secrets from each other—but even those secrets are built upon a shared foundation of loss and loneliness and duty. Those things aren't unique to our weird little community. People have been forging alliances and pledging fealty based on those things since there have been people in the world. But the specific recipe that we follow, the *blend*, that's all us. That's unique.

Something warm and soft touched my skin. I looked down. Sam's tail was looped in a tight knot around my wrist, providing an anchor without slowing me down.

"You're not alone," he said.

Warmth seemed to flow through my veins, a cousin to the fire that lingered in my fingers, but different, more diffuse, less dangerous. "I know," I said, and we kept walking, a human disaster and a fūri heading toward the inevitable, leaving safety in the rearview mirror, as we had already done so many times before.

This wasn't the first time I'd been in Lowryland after dark—far from it, in fact; my first nocturnal roller skating expedition had followed my employment by less than a month—but it was the first time the Park had seemed actively hostile. The shadows were too deep and the edges were too sharp, as if painted by an inimical hand. Out of the corner of my eye, I could see light flashing off window panes and bits of polished plastic, seeming more like the eyes of hostile creatures than any simple trick of light and shadow.

"Shades of Lovecraft," I muttered.

"What's that?"

"Nothing."

We were approaching the gate that would take us out of the backstage employee areas and into the main body of the Park. It wasn't locked. What would have been the point? Once someone had made it into Lowryland, locks would only give them incentive to break things. Locks were for areas where guests could get seriously hurt or do substantial amounts of damage, not for the great expanse of open space and twisting trails that made up the majority of the Park's real estate.

"You ready?" I asked, looking back at Sam.

He unwound his tail from around my wrist, knowing I was going to need my full range of motion. I nodded appreciatively and pushed the gate open, revealing the gleaming chrome and low nighttime lighting of Metropolis, Lowryland's answer to Disney's World of Tomorrow. Loosely themed after the futuristic utopia of 1927's (thankfully public domain) *Metropolis*, the Lowryland version owed less to Weimar, Germany, and more to the pulp covers of silver age science fiction novels. During the day, robots, androids, and space explorers roved the neon walkways, delighting guests and luring them onto the sleek, chrome-plated rides.

At night, Metropolis was less a dream of a future that had never come and more a graveyard of ideas that had never been able to come to fruition. The spidery legs of launching pods and "spacecraft" seemed menacing and vaguely animate in the shadows, like they could reach for us at any moment.

I didn't say anything, only pointed to my right, indicating that Sam should follow me along the walkway to the Deep-Down. He nodded, letting me lead the way.

As we walked, the Park became less futuristic, more drowned and damaged, worn away by the forces of time and entropy. Atlantis skirted the edge of the two sections, blending them in a way that delighted the Park's designers and horrified the marketing department. It was hard to explain something so high-concept that it required the shared themes of two entire areas to shore it up. But the kids loved it, and the merchandise sold, and so no one messed with Atlantis, and no one messed with the Deep-Down.

It wasn't my area. That's the only excuse I can give for forgetting that a roller coaster runs right through the heart of the Deep-Down, slicing through the Kraken's Lagoon in a self-contained tunnel. It's called the Sea Dragon, and it's the largest, most powerful coaster the Park has, utilizing every trick the engineers know and a few dozen I would have sworn they didn't to get the job done.

We were halfway through the glass-walled tunnel to Fairyland when a roaring sound reverberated through the water around us, magnified by the liquid until it seemed to come from nowhere and everywhere at once. Sam jumped. I froze, fire surging into my fingers, hands balling automatically into fists.

"Uh, Annie? What—"

The sound was getting steadily louder, and closer at the same time, filling the world. The water was dark, but I could still see the movement through the glass—and it wasn't sticking to the outline of the tracks as it raced toward us.

I did the only thing I could. "*Run!*" I shouted, and grabbed Sam's hand, sprinting for the end of the tunnel.

We almost made it before the train slammed into the tunnel's glass wall, and the air was gone, replaced by the crushing force of a tsunami filled with shards of shattered glass. Sam's hand was ripped out of mine.

Everything went black.

Twenty-four

"We don't decide to win. We don't even decide to play. But sometimes we decide to lose."

–Mary Dunlavy

Drowning

THE TUNNEL WAS NARROW enough that the first swell of water slammed me into the ceiling and held me there, shards of glass cutting my arms and legs as the artificial currents buffeted my body. There was no light. There was no air. There was no way for me to know where Sam was, whether he'd been swept entirely away or whether he was only a few feet from me, struggling to find a way to renew our connection.

I closed my eyes. They weren't doing me any good, and the last thing I needed was to get a piece of glass embedded in my cornea. Blinding myself wouldn't improve the situation.

It might not make the situation worse. I was trapped in crushing darkness, and while I have reasonably good lung capacity, I was going to run out of air soon. Sam was ... Sam was somewhere. That was as far as I was willing to let myself go. Sam was somewhere, because the alternative was accepting that Sam might be dead, and if Sam was dead, I was going to burn this whole goddamn place to the ground, fire in my fingers or no. Magic is nice, but napalm is reliable.

No one kills my people. No one but me.

My fingers were heating up again. It wasn't enough.

Even if my fire had somehow been back to its full strength, it wouldn't have been enough. I couldn't produce the kind of flame necessary to boil away this much water, not when there was no air for me to burn. I couldn't do anything.

Well. I could do one thing. Water still buffeting me against the top of the tunnel, I forced myself to relax as much as I could, wishing I had the ability to take a deep breath—wishing I had time to *think* about this. There wasn't time. In the end, I guess there never is.

I didn't have much left in the way of air. I had enough to open my mouth against the frigid, bitter current and spit the words into the water:

"All right, Mary," I said. "I want to make a deal."

The water stopped. It didn't recede, it didn't disappear: it *stopped*. It didn't freeze, either. Freezing would have implied that it had suddenly become colder, suddenly turned hard, and it hadn't done that. It was water, fluid and free and motionless, holding me effortlessly up. I couldn't breathe. That didn't matter, because my lungs didn't hurt anymore, and while I would have sworn my eyes were closed, it seemed that I could see a little better, like the world was becoming suffused with golden light. It was the sort of light that shines on country roads when the sun is going down, slanting through corn husks and glittering with dust motes, rural and rare and impossible to replicate in any other situation. It was an old-fashioned kind of light, a dustbowl dream, and it was getting stronger by the second.

Maybe this was what drowning did. Maybe when people said they'd had a near-death experience and seen the light beckoning them home, they'd really been dreaming of farm country, of corn and wheat and the sickle and the scythe. But I didn't think so. This felt too personal, like it was something intended only and entirely for me.

The light shone, and because light is nothing without something to illuminate, it shone on a mile of empty country highway, asphalt cracked and broken from spending decades baking in the summer sun, shoulders choked with nettle-bush and briars. Past the shoulder

came the corn, and it grew tall and lush and somehow
terrible, as if whatever watered it had less to do with
what I was drowning in and more to do with what I was
keeping, hot and captive, in my veins.

The road appeared, and because a road is nothing
without someone to travel it, a woman walked along the
center line, her jeans faded asphalt-gray, her hair white
as corn silk or cobwebs, her eyes echoing the scene again
in miniature, in microcosm, until she became a Ferris
wheel that turned for nothing good, part of a carnival
whose tickets were too dear to buy with anything but
dreams.

"I told you not to call unless you had to," she said, and
her voice was sorrow, her voice was shame, and there
were tears on her cheeks, tears for me, the first of her
charges in three generations to call upon the crossroads.
"Dammit, Annie, I *told* you."

"I'm sorry, Aunt Mary," I said. "I tried, and you said
that if it was this or the cemetery . . . I tried so hard."

She sighed. "I know, baby. I know."

What she didn't say was that she'd always known it
might come to this, the youngest of the family looking at
the oldest—oldest still walking in the world, anyway—
and requesting the kind of help that hurts more than it
heals. I was the one who'd spent the most time with her,
the Price girl who'd never outgrown her babysitter. She'd
stayed with me because she liked me, and because I was
lonely, until the situation had changed, and she'd started
staying with me because I needed her again. With that
kind of exposure, that kind of familiarity leading to con-
tempt, it had always been almost inevitable that I would
one day ask for something I'd have to pay for.

"Are we there?" I could talk, I could breathe—or
maybe I didn't need to breathe; it was hard to say—and
I could feel fire in my fingers. This could be the crossroads.

"Almost." She looked at me solemnly. "As your representative in this negotiation, I sincerely recommend that
you rescind your request. Change your mind, baby girl,
before it's too late. Walk away from this."

The world was still drowning in darkness, when I focused my eyes to look past the golden light and the corn. The water was still there, no matter how hard the crossroads worked to conceal it. Nothing had changed. Everything was changing. "If I do that, am I going to survive?" I asked. "Is Sam?"

Mary looked away, but not before I saw the flicker of regret in her empty highway eyes. "I can't tell you that one way or another. Not for sure."

"The water—"

"Is a natural death. If it takes you, you go down free."

The idea that she would let me drown, let me *die*, when she could have done something to save me . . . it burned. She was my Aunt Mary. She was the woman who had wiped my runny noses and kissed my bruised knees, all while teaching me the strange, careful rules that dictated her existence among the living. She loved me. I knew she loved me. She wasn't supposed to be willing to stand back and let me go. Even knowing that she had no choice in the matter couldn't stop my heart from aching.

"You told me to call you if I got into trouble," I said softly.

Mary turned back to me. Her hair was starting to move of its own accord, not writhing like Megan's snakes, but rising off her shoulders until it surrounded her head in a luminous cloud. She was glowing. When had she started glowing?

"You called," she said. "I came. Antimony Price, you stand before the crossroads, where all things are possible, where all things are forbidden. What is your purpose here?"

The water should have been pinning me to the ceiling of the tunnel. Instead, my feet drifted down to the meet the road, and all that there was above me was sky, endless, dust-colored sky, stretching out from hope to horizon. I flexed my fingers again, calling the fire closer to the surface. I might not be able to see or feel the water anymore, but I was cold. I was so damn cold.

Death is cold. "I need to live. I need Sam to live. I need to save my friends."

" 'Need' is a big word, little girl," said a voice—a new voice, buzzing and sharp as a cicada's whine, devoid of all humanity. I turned.

Behind me stood a figure made of absence. It was neither light nor shadow, neither form nor void: instead, it was nothing at all, a bend in the landscape that somehow created the impression of a person. Only it was more substantial than that at the same time, pulling tricks of the horizon into itself, becoming present in a way that should have been impossible. I wanted to step back, away. I wanted to flee. Every animal instinct I had was screaming at me to do exactly that, to risk death by water rather than whatever this figure had in store.

But Sam was out there somewhere, marooned in the drowning dark. He needed me. Fern, Megan, and Cylia were out there, captives of people who would never have known they existed if I hadn't intervened. They needed me. Running away might have been the instinctive option, but it wasn't mine. Not anymore. I had given that away once I started assembling people who depended on me. My parents had raised me to survive, but not at the expense of my allies.

Guess there's something to being the one who comes after the heir and the spare. Even if I fucked up bad, the family would endure.

"I'm here to make a deal," I said.

The shape that was and wasn't a person somehow smiled. "I thought you might be," it purred. It looked past me to Mary, smile blossoming into a triumphant grin. "We get another one. You kept your precious pets away from us for generations, and now we get another one. How's that make you feel, Mary-girl? You feel like moving on yet? Let us get another ghost. You're about used up."

"It makes me feel like I'm still needed, and like I'll be damned before I leave my family alone with *you*," snapped Mary, stepping up and resting her hand on my shoulder. There was an electric current in her skin that crackled and burned where it touched me. It was oddly reassuring to have her there, like her presence meant nothing was going to touch me without going through her first. "I am her advocate in this negotiation. I speak for her."

"Seems to me there isn't going to be much of a negotiation," said the shape. It was still smiling. Even looking at that impossible expression hurt my mind. "She's already told me what she needs. She's a greedy one, asking for three things when most people come here asking for one."

"She's only requesting two," said Mary, shooting me a look that warned me not to argue. "The lives. She can perform the rescue herself, as long as she survives."

"His survival and mine are the same thing," I said, picking up the thread of her argument. "The water took us both."

The shape turned its eyes on me, smile fading, and I revised my earlier impression of its smile as the most terrifying thing about it. Its calm regard was a hundred times worse.

"No," it said. "You haven't drowned yet. You're light, buoyant—you're *human*. The man you ask after is different. His own bones weigh him down. He's further gone than you are, Healy child, Price girl, and he hasn't much time. Don't let your friendly ghost trick you into a slow negotiation. She has her own agenda as much as you or I do, and she'll only stop you from saving him."

Mary's hand tightened needlessly on my shoulder. I recognized a trick when I heard one. Still, it took everything I had to draw a shuddering, impossible breath, and smile, keeping my expression as close as I could to serene.

"I think it's important that we do this the right way," I said.

The shape continued to look at me. "Your grandfather sold his future for your grandmother's breath, you know," it said. "People have probably been telling you how much you remind them of him your whole life. How surprised they'd be, to see you here! Or maybe not surprised at all. Maybe they knew this was inevitable from the moment you first cried. You were always going to come to us. You were always going to walk the road already drawn for you. We only wonder why you took so long."

"You didn't have anything I needed," I said. "I need to live. I need Sam to live."

"Ah," said the shape. "But what will you *pay*?"

"I brokered the deal between Thomas Price and the crossroads for the life of Alice Healy," said Mary. "I witnessed its clauses. You are not allowed to take back what has been given. Her life is not a part of this deal."

I glanced at Mary, startled. She didn't look at me. All her attention was on the shape, jaw set, expression grim. She looked like she was fighting a battle I wasn't equipped to understand, and I realized I didn't *want* to understand it. I wanted to survive it. I wanted to save my friends. That was all.

The shape glared at her without eyes, irritation crackling in the air around it. "Fine," it said sullenly. "Alice Healy's life is off the table. Still. The latest apple of her orchard requests two boons of us—three, if you'd let her. We have the right to demand payment."

"Not in blood," said Mary.

"Not in *her* blood," corrected the shape.

"Not in Sam's blood either," I said. They both turned to me. It was hard to shake the feeling that I wasn't supposed to open my mouth during this discussion. I swallowed hard and said, "I'm not bargaining for his life just so you can kill him afterward."

"No blood from you, no blood from him ... why should I give you anything at all?" The shape sneered. "Our little maidservant reminds me that we can't kill your grandmother, however much we may want to. So? All I have to do is refuse to deal and you're dead, drowned and gone and washed away. That would be plenty. We could have our revenge without raising a finger."

"Not a very satisfying revenge, though," I said. "I mean, really? Your revenge on my grandfather is letting me drown? Not proving him wrong by making a deal with me and tormenting him in the great beyond?"

The shape seemed amused as it asked, "The great beyond? You mean the afterlife?"

"Yes." I paused. "Wait—do you mean he isn't dead?"

"Your grandfather's fate would be a different deal, and a much dearer one." The shape took a step closer, suddenly predatory, suddenly crackling with menace. "Would you prefer it?"

"No," I said firmly. "I need to live. I need to save Sam."

"She will not pay in blood," said Mary. "Remember that."

The shape shot her a sour look. "We erred when we saved you from the shade," it said. "Yes. I remember. She will not pay in blood. But she is a child of her bloodline, isn't she? I can feel it in the air around her. She allowed her magic to be half-severed and removed from her once before . . ."

The shape didn't have to finish its sentence for me to know what it was going to charge me. Instead of alarm, I felt . . . relief. All I did with my magic was destroy things. I was a menace without someone to teach me, and look what had happened when I'd accepted an offer of education. At least if the crossroads stole the fire from my fingers, they wouldn't be setting up a funnel to drain the energy of everyone around them. Mary wouldn't let it happen.

Mary frowned. "Not forever," she said.

The shape looked amused. "Why not, little ghost? What possible reason could you have for such a restriction?"

"She's not asking for immortality. Taking her magic forever when her life is constantly in danger would go against the spirit of the agreement—or do you want it known that you would cheat those who petition you?" The corner of Mary's mouth twitched in the beginnings of a smile. "You would, of course. Everyone knows you would. But knowing and having proof are very different things."

The shape's amusement faded into irritation. "Very well. We will give her what she asks—her life, and the life of her lover—in exchange for her power, as collateral against a task to be performed later, at our discretion. We will decide what to ask of her when the time arises."

Mary grabbed my arm. I turned, startled, to find myself looking directly into her empty highway eyes. They were darker than usual, like an accident had happened just beyond the edge of her irises, sending smoke billowing into her impossible internal sky.

"If you take this, if you do this, you won't be able to refuse them," she said, voice low. "When the crossroads call, you'll have to answer, and if you try to say 'no,' they'll have the right to make you pay. Do you understand? They can enforce your obedience. They'll have your magic, and that means they'll have *you*, no matter how far you run from the road."

"But I'll be alive," I said. "*Sam* will be alive. We can save the others."

She nodded minutely. Then, to my surprise, she smiled.

"You people," she said. Her voice was sad, and fond. "If I hadn't died before I met you, I'd expect you to be the death of me."

"Love you, too," I said.

Mary turned back to the shape. "Antimony Price will accept your offer of her life, and the life of Samuel Taylor, in exchange for her magic to be held as collateral against a future task to be set by the crossroads and communicated through me, as her advocate and representative. Once the task is performed, her magic will be returned. Should she fail the task, her magic may be withheld indefinitely. Her life, however, cannot be revoked, nor can the life of Samuel Taylor. Do we have an accord?"

With a predatory smile, the shape extended what could charitably be referred to as a hand. "We do," it said.

My skin crawled from the proximity to the whatever-it-was. It was difficult to resist the urge to step backward, well out of its reach. Mary nudged me.

"Shake," she said. "That seals the bargain."

Of course, it did.

I reached out and took the shape's hand in mine. There was no substance to its fingers, and yet somehow, they were entirely unyielding, refusing to bend or give under the pressure of my own. It grasped my hand firmly, still smiling as it shook.

"The compact is sealed," it said. "You'll live."

The fire in my fingers blazed, going from an ember to a forest fire in the matter of a moment. I cried out, trying to pull away, and the shape gripped me even harder, pinning me in place until the flame died, leaving me cold and empty. Then it pushed me away, and the country road was gone, and the sunlight was gone, and *Mary* was gone, and the water—which had never really disappeared, only faded into inconsequential distance—came surging back, and I was gone, just like everything else.

I was gone.

Twenty-five

"Oh, my sweet girl. I will always love you,
no matter what. Now get out there, and kick
their asses back to the Stone Age."

–Evelyn Baker

*Lowryland, about to have an even worse night, which
is sort of an accomplishment right now*

I WOKE UP PRESSED against the base of the bronze Laura
and Lizzie statue at the center of the Fairyland hub, my
left arm pinned under my body, one leg slung up onto the
statue itself, leaving me in an inelegant spread-eagle position that made me incredibly grateful for the existence of
jeans. I groaned. The sound awoke a pounding in my head
that was almost worse than the tingling in my arm.

Pain meant I was alive. The crossroads had kept their
side of the bargain. With the thought came the realization that I couldn't feel my magic anymore. There was no
fire in my fingers and no void in the pit of my stomach
for Colin to use as a drain. Regret grew heavy in my
chest. My magic had been so happy to see me when I had
stepped through the broken mirror. It had stopped hurting me as soon as I had apologized, and now I had sold
it to something I didn't understand but knew enough to
be afraid of. I didn't deserve to get it back. Even if I did
whatever the crossroads would eventually ask of me, I
didn't deserve it.

That was a moral dilemma for later. Right now, I
needed to find my friends. I needed to find Sam. If the
crossroads had saved me, they should have saved him,

too—but I had a lifetime of Mary warning me about the kind of tricks they liked to pull. They were a malicious genie trapped in a bottle that spanned the globe, and they would cheat if they had the opportunity to do so. They might save Sam from drowning, only to leave him washed up on the roller coaster tracks, ready to be crushed to death when the trainspotter tried to pull another fast one. They might do almost anything. I had to move.

That was easier said than done. What felt like every muscle in my body protested as I levered myself away from the statue and off the ground. The last time I'd hurt this much, it had been because I'd been hip-checked into the rail around the track by a blocker twice my size. She'd gotten a trip to the penalty box. I'd gotten a bruise that ran the length of my right thigh, black and yellow and blooming like a flower.

The thought reminded me of something else: when the wall had cracked and the water had come crashing down, I'd been wearing my backpack. I wasn't wearing it now. I looked around, finally spotting the nylon strap in the bushes to my left. I couldn't run, but I could walk quickly, and that was exactly what I did.

Like everything else, the backpack was drenched. Anything paper that had been shoved in there was ruined now. My skates were soaked. They were still skates, and they still fit my feet, even wet. Hell, the rest of me was so wet that I barely even noticed the discomfort as I kicked off my sodden shoes and yanked the skates on over my equally sodden socks. Everything squelched. I tied the laces tighter. The blisters I was going to get from this were tomorrow's problem. Right now, I had bigger things to worry about. Like Sam.

Stopping to put my skates on might have felt like a waste of time, but it was actually anything but. Skating bruised and battered is what derby girls *do*. I might not be able to walk faster than a hobble for the next few days, and that was fine, because I could still skate like the top jammer of the Slasher Chicks.

"I'm the Final Girl, you fuckers," I muttered, and

pushed off, steadily gathering speed as I began to skate through the area, looking for my boyfriend.

Sam was a big guy; he wouldn't have been thrown into any trees, or at least he wouldn't have stayed there once the water rolled back. If he'd been knocked out—which wasn't a bad assumption—he would also be in his heavier fūri form. That was what really worried me. Monkeys have denser bones than humans do, and as a yōkai, Sam had more in common, physically, with the simian side of his heritage. The water had pinned me to the tunnel roof, but Sam? He would have sunk like a stone. There was no telling how much water he'd inhaled while I was bargaining with the crossroads for our lives.

They'd promised me he would live. They hadn't promised immortality, or indestructability, or even that he'd still be in one piece when I found him. Even with Mary there to keep me from screwing up completely, the situation had been too dire to allow for the sort of careful negotiation that had really needed to happen. I skated faster, my heart hammering in my chest, my mind spinning out every dire scenario it could come up with—and there were quite a few of those. The curse of an active imagination.

The most active imagination in the world couldn't prepare me for coming around a bend in the path and finding Sam sprawled, motionless, in the middle of a flowerbed.

"*Sam!*" I skated to his side as fast as I could, dropping to my knees before I'd come to a complete stop. I immediately regretted my lack of kneepads as the pavement stripped away several layers of skin. That was going to sting. And it didn't matter, because he still wasn't moving.

Fighting to keep it together, I pressed my ear against his chest, relaxing only when I heard the distant, steady beat of his heart. He was unconscious. He wasn't dead.

"Hey." I sat up, gripping his shoulders and giving him a shake. His head lolled, but he didn't respond. I shook harder. "*Hey*. Wake up. We need to go fight a bunch of asshole Harry Potter wannabes to get our friends back."

Still he didn't respond. I sighed.

"I didn't want to do this," I said, and slapped him.

Hitting your friends without their consent is generally not a good idea, and is a good way to end a friendship. Hitting your significant others without their consent is the sort of thing that leads to breakups and restraining orders. Under the circumstances, and in the absence of smelling salts, I figured he'd forgive me.

Sam groaned. I slapped him again. He groaned louder. I pulled back my hand for one more hit, and stopped as something grabbed my wrist—something wet and hairy and flexible. A glance confirmed that it was Sam's tail, and I felt something in my chest unsnarl, even before I turned to look at him. His eyes were open. He looked confused, but his eyes were open, and he was looking at me, and he was alive. The crossroads might have tried to cheat. They hadn't quite succeeded.

"Annie?" he said, bewildered. "What the fuck . . . ?"

"Their trainspotter threw a roller coaster at us."

He blinked. "I hate that those words made sense in that order. But it does explain why I feel like I've been hit by a train."

"Because you were." I stood, bracing myself to keep from rolling away before I offered him my hands. "Up. We have to move. They probably think we're both dead, but that's only going to last until their routewitch talks to the paths, or someone thinks to come out and look for a body."

"More hate," said Sam. He took my hand, wobbling as he got his feet under himself and slowly, awkwardly stood. Then he shook himself, sending drops of water scattering in all directions. When he was done, he was dryer, and fluffier than I had ever seen him.

It was enough to make me smile, if only for a moment. "Nice hair."

"You're one to talk." He ran a hand over the top of his head as he looked around, tail curling and uncurling anxiously behind him. "You know this place better than I do. Where do we go?"

"This way," I said, and pointed before I started to skate.

Neither of us was at our best, but I'm a good enough

skater that I was able to build up a good head of steam, and when something went whipping by to my left, it was no surprise to see that it was Sam, using the lights and overhanging tree branches to travel through the Park at an impressive speed. He was holding back, circling me, allowing me to be the one who guided us to the goal. I flashed him a thumbs-up and turned, heading down a narrow side path toward the Midsummer Night's Scream.

Their trainspotter had been strong enough to wrest the Sea Dragon off its tracks, but that would have taken a lot out of him, and unless they were running a coaster somewhere else in the Park—which I was pretty sure I would have been able to hear—he was still going to be drained. That was good. He couldn't hit us with another train. That didn't mean Emily was at anything other than full strength, and while routewitches are more defensive than offensive, they're still dangerous.

With the two witches dead, we were down to a route-witch, an ambulomancer, a trainspotter, and a sorcerer. Not the sort of spread that seemed like a good time, but at least none of them were particularly complementary. Their powers weren't designed to work together. The witches had probably been able to bridge the gaps, making the cabal more cooperative, less competitive. Now they were gone, and we were racing toward a four-way boss fight.

"Sam!" He stopped swinging and waited for me to catch up, moving more slowly to keep pace as I said, "Joshua's the trainspotter. Don't get between him and anything with more than four wheels. Emily's going to have trouble getting a fix on you if you stay off the ground."

He looked concerned. "What about you? You're on the ground."

"I'm hoping the roller skates will confuse her." It was a foolish hope. Wheels have never confused a routewitch before. I was more hoping I could deliver an elbow to her chin before she had a chance to do anything.

"Nope," said Sam, and grabbed my shoulders with his feet, wrapping his tail around my waist for good measure before he resumed his forward momentum. "Not going to go on a hope. Going to go on a 'definitely and also we're going to survive.' Now tell me where to turn."

I thought about arguing, and decided against it just as quickly, gripping his ankles to stabilize myself as I said, "Head left. The coaster will be right ahead of us."

"Got it." He didn't seem to be weighed down by my extra mass at all, and kept swinging smoothly onward, expression grim. "What else do I need to know?"

"Without his wand, Colin has a lot of technique, but not that much raw power. I think that's why he was siphoning mine." A sorcerer who didn't have the strength to back up his threats would be easy pickings in the wider world—unless he surrounded himself with allies and occasionally tricked a younger, stupider magic-user into doing something that they shouldn't. I had made him stronger. I had made him *legitimate*.

I had never felt so foolish in my life.

"What about the other lady?"

"She's an ambulomancer. She draws power from distance traveled, but only when she does it on her own two feet." I hated trying to unsnarl the delicate distinctions between the different types of magic-users. The fact that Sam wasn't slowing down and I had to keep pulling my legs up to keep from slamming into things wasn't helping. "A routewitch gets power from distance, period. Roller skates, bare feet, cars, whatever. As long as they're on the ground, they're gaining strength. An ambulomancer gains power faster, but has to keep their feet anchored."

"What do they do?"

I was about to answer when Sam swung into an invisible barrier, losing his grip on the branch he'd been using and sending us both toppling toward the ground. I only had a few seconds to figure out my landing. Calling on everything I'd learned from gymnastics and cheerleading—and a few things I'd learned from roller derby—I bent my knees, braced my shoulders, and hit hard.

Dropping eight feet onto pavement in roller skates may never rank among my top ten favorite activities. At least I was in footwear designed to protect my ankles.

I've seen my sister do similar drops in high heels, and somehow her legs are not shapely sacks of gravel barely held together by her muscular system.

Sam dropped next to me, landing harder, but with a little less visible pain. He gave me a wide-eyed look. "Assuming that's what they do," he said.

I nodded. "Yeah. Barriers. Ambulomancers are the reason that sometimes a road goes on forever, and sometimes it's like a quarter of a mile long."

"So how do we fight it?"

Normally, this was where I would have called for Mary, or better yet, Rose. Normally, I wasn't also dealing with a routewitch. I frowned at the nothingness in front of us before saying, "They want us there. They *want* us to come to them. So there has to be a way in."

"Won't that be like running into a blind canyon because the villain wants you to?"

"It would be, except that it's not possible to have only one way in. That would mess up the pressure." I looked wildly around, finally spotting the charred wall near the site of the first accident in my recent chain. "This way."

I skated for the employee door with Sam on my heels. When I found it locked, I pulled one of the knives from inside my shirt—how I hadn't been shredded by my own weapons when the water pinned me to the ceiling, I had no idea—and slammed it down on the hasp, breaking the cheap padlock. Sam blinked, looking impressed, and didn't say anything. He just followed.

We made our way across the employee walkway to the first tunnel door. Unlike the gate, it wasn't locked. I pulled it open, and Sam grinned, a sharp, virtually feral expression.

"Got it," he said.

"Good," I said, and stepped into the tunnel.

The thing about road witches, whatever their type, is that they're limited. Roads and feet and trains. Boats and planes and once, when we were more dedicated to sending people down into the bowels of the earth to bring back armfuls of riches, mines. An ambulomancer could no more wall off a tunnel than a trainspotter could read the story of a road. But the tommyknockers have been rare or entirely gone for decades now, outside of places like Kentucky, where the coal mines still thrive. Colin didn't have one. His ambulomancer didn't have the employee passageways.

Sam didn't have any of that background. He just knew that I'd gone for the tunnels, and he trusted me enough to follow me underground. It was a humbling thought, knowing that he trusted me that much. I was going to do my best to make sure I deserved it.

It was hard to follow the twists and turns in the dark. I had been working mostly in Fairyland for long enough that I knew the way I had to go, and after only two false starts, we were standing at the door that would take us into the landscaping of the Midsummer Night's Scream.

I put a finger to my lips in an exaggerated hushing gesture. Sam nodded. Then he leaned in, pushed my finger aside, and kissed me.

His lips tasted like chlorinated water, and he smelled of wet fur, and I grabbed his arms and clung to him, counting off the seconds I felt we could afford to spend on this small, utterly self-indulgent gesture. When I reached ten, I let him go, offered a tight smile, and opened the door on the dark tangle of the bushes that hid it from casual view.

The voices reached us immediately.

"Joshua should be back by now. Are you sure you didn't make your shell too strong?" Colin. He sounded peevish and unnerved, which was fine by me. The more off-balance he was, the better our odds were.

"Something hit it," said a female voice. The ambulomancer. I wished I'd taken the time to learn her name. I'd been too trusting. I'd allowed them to lull me into a false sense of security—and I'd done half the work for them, treating Lowryland as some sort of magical, uncrackable safe haven against all the people who would do me harm. I'd been so focused on the threat of the Covenant that I had never considered the possibility of danger from within.

"That's what happens to shells," said Emily.

"Yes, but something hit it without *shattering* it," said the ambulomancer. "Your little apprentice is probably walking around the edges, looking for the door I left her. She'll be here soon, or she's unconscious on the ground and Joshua will bring her back. Either way, I did my job, and either way, she's only still a threat because you did your part wrong. She should be loyal by now."

"You enjoyed her power as much as the rest of us," snapped Colin. "Don't be a child, Andrea. If I'd drained her any faster, she wouldn't have been able to regenerate for years, and we would have lost all the good she's done us."

I turned to Sam and pointed upward. He nodded, catching my meaning, and I barely had time to take a breath before his hands and tail were around my waist and he was propelling himself nimbly into the air, carrying us past the brush in a single powerful leap. We landed in front of the cluster of magic-users, him with bent knees, me standing as straight and seemingly effortless as any pom-pom girl since the dawn of cheerleading time. Sometimes it's all about making an entrance.

Emily jumped. The ambulomancer—Andrea—clapped a hand over her mouth to stop a shriek. And Colin, whose back was toward us, went ramrod straight and tense, his shoulders forming an iron bar beneath the jacket of his tailored suit.

"I asked you to teach me, not rob me," I said coldly. "Give back my friends and this can be over."

"Demanding as always," said Colin. He turned slowly, looking first at me and then at Sam. His lips pulled back in a sneer. "Beauty and the Beast indeed. Have you considered what the children will look like? It's a disgrace."

"Nah," I said broadly. "My family will be cool with it. We've been cool with stranger." Now was the moment to put that dramatic entrance to good use. I took a step forward, Sam's tail obligingly uncoiling from around my waist, my eyes fixed on Colin and my hands spread by my sides like the fire was still there.

Cheerleading and roller derby have this much in common: image and attitude are sometimes everything.

You're going to eat grass and track no matter how good you are. What people will remember is how you get back on your feet. So I advanced on those people like Dany emerging from the fire, like Jean stepping out of the Phoenix Force, like . . .

Well, like me. Antimony Price. The girl who burns and does not die.

"I don't believe we've been properly introduced," I said. My hands moved, plucking knives from the waistband of my wet jeans and holding them low against my hips, as deadly as the fire I had given to the crossroads, and a lot harder for unethical sorcerers to steal. "My name is Antimony. Antimony Price. Maybe you remember my grandparents?"

Andrea went white, taking a quick step backward and almost tripping over one of the low decorative walls used to shape the walkways. "You're a *Price*?"

"It's hot when your name scares the shit out of people," Sam observed.

"She's lying," said Colin dismissively. "Don't listen to this foolish little girl who thought she could take advantage of our kindness and wound up in over her head. She's not a Price. They're all dead."

"She stinks of travel and the grave," said Emily. Her tone was uneasy, and she was looking at me with a new intensity. "Alice Price grew up among ghosts, and her godmother was an ambulomancer. We knew her very well."

"Thomas Price was a fool who chose to fritter his potential on a farm girl," snapped Colin. "He died childless."

"He *disappeared* the father of two, after making a deal with the crossroads for the life of his wife, my grandmother," I said, keeping my voice calm, keeping my hands steady. "I take after him in so many more ways than you can imagine. If you're not with me, you're against me—and I don't think you want that, do you?"

"She's bluffing," said Colin—but there was a note of unease in his voice now, like he was reviewing every interaction we'd had, and finding at least a few of them questionable.

I took another step forward. Andrea took another step back.

"No," she said, voice clear and only shaking a little. "She's not. I'm out. I don't have the chops for this shit." Then she turned and fled, racing off into the darkness of the Park.

Colin scowled. "Is this your plan, child? Say dire things and frighten us all away?"

"No," I said, and raised my right hand.

The knife flew straight and true, embedding itself in Colin's left shoulder before he had a chance to realize what I was about to do. He bellowed, pain and rage and shock all mixed together into a single primal sound. That was Sam's cue. He leaped straight upward, crashing down on Emily while she was still gaping, wide-eyed, at the blood soaking into Colin's sleeve. She went down like a sack of potatoes, Sam crouching on top of her, pinning her to the ground. He rolled his lips back, showing his teeth. She froze. Smart girl.

Colin grasped the knife in his shoulder, yanking it loose and flinging it to the ground. "You ungrateful little *wretch*," he snarled. "How dare you? Don't you know who I am?"

"Yeah," I said. "You're the guy whose ass I'm about to kick."

Stan Lee is a human dude from New York. I don't know whether he's ever met a superhero in real life. (He's definitely met a cryptid—the cryptid population of New York and New Jersey is *staggering*—but that doesn't mean he knew it was happening.) Still, there's one thing he got absolutely right: if you can quip and joke and one-liner your way into a fight, the odds are good that it will throw your opponent off at least enough to make them forget about a few things.

Like the fact that I was on roller skates.

I threw myself into the motion, crouching low and skating as hard as I could across the concrete, smoothed and evened out by the feet of a hundred thousand tourists, maintained nightly by the Lowryland staff. Colin barely had time to realize what was happening before my shoulder slammed into his stomach. At the same time, I punched him hard in the stab wound I had created, taking him down to the ground with my arm forming a bar across his throat. He landed even harder than Emily had. I couldn't feel bad about that.

He glared at me, eyes burning with hatred and with flickering, deep-buried magic. His lips moved as he tried to speak. No sound emerged. I had knocked the air completely out of him, leaving him temporarily silent.

Good. I jabbed him again in the stab wound before hissing, "Last chance, asshole. Where are my friends? Give them back to me, and maybe you walk away from this."

Colin glared at me. He knew I was lying. I knew I was lying.

I knew how this ended.

Colin and his cronies had been hurting people, using Lowryland as the engine of their mischief, for a very long time. Losing the boost from my magic wasn't going to stop them. It might slow them down a little, but they would start up again. Andrea was gone. She was also an ambulomancer. She couldn't do this sort of thing without someone to help her. Emily was going to have other things to worry about as soon as Rose told the Queen of the Routewitches what she'd been up to. Colin . . .

Colin was a sorcerer. Colin wanted power more than he wanted to survive. If we walked away and left him breathing, he'd start the whole thing up again as soon as he had a new wand. There was no other outcome. I had to kill him.

Behind and above us, there was a snarl as the Midsummer Night's Scream rumbled to life. I glanced up, shocked. Colin laughed. When I looked back down, he was smirking.

"Where are your friends?" he asked. "About twenty seconds from dying."

The whole scenario unfurled like a terrible flower, each piece leading seamlessly to the next as it all came together. I shoved myself away from Colin, looking over my shoulder to find Joshua standing there, his eyes glowing faintly, like a cat's, and his hands raised above my head.

"Shit," I hissed.

Joshua was a trainspotter, and while he might be almost out of juice after his trick back in the Deep-Down, he could still whisper his wanting to the trains—to any train—and be answered in the affirmative. He could turn the coaster on from a distance. He *had* turned it on. And Colin was a sorcerer. Which meant that blood sacrifice would make him stronger.

Colin's smirk grew, becoming an outright grin. "I think you'll find I'll have a new wand in no time," he said.

The train would crush Fern, Cylia, and Megan, imbuing the train, the wheels, everything around it with the trauma of their intentional and carefully orchestrated deaths. Colin would be able to take his pick of materials, crafting a new wand capable of channeling his mystical energy. Everything we'd done would be for nothing. The cabal would be back in business without missing so much as a step.

"No," I said, and skated toward Sam, moving fast, trusting him to know what I wanted.

There are advantages to having a preternaturally strong, incredibly swift boyfriend. Sam saw me coming, saw the lights coming on along the roller coaster's tracks, and knew what I wanted him to do. If he had issues with it—if he didn't like the idea of flinging me headlong into danger while he stayed with the danger we already had—there wasn't time to discuss it. He stood, making a basket with his hands, and when I was close enough, I jumped, knees together, wheels spinning against the empty air.

Sam's hands grasped my calves for only a second before he was flinging me upward as hard as he could, away from the remnants of the cabal, toward the distant but rapidly nearing shape of the Midsummer Night's Scream.

Guess it was time to come up with a plan.

Twenty-six

"The survivors decide how well the show went. Always survive."

–Frances Brown

About to slam into the side of a massive roller coaster

T**HE** M**IDSUMMER** N**IGHT'S** S**CREAM** was built in the 1990s, after the first wave of wooden coasters but before they became trendy again. As a consequence, the only wood involved is in the structures surrounding the track, most of which are actually plastic and steel, both of which require substantially less maintenance. I had never approached the train from this angle, and I didn't have much time to decide where I was going to land.

When all else fails, go for the path of least resistance. I braced myself as best I could, and when I reached the sculpted metal "trees" next to the mouth of the big tunnel, I grabbed on, feeling the metal edges of the "branches" bite into my palms. My momentum died with a bone-shaking jolt, and I was suddenly hanging there, as vulnerable to physics as anyone.

The train was still snarling and growling in its launching bay. It hadn't started moving yet. Why hadn't it started moving yet? It would have made sense to tie my friends to the coaster track, and I knew Colin would want them all to die at the same time, for the sake of grinding their last moments as deeply into the structure as possible—

But that didn't mean they had to be tied at the same point. I had to think about this logically. Normally, riders would wind slowly up a wooded path, traveling deep into "goblin territory" before joining Laura and Lizzie on their lightning-swift journey to freedom. Maintenance crews could ride the ADA-mandated elevator or climb up the stairs built into the structure. That gave three access points, and that would probably have felt like two too many to Colin and his flunkies. They'd want something that could only be reasonably accessed one way. Via the track.

The train was still warming up. Turning on a modern, high-tech roller coaster with nothing but magic probably wasn't easy. That didn't mean I had much time. Pulling myself up with shaking arms, I swung my feet over, onto the track. My skates, formerly an advantage, made it virtually impossible for me to get my balance back. I ground my teeth and kept trying until I felt steady enough to let the tree go.

The track had been built to be maintained, thankfully, and there was room for both my feet. I caught my breath, testing the faint downward slope of the hill's ledge. Then, with a silent prayer and a lot more silent cursing, I lifted my toes, releasing my brakes, and let go.

Fun facts about roller skates: the only brakes they have are the ones on the toes. Otherwise, physics does most of the hard work. Which meant that when I released my toe stops at the top of a coaster hill, gravity kicked in and kicked my ass, pulling me down what felt like a sheer drop until my hair was whipping straight out behind me and my lungs ached with the effort to keep myself from screaming. All my focus was on staying on the tracks, keeping myself yoked to the great steel structure that had never been designed for something as soft and squishy as a human being.

I'm going to die, I thought, as I hit the bottom of the hill and started up the next one, propelled by nothing more or less than my own momentum. *I'm going to hit the loop-de-loop, and there's going to be nothing to keep me on the track, and I'm going to die. I'm going to—*

A dark hole loomed up ahead of me, lit by a flickering rainbow sheen, like bioluminescent fungus. This time, I gave up and screamed. I'd been so concerned about the big loops that I'd forgotten the goblin caverns at the bottom of the ride.

I dropped into the darkness, my skates suddenly soaked through again as I hit the artificial lake at the bottom. It wasn't deep, designed to kick up water and delight guests, but it was there.

And it gave me an idea. I threw myself to the side, abandoning the track for the water, and splashed down hard, sliding a few feet before the water finished absorbing the shock of my landing. I came up gasping, no longer bound to the structure of the track—and no longer aided by its merciless progress, either. That was fine. I needed some control over where I was going, given what was likely to come next.

From here, the track rose up into the darkness, the flashes of rainbow light becoming less frequent, while never quite stopping altogether. Total darkness was terrifying: near darkness was exhilarating. I wiped my wet palms against my wetter jeans, and started climbing.

I was almost to the top of the first hill when my hand hit something that wasn't metal. It was soft, yielding, and mammalian. I paused, considering the silence of the something, and touched it again, more intentionally.

"Fern?" I whispered.

"Annie?" She sounded hopeful but wary, like she knew this couldn't possibly be anything but a trick. "Is it really you?"

"Why didn't you make a sound when I touched you?"

"I thought you were them, and I thought they'd leave me alone if they thought I was still knocked out." Fern's voice was even wispier and softer than it usually was. She was clearly fighting to remain calm. "Are you here to save me?"

"Well, of course, I am. Couldn't leave a teammate, could I? Slasher Chicks forever." I felt along the edge of her body, finding the ropes that bound her to the track. I had knives. What I didn't have was a good way of catching her. "Fern, I need you to reduce your density as much as you can, all right? When I cut you loose, you're going to fall. You need to be ready to fall."

"I'm ready," she said bravely, and I had never loved her more, or felt worse about sucking her into my fight.

It only took a few seconds for me to slice away the ropes that bound her. Fern dropped immediately, knocking against me as lightly as a balloon before slinging herself over the track's edge and hanging on by her fingertips.

"Now what?"

I took a breath. "Now I find the others."

I couldn't see Fern, but I could hear her concern as she said, "I don't know where they are. I woke up here."

"I know they're on this track." I knew that Colin wanted their deaths to be painful, swift, and grouped together—but when I was talking about something that moved as fast as a roller coaster, as long as hitting Fern didn't derail it, it would be able to finish climbing the hill in a matter of seconds. "Sam's outside. Go help him."

"But I—"

"Please." The coaster would finish powering up soon. I needed Fern clear.

She lightly touched the top of my hand. "Be safe," she said, and was gone, drifting down to the dark waters below.

I resumed my climb.

I hadn't gone far when a new sound entered the equation: a faint but steady hissing. Megan was tied to the tracks in front of me. I stopped where I was, unwilling to reach out when I didn't know where those snakes were. "Megan."

No response.

"*Megan.*"

A faint moan, this time, like a larger snake stirring in its nest. (Not that snakes actually moan, outside of SyFy Original Movies.)

"Wake up and tell your hair not to bite me, before the roller coaster crushes us both."

There was a sharp gasp then, before Megan asked warily, "Annie?"

"It's me. Where's your head? Keep talking so I can cut you free."

"What the hell is going on? Where *are* we?" The

snakes continued to hiss angrily as she spoke. At least now I could tell where they were. That was a nice, potentially nonvenomous change.

"You know the Midsummer Night's Scream?" I asked, as I started to cut.

"Of course, I know the—no. *No.*" Megan sounded rightly horrified. "You are *not* telling me that."

"I am." I cut another rope. "You're going to need to climb down once you're loose. I still have to find Cylia, and their trainspotter is working on getting the coaster moving."

There was a pause. "I hate that that was a sentence."

"I'm getting that a lot today. I think this is the last rope. Hold onto something."

"It is." There was a rustle as Megan grabbed the track. I sliced through the rope. "You humans need better night vision."

"I'll put it on the mad science wish list. Can you get down?"

"Do I have a choice?" Megan began climbing past me. I felt a snake's tongue caress my cheek, light as a whisper, and then she was gone, descending toward the water. That would have been the smart thing to do.

I started climbing up instead.

Light was beginning to seep into the tunnel, flowing through the hole where the train would emerge, triumphant, from the animatronic underworld, when I found Cylia. Her eyes were open, scanning the darkness below her. She relaxed slightly when she saw me.

"I was wondering whether the cavalry was coming," she said.

"We don't have much time," I replied, and grabbed the first loop of visible rope. "Hold on, I'm getting you out of here."

From behind us, the sound of a train whipping along the track made it clear how little time we actually had. Cylia closed her eyes.

"Wake me when we're dead," she said.

"No," I snarled, and kept cutting. "No, and no, and

no." We were maybe thirty feet above the artificial lake, which I knew got deeper around the tracks, for the sake of the illusion. If we fell right, if we were *lucky*—

The rope gave way. I grabbed Cylia, flinging both of us away from the tracks, dropping like rocks into the dark below. Cylia shrieked. The Midsummer Night's Scream passed by harmlessly overhead, a great rocketing mechanism of sound and steel and mayhem. And we were falling, and there was nothing I could do but close my eyes and let it happen.

The shock of hitting the water knocked my eyes *right* open. Cylia and I were driven below the surface, and my feet hit the bottom before I kicked and pushed us up again, sputtering and soaked, into the drier dark. Cylia clung to me. I clung to Cylia. Then, in relief and surprise, we started to laugh.

"We're alive!" she shouted.

"Yes!"

"We didn't die!"

"No!"

"We . . ." Cylia stopped. "Is this over?"

"No," I said again, my own levity fading. "But it will be soon. Come on. Let's find a maintenance door."

Dripping, shaking, and exhausted, we made our way toward the edge of the lake, moving one step closer to safety. We had a long way yet to go.

When we emerged from the maintenance door in the side of the structure, we found ourselves faced with the usual nest of tangled landscaping and complicated design, intended to keep guests from stumbling over anything they shouldn't. We climbed over it all, Cylia helping me when my skates made it difficult to balance, until we reached the fence to the queue area. After hopping that, it was a simple matter to head back to the front of the ride.

Sam was still there, standing on Emily's shoulders, keeping her pinned down. Fern and Megan were behind him, looking warily at Colin and Joshua. I didn't know why they hadn't run away. I would have run, if one of my enemies had been planning to come back with reinforcements.

Maybe they had more loyalty in them than I'd expected. Maybe they had stayed for Emily.

"It's not too late," said Colin, his eyes clearly fixed on me. "I hurt you; now you've hurt me. With your power, and my skill, we could find a cleaner way to accomplish all our goals. You could help me truly realize Lowry's dream."

"Okay, one, if Lowry was a sorcerer, I don't want to know," I said. "Two, I am not working with you. And three, I don't have any power to offer. I sold it for the chance to beat you."

I'd sold it for so much more than that, but my little white lie was absolutely justified by the look of horror and disgust that crossed his face. "Impossible. No one would give up that kind of power."

"I don't know. Sailor Moon did, at least twice. I will diminish and go into the west, but not before I kick your ass."

Colin sneered. "You'll fail. You and your little collection of monsters can't possibly—"

He froze. Literally. Both he and Joshua stopped where they were, not moving, not visibly breathing. I started to turn.

"I wouldn't do that if I were you," said Megan wearily. "Let me get my glasses back on."

"Why did they let you *keep* those, instead of just blindfolding you?" asked Sam. He glanced at me and smiled, just a little. "Hey. Missed you."

"Well, you know. Places to go, people to save." I shrugged extravagantly. "I lived."

"What did you mean about selling . . . ?"

"Later." I offered what I hoped was an encouraging smile. "I'll tell you later."

Sam nodded. "I'll make sure you do," he said.

"How about you can the sweet moment and let me up?" demanded Emily. "You can't keep me here forever."

"No," I said. "We can't. But you're probably going to wish we had."

She didn't have an answer for that.

Getting Emily to drop the shields keeping the dead out of Lowryland wasn't really an option, and so we did the next best thing: we walked. Sam used his tail to pin her arms to her sides and Cylia and Fern carried her, while Megan walked alongside as a constant reminder of what would happen if she tried too hard to escape. The memory of what had happened to Colin and Joshua after Megan got close to them was clearly very fresh in Emily's mind, because she didn't fight.

(The gaze of the Pliny's gorgon doesn't petrify; it only stuns. But their venom is one of the strongest petrifying agents known to man, and the snakes on their heads make an excellent delivery agent. I had been trying to figure out how I was going to find the will to kill two men. Megan had just walked up to them and allowed her hair to bite them. In the morning, the groundskeepers were going to find two really weird new statues. I didn't know how to feel about that yet. I was pretty sure I was going to be okay with it. I was equally sure that that would mean there was something wrong with me.)

Mary and Rose were waiting just outside the Park gate. Both were wearing what I thought of as their funeral clothes, Mary in a knee-length skirt and a white blouse with a Peter Pan collar, Rose in a green silk prom gown. Emily, who had been quiet up until that point, started to kick and scream when she saw them.

"No!" she shouted. "No, no, no! Turn me to stone! Kill me! I don't care! Not this!"

"You earned this," said Mary, in a voice like a tomb door swinging closed, and there was nothing else to say, and no other way for this to end. Rose and Mary each took Emily by an arm, taking a step backward. The air grew hazy around them, creating the impression of a long road running off to nowhere.

"Wait," I said. They stopped, looking at me. "What's . . . what's going to happen to her now?"

"She swore by the Ocean Lady that no harm would come to you while you were in her company," said Rose. "Maybe she shouldn't have done that. What comes next is of her own creation."

Emily was screaming when the three of them disappeared, leaving the rest of us to stare silently at the place where they had been.

Megan spoke first.

"Fuck this," she said. "I'm going back to the hospital and finish my residency."

Epilogue

"Well, hell. Now what?"

–Enid Healy

A shitty company apartment five miles outside of Lakeland, Florida

Three days later

"YOU'RE SURE YOU WON'T change your mind?" asked Sophie.

I looked at the keys in the palm of my hand. They were little and rusty, worn smooth by dozens of hands. They were mine. They were Melody West's. The door they unlocked was small and safe and far from the Covenant of St. George, and while I had lived behind it, I had been small and safe, too.

"I'm sure," I said, and held them out to her with a quick, sad smile. "Better not ask again. People will think you're showing favoritism."

"I can't show favoritism," she said. "You don't work here anymore." Then, making no effort at all to hide her tears, she reached out and pulled me into a hug.

I let her. She'd earned it. And as I hugged her back, I couldn't help feeling like I'd earned it a little bit, too.

When we pulled away from each other, Sophie kept my hands and said, seriously, "You promise me you're not going back to him. You *promise*."

"I do," I said. Not turning, I gestured to the car waiting by the sidewalk, avocado green and already packed with the strangest road trip buddies I would ever have.

Fern was perched on the roof, light as a feather. Cylia was standing next to the driver's side door, waiting for me. Sam . . .

Sam was on the sidewalk, and I knew that if I turned, he'd be smiling, glad to go anywhere with me, as long as I didn't send him away again.

Sophie glanced over my shoulder, and she saw that smile. I know she did, because she squeezed my hands, leaned in a little closer, and said, "I like this one. Take care of him."

"I will," I said.

Then she let me go, and I turned, and walked away.

Colin and Joshua were officially missing. I didn't know what happened to their weird statues, and I didn't want to. The disaster in Deep-Down had accomplished the unthinkable, closing all of Lowryland for a week while a full safety review was conducted and the rides were repaired. It was probably costing the company millions in lost revenue and bad publicity. Guess without the cabal redistributing things, their luck had finally run out. That was okay. If Lowry Entertainment could survive the dry spell, their luck would rebalance, and they'd endure. There's always room in the world for a little more magic.

There was room in me for a lot more magic. The fire in my fingers was officially gone, ceded to the crossroads as collateral against whatever they were going to ask for. I was willing to wait to find out what that was. Mary was right about one thing: whatever the crossroads asked of me was probably going to be more than I was willing to pay.

Only probably. As I looked at Sam, standing there, waiting for me, *alive*, I was fairly sure that there was no price I wouldn't have been willing to pay for the opportunity to be here.

"Got everything?" he asked.

I hefted my backpack. "Everything worth taking," I said.

"Got any idea where we're going?"

"Cylia's driving," I said. "She'll get us where we need to be."

"And on that note, get in, losers," said Cylia. "I want to be in South Carolina before morning."

"What's in South Carolina?" asked Fern.

Cylia grinned. "I have no idea, but it's on the way to Maine."

Fern slid off the roof and into the front passenger seat, leaving me to fold myself into the backseat with Sam. Cylia turned the air-conditioning on. Sam squirmed into a hoodie that would have been way too warm to wear outside, and as soon as the hood was up, I felt his tail wrap around my ankle. Fern was happily singing along to some piece of crossover pop country fluff, and as I let my head droop to rest against Sam's shoulder and closed my eyes, I knew one thing for certain:

Wherever we went next, I was better off in the company of friends.

The road rolled by under our wheels, and I drifted slowly off to sleep, finally safe, finally secure, and finally a little bit closer to home.

Read on for
a brand-new Aeslin Mice novella
by Seanan McGuire:

THE RECITATION OF THE MOST
HOLY AND HARROWING
PILGRIMAGE OF MINDY
AND ALSO MORK

"Remember who we were. Remember who we are. Remember that one day, all of this will change. The gods provide. All else is up to us."
— from the Aeslin litany of Faiths Forsaken and Yet to Come.

The parking garage of the Minneapolis-St. Paul International Airport

Two weeks and three days after the departure of the Precise Priestess, may her blades fly ever true

🐁

SAM

Sam looked at the mice standing proudly naked on his palm, and wondered what the hell Annie had been thinking, telling him to bring them here. They were so small. They could speak English and pick locks. They were distressingly adept at both stealing and figuring out the password on his phone, enough so that he'd had to disable in-app purchases in Candy Crush. But they were still *mice*, and they were still so *small*.

"You're sure about this," he said. "If you wanted to stay with me and Grandma, you could. We're going to be wintering in Indiana, in one of the permanent boneyards.

I could put out some calls, find someone we can trust who could get you to the Campbells—"

"Peace," squeaked the smaller of the two mice. It was sleek and brown and getting fat a little faster than Sam thought mice were supposed to get fat, even with the way they kept sneaking into the cheese supply. He was pretty sure there were going to be more mice soon, and oh, God, was he sending a pregnant mouse off to get stepped on by some TSA asshole?

Annie was going to *kill* him.

"Peace," repeated the mouse. "We have made Pilgrimages before. They are a rare honor. We will be Tested as so few of our generation have been, and when we are Triumphant, none among the colony will question the Sincerity of my mate, nor the provenance of the New Rituals we carry."

Sam rubbed his forehead with his free hand and tried to figure out when his life had gone quite this far sideways. It was probably Annie's fault. Everything seemed to be, anymore. "How do you decide which words to capitalize when you're talking? It's weird. I'm not sure there's a grammar for that."

The two mice exchanged a long-suffering look. Apparently, he wasn't the first to ask. The smaller one—Mindy—pushed her whiskers forward, and said, "If you were of the colony, you would understand."

"If I were of the colony, I'd be too small to carry you."

"Balance is inevitable, even when it is Undesired," said Mindy. She stepped forward, putting a paw on the pad of his thumb. It was probably meant to be a reassuring gesture. All it did was drive home the difference in their sizes.

They were going to die. Annie's mice were going to die, and *Annie* was probably going to die, and with his luck, she wasn't going to take after her dead aunt. She'd just be gone, forever, and he'd never get to tell her he was sorry.

"We will be Careful," said Mindy solemnly. "We will be Cautious. We will be all the things one must be when undertaking a Holy Mission. We must. The colony needs to know what only we can say, and the Lost Ones must be brought home."

"Does that include Annie?" The question escaped him before he could think better of it.

Mindy pushed her whiskers forward again: the Aeslin answer to a smile. "The Precise Priestess is not Lost. She is merely Missing. When she returns to us, in glory, we will be rewarded for our Faith. Now put us down. We have very far to go."

Reluctantly, Sam bent and placed his hand against the cool concrete. The mice scampered from his palm, heading for the nearest drainpipe. In a few seconds, they would be gone.

"Wait!" he cried.

The mice stopped, looking back over their shoulders at him.

Feeling awkward, feeling confined by his artificially human skin and wishing he had a tail that he could twine around his ankles, Sam asked, "How can you be so sure that she's okay?"

"We believe in her," said Mindy. "You should do the same."

Then they were gone, leaving Sam to search for any unnecessary capital letters in their parting statement. He couldn't find them.

Shoulders slumped, he started for the car. Better not to hang out here any longer than he had to. Going to jail would probably interfere with his "track your missing girlfriend across the country whether she wants you to or not" plans for the weekend.

Five dollars to pay for parking and he was gone, heading back to the carnival, leaving the mice behind. Hopefully their gods would help them, because if they got killed, Annie was going to have his head.

Although at least then, he'd know where she was.

Head filled with dark thoughts of missing girlfriends and Covenant strike teams, Sam Taylor drove on.

MINDY

Humans do not often consider the scale of their works. They might take more care to block access to them, if they did. Or they might not. Who can know the thoughts of humankind? Not us, who merely scamper around the fringes, cleaving to our gods and hoping for enlightenment. Not even such as the Heartless Ones, who pluck thoughts from the air as we pluck berries from the vine, can fully understand the thinking of the humans. And so:

The drainpipe which had been left exposed in the parking garage was not blocked or barred in any way. It provided a clear highway for such ordinary mice and rats as might wish entrance to the good things inside the airport, and we kept our wits about us, my mate and I, as we raced along its length with our whiskers bristled and our teeth ready. We ran bereft of all adornment, that any who saw us might take us for those same ordinary mice, and I felt a small pang of regret for the many good things we had been forced to leave with Samuel Taylor, suitor to the Precise Priestess, whose godhood was not yet guaranteed, but which could safely now be assumed.

He would make a fine, strong god, and a fine, strong protector for the Precise Priestess. She would do well, so long as she was standing by his side. Our Priestesses are rarely in need of rescue, but neither are they frequently willing to accept help from outside the bounds of family. It is an understandable form of self-restriction—few who are not family have ever proven themselves to be worth trusting—but we would rather they had aid.

My mate, the one the Precise Priestess referred to as "Mork," ran by my side. He moved carefully, staying close enough that I could feel his presence, not so close that he could hamper or hinder me. Of the two of us, he was the one more inclined to agree with Samuel Taylor, who thought we should have remained hidden and safe until they could find a way to reunite us with the kin of our gods.

Mork had been too long among the halls of the unbelievers, born and raised in exile, paying each day for the sins of his parents and forbearers. The ways of true faith were as yet unfamiliar to him. I could run in certainty, knowing the gods would claim and keep me, knowing that if I should fall, they would be waiting to raise me up into the heavens. He had yet to behold the divinity of any save for the Precise Priestess herself. In her absence, his faith was flagging.

It would be a problem, if our journey lasted too long. Aeslin have faith. It is what distinguishes us from all other creatures of the forest and field, what allows us to endure in the face of all adversity. We are rational creatures: we know our faith is not always, in and of itself, rational. But when we are threatened, when we are called upon to do things no ordinary mouse could do, we hold to that faith to bolster us up.

There is a litany, recited in secret, when the family who watches over us and is watched over in turn is sleeping and unaware. We remember the faiths we have forsaken, the beliefs we have left behind in our quest to survive. We remember the old gods, the fallen gods, the blasphemous and broken gods. We remember who we were, before we came to the good safety of the Kindly Priestess and her descendants. We must, for to forget would be to become less than Aeslin, and more—and worse—to lose the gratitude we must each bear, each and every day, for the gods who keep us now.

We love them. We believe in them. We will die for them and consider our brief lives well-spent, if only it makes them smile for a moment in our memory. We do what we must do, and we have no regrets. Those of us who are lost in service are never truly lost. They await us in the Halls of Heaven.

Mork, though . . . if his faith was wavering, I did not know whether death would carry him to those Halls, or whether he would find the holy light of some other object, some other ideal. I could not let myself be swayed from my devotion, not even for the father of the pups stirring in my belly. If he lost the way, he would be lost to me, and to his descendants, for all of time.

I stopped. Mork stopped with me, ears flat, eyes pleading.

"We must run," he said. "There may be predators here."

"I smell no such things, nor poisons, nor other dangers," I said. "I must pray."

Our names are things of scent and gesture, intended to be exchanged during catechism and ritual without disruption of the rites at hand. As I must recite this, I shall use the names given to us by the Precise Priestess, for they are meant to be spoken aloud, as part and parcel to the moment.

Mork wrung his paws and twitched his tail and said, "Prayer can wait. We must run."

"The running will go better and more smoothly if you pray with me." I looked at him gravely, hoping he would see the necessity in my actions. "Please. Let us remain united in our faith."

His faith was weaker than mine, more frayed, and yet he was Aeslin: the lure of veneration was more than he could resist. He nodded, whiskers bristling.

"We will pray," he said. "But we will pray quickly."

"Yes," I agreed, and bowed my head, and began: "When first the Precise Priestess was brought before us, She was red of cheek and furious of voice, and those who had been pledged into Her service before even Her mother, the Thoughtful Priestess, knew of her approach rejoiced, for they had a new Priestess to serve in glory—"

Mork echoed what words he could, and we huddled together in the drain that would lead us into the airport, and we had so far yet to go, with only our faith to protect us.

SAM

The first thing Sam saw when he reached the motel currently serving as a temporary home to the carnival folks was almost enough to make him turn around and keep on driving, choosing discretion as the better part of valor:

His grandmother, Emery Spenser, standing in front of the ice machine with her arms folded and a sour expression on her face. There was no way she could have known when he was going to get back, especially since he hadn't exactly told her he was going. Which meant she'd been standing there for a while. Maybe for hours.

Which meant he was a dead man.

"At least I know there's life after death," he muttered, pulling into the first open spot. He was pretty sure Annie wouldn't want to fool around once he was a dead aunt. But he knew Mary could touch stuff, so maybe it wouldn't be so bad. It wasn't like he had a choice, seeing as how his grandmother was about to murder him.

He was tired. The scrape on his forehead where the bullet had bounced off still hurt, and maybe it was vain of him, but every time it ached, he worried about whether it was going to scar, which just seemed to make it ache more. He'd been holding it together and human-looking for hours, and all he wanted to do was go to his room, relax, and take a shower long enough to qualify as a drought risk. Was that so much to ask?

Apparently. Because the second he stopped the engine his grandmother came stalking toward him, shoulders set and hands clenched in a way he knew meant trouble. Well, maybe she'd just call him "Samuel" instead of Sam, and—

"Samuel," she said, through gritted teeth. "Coleridge. Taylor."

She was using his middle name. He was screwed. "Uh, hi, Grandma," he said, rubbing the back of his neck with one hand. At least being yelled at would make it easier to stay tense and hence human. "How's things?"

"You *disappeared*," she spat. "I thought you were *dead*. Where the hell have you been?"

"Gosh." He took an exaggerated look at the parking lot around them. Why was he spending so much time in parking lots? It wasn't fair. Not even a little bit. "This sure is a big, exposed, public place. We should totally discuss family business here."

Emery narrowed her eyes. "You think I won't raise my voice to you in private, young man?"

"No, Grandma, I know you'll raise your voice to me in private, but at least in private, I'll feel comfortable raising my voice *back*." There had been a few incidents, when he was younger, times when his anger had outweighed his ability to focus on the small flexion that kept him looking like a human being and not like a fūri.

(When Annie had asked him to describe the sensation of holding human form, he'd hemmed and hawed and finally said it was like carrying an egg in a spoon. Sure, it was easy enough to start, but the longer he had to focus on the egg, the harder it got to keep it balanced, and to keep himself from saying "to hell with it" and throwing it at the nearest window. Humanity was an effort. Sometimes more of an effort than it was genuinely worth.)

Emery paused before she said, grudgingly, "Come to my room."

"Okay, Grandma," he said, and ambled after her, all too aware of the curious eyes watching them through parted motel curtains. If all those eyes had belonged to carnival folk, he would have been a lot more comfortable. Sadly, while they had the numbers, and they had the initial insurance payout keeping them housed, they had yet to displace all the people who'd rented their rooms before the carnival came to town. As those rooms became available, more carnies would move into them, until eventually, they had the whole place to themselves.

This was never going to be more than a brief waystation, but Sam found himself counting the hours until checkout every morning, eagerly waiting to see how many unfamiliar faces would flicker in the lobby and then disappear forever, off to their lives, leaving him alone.

Emery unlocked the door to her room—ground floor, conveniently close to the ice machine and the lobby, where a continental breakfast of bad coffee and worse pastries was set out every morning—and waved Sam imperiously inside. He went, fighting the urge to duck his head and mutter like a naughty child.

As soon as she was inside and the door was closed he relaxed, allowing his body to shift into the form it preferred. The hair atop his head thickened as it became fur, and his tail, always an unwelcome absence, re-extended from his spine and snaked along his leg, finally wrapping tight around his ankle.

Emery watched this process with her usual grim patience—an expression he'd often mistaken for disapproval when he'd been young and stupid and afraid she loved him less because he wasn't human. It wasn't that she loved him any less, she'd explained, once she'd finally grasped the root of his concern; it was that she had less respect for the world because it couldn't allow him to be himself.

"The world doesn't know what it's missing, my brave boy," she'd said, and he'd never worried about being himself in front of her again.

"Samuel," she said now, her tone filled with regret and disappointment. "Where in the world did you go that was so important you couldn't tell anyone? Not even me?"

"The airport," he said. "I didn't tell you because I knew you'd say not to go."

Her eyes grew wide. "The *airport*?" she demanded. "Sam, you know better! That sort of place—there's cameras everywhere, government agents, the *Covenant*—"

"Annie wouldn't have asked me to take her mice to the airport if the Covenant was going to be there."

"Annie." Emery's voice was suddenly hushed. "You mean the girl who led the Covenant right to us, then burned down our carnival to stop them? The girl who lied to us about everything?"

"Not everything," he muttered.

It didn't matter: Emery was on a roll. "I found you bleeding, shot in the *head*, Sam. Do you know how easily you could have died? I could have been tracking your mother down right now to tell her that her only son was being dissected in some black ops lab, and all because of *Annie*."

"At least then you'd know where she was," said Sam.

"Don't talk about your mother that way," snapped Emery. "We're discussing your shortcomings, *not* hers."

"Right," said Sam, and scowled. His mother had taken one look at her bouncing baby boy—complete with prehensile tail and sideburns at two hours of age—and run for the hills, leaving Emery to clean up her mess. His grandmother always said he shouldn't blame her, that his mother had known too much about the difficulties he was going to face living as a yōkai in a world dominated by humans, and she hadn't been able to handle it.

If she'd been that concerned about him, why hadn't she insisted his father wear a condom, or gone and gotten herself knocked up by some nice, run-of-the-mill human guy? He couldn't imagine wanting to be anything else, but no one in his life had ever managed to make him feel like as much of a monster as his own mother had.

"Honestly, Sam, what were you thinking? You could have been seen. You could have been *taken*."

"I was thinking Annie didn't lead the Covenant to us, Umeko did. Remember Umeko? The one who was killing people? As soon as she started doing that, the Covenant knew who we were and that we were harboring a threat. An *actual* threat, Grandma, not just the Covenant being weird about us because we were monsters." Sam shook his head. "If Annie hadn't been there, we would have all died. The purge would have happened, and they would have burned our bodies. Instead, we got another shot. We can rebuild the carnival, and we can start over. Annie did that for us. We owe her our lives."

"She still lied. She still hurt you."

"I'm a big boy. My heart can handle it."

The look Emery gave him was quietly disbelieving. "Why don't you let me be the judge of that?"

"Because I'm not eight years old anymore, for a start."

"Samuel—"

"She lied to us. She apologized. She did everything within her power to make it right. She saved my life. She probably saved *all* our lives, since she's the reason we had any idea at all that the Covenant was coming." Sam raked a hand through his hair, frustrated. "Did she mess up? Yeah. She messed up a lot. But I'm pretty glad she did, since otherwise, I'd think she was too good to be true."

Emery opened her mouth to reply. Then she paused, giving her grandson a narrow-eyed look, and said, "You still like her."

Sam's cheeks reddened. "Uh, well. She's okay, I guess. She doesn't mind the whole 'monkey' thing I've got going on, and I don't know if you've noticed, but we're not exactly dripping in fūri around here. So that's a point in her favor. She's pretty good with knives, too."

"She's a *Price*, Sam. Do you understand what that means?"

"Not really." He shrugged. "I don't think you do either, though. Because what she says about her family and what you say about her family doesn't exactly match up. You're the one who taught me that when you have two conflicting stories, the truth is usually somewhere between them."

"They were *Covenant*," Emery said.

"They quit. A long time before Annie was born. That part's consistent in both your story and hers. The Prices quit, and now the Covenant wants them—and by extension, her—dead almost as much as they want people like me dead, which seems like a good way to be sure we'll always have something to talk about." Sam shrugged again, more vehemently this time. Something about arguing with his grandmother always made him feel like a sullen kid. "She asked me to get her mice to the airport,

I told her I'd do it, I did it. I don't understand why this has to be some kind of federal case."

"Because I can't lose you, too!" Emery clapped a hand over her mouth, looking stricken.

Sam was silent.

It was no secret among the carnies that Emery felt she'd failed her only daughter. Delilah's rebellion had taken the form of running away to join the business world, as far from the lights and sawdust of the carnival as she could get. Presumably, she was still out there somewhere, sitting in boardrooms and wearing pencil skirts and trying not to think about the world of monsters and midways she had left behind.

Sam tried not to think about her when he didn't have to. He didn't hate her—not anymore, anyway; not since he was eight years old and realized that if she'd tried to keep him with her, he would have been her little secret, always stuffed into his human form, always hiding—but he didn't like her either. She was the woman who'd taken one look at him before giving him away. That sort of thing was kind of tricky to forgive.

Finally, carefully, he said, "You're not going to lose me just because I like a girl, Grandma, or because I try to keep my promises. You raised me better than that. But if you try to keep me from doing what I know is right, that's where we're going to have some problems."

"You scared me," said Emery in a small voice.

"It's a scary sort of time," he allowed, and gave her a pleading, almost sheepish look. "Now can I have a hug?"

"Of course you can, sweetheart," she said, and went to him, and held him like her life depended on it. "Of course you can."

Sam, watching the wall over her shoulder, knowing how close he was probably going to come to breaking her heart, didn't say anything at all.

MINDY

Prayer helped us both, as prayer always does: Mork ran alongside me with more serenity now, his tail brushing against mine in peaceful solidarity. We did this for the sake of our gods, long may they watch over us in all things, and for the sake of the Precise Priestess, who walked now as none among our family had walked in years beyond measure.

She walked alone.

If Aeslin live in the halls of believing, our gods live in the halls of memory. It is our duty, and our honor, to remember all that happens to them, preserving it against the ravages of time. We codify history into ritual and rite. When the Thoughtful Priestess, long may she light the way, asks for the stories of those who came before her, we are eternally prepared.

Mork and I ran because we were burdened with a sacred duty: to carry the last months of the Precise Priestess home to the rest of the colony, that they might never be forgotten. That the word "last" can mean many things had not escaped either one of us. These months might be one side of a gap, a place where the catechism would grow vague, suitable for enthralling generations of scholars, teasing them with the unclear. When we are present, we can be sure every detail is perfect, that nothing is left behind. Without us, we would be bound to human recollection, and what a human—even one as glorious as our Priestess—saw fit to share.

These months might also represent the final entries into her litany, the pieces that would cap and conclude her too-brief time upon this world before she transcended flesh and left us for the heavens. The thought was enough to raise the fur along my backbone. We know the gods can die. We know the priestesses must, in their time, do the same. We know also that our time with them would be longer were their mission not so essential. They must fight, and all who fight must one day fall. We treasure our time with them all the more for knowing that it might end.

The Precise Priestess was young, and strong, and clever. She would not allow herself to be lost to us. It was upon me, and Mork, to carry her words and warnings home.

The drainpipe leveled out for a long stretch before it began climbing upward, sloping and slanting below the airport's foundations. We ran until the good greasy smell of frying potatoes addressed our noses. Then we stopped, in perfect tandem, whiskers twitching. My stomach growled.

Mork looked first to my face and then to my belly, where the pups we had gotten together waited to be born. "You must eat," he said.

"We can eat once we have achieved our goal."

"No," he said, firmly. "For did not the Precise Priestess say, lo, You Can Eat Once We Get Past Security? We have passed the checkpoint of the humans. Now is the time of eating."

"All praise her wisdom," I murmured. Absent our usual tools and clever carrying devices, we were as mice, unable to lay in stores against the journey. I had never taken a plane from Minnesota to Oregon before. It could be hours before we landed, and there was no way of knowing whether there would be provisions upon the plane.

"I will go," said Mork. He bristled his whiskers against mine, and then he was gone, darting along the length of the pipe and disappearing into whatever waited beyond.

My belly rumbled again. I pressed my paws against it, feeling the pups move inside me, and waited for his return, straining my ears for any sound and my nose for any scent more powerful than that of frying potatoes. None came to me.

Once, according to the oldest rites, the litanies of faiths long marked as heretical and abandoned, Aeslin colonies were plentiful. We found the objects of our worship in field and forest, building our homes around them, and when we grew great enough in number, we would experience a religious schism. Half the colony would go, off to find and follow a new god, and they would be forgotten to the rest, marked anathema and untouchable. It was necessary in those days, to forget. Many who went out into the world to find a new faith would not survive the journey.

Still, we flourished. Still, we walked in a world filled with wonders, and we worshipped as we saw fit, making of creation our cathedral. Yes, we were preyed upon, sometimes by larger beasts, sometimes by our own gods, but we were Aeslin. We were quick and we were clever, and we endured.

Until the coming of the Covenant, may they never know peace nor the company of their own corrupted gods. They beheld us at our devotions and marked us as devil-born, creations of purest evil, and they set themselves against us. We, who were but mice in comparison to them, who were small and soft and defenseless. We would have worshipped them, had they but asked us to. We would have built shrines in their honor and become keepers of their history, preserving it against the ravages of time. But no. Such was not suitable for their ideals. They slew us where they found us, and as they knew us, they found us with ease.

I was raised knowing that my colony, our shared faith, might be the last vestige of the Aeslin in this world, with all others gone to their scattered afterlives, nevermore to be united. Might: we knew there was the possibility of another, if they had been clever. If they had been quick.

When the Precise Priestess had come to her clergy and requested one of us accompany her across the great sea, reversing the voyage of the Patient Priestess and the God of Uncommon Sense, we had seen our opportunity. She thought well of me, for I had volunteered, and it will forever be my own small shame that she may not know the reasons for my eagerness. She knows we suspected the presence of the Lost Colony, and does not resent us for keeping that knowledge from her.

She does not know that I was chosen because I was young, and likely to be fertile, and unmated. Mork knew before he bedded me. Mork *understood*. When there are so few Aeslin left in the world, we cannot allow anything to prevent the making of more.

Had he proven unsuitable, I would have left him in England when my Priestess carried me away, and I would have taken our pups with me, and my colony would have grown greater for my labors. But he was not unsuitable. His colony has labored in secret and in shame all this time, and finally, finally, they are ready to come home.

All praise to the Precise Priestess, who carried me across an ocean and returned me home with my mate by my side. All praise to her, who understood that while she would miss us, carrying word of the Lost Colony home mattered as much as her own journeys. We had, in that moment, two sacred duties, to our gods and to our species, and she saw the conflict with clear and open eyes. She chose its resolution.

May all those who came before her guide her and keep her safe, for we can do so no longer.

I stood in the dark, paws pressed against my belly to feel the movement of both hunger and young, and waited. If Mork wished to betray me—if he was loyal to the Covenant's gods—this would be the time. He could run for the familiar. He could lead them to me, and unveil all of my family's secrets. It is the Aeslin way to have faith in the divinities which guide our lives. In this time, in this moment, I was choosing the hardest path of all. I was choosing to have faith in him.

The sound of paws running through the pipe ahead of me pulled me from my contemplations. I tensed, ready to run or fight, if either proved necessary. Even without a weapon, I have training and awareness, things lacked by common predators. I could not defeat a cat, however hard I fought. A mouse, on the other hand, would find me a troublesome foe.

Mork scurried into view, body low to the ground, a French fry clutched in his jaws. I relaxed. He ran faster, stopping in front of me and sitting up on his hind legs, dropping the fry into his paws and holding it out to me as if in offering.

"The pipe empties into a space of flame and grease," he said. "It is a restaurant. None saw me, for I was quick and clever. If we are quick and clever together, we may transverse their floors and make our exit."

"Where would we go?" I asked, before taking the fry and beginning to delicately nibble.

"There were two ways. One to a place of carpets, where many people walked, and another to a place of stone floors and few people."

The front and back of the airport, public area and staff halls, then. That was useful to know, even if it required entering a kitchen. Humans can be odd about mice in their cooking spaces. Years of raiding hotel kitchens during the Precise Priestess's conventions and field missions had trained me to face the most aggressive of chefs, but we did not wish to attract attention if we could help it.

Thoughtfully, I chewed my fry. Finally, I swallowed and said, "We must find the holy Departures Board. It will tell us where the planes are going, and more, which will take us closer to our goal." Portland was our final destination. Seattle would work almost as well. Planes flew between the two all day, on what were known as "commuter hops." If we could reach one, we could reach the other.

"Where is this holy Board?" asked Mork.

"I know they are located in the passenger areas, but we are more likely to cause a Hue and Cry there," I said. "Let us first search the staff area. Will you lead me?"

Mork pressed a paw over his heart. "It would be my honor," he said gravely.

We ran through the pipe, our flanks brushing, and I

had never felt more free, nor more in tune with what it means to be of the Aeslin. We were serving our gods and our colony, and we were doing it together. Oh, what bliss. Oh, what joy, to be born into the never-ending spiral of true faith. How small the worlds of those who did not believe seemed to me in that moment, as we ran on.

ι

SAM

Sam lay sprawled on his shitty motel bed, staring at the shitty, water-stained ceiling, and wondered how *anyone* could handle living in a place that never moved. The view out the window—also shitty, although he guessed his standards for windows were lower than his standards for, y'know, *mattresses*—was always the same, parking lot and narrow slice of street and shitty little stores on the other side. No mysteries. No surprises.

It wasn't like that in the boneyard. The carnival only ever put down shallow roots, clinging just hard enough to keep from being blown away. When they wore out their welcome they were gone, moving on to the next town, or heading for whatever rental property they were using for the winter. Permanence had never been the goal, not once.

Annie wasn't like that. She hadn't been willing to say much about where she'd grown up, which made sense, given the whole "actively being hunted by the Covenant of St. George," but her calendar had been the opposite of his. Summers with the carnival, seeing as much of the world as she could from the boneyard and the midway, and the rest of the year spent under a fixed roof, with a view that never changed.

He rolled onto his stomach, wadding a pillow to support his chin. If their circuit had ever taken them further west, he might have met her sooner. Gawky teenage

Annie hanging from the trapeze and criticizing his form. College Annie throwing things and telling him to get faster, what did he think this was, some kind of *game*? It was like there was a whole life they never got to have together because of stupid geography, and now they weren't getting to have *this* life together either, because of the stupid Covenant.

Sam groaned and rolled over again, automatically whisking his tail out of the way so he wouldn't pin it with his own leg. "This *sucks*," he informed the empty room. "Everything about it is awful and I hate it."

"You and me both, kiddo," said a flat female voice.

Sam froze.

On the one hand, maybe not the *best* response to suddenly hearing an unfamiliar woman in his room, having somehow gotten past the locked door without him noticing: he was still in his natural form, after all, and even robbers with shitty ideas about where to look for the next score were likely to notice the giant humanoid monkey in pants. Monkeys did not normally wear pants, or have proportions this close to human, or—

He was spiraling. Great. Well, no. The opposite of great. He should have moved, should have bolted for the bathroom or leapt for the sound of that voice. There was almost nothing in the world as fast as a fūri, except for maybe another fūri. And while the universe could be cruel, he didn't think it was cruel enough to throw a girl fūri at him while he was busy panicking about his missing, all-too-human girlfriend. That wasn't funny. That was *mean*.

"I know you're not dead," said the voice, still sounding rather, well, obnoxiously disinterested in the whole situation. She was the one who'd started this. The least she could have done was sound like she meant it. "I have what you might call a second sense for dead people."

Dead ... Sam sat up, turned, and scowled at the white-haired woman sitting in the threadbare armchair next to the window. "You're Annie's dead aunt," he accused.

"And you're smarter than you act," she replied, with a quick, frosty smile. "Hi."

She looked younger than Annie, somewhere in her late teens, with long white hair and eyes that made him oddly uncomfortable, although he couldn't put his finger on exactly why. There was something in the way they reflected the world—or didn't—that made him want to turn and run and never look back. Humans were predators and so were fūri: he got a certain bloodthirstiness from both sides of his heritage. But this woman . . .

Something in him knew her for a bigger, better predator, and had no interest whatsoever in attracting her attention. Let her sit there in her jeans and yellow peasant blouse, looking utterly innocent. It didn't matter. The part of him that had evolved to stay alive knew better.

"Uh," he said. "Hi."

"It's Mary, in case you've forgotten. Mary Dunlavy."

"Right."

"I thought you might like to know that I've been keeping an eye on you, and that I'm still looking for Annie. But she's not dead. I'd know it if she were. She's out there somewhere, stubborn as ever, and I'll find her soon."

Just like that, he was off the bed and standing in front of her, tail wrapped tight around his ankle like he thought he could keep himself from coming untethered from the floor and floating away. He began to reach for her, to shake her until she told him what he wanted to know, but a glance at those eyes made him think better of the idea, and he froze again, hands only half-raised.

Mary looked amused. At least one of them was.

"Where is she?" he asked, somehow managing to make the question sound more like a plea than a demand. "She shouldn't be out there by herself. She doesn't even have her mice. She's going to get hurt. So where is she?"

"Stop," said Mary. There was ice in her voice, an avalanche packed into that single syllable. Sam shied back before he could stop himself, feeling the hair stand on end all the way along the length of his spine. "You can't ask me questions, Sam, and you can't ask me for things. Those are the *rules*. If you break them, you'll be sorry."

"What—" He stopped, catching himself, and eyed her

warily. "It sure would be nice if I understood why that was the case, dead aunt lady."

"Again, it's Mary," she said. "How much do you know about ghosts?"

"It sucks that you can ask me questions and I can't return the favor," he grumbled. "Ghosts. People leave them behind when they die, sometimes. Nobody really knows why for sure. They haunt houses and stuff, and Grandma has an umbramancer come by the boneyard once a year to make sure none of them have attached themselves to the show. Something about how phantom carnies really mess with insurance rates."

"That's a start," said Mary. "Ghosts are like cryptids or yōkai: one name to describe hundreds of different things. It would take too long to list the things I'm not, so I won't bother. I am a very specific kind of ghost. I don't haunt a place: I haunt a concept."

Sam hesitated. "When Annie introduced us back at the carnival, she mentioned the crossroads. Did she mean . . . ?" He caught himself and groaned. "Fuck I am *not* good at not asking questions."

"That's one of the few you're allowed to ask." Mary's smile contained no pleasure. "You can't deal with the crossroads if you don't know what they are, which means the only debt you incur by asking about them is their attention. Normally, I'd say that was debt enough, but I've met you, and I know Annie well enough to know what kind of man she'd fall for. You'll have the crossroads interested in you one way or another."

"Because that doesn't sound dire and horrible," grumbled Sam. "What are the crossroads?"

"They're where you go when you want something so badly that you're willing to bargain everything you have against the chance that you might get it." Mary looked at him calmly. "They're where brave men sell their souls and good men sell their futures, and bad man sell everything they have. When you go there, when you're taken there, you tell the shadows what you want. I'm the ghost who tries to talk you out of it."

"Oh," said Sam, in a voice that was suddenly small,

yet seemed to be too big for the room around them. He felt like he was shouting. "I guess that's an important job. I still don't get why I'm not allowed to ask you questions."

Mary actually smiled at that. "Nicely phrased. You're catching on. Because I work for the crossroads, because I work *through* the crossroads, when you talk to me, you're also talking to them, in a metaphysical sense. I don't know where Annie is. At the same time, if you said 'hey, Mary, where exactly is Annie,' I could take you to the nearest crossing so they could tell you. All you'd have to do is make a deal. It's just that some—most—of those deals aren't nice."

"So you're the asshole rabbit from *Madoka*?"

"All right, I can see why Annie likes you so much, but no. The crossroads are the asshole rabbit from your little cartoon. They want you to make deals you can't live with. They want you to give them everything—*everything*—in exchange for things you never really needed in the first place. It's my job to take you to them if you ask. It's also my job to make you reconsider. Leave the crossroads alone. They're not for you."

"Sort of seems like you're saying they're not for anyone."

"That's exactly what I'm saying. Do you understand the rules now?"

"Don't ask you questions, which is sort of a bummer, don't go to the crossroads, don't sell my soul." Sam ran his hand through his hair, leaving it in spiky disarray. "I guess I'm sort of curious about why you're here, though, with so many rules."

"I'm here because I figured you'd want to know that Annie is okay, even if I'm not in a position to tell you where she is right now." Mary gave him a wry smile. "You're not family, but you're family-adjacent, and that means I'm allowed to check up on you from time to time. Before I was a ghost, I was a babysitter, after all."

"This is weird," said Sam.

"Yes," agreed Mary.

"Very weird," said Sam.

"If you start singing show tunes, I'm leaving," said Mary.

"What?" asked Sam.

Mary rolled her eyes. "Never mind. Kids these days, I swear. You get the mice to the airport okay?"

"I did," Sam said. "I, uh … I sort of want to ask if they're going to be all right out there. They're awfully small."

"I know," said Mary. She sighed. "Aeslin mice always are."

MINDY

At the pipe's end was a Kitchen such as I had never seen before, not even at Penton Hall, where they fed so many people each day that it was dizzying. This Kitchen was vast, shared between multiple groups of humans, who moved from station to storefront and back again as they worked.

Mork and I froze in the shelter of the pipe, watching the humans move, counting out their steps. Once we knew the pattern, once it was committed to memory, we left our shelter, and we ran. Pipe to table leg, while all backs were turned, all eyes were lifted; table leg to the side of the freezer while the man who worked nearest to it was consumed with staring at a pretty co-worker. Freezer to door.

Door to crevice, and crevice to hall, and suddenly we stood in an echoing room with floor of concrete and ceiling of high, naked beams, all steel and glass and the smell of cleaning fluid. We moved quickly, darting behind the nearest object: a metal bookshelf laden with heavy binders.

People moved here as well, but not as many, and not with as much purpose. We were behind closed doors, where the public could not go.

Mork looked to me, and I felt my chest swell with pride. I was a Leader. I was bringing him to true faith, and I was bringing him home. Truly, those who had sponsored me into the priesthood would feast and dance on our arrival.

"Where do we begin?" he asked.

"The holy Departures Board in the airport where we began was black, and mounted high upon the wall," I said. "I do not believe they would put such effort into Form here; this is a place for Function. Seek things whose Function seems to be the spreading of information, and meet me here in the time it takes to recite the first Catechism of the Kindly Priestess."

"A wise thought," he said, and pushed his whiskers lightly against my own before he scampered away.

I took a breath. "On the fifth day of summer, after a week of poor forage," I began, and scampered in the opposite direction, reciting all the way.

My eldest sister was called to the services of the Kindly Priestess. She knows all the rituals, even the ones so obscure that they are no longer performed within the main colony. She can perform the Calling of the Chickens, and sing the lullabies for the children whose names were willfully removed from the ranks of the divine, who wished only to forget their mother's strangeness and live as did their peers. We treat our gods as a single branch, stretching straight and true, but we cannot forget that we were the ones to prune them so, at their own requesting.

There are no other Lost Colonies, however much we might wish it so. It took crossing an ocean to cause a schism in our current faith, and that has only happened the once. We are, and we remain, the last.

This place, designed as it had been for the ease of humans, afforded plentiful hiding spots. I ran, keeping close to the wall, looking in all directions for a Departures Board, and found nothing. When I reached the middle point of my recitation I stopped, made the sign of the Kindly Priestess across my chest and withers, and turned to run back in the direction from whence I had come.

The Lost Colony kept its liturgies well: Mork and I

arrived back where we had parted at the same time, both of us mouthing the final words of the rite. He twitched his ears, greeting and apology, and said, "There was no Departures Board in the direction I chose. Only men, and bags, and a room of computers."

Were the God of Chosen Isolation with us, he could have made those computers tell us everything we needed to know. But had he been with us, we would have had no need of the knowledge. He would have placed us in his bag and carried us onto the airplane, even as the Precise Priestess had done, and our only task would have been to mark his actions.

A pang of homesickness grew where my heart should have burrowed. How I missed the safety of my gods, who were large and powerful and walked in a world built to their scale, carrying us, their faithful, with them. This would all have been so much easier, had we not been alone.

But that was what made it a trial, and not a vacation. Slicking back my whiskers in defiance and acknowledgment, I said, "There was less in the direction I chose, but I saw there a door, labeled 'Open Slowly,' which I believe led to the Place of Passengers. Let us go there together. We do not need to Open Slowly. We do not need to Open at all. We can find the Board of Departures, and from there decide which plane will carry us most quickly home."

The Precise Priestess had lived up to her name and title when giving her directions: either Portland or Seattle would do, although Portland was to be preferred, but if necessity demanded we choose between a direct flight to Seattle and a connecting flight to Portland, we were to go to Seattle. Changing planes would mean putting ourselves in active danger a second time, and it would be better if that part of our journey were finished as quickly as possible.

"Yes." Mork hesitated, and then, with the shape of my name on his whiskers, he asked, "Will they truly welcome me? Me, who was outcast, who was lost?"

"You were never outcast, nor were any of your

ancestors," I said, moving closer, touching my tail to his. How strong he was, and how frail! My children would be blessed in their father, to be sired by one so brave. "Those who chose to stay did so from devotion. We have never doubted your faith. You will be lauded when you return home by my side, the lost son finally returned to us, filled with the moments we have yet to learn. Those who keep the devotions of the God of Bitter Honesty and the Obedient Priestess have been waiting *lifetimes* for your arrival. We need only to reach them, and you will see. You will understand."

"I believe you," whispered Mork, the sweetest words that any lover has ever spoken. Together once more, we turned and ran for where I had seen the door. We would continue. We would prevail. We were Aeslin, and together, we would be strong.

SAM

"You can't tell me where Annie is, and you won't let me give you my number for when you see her, and you won't promise to remind her that it's a serious dick move to run out on your boyfriend so you can be martyred by a bunch of asshole monster hunters." Sam folded his arms and scowled. "I'm starting to wonder whether there's anything you *will* do."

"Well, for one thing, I appear to have taught you how not to ask questions, which is a skill that will serve you extremely well if you're going to continue hanging around with Annie. I love her to death—which is completely true when I say it, since I'm already dead—but I swear asking her questions is like taking the midnight train to oh god why would you do that no, no, please stop talking-ville. She's a good kid. I'm not trying to warn you off her. I just hope you have an incredibly high threshold for awful."

"I grew up with a traveling carnival."

"Then you're going to be fine."

Sam rolled his eyes. "Are all ghosts jerks, or just you?"

"All ghosts who willingly associate with the Price family are jerks, because we're trying to keep up with the rest of the group. And don't roll your eyes. They'll stick that way, and you'll start swinging into things."

"I'm not Spider-Man," grumbled Sam.

Someone knocked on the door.

Both Sam and Mary froze before turning, slowly, to look at the door. Sam straightened, tail vanishing as he shifted back into his human form. "Uh, who is it?" he called.

"Samuel? Who are you talking to in there?" The voice was Emery's.

Sam winced. "Uh, no one? I have the TV on."

"Don't you lie to me, young man, I know the difference between a commercial and a conversation."

"Shit," muttered Sam. He looked to Mary. "If you're going to vanish, this is when you do it. Like, right now."

"No, no, this is way more entertaining," said Mary. She flickered, disappearing from the chair and reappearing next to Sam. Her clothes had changed during the transition, becoming grayscale—gray jeans, black sneakers, white peasant blouse with crows and tombstones embroidered around the neck and wrists. She beamed at him. "Think I look believably dead?"

"I think you look believably like me getting grounded," said Sam direly. Emery knocked again. He sighed. "Coming, Grandma!"

Sam barely had the door open before Emery was pushing her way inside. She stopped dead when she saw Mary.

"Oh," she said. "Hello."

Mary smiled. Not brightly, but sadly, with the weight of a whole lot of very long roads weighing it down.

"Hi, Emery," she said. "Long time no see."

Sam looked back and forth between the two of them, eyes going wide as he added two and two together and came up with a number that was something like four and something like "oh, fuck." Finally, he managed to squeak, "You two know each other?"

"Your grandmother came to the crossroads a long time ago," said Mary, voice gentle, like she was trying to explain some terrible idea to a child. "She was worried about a lot of things. Her own daughter, mostly. This was before you, Sam, before you were even a shadow on the horizon. She wanted to purchase a guarantee of a happy future. And I talked her out of it."

Emery burst into tears and ran the last few feet to Mary, throwing her arms around the other woman's neck and sobbing into her shoulder. Sam blinked.

"I feel like I'm missing like, two-thirds of this story, and it's the part that makes it okay for you to make my grandmother cry and say you talked her out of buying a happy ending, so it would be *awesome* if someone could tell me why I'm not supposed to be angry right now."

"Because, silly boy, she would have been narrowing her life from a highway to a side street," said Mary, patting Emery on the back. "No more questions, no more choices, just a single pre-determined path that she would have had no choice but to follow. You, for example. I can guarantee you wouldn't exist, because you're way too much of a wild card for the crossroads to be comfortable having in their deck. A half-fūri trapeze artist? Please. You're a nightmare to any organized plan. Buying a future means selling the ones you didn't use. That's a lot of power to waste on making yourself miserable."

"But she said *happy* ending," protested Sam.

"Uh-huh. Ever done drugs?"

Sam froze, looking guiltily between Mary and Emery for several seconds before he said, "I, uh, smoked some weed with Ananta once. She offered, and I was curious, and the carnival wasn't open. Um. Sorry, Grandma."

"How did it make you feel?" asked Mary, before Emery could say anything.

"I don't know. Floaty. Sort of silly. My feet were fascinating, which was good, since I couldn't tense enough to change forms. Which freaked me out, once I realized it, and then I got into an argument with one of the cobras over whether I was being insensitive for being angry that I couldn't pass myself off as human anymore."

"How do you get into an argument with a cobra?" asked Mary.

"The tips of their tails are really flexible. They can use a stylus, and wow, do they know how to swear." Sam shook his head. "The whole thing made me feel really stupid and sort of trapped, like I didn't get to decide what I was going to do, I just *did* it."

"Great," said Mary. "Now magnify that feeling. Imagine waking up every morning and just *doing* things, going through the motions of your life without making any actual decisions. You wouldn't go to the store because you looked in the pantry and realized you were out of noodles, you would go to the store because your feet had you halfway there before you noticed you were out of bed. Everything would be kismet, which sounds great until you realize that you haven't *decided* to do anything in years. Everything happens. You can't make it stop."

Sam grimaced. "Okay, that sounds really awful."

"That's why she talked me out of it," said Emery. She reached up and touched Sam's cheek lightly. "My silly little ideas of what it meant to be happy could never hold a candle to this world."

"Glad to help," said Mary. "Now can we talk about how you went and got *old*? Hen's teeth, Emery, last time I saw you, you were the hottest thing in six counties. Now you're down to like, three."

"Last time I saw you, my daughter was three years old, and I was terrified that raising her on my own would do something to hurt her," said Emery. "Between her and Sam, I've been a mother twice over. That sort of thing ages a body. You don't look any deader."

Mary grinned. "Good thing, too. I never did feel much like rotting."

"What brings you here? Are you—" Emery's

expression hardened, shuttering itself, until her face had become a fortress. "Absolutely not. Samuel Coleridge Taylor, I forbid you to have any dealings with the cross-roads."

"I wasn't," Sam protested. "I didn't even know they existed until Mary showed up and started lecturing me about leaving them alone. Can you please only yell at me for things I've actually *done*?" He realized his mistake too late, and winced.

"You mean like sneaking away to take *some girl's* Aeslin mice to the airport?" Emery asked.

"Wait," said Mary, holding up her hands. "You're mad at him because he helped the mice? Antimony's mice? You're serious?"

"You know her?" asked Emery sharply.

"I'm her babysitter," said Mary. "I've been the Price family babysitter since shortly after I died, back when they were still the Healys, and still believed the rest of the world would eventually allow them to put the Covenant behind them. You're honestly mad about this? For the love of Hades, Emery, that girl did nothing but save you—"

"She burned my carnival!" Emery snarled.

"You have insurance! You'll get it back, you'll get it all back, and she *saved* you, as surely as I did, by *doing her job*. That little girl—that *child*, because they are always children to me, Emery, the only children I'm ever going to have—risked her life on your behalf, and this is the thanks she gets? You berating her boyfriend because he dared keep his word to her? Come on. I thought better of you. Honestly, I'm astonished that you didn't think better of *yourself*."

Mary's glare had an almost physical presence. Emery held up under it for a few seconds before she wilted, shoulders slumping, and turned her face away.

"Do you have any idea how hard it is to raise a child, to make him happy and healthy and secure in himself, when you know every minute that the world is full of people who would hurt him if they could, all because of things he didn't choose? I love my boy. I love him for who and what he is, and I wouldn't change it. But that girl was every nightmare I've had in the past twenty years all wrapped up in one."

"Her name is Antimony," said Mary. "She saved you. I won't ask you to be grateful, because it seems like that would be pushing it, but I will ask you to be respectful. She's earned that much. Sam?"

"Uh, yeah?"

"If you need me, call. I always hear when my kids call, and I'll do my best to come. I can find you." Mary took one last look at Emery, and then she was gone.

"Oh, God." Emery put her hands over her face. "What have I done?"

Sam didn't answer.

MINDY

We squeezed our bodies beneath the door, the weight of my belly making the task more difficult than it should have been. It was good, that we undertook this journey now: had we waited, I might have found myself unable to move easily through the airport, and all would have been lost.

On the other side of the door, the floor was covered in dull red carpet, and smelled of many feet. It had been cleaned recently, for there were no smells more than a few hours old, and yet it had already been transformed into a highway of informative filth.

Humans walk through a world filled with information they can neither access nor understand. I pity them for that, even as I rejoice that we have something that they do not, that we can be *useful*. Some of the people who had passed through this place had come from home. Their footsteps left traces of Portland soil, of Portland flora, behind. But unless we wished to track them down, presume they were visitors to this place and would be returning home in the fullness of time, and stay with them until their pilgrimages ended, knowing where people had *been* was of less use.

Long stretches of wall were exposed, leaving no cover. But people walked in all directions towing small cases behind them. If we timed this correctly . . .

"Follow me," I said. Mork nodded, and we moved to the edge of the large metal rack which offered our current concealment. A woman in very tall shoes walked by, towing a black bag with many zippers. I ran, leaping to the side and climbing onto the top. Mork did the same. The woman did not notice, but walked on, pulling us with her.

Humans are predators, for all that they prefer their food pre-killed and packaged for their convenience: motion catches their eyes more than any other thing. Having made it to the safety of her bag, we were likely to remain safe until needs forced us to move again. I held my whiskers perfectly still, forbade my ears to flick, and focused only on charting our surroundings. We would need to be able to navigate this airport if we were to transverse it without unnecessary difficulty.

"Look," breathed Mork. I turned my head the smallest of fractions, and beheld what had captured his attention: a black rectangle hung high on the wall, covered with numbers, times, and the names of cities.

Our helpful transport was no longer so helpful. We were passing a row of empty seats. I leapt, Mork close behind me, and no one screamed or threw anything, leaving me to believe that we had once more escaped notice. It couldn't last forever. I was going to take full advantage while I could, for did not the Violent Priestess say, lo, The Best Offense Is a Sneak Attack?

According to the board, there were four flights departing for Portland within the next two hours. One—the soonest—was on the opposite side of the airport. I dismissed it as an option. By the time we could make our way there, the plane would likely have departed, and then we would be too far from the other three. Each of the other flights presented its own disadvantages. I bristled my whiskers.

"Have you any scripture?" I asked.

"Not . . . not that you would know," said Mork awkwardly.

I glanced at him. "You speak of a Priestess known to the Lost Colony?"

"The Obedient Priestess."

"Ah," I breathed. "We know her as a child. We were denied the glory of knowing her as a woman. What would she have said?"

"She did say, lo, Aim For The Middle, For When You Strike True, It Is a Bullseye, and When You Miss, There Is Much More Target."

"So be it," I said, unable to stop the thrill that ran down my spine as I heard new holy words, words we had been so long ignorant of. "Truly, she was wise, and we will be enriched beyond all measure by growing to know her better. The second departing flight, then. If we can achieve it, we will be home before the clock strikes nine. If we cannot, we will take the next. Thus will we chip away at our obstacles, and find ourselves well-redeemed."

The second flight was in the same part of the airport as our current hiding place, if the numbers on the gates were to be considered accurate: we would still need to travel a great distance, but it was not overly ambitious, nor beyond our means. We could do this.

We *would* do this.

A man walked by, heading in the direction we needed to go, toting another case like the one we had ridden before. I glanced to Mork, flicked an ear, and leapt. He leapt with me, into the next step on our adventure; into the future.

SAM

"I don't hate you, but I'm not going to let you draw anti-possession wards all around the border of my hotel room, and even if I wanted to let you, you wouldn't do it, because we can't afford to have the room cleaned," said Sam, for what felt like the fifty-seventh time. "Mary didn't try to possess me. Not once. She looked at me sort of like I was six years old and needed to learn how to clean my room, but that doesn't feel like a precursor to possession. A time-out, maybe. She's a babysitter."

"You don't understand the forces you're toying with, Sam," snapped Emery.

Sam relaxed a little. If he was back to "Sam" instead of "Samuel," she was calming down. Anti-possession wards notwithstanding. "I understand that she cares about Annie, and that she's actively looking for her, which means I don't have to. I want her to keep coming around, if only so I can sleep at night."

Emery paused. "What do you mean?"

"I met a girl, Grandma. A girl who liked me. *Liked* me-liked me, not just 'better be nice to the boss's son.' She kissed me when I was like this, you know?" He waved a hand, indicating all of himself. "She didn't pull back or ask if she was going to get fur in her mouth or say anything weird about how kissing a dude with a tail was sort of kinky. I know you love me, I know you don't care, but my dating life has never been totally awesome. Human girls get weird."

They had done more than kiss while he was relaxed enough not to look human anymore. Somehow, he didn't think his grandmother would appreciate hearing that. He was also pretty sure Annie wouldn't appreciate him *telling* that, and while she was probably hundreds of miles away playing roller derby under an assumed name,

Mary was only ever a thought from smacking him in the back of the head.

Having ghosts around sure was a good way to learn how to watch his mouth.

"I don't like her," said Emery. "She's a Price. She'll only get you hurt."

"I don't think you need to like her, Grandma," he said. "I'm pretty sure the only one here who needs to like her is me. And I like her plenty."

"She's dangerous."

"I'm dangerous."

"You're not, baby, you're not." Emery started to reach for him, then seemed to think better of it and pulled her hands back. "You're special."

"Grandma, I'm a monkey." Sam shrugged. "I'm not complaining. I like being a monkey. I like being able to go back and forth. I can walk around in the human world, doing whatever, and then come home and know that I'm stronger and faster than they could ever hope to be. But even if I didn't like it, that wouldn't make it change. I am always going to be what I am, which means I am always going to be looking over my shoulder for Covenant assholes and bigger monsters. I'm not going to go to college and have wacky hijinks. Jimmy Wong isn't going to play me in the movie. I'm totally cool with all of these things. I like who I am, I like my life. But you don't get to tell me Annie's dangerous and I'm not. Maybe I'm a different kind of danger. I don't think so, though. I think we're pretty much the same kind of health hazard."

Emery sighed, pressing a hand to the hollow of her throat, like she was trying to trap her breath inside. Like she thought she could keep herself from shaking into pieces. "I don't want to lose you."

"You're not going to lose me. You're my *Grandma*. You raised me. When I was little, I always wondered why you didn't do like the young grandparents in Lifetime movies and tell me you were my actual mother."

"I let you watch too much television," Emery sniffed. "And I didn't want you to think I could answer questions about your father, or that you were adopted. You needed to know you were mine, but that there were things I couldn't tell you, because they'd never been mine to know."

"See?" Sam smiled encouragingly. "We have so many years of just us. We have bad jokes and too much TV and 'don't hang from the ceiling, it's uncouth,' and setup and teardown and *everything*. You're never gonna lose me."

Emery opened her mouth to reply. Then she paused, eyes narrowing as she really *looked* at her beloved, boneheaded grandson. When had he gotten so tall? When had the fur on his cheeks gone from baby fuzz to something that looked like it could break a razor in two? When had he grown up, and why hadn't she found a way to stop it?

"You're going to go after her, aren't you." It wasn't really a question.

Sam's smile wilted a little, losing its edge of encouragement, gaining an edge of melancholy. "Wouldn't you? If you were in my position, if someone you lo—liked a whole lot was out there somewhere alone and maybe scared, wouldn't you go after them?"

"Yes," she said. "My brave boy, yes."

"Good," said Sam, and folded his grandmother into a hug, staring over her shoulder at the wall.

He was going to go after her. Just as soon as he knew where to *go*.

MINDY

The first man stopped at a gate some distance shy of our destination. We hopped down before we could be seen and rushed to the shelter of the nearest trash can, sticking close to its base, where we could be reasonably sure we would go unseen. A Dorito greeted us there.

"Praise the divine," Mork murmured, and broke it in two.

"Praise the divine," I echoed, and pretended not to notice when he passed me the larger of the two pieces.

We sat in peace for a moment, enjoying our scavenged treat, watching the people come and go. There were so many of them, humans in unbelievable array. Some were dressed as for ritual purposes, garments all of one color, tight-fitted and tidy. Others looked as if they were preparing for a very long nap. None of them saw us. We moved through their world but apart from it, separated by scale.

Mork followed my gaze, and asked, "Do you envy them?"

"Envy them what?" I looked to him, ear cocked to show curiosity. "Their size? It would be nice, to be so protected from predation. But look how much they need! What fills my belly is but a crumb to them. They are endless hunger. They will devour the world, and they still will not be fulfilled. And lacking predators to turn their hands against, they turn so very often on each other. No. I do not envy them their size."

"I envy them," murmured Mork. He looked down. "They do not depend on faith to steer themselves. I have seen humans who believed in nothing but their own decisions. Humans who served the Covenant because it was convenient, not out of any sincere desire to better the world. It would be ... pleasant ... not to believe that the gods are aware, and judging, at all times. It would be good not to be found wanting."

"You have not been found wanting." I brushed my palm over the tips of his whiskers. "You have been found by *me*, who was carried to you by an envoy of the gods, who has found you perfect in all ways. You are gloriously good, and we will be so glad of having you."

"Truly?"

"Truly." I fanned my whiskers at him. "I would not have chosen you to sire my children, were it not so."

He squeaked amusement, and bumped his head against my belly. "Then where are we to go?"

"There." I pointed down the length of the airport. "We continue this way. And look: a good thing comes."

A vehicle was rolling down the carpet toward us, long and gray and open-topped, carrying a scattering of humans and their bags. It moved slowly enough that we could catch it easily.

Mork nodded. We tensed. The vehicle rolled closer.

"Now," I said.

We ran.

It was a short distance in the open; short enough that I anticipated no problems, and perhaps there would have been none, had not the vehicle slowed to a stop. I leapt, grabbing hold of the undercarriage and securing myself out of sight. Mork leapt in turn—

—only for the swinging foot of a dismounting human to catch him square in the gut and send him flying. He impacted with the wall; he did not move when he landed on the carpet. Someone screamed. Humans began to point. I clung, frozen with indecision, to the pipe where I had secured myself, and saw someone drop an empty cup over his half-curled form.

He was lost.

SAM

After his grandmother left—which was honestly something of a relief, since he hadn't been sure how many more reassurances he didn't entirely believe he could offer before he started shrieking—Sam's motel room seemed to contract, becoming more like a cell than ever. She knew he wanted to go after Annie. She had even, in her stilted way, told him that she wouldn't blame him when he did. All that was great.

It was just that he had no idea where Annie *was*, and until he knew that, "going after her" was pretty much another way of saying "running away from home." That, his grandmother was not going to go for.

And the carnival needed him. He knew that. They needed him to be there to talk to the insurance investigators, to be visible as the owner's grandson, rather than missing as the possible arsonist. As long as Mary said Annie was okay and didn't need him rushing out there to find her, this was where he belonged.

"Fuck," he muttered, tail lashing, and stalked toward the bathroom.

One nice thing about growing up in a trailer: basically anyplace with plumbing had a mind-blowingly awesome shower in comparison. He relaxed under the stinging spray, pushing it hotter every few seconds, letting it blast the tension out of his back and shoulders. Clouds of steam billowed through the room.

(Once, they'd stayed at a bogeyman-owned motel with a hot tub, and he and Ananta had snuck down at two o'clock in the morning, when all the good humans were asleep and the bad humans were too stoned to process what they were seeing. They'd luxuriated in the hot water for hours, him and the snake who walked like a woman and her two baby brothers who actually looked like snakes. It had been one of the best nights of his life.)

"Do you even *get* wrinkly, or do your magic monkey powers keep that from happening?"

This time Sam didn't freeze, even though that might have been the safer response. He yelped, jumping, and yelped again as his feet tried to go out from under him. Flailing wildly, he grabbed the shower curtain, which promptly came off in his hands, leaving him soaking wet, stark naked, and holding a sheet of opaque plastic over his genitals.

Mary, sitting on the sink and filing her nails with a bright pink file, offered him a tight-lipped smile. "Don't worry, buddy, I'm not here to check out your junk. Your modesty is safe with me."

"Bathroom," Sam squeaked.

"Yup. It is." Mary went back to filing her nails. "I'm glad you have that down. I'd be really distressed if you didn't know what a bathroom was. Carnie childhoods can be weird, but you should still know about showers."

"If I throw the soap at you, do I somehow piss off the unspeakable eldritch entity that you serve?"

"Nope." Mary studied her thumb. "But I do disappear, and then you have nobody to talk to."

"I don't like to have conversations while I'm *naked*."

"I'll be sure to let Annie know."

Sam threw the soap.

Mary disappeared.

Sam waited for a count of five before letting go of the shower curtain and turning off the water. Even if he'd trusted her not to reappear, which he didn't, the moment was gone; all the tension he'd been trying to wash away was back, and it had brought some friends along, to make sure it didn't get lonely. At least now he was clean.

Rehanging the shower curtain was tricky and annoying, and much of the bathroom received a thorough dousing before he was done. Including his clothes, and the towels. Sam looked down at himself, groaned, and hopped back into the tub before tensing in that so-specific way and shifting back into his human form. The water that had been trapped in his fur—which wasn't plentiful, but was *dense*—dropped to the floor with a loud splatting sound and ran down the drain.

"Everything about this day can die," he muttered, getting out of the tub a second time and scanning for something dry enough to cover himself. The options were slim at best.

"Oh, I am going to regret this," he said, and gripped the doorknob before saying, loudly, "Mary, if you're out there, please leave for like, five minutes so I can cover my ass. Literally."

When he opened the door, there were no visible ghosts in the room. He supposed she could be there and *in*visible, as could any number of her friends. There could be a whole ghost convention going on, all of them snickering behind their phantom hands and pointing at—well, pointing at stuff. Stuff he didn't want ghosts to be pointing at. He hurried to the dresser, digging out a pair of sweat pants and yanking them up over his waist before letting out a relieved breath.

"Okay," he said. "I can do this. I can deal with this." He looked down at himself. If he was already walking around looking human, he might as well take advantage of it and visit the vending machines.

Ananta was there when he came strolling up, a half-filled cooler in her hands, kicking the ice machine to keep it spitting out ice. Sam stopped, raising an eyebrow.

"Are you gonna build a snowman?" he asked.

"I'm cold-blooded, Sam," she said, and kicked the machine again. "If I built a snowman, I would slip into a state of hibernation, and no one would get me out of it until next spring. No, I am not going to build a snowman."

"There are these things called 'gloves,'" he said. "You wear them and your hands stay warm, and then you can build all the snowmen you want."

"Asshole," she said fondly. "My room doesn't have a fridge, so I have to keep the dead rats on ice. And we go through a *lot* of rats in my room." Her room, and the trailer she kept parked right outside of it. CAUTION: LIVE REPTILES was stenciled on both sides and the rear doors, and Sam was pretty sure it was the safest vehicle any of them had. No sensible car thief would go straight for the one thing on wheels that was guaranteed to be full of snakes.

"Doesn't that get, you know, old?" Sam asked uncomfortably, thinking of the mice and the way they had bowed to him, their clever little paws that were really hands cast in a very different scale. There were so many things in the world that could hurt them, or devour them, and he had put them down and walked away.

"If you have a suggestion on how to convince my brothers to eat pizza, you have my attention." Ananta kicked the ice machine again. Another spray of cubes flew out. "As it is, I'm lucky when I can get them to eat their rats. They want hamsters all the time, spoiled little brats that they are."

"Okay, well, I know that this is both your culture and your biology, but I'm a mammal, so this is taking a sharp left into Creepytown for me," said Sam, rubbing the back of his neck with one hand. "Sorry."

"Don't worry about it," said Ananta. "*I* can eat pizza."

"Yeah, but you put raw chicken gizzards on top."

"It's still pizza. That is, in fact, the beauty of pizza." Ananta lifted the cooler onto her hip, giving Sam an assessing look. "What brings you out here? Your grandmother was ready to murder you earlier. I figured you'd be on house arrest."

"We talked it out."

"You mean you yelled it out."

"Same difference." He moved toward the soda machine, digging in his pocket for the quarters he'd snatched off the dresser. "We're cool. We just had to have the Annie talk. You know, the whole 'I am not abandoning my . . . Annie because you don't like her family, and it's not reasonable for you to expect me to' thing."

"Uh-huh," said Ananta. "This makes what, round twelve?"

"I think fourteen." He jabbed the button for a Pepsi. The machine made a clunking sound. Sam scowled at it. "I think maybe we're cool now, though. She really seemed to be listening."

"Uh-huh. Didn't she seem to be listening last time? And the time before that? And the time before that?"

Sam hit the machine. His soda still did not appear. "She's going to have to admit that I'm an adult eventually. It's sort of scaring her. After Mom, she's way worried about me disappearing."

"That's good, because you're going to." When Sam shot her a wounded look, Ananta shrugged. "It's true. No shame in it. Young things grow up and run away to find a place where they can be adult things without being treated like they're never going to understand the world. When I finish escorting my brothers around the country and settle them somewhere, I'm going to go home to my parents, and they'll treat me like an adult, because they had that break between me leaving as a child and me returning as a woman."

"Oh," Sam said. He hit the machine again, hesitated, and asked, "Why are you going back to them?"

"Lots of reasons, chief among them that I'm too old to marry." Ananta's smile was brief and wry. "Biology is not on our side when we're forced to live the way we are now. For me, my window to meet a boy and decide he was the one for me closed with puberty. I needed time to acquaint myself with his venom. Not to become immune to it—I'm immune to all venom, wadjet or no—but to teach my own to sing in harmony with his. Otherwise, no eggs."

Sam paused. "Uh."

"It's weird. If you're a mammal, it's weird. For us, the idea of unplanned pregnancy and cross-breeding with related species like it's no big thing is weird. We are separated by a gulf of 'biology shouldn't work that way,' and it's all very sad. Let me." Ananta put down her cooler and walked over to crouch next to the soda machine, sticking her arm in the slot. "Anyway, I had two older sisters, and there are never that many potential husbands to go around. And it's not like I tried all that hard. I like being a big sister. I'm excited to be an aunt. I never particularly wanted to be a mother. Part of our social structure involves unmarried, unimprinted females who can move freely through the territory of mated adult males without causing problems, so my parents don't care."

Ananta bounced back to her feet, holding a can out to Sam with a small smile on her face. "Think it's going to be as easy for you?" she asked.

"I don't understand how you can talk about this stuff in the open like it's not going to get us all killed," he muttered, cheeks red, as he took the soda.

"Easy: I know it's not going to get us all killed." Ananta retrieved the cooler. "There's caution and then there's paranoia. My baby brothers are cobras who like to watch Cartoon Network and write angry Tumblr posts about mistreatment of snakes. I chose to be a spinster when I was nine years old, and I never looked back. I'll always be cautious. But I refuse to let a bunch of human assholes force me to live my life in fear. See you at breakfast." She waved and walked back to her room, leaving Sam to watch her go.

"Huh," he said, and cracked open his soda.

Maybe Mary was back by now.

MINDY

The cup was paper; the person who had dropped it was running away, perhaps in fright, but more likely, I feared, to find one of the humans who patrolled the airport. My time, such as it was, was short.

Leaping down from the vehicle, I ran to the cup, darting around the feet of startled travelers. A few of them stomped at me, but they were slow and I was quick, and I evaded them with ease.

Someone screamed. I ignored them, even as every instinct I possessed told me to run, to flee, to Not Be Seen. I wore no finery, no regalia that might identify me to the uninitiated as a priest of the Precise Priestess. They would see only an ordinary mouse.

Let them think this airport infested. Let them think whatever small, human things they liked. They would not approach the borders of the truth, and I had something left to save.

The cup was paper. Paper can be shifted. I reached it and threw all my weight against it, trying to topple it onto its side, away from Mork. Someone gasped.

"Look, it's trying to get to its friend," one of the humans said, in a puzzled tone, like they could not comprehend fellow-feeling from something as small as Mork or I. I flung myself against the cup again and again, until it began to shift, until it began to topple.

The cup was paper. Paper yields. I struck the cup again and it fell. Mork was there, curled into a ball, trembling with fear. I ran to him, butted my head against his flank, touched his ear with my paw.

"Come," I squeaked, voice so low that I knew the humans would not hear, not with all the noise and bustle of the airport. "We must go."

He uncurled, and when he beheld me, there was nothing but wonder in his eyes. I fanned my whiskers, bumping my head into him once more before I ran, and he, O thanks be to all the gods who have come and gone and who have yet to be, he ran beside me, keeping pace, uninjured enough to do so.

A few humans screamed. We did not slow or look back at them. Let them shriek. They might make our passage more difficult, but they would not prevent it. We were together. We were, in the moment, invincible.

Ahead was a small semicircle cut out of the airport passageway, filled with eating places. It was not where we had entered, but we recognized the design all the same, and darted into its dubious safety. The shrieks faded behind us. We ran under a counter, and from there into a kitchen, and from there to the door which led to the employee tunnels, out of public view.

It was much quieter there. We concealed ourselves behind a stack of boxes. Then, and only then, did I turn to Mork and begin running my paws over him, searching for signs of injury. He squeaked when I pressed on the side of his chest; I suspected a broken, or at least bruised, rib. His breathing was steady and even. His limbs moved with ease.

I put my paws over my eyes, sank down onto my haunches, and trembled.

"O my love, who is my love, who is my beloved," he squeaked, nosing at my ears. "I am well, I am well. See, only look, and see me here revealed."

Some words—some rituals—predate any of the religions we have known, go all the way down to the root of what it is to be Aeslin, the place where our faith cleaves close to our long-shadowed beginnings. He spoke to me as one half of a formally mated couple, wed under the auspices of the gods, blessed by our trials together. It was the wrong choice. It was the only choice. After what we had been through, any other wedding would be a sham and a show, intended only to confirm what the gods already knew.

I trembled harder, shaking as if I no longer understood the shape of my own skin. "I thought you were dead," I squeaked.

"I know, and I am sorry." He nosed my ears again, whiskers tickling. "Look at me."

I lowered my paws. He touched his nose to mine, whiskers pressed so far forward that his lips lifted, exposing his teeth. I did the same, and as our whiskers intertwined, I knew that this was real. He had survived. I had saved him. We were still terribly far from home, but we were still together as well. Perhaps we could yet be victorious.

"There you are," he said.

I slicked my whiskers back with a small, hiccuping laugh. "You *frightened* me."

"I was afraid as well. The foot which struck me came with great speed. I thought I might be joining the gods this day." Mork looked suddenly unsure. "Would they have me, who is so near to being a heretic?"

"If they refused you, I would scale the walls of Heaven to break the locks and welcome you inside," I said gravely.

He brushed his whiskers against mine again, and I was not so pregnant, nor was our position so precarious, that I could not accept his invitation for what it was. We moved to the deepest shadow and performed the oldest ritual of them all, which worships the Aeslin and our continuation, and has no need for any outside gods.

When we were finished, he licked the fur atop my head back to acceptable smoothness and we ran, the two of us together, moving in matching, harmonious strides as we raced the length of the hall. We knew the direction of the gate we sought. We would need to return to the public halls soon enough, to find a way to board the airplane without being caught, but for now, it was safer to stay here, out of sight, running.

Running, together, and free.

SAM

Everything about this day was conspiring to give Sam a headache. It was the kind of day that would normally have had him fleeing for the trapeze, where he could work some of the stress out through sheer physical activity. Not really an option when they were all crammed into tiny motel rooms. Jogging laps around the parking lot might work, only it would probably attract attention and maybe someone would call the police.

In the end, he had resorted to the only thing that seemed even halfway sensible: the roof. Getting up there wasn't hard. All he had to do was take the stairs to the third floor, climb the maintenance ladder to the locked hatch, reach around to the edge of the roof itself, and then pull himself up. No big deal. He tried not to do it, like, *every* day, since he could only get caught once before it was forbidden, but at least it was a big open space where he could be alone.

(He had to stay human while he was up there, damn the luck, since several of the surrounding buildings were taller than the motel. But even humans could do yoga, and sit-ups, and since he was weaker in this shape, it was probably better to wear it while he was working out. The benefits of improving his human muscle tone were magnified when he transformed, rather than being reduced.)

First he wandered around the rooftop for a little while, making sure he hadn't been followed. Then he did a few sets of squats, trying to force himself to relax through endorphins alone. Finally, he sat down on the rooftop refrigeration unit, and said, "Sorry about the soap."

"It's all right." Mary walked out from behind a big metal rectangle he still didn't know the purpose of. She was back in color, her hands shoved into the pockets of her jeans, moving at an easy slouch. She looked utterly relaxed, like all of this was normal.

"This isn't normal," Sam blurted. Mary raised an eyebrow. "Us. Me, you, Annie being missing, you and me worrying about her, it's not normal. This isn't how it's supposed to go."

"Maybe and maybe not, but here we are," said Mary. "Annie's a brave girl. She'll be all right until she isn't, and once she isn't, we'll figure out how to help her."

"You know, it would be better if we could help her *before* she was in trouble."

"Probably," Mary agreed. "But then she'd never believe us when we said that we'd only be trying to help. She'd say everything had been under control, and why did we feel like we needed to butt in."

"And then she'd be mad," said Sam.

"Then she'd be mad," said Mary. "I try not to make my friends mad when I can help it."

"So what, you're going to hang out haunting me until it's time to ride to the rescue? Because if that's the case, we're going to need to talk about boundaries. Like when I'm in the shower, that's a no-haunting zone. There are things you don't need to see."

"I like how you assume I haven't already seen them," Mary drawled. Sam shot her a stunned, borderline offended look. She burst out laughing. "Chill, chill, Mister Monkey. I have not been spending my afterlife peeping in the showers of men much too young for me. And before you make some comment on my looks, I've been dead so long that I'm not even a cougar. I'd be a sabertoothed tiger at best. I meant more in the greater 'spend seventy years or so dead, you're going to see every possible kind of mammalian genitalia, and some kinds you weren't sure were physically possible' sense."

"Oh my God," said Sam. "Annie's dead aunt is a weirdo pervert."

"I prefer 'bores easily,' but whatever makes you happy." Mary hoisted herself up onto a refrigeration unit and sat. "No, I'm not going to be haunting you full time.

I've been checking in to make sure you were okay—
Annie's bound to ask about you, and I want to know
what to tell her—but when I saw that you'd finally deliv-
ered the mice to the airport, I figured it was time to give
you a little reassurance. As a reward."

"What do you mean, 'finally'? I got them there as
quick as I could."

"I know. Remember, this hasn't been easy on any of
us. You're here, with no way of reaching her; she's cut off
from her entire support structure, her entire family; her
family's worried sick; and I'm the only one with any potential to move between all three of you, and there are
so many rules governing what I can and can't say that I
could scream."

"Are you . . ." Sam hesitated. "You're allowed to tell
me that she's okay, once you find her. Once you know for
sure."

"Yes, as long as she words it right."

"I guess that means you're allowed to tell her that I'm
okay, too."

Mary smiled. "I am, in fact, allowed to carry that sort
of small, observational update. And I intend to. This may
surprise you, bon vivant that you are, but our Annie has
never been one to make friends easily."

Sam snorted.

"I know, it's shocking, with the snarkiness and the
cynicism and the random acts of violence, but there you
have it. She holds herself back. She doesn't *connect*. I
blame her siblings, mostly. They bonded with each other
so tightly that they didn't leave much room for her.
Three's a hard number. You, on the other hand," Mary
leveled a finger at Sam's chest, "she likes you. She cares
about you. She wants you to be happy. She also wants
you to be safe, but I'm pretty sure those two goals are
going to be mutually exclusive at some point."

"What do you want?" asked Sam. He paused. "Uh. If
that's not the kind of question where answering it means
something creepy shows up and tries to buy my soul. If
it is, I take it back."

"Clever," said Mary. She drummed her heels against the refrigeration unit. "What do I want? I want my family to embrace the merits of dying in their beds, peacefully, of extreme old age. I want them to learn about self-control and nonviolent solutions and being *careful*." Something about the way she spat that last word made Sam think there was a story there, and more, that he didn't want to hear it. "I'm not going to get what I want, and I'm okay with that, since people who live the lives I want for my family don't tend to be the sort to encourage ghosts to hang around for no good reason. But I'm going to do my damnedest to make sure they're happy, when I can."

"Huh," said Sam. "I guess that makes sense."

Mary smiled a little. "Wait until she takes you to meet her parents."

Sam's eyes widened. "Whoa, hold on. We're not, like, serious or anything."

"Uh-huh," said Mary. "I know. But you'll still have to meet them eventually. So much about Annie will make sense once you meet the rest of the family."

"I dunno," said Sam. "So much about her started making sense when I met *you*. I'm not sure what else is necessary."

"Just stay alive until I can find her and get her to give me permission to tell you where to find her, okay?" Mary smiled lopsidedly. "It shouldn't be *too* difficult a job, even for you."

"What's that supposed to mean?"

"You're dating Annie. Clearly you have a Price-worthy sense of self-preservation."

"Hey," protested Sam.

Mary laughed, and disappeared. Sam scowled at the place where she had been.

"Okay," he said. "That's annoying."

MINDY

We emerged into the public concourse with caution, squeezing our bodies beneath the door and out onto the carpet. The numbers overhead told me that we had moved well in the correct direction; the gate from which our flight was intended to depart was nearby.

"Come," I murmured, and began to scamper, close to the wall, hopefully out of sight. Mork followed close behind me, the two of us forming a single unbroken line as we ran.

The gate was filled with a scattering of humans. Humans, and—I paused, sniffing at the air, ears swiveling. Mork looked at me with some concern.

"What is wrong?" he asked. "What do you smell?"

"If we are blessed, salvation," I said.

The large vehicle approached. I signaled for Mork to accompany me, and together we ran across the open space, darting under the vehicle just behind the front wheels, and darting away from it just ahead of the rear wheels. No shout was raised. Our clever obfuscation had gone unnoticed. The urge to hail and rejoice rose in my breast. I forced it down. The Precise Priestess had chosen me above all others for this mission because I could hold my tongue, and I would not disgrace her now.

My silence is a rare talent, practiced and honed since my youth, since the Precise Priestess came to us and spoke of the need for subtlety, for secrecy. All Aeslin know how to hide, how to conceal, but I am rare, for I can do those things even in the presence of family, even when the need to rejoice has taken root deep within my soul. Mork . . .

Mork, too, is silent. Mork, too, can conceal himself even when most of our kind would bubble forth in religious ecstasy, unable to hold their tongues a moment longer. But his silence is not rare. All among the Lost

Colony share it, for their fear of discovery is greater than any I have ever seen. Discovery not by the wide and terrifying world, which is so full of dangers for such as we: discovery by their gods. Discovery by the ones they believe in, who should keep them Safe, who should keep them Secret, who have kept them Sacred.

It is a crime, what they have done to the Lost Colony, and I am beyond grateful for my own gracious, beloved Priestess, for were she any less, my own faith might have begun to waver.

We ran into the shelter of a trash can and I sniffed again, ignoring the tempting scents of half-eaten food drifting from the garbage, focusing instead on what I had detected before. There were people everywhere, gazing out the windows or at their small electronic devices. They seemed resigned to their wait.

And there, standing at a half-circle counter with the flight time displayed on the wall behind it, was a woman in a simple polyester uniform, wearing flat shoes and tapping on a keyboard. I inhaled again. The scent of her was unmistakable.

Dragon.

"Come," I squeaked, and launched myself across the open space before Mork could ask why. When we reached her side, I did not hesitate, but flung myself onto her ankle and raced up her leg, gripping carefully at her stockings. She would not thank me if I required their replacement. Mork followed me.

The dragon did not stop her typing as we ran along her leg, did not betray in any fashion that she was in distress. This, I had expected. Dragons survive by failing to attract attention beyond that which is necessary. This dragon might attempt to pop us into her mouth if given the opportunity, but she would neither scream nor slap us away unless someone else gave voice to our appearance.

Once upon the counter, I darted behind her keyboard, where I would not be visible to any who might approach. Mork matched me more timidly, clearly confused by my actions. I sat back on my haunches and waved a paw. The dragon looked at us, raising an eyebrow, and said nothing.

"Hail and well met," I squeaked. "Hail to you, Dragon."

Her other eyebrow joined the first. "Hmm," she said.

"We require passage to Portland," I informed her. "This plane is going to Portland. Can you please arrange for our placement on the plane?"

The woman stopped typing and lifted the receiver of a black telephone. Anyone not looking would have been unable to tell that the forefinger of her other hand was occupied with depressing the button to keep the phone from knowing that it had been disturbed.

"Today's flight to Portland, Oregon is two-thirds full, and seats are available," she said. "How would you like to pay?"

"We have no money," I said, showing her my empty paws. "We will not occupy a seat. We will hide, and hide well. My family has dealt often with dragons, and Aeslin mice do not forget. Tell us your name and you will be rewarded for your actions."

The dragon froze, more completely than anything mammalian could ever have done. She mimicked the human face and form with the perfection of the desperate, even down to quirks of anatomy that had no business appearing on anything that did not feed its young of its own body, but there were things that would always tell.

"Please," I whispered. "Please, you must move. Someone will see you and think you strange. You will be Found Out."

Her shoulders relaxed as the smile returned to her face, pretty actress falling back into a practiced role. "Yes, sir, I understand," she said. "What you're describing *is* a fairly unique circumstance."

She could not speak freely. I hesitated before asking, "You know who we belong to, yes?"

"Oh, absolutely."

"Our family can pay in favors, or in gold. We cannot set the price for them, but we can speak to them of your goodness and kindness, of the risk you took on our behalf. We can make you a miracle in their eyes."

Her expression hardened slightly. "Oh," she said. "I think you can do a little better than *that*."

SAM

"Grandma?" Sam knocked again, a little harder this time. "Hey, it's almost dinner time. I was thinking KFC. How do you feel about chicken?"

There was no reply. He sighed and knocked again.

"See, I know you're in there, because the truck's here and also I saw someone moving behind the curtains right before I started knocking. Pretending you're not is only going to annoy me, and you know what I do when you annoy me? I annoy *you*. So unless you want me hammering on your door and singing the 'Happy Banana' song at the top of my lungs—"

The door swung open. Emery looked at him wearily. "You *hate* that song."

"Yeah, but you hate it more," he said, and stepped past her into the room. "The enemy of my enemy is my friend; the earworm of my grandmother is my weapon. Do you want chicken?"

"I'm not hungry."

"You're not a very good liar, either." Sam shrugged. "I'd say I was sorry about barging in, but Mary's been doing it to me all day, and you know what? It works. Like, really well. Once somebody barges in, you sort of have to deal with them, whether you want to or not. So now you have to deal with me."

"Samuel, please." Emery looked at him wearily. "I'm not in the mood."

"Because I ran off to take Annie's mice to the airport and then I refused to back down on that whole thing where I'm not human and you don't get to pretend I am when you're trying to decide what kind of happy ending would be best for me."

Emery glared. Sam shrugged again, transforming at the same time, so that he finished the gesture with his tail wrapped around his ankle and his toes gripping the carpet.

"We both got pretty pissed at Annie for lying to us. Shouldn't that mean we tell the truth?"

"You're too young to understand how dangerous this all is."

"Grandma, I've known how dangerous the world was since I was six years old and you fired that roustabout for talking about how much money you could get if you sold me to a freak show."

Emery went still.

"I mean, I say 'fired,' but I'm pretty that if I went looking for him tomorrow, I'd find out he disappeared with no forwarding address a long time ago, wouldn't I? On account of how he never came back to kidnap me and make his fortune. The world has never been a safe place, for anybody. Maybe you inherit a tail from your dad and maybe you get hired by a carnival that tempts you more than you can resist. Or maybe you're born into a family of monster hunters and feel like your back is up against the wall. We don't get *safe*. We just get to choose what kind of dangerous we go after."

"You already told me you were going to go after her, and I didn't fight you," said Emery. "What else do you want from me?"

"I want you to say you understand, maybe, or that you like Annie even though she's a Price, and you're okay with her being the reason I finally found something I wanted more than I wanted to take care of you," said Sam. "I want you to say you'll love me no matter what I do or where I go. I want you to mean it. Can you mean it? Please?"

"Of course I'll love you no matter what you do or where you go," said Emery. She sighed, sitting on the corner of the bed. "You know, in my day, it was a given that the next generation would stay and run the carnival. Let our elders retire gracefully."

"The only way you're going to retire gracefully is if the gravedigger hits you with the shovel until you stop trying to climb out," said Sam.

Emery laughed. "Maybe so. Maybe so. But I always thought you'd take over."

"Maybe I will." Sam smiled. "I love the carnival. I don't know if I could ever be happy living under a roof that never moved, waking up every day in the same place. And I'm not saying Annie and I are going to run off and live happily ever after. Maybe I'll come back after getting it all out my system, and settle down and learn how our insurance works."

"Or maybe you'll bring her back with you," said Emery.

"Also an option. I'm not leaving forever. I'm not even leaving right now."

"Not until *Mary* tells you it's time to go." Emery couldn't keep the bitterness out of her voice.

Sam frowned. "Okay, I'm missing something. Why are you mad at her? She kept you from doing something that would have meant I never existed. I like existing. It's one of my favorite things."

"She never came back," said Emery. "Not even when the show passed through the town where she'd found me, not even when I called her name. She never came back and she never said hello, and now she's in my grandson's room like it hasn't been thirty years since the last time I saw her? I'm allowed to be a little hurt."

"She didn't come back because she was trying to keep the crossroads from realizing you got away," said Sam. "Seriously, whatever those things really are, they're *jacked*, and I don't want anything to do with them, like, ever. She has so many rules about what she can and can't say that I'm a little bit amazed she's not more of a jerk. Although she is a *major* jerk. Annie has awful taste in dead aunts."

"Really?"

"Really-really." Sam nodded vigorously. "Half the conversations we've had so far have been her teaching me the rules of talking to her. I think she's probably pretty lonely a lot of the time? But she can't go making friends, because she's dead, and also because somebody says the wrong thing and suddenly she's dragging them to her bosses to sell their souls. It sort of sucks to be Mary."

"Oh," said Emery, sounding subdued. "I think . . . I think I may have been uncharitable toward the girl."

"It's okay. It's not like the rules are the sort of thing we have easy social conventions for. I wouldn't be handling them this well if she weren't my only way of getting to Annie." He paused, looking at Emery. "I may not have a lot of warning before I need to go. When Mary says she's ready for me to help, I'm leaving. Middle of the night or middle of the day, whatever, I'm gone."

"Say goodbye if you can," said Emery. "Leave a very clear note if you can't. I can stomach you running off to play the brave hero and rescue the lady, but if I think there's *any* chance the Covenant has snatched you from your bed, I will rain down hell itself on their heads. I'll make them wish all they had gunning for them was a little girl with fire in her fingers and lies on her lips. Are we clear?"

"As crystal," said Sam. "Can we loop back to the question of whether chicken is good for dinner?"

Emery laughed, the sound tapering into a hiccup that made it sound like she was about to cry. Sam tensed as she wiped her eyes. Then she smiled at him.

"Best thing I ever did in my life was decide that the crossroads weren't for me," she said. "If you ever wonder about that, you just remember this moment. And promise me, Sam. Promise me nothing will ever be tempting enough to make you take that walk."

"I promise, Grandma."

"Good boy." She stood. "I'll come with you. Chicken is fine, but you never get the right sides."

Sam laughed, pulling himself back into his human guise, and started for the door.

Things were going to be all right.

♦

MINDY

Our new friend had stepped away from the desk after calling someone to relieve her, and had offered us solace in the safety of her handbag, which was large and leather and smelled most temptingly of breath mints. We had been contentedly exploring its contents ever since, while she stood nearby and spoke quickly and quietly into her mobile phone. When she was done, she picked up the purse, dropping the phone next to Mork, and hissed, "Come with me," before slinging us up to her shoulder and striding across the walkway.

Mork gave a squeak of pained dismay. I put a paw upon his haunch to calm him.

"Peace," I said. "For did not the Arboreal Priestess say There Is No Need To Fear A Dragon Who Has Yet To Be Paid? We have incurred a debt against our family on this day, and we are in no danger until it is discharged."

Mork looked uncertain of my words. I pushed down a pang of irritation. He was still learning to trust this expanded pantheon, and lacked the benefit of the many lessons gleaned from the Arboreal Priestess's dealings with the dragon world.

Mine is not the path of the Arboreal Priestess's clergy, nor would I ever wish it to be, for my defection would damage the Precise Priestess heart and soul. But I may admire all members of our pantheon for their graces, and hers is the dance of diplomacy, the bending and weaving of different goals into a single coherent whole. Through her we have become, if not allies to the dragon race, then at the very least valuable beyond measure.

Had the desk clerk been of any other species, I would have been hesitant to approach her, for there are those who would put money against Aeslin lives, those who believe a colony of their own would bring them fame and fortune beyond all measure. For the dragons, however, who have lived for centuries by gold alone, we represent something more valuable than money.

We represent hope.

A door opened; a door closed; a lock was thrown, before the purse in which we rode was tossed unceremoniously onto a sink. "Come out, mice," said the dragon.

We emerged, cautiously, into the light of the family restroom. It was meant for a single user; there were no stalls, and the door between us and the rest of the airport was locked. The dragon loomed over us, frowning hard to conceal her anxiety.

It is only polite to allow people their masks. "Hail," I squeaked politely. "Will you aid us?"

"One of my sisters is on her way now," she said. "She will be escorting you to Portland, and providing you with a safe berth on the plane. In exchange, you will arrange a meeting for her with your family."

I pressed my whiskers forward in distress. "We cannot negotiate—"

"I know *that*," she snapped, cutting off my objections with a wave of her hand. "If you claimed you could, you would be lying. What I want is for you to get back to Oregon, call your family, and have them send a representative to the airport to collect you and sit down with my sister in a public place. She will make an appeal on behalf of our Nest. They will hear it fairly. I know they will, because you're going to promise on their behalf. If they feel we are worthy, they will assist us in bringing our suit before the dragons of New York. I know your family has brokered a successful deal on the part of the Los Angeles Nest. We're only asking for the same treatment."

I bowed my head, acknowledging her words.

Before our gods left the Covenant of St. George— may they wander lost for a thousand years—they were complicit in perpetrating a great wrong against the dragons, whose females could pass for human, but whose males were never seen as anything more than monsters. For centuries, the world had believed the male of their species extinct, and without him, all hope for their future.

The females could continue to reproduce on their own, but only more like themselves. The skies would never again know the kiss of leather wings.

Then the Arboreal Priestess, in defiance of her title, had traveled beneath the Manhattan streets and discovered a male dragon, sleeping the centuries away. Since then, his Nest had begun to be blessed with male children. This woman, this dragon, only wanted the same as her sisters—the same as my colony and I. She wanted a future.

"It Will Be So," I intoned, and the dragon smiled.

SAM

"Hey, Mary, I don't know if you, like, eat or anything, but if you do, I have leftover chicken," said Sam, sitting down on the roof.

There was a scuff from behind him, like a sneaker scraping across gravel. "I could eat," said Mary.

"Cool," said Sam.

He watched the dead girl walk around him and settle, cross-legged, to dig through the red and white striped bucket of legs and thighs. Once she had a drumstick in her hand and was picking off the skin, eating it one methodical strip at a time, he cleared his throat.

"So you know, and without me asking for anything, my grandmother knows that as soon as Annie needs me, I'm gone," he said. "And I mean it, no matter where I am, no matter what I'm doing, I'm gone. I hope you won't forget that while you're off doing your ghost stuff."

Mary smiled at him around her food. She swallowed her latest mouthful of chicken skin, and said, "Don't worry, fella. I never forget a pretty face."

"Cool," said Sam again, and they sat quietly on the motel roof, eating chicken as the moon came out above them, and Annie was very far away, but somehow Sam wasn't scared anymore.

He was going to see her soon.

$$\lambda$$

MINDY

Our dragon's name was Jessica; her sister was Angelica.

Her sister's daughter, no more than seven years old and doubtless included on this voyage because she provided an adorable reminder of what was at stake for their species, was Allison. It was her backpack that had been outfitted for our comfort, containing as it did several pieces of repurposed doll furniture, a package of graham crackers, and a large wedge of cheddar cheese.

Mork and I nestled together on a soft square of artificial fur meant to be a blanket for the plastic bed beneath us, his head across my neck, our tails tangled together in a comforting weave. Around us, people talked and went about their business, while Angelica filled out spreadsheets on her laptop and Allison charmed inflight snacks out of the flight attendants.

"We will be home in short order," I murmured.

Mork exhaled, ruffling the fur along my neck. "And they will like me?"

"O my love, who is my love, who is my beloved," I replied, folding my paw over his and holding him tight, he who had come so far to make this voyage with me, he who had come with me to find a future. "They are going to love you even as I do."

The words are said: the ritual is performed. The things done outside the reach of the family's walls are here protected and entered into record, to be known and kept forevermore.

We are Aeslin. We believe, and we endure.

So be it.

Price Family Field Guide to the Cryptids of North America
Updated and Expanded Edition

Aeslin mice (Apodemus sapiens). Sapient, rodentlike cryptids which present as near-identical to non-cryptid field mice. Aeslin mice crave religion, and will attach themselves to "divine figures" selected virtually at random when a new colony is created. They possess perfect recall; each colony maintains a detailed oral history going back to its inception. Origins unknown.

Basilisk (Procompsognathus basilisk). Venomous, feathered saurians approximately the size of a large chicken. This would be bad enough, but thanks to a quirk of evolution, the gaze of a basilisk causes petrification, turning living flesh to stone. Basilisks are not native to North America, but were imported as game animals. By idiots.

Bogeyman (Vestiarium sapiens). The thing in your closet is probably a very pleasant individual who simply has issues with direct sunlight. Probably. Bogeymen are close relatives of the human race; they just happen to be almost purely nocturnal, with excellent night vision, and a fondness for enclosed spaces. They rarely grab the ankles of small children, unless it's funny.

Chupacabra (Chupacabra sapiens). True to folklore, chupacabra are blood-suckers, with stomachs that do not handle solids well. They are also therianthrope shape-shifters, capable of transforming themselves into human form, which explains why they have never been captured. When cornered, most chupacabra will assume their bipedal shape in self-defense. A surprising number of chupacabra are involved in ballroom dance.

Dragon (Draconem sapiens). Dragons are essentially winged, fire-breathing dinosaurs the size of Greyhound buses. At least, the males are. The females are attractive humanoids who can blend seamlessly in a crowd of supermodels, and outnumber the males twenty to one. Females are capable of parthenogenic reproduction and can sustain their population for centuries without outside help. All dragons, male and female, require gold to live, and collect it constantly.

Fūri (Homo therianthrope). Often proposed as the bridge between humans and therianthropes, the fūri is a monkey—specifically, a human—that takes on the attributes of another monkey—specifically, some form of spider monkey. Fūri transform instinctively, choosing their human forms for camouflage and their more simian forms for virtually everything else. A transformed fūri is faster, stronger, and sturdier than a human being. Offering bananas is not recommended.

Ghoul (Herophilus sapiens). The ghoul is an obligate carnivore, incapable of digesting any but the simplest vegetable solids, and prefers humans because of their wide selection of dietary nutrients. Most ghouls are carrion eaters. Ghouls can be easily identified by their teeth, which will be shed and replaced repeatedly over the course of a lifetime.

Gorgon, Pliny's (Gorgos stheno). The Pliny's gorgon is capable of gaze-based petrifaction only when both their human and serpent eyes are directed toward the same target. They are the most sexually dimorphic of the known gorgons, with the males being as much as four feet taller than the females. They are venomous, as are the snakes atop their heads, and their bites contain a strong petrifying agent. Do not vex.

Hidebehind (Aphanes apokryphos). We don't really know much about the hidebehinds: no one's ever seen them. They're excellent illusionists, and we think they're bipeds, which means they're probably mammals. Probably.

Jackalope (Parcervus antelope). Essentially large jackrabbits with antelope antlers, the jackalope is a staple of the American West, and stuffed examples can be found in junk shops and kitschy restaurants all across the country. Most of the taxidermy is fake. Some, however, is not. The jackalope was once extremely common, and has been shot, stuffed, and harried to near-extinction. They're relatively harmless, and they taste great.

Jink (Tyche iynx). Luck manipulators and masters of disguise, these close relatives of the mara have been known to conceal themselves right under the nose of the Covenant. No small trick. Most jinks are extremely careful about the way they move and manipulate luck, and individuals have been known to sacrifice themselves for the good of the community.

Johrlac (Johrlac psychidolos). Colloquially known as "cuckoos," the Johrlac are telepathic ambush predators. They appear human, but are internally very different, being cold-blooded and possessing a decentralized circulatory system. This quirk of biology means they can be shot repeatedly in the chest without being killed. Extremely dangerous. All Johrlac are interested in mathematics, sometimes to the point of obsession. Origins unknown; possibly insect in nature.

Jorōgumo (Nephilia sapiens). Originally native to Japan, these therianthropes belong to the larger family of cryptids classified as "yōkai." Jorōgumo appear to be attractive women of Japanese descent until they transform, at which point they become massive spider-centaurs whose neurotoxic venom can kill in seconds. No males of the species have ever been seen. It is possible that the species possesses a degree of sexual dimorphism so great that male Jorōgumo are simply not recognized for what they are.

Laidly worm (Draconem laidly). Very little is known about these close relatives of the dragons. They present similar but presumably not identical sexual dimorphism; no currently living males have been located.

Lamia (Python lamia). Semi-hominid cryptids with the upper bodies of humans and the lower bodies of snakes. Lamia are members of order synapsedia, the mammal-like reptiles, and are considered responsible for many of the "great snake" sightings of legend. The sightings not attributed to actual great snakes, that is.

Lesser gorgon (Gorgos euryale). One of three known subspecies of gorgon, the lesser gorgon's gaze causes short-term paralysis followed by death in anything under five pounds. The bite of the snakes atop their heads will cause paralysis followed by death in anything smaller than an elephant if not treated with the appropriate antivenin. Lesser gorgons tend to be very polite, especially to people who like snakes.

Lilu (Lilu sapiens). Due to the striking dissimilarity of their abilities, male and female Lilu are often treated as two individual species: incubi and succubi. Incubi are empathic; succubi are persuasive telepaths. Both exude strong pheromones inspiring feelings of attraction and lust in the opposite sex. This can be a problem for incubi like our cousin Artie, who mostly wants to be left alone, or succubi like our cousin Elsie, who gets very tired of men hitting on her while she's trying to flirt with their girlfriends.

Madhura (Homo madhurata). Humanoid cryptids with an affinity for sugar in all forms. Vegetarian. Their presence slows the decay of organic matter, and is usually viewed as lucky by everyone except the local dentist. Madhura are very family-oriented, and are rarely found living on their own. Originally from the Indian subcontinent.

Manananggal (Tanggal geminus). If the manananggal is proof of anything, it is that Nature abhors a logical classification system. We're reasonably sure the manananggal are mammals; everything else is anyone's guess. They're hermaphroditic and capable of splitting their upper and lower bodies, although they are a single entity, and killing the lower half kills the upper half as well. They prefer fetal tissue, or the flesh of newborn infants. They are also venomous, as we have recently discovered. Do not engage if you can help it.

Oread (Nymphae silica). Humanoid cryptids with the approximate skin density of granite. Their actual biological composition is unknown, as no one has ever been able to successfully dissect one. Oreads are extremely strong, and can be dangerous when angered. They seem to have evolved independently across the globe; their common name is from the Greek.

Sasquatch (Gigantopithecus sesquac). These massive native denizens of North America have learned to embrace depilatories and mail-order shoe catalogs. A surprising number make their living as Bigfoot hunters (Bigfeet and Sasquatches are close relatives, and enjoy tormenting each other). They are predominantly vegetarian, and enjoy Canadian television.

Tanuki (Nyctereutes sapiens). Therianthrope shapeshifters from Japan, the Tanuki are critically endangered due to the efforts of the Covenant. Despite this, they remain friendly, helpful people, with a naturally gregarious nature which makes it virtually impossible for them to avoid human settlements. Tanuki possess three primary forms—human, raccoon dog, and big-ass scary monster. Pray you never see the third form of the Tanuki.

Ukupani (Ukupani sapiens). Aquatic therianthropes native to the warm waters of the Pacific Islands, the Ukupani were believed for centuries to be an all-male species, until Thomas Price sat down with several local fishermen and determined that the abnormally large Great White sharks that were often found near Ukupani males were, in actuality, Ukupani females. Female Ukupani can't shapeshift, but can eat people. Happily. They are as intelligent as their shapeshifting mates, because smart sharks are exactly what the ocean needed.

Wadjet (Naja wadjet). Once worshipped as gods, the male wadjet resembles an enormous cobra, capable of reaching seventeen feet in length when fully mature, while the female wadjet resembles an attractive human female. Wadjet pair-bond young, and must spend extended amounts of time together before puberty in order to become immune to one another's venom and be able to successfully mate as adults.

Waheela (Waheela sapiens). Therianthrope shapeshifters from the upper portion of North America, the waheela are a solitary race, usually claiming large swaths of territory and defending it to the death from others of their species. Waheela mating season is best described with the term "bloodbath." Waheela transform into something that looks like a dire bear on steroids. They're usually not hostile, but it's best not to push it.

PLAYLIST:

Everybody needs a soundtrack, and Antimony is no different. Here are some songs to rock you through her adventures.

"I'm Sexy, I'm Cute" . . . .*Bring It On*
"Work, Bitch" . . . . .Britney Spears
"Brilliant Disguise" . . . . .Bruce Springsteen
"Don't Threaten Me With a
   Good Time" . . . . .Panic! At the Disco
"The Secret Lives of the Dead" . . . . .Tettix
"Ghost" . . . . Belle Histoire
"Mad World, Outlive Me" . . . . Amelia Curran
"Stick It To The Man" . . . . *School of Rock: The Musical*
"Burn" . . . . Mad at Gravity
"Help, I'm Alive" . . . . .Metric
"Teach Me To Be Bad" . . . . Thea Gilmore
"Situation Critical" . . . . *Overwatch* original soundtrack
"Hold Me Up" . . . . .We're About 9
"Please" . . . . .Ludo
"Nothing to Remember" . . . . Neko Case
"All This and Heaven Too" . .Florence and the Machine
"Lucky Me" . . . . Sarah Slean
"Get Lucky" . . . . Halestorm
"Haunted" . . . . Taylor Swift
"Rock All Night" . . . . Court Yard Hounds
"Hit Me With Your Best Shot" . . . . Pat Benetar
"Falling in Hate" . . . . Five Finger Death Punch

"Bend the Rules"...........................Saybia
"Cry Baby"..................... Melanie Martinez
"Crossroads"........................ Bekah Kelso
"Heads Will Roll" ....Yeah Yeah Yeahs
"Any Way You Want It" ....Journey
"Girl in a Car" .... Kris Delmhorst

ACKNOWLEDGMENTS:

Here we go again: Antimony Price, best jammer in the family, is still on the track and refusing to step aside. She's done enough to earn herself a bonus lap, and she'll be back for book eight, *That Ain't Witchcraft*. Honestly, I couldn't be happier. This series is a joy to write, and Annie only makes it better. I can't wait for you to see what she gets up to now that she's finally put her dream team into action. It's going to be a lot of things. It's sure not going to be boring.

This book really delved deep into my knowledge of theme parks, and thanks go to everyone who has ever accompanied me to one of those dream destinations, especially Vixy, Amy, Brooke, and the glories of the Chicago contingent. Thanks to Anthony, Doc, and David for answering questions, and to Kelly and Daniel for putting up with my idiosyncratic approach to tourism. Thanks to my newest theme park buddies, Torrey and Wish, and to Alexis, for not getting mad when I started breeding giant insects in the front room.

Phil remains responsible for much of what goes on around here, and I sometimes feel like we don't thank-slash-blame him enough. So thanks, Phil. Also thanks to Megan, the real one, who didn't know that she was going to be joining the Lowry medical program, and to Priscilla Spencer for her amazing map of Lowryland.

The machete squad continues to be absolutely amazing, and I would be lost without them. Kory Bing illustrates the amazing Field Guide to the Cryptids of North America, which you can visit at my website—bring a net—while Tara O'Shea's dingbat and website design remains top-notch. I have the best team, y'all. Thanks to everyone at DAW for continuing to put up with my antics, and to my wonderful publicity team at Penguin Random House.

You may have noticed that our cover art has changed a bit. Aly Fell was unavailable for this book, due to personal reasons, and Lee Moyer was able to step in at the last moment. I am so grateful to both of them for helping to keep the "look" of the series consistent.

I have settled comfortably in Washington State since our last little chat, and I love it up here. My mother, Micki McGuire, has been key in making sure our new little household runs smoothly, but she's not the only one. Jennifer Brozek has been tapped repeatedly for cat-sitting duties, while Michelle Dockrey has fully stepped into her role as my local personal assistant, and makes sure my email doesn't actually eat me. It's a risk. Thanks to everyone here in the Seattle community for being so welcoming. You're great.

Thanks to my various tour buddies of the last year, including Mishell Baker and Sarah Gailey; to all the bookstores that have hosted me while I wandered around the country; to everyone who sent good wishes when my cats became ill; and to my beloved Cat Valente, for the cupcakes. Thanks to Borderlands Books, for putting up with me. And to you: thank you, so much, for reading.

Any errors in this book are my own. The errors that aren't here are the ones that all these people helped me fix. I appreciate it so much.